RECORD OF THE PALADINS:
BOOK OF IVON AND IVOIRE

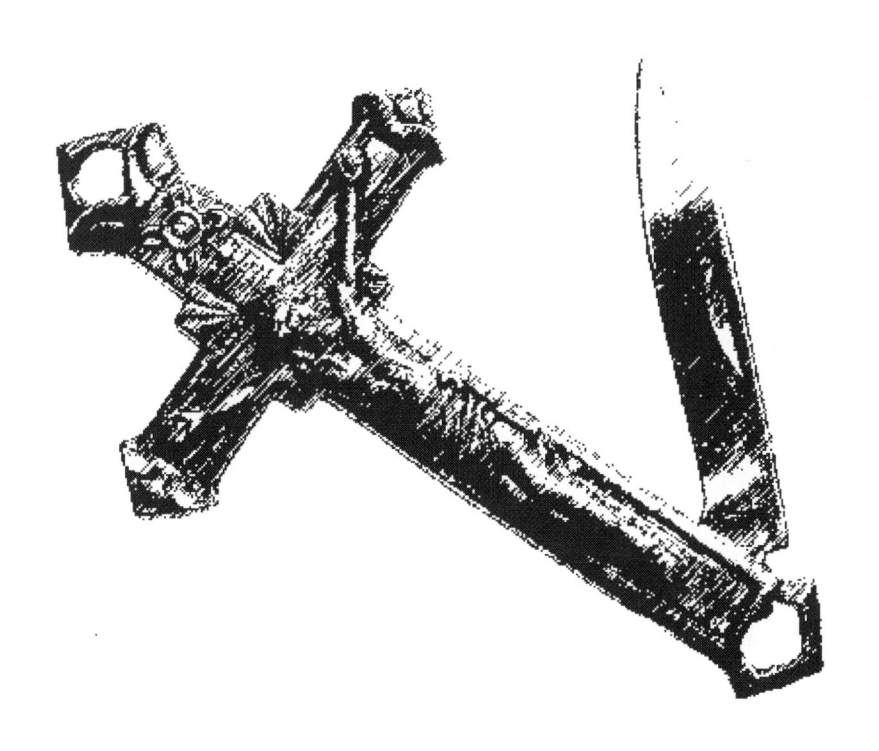

BP McCoppin

Text Copyright 2024 by BP McCoppin
Illustrations by BP McCoppin

All rights reserved. Associated logos are trademarks and/or registered trademarks of BP McCoppin

Record of The Paladins and all related characters and element are trademarks of BP McCoppin.

No part of this publication may be reproduced in whole or in part, or stored in a retrieval system, or transmitted in any form by any means, electronic, mechanical, photocopying, recording, or otherwise, without written permission from the author.

Cover art by BP McCoppin

DEDICATION

This book is dedicated to my parents, Neal and Nancy McCoppin.
They are the storytellers who have given me this passion.

"Sorry for killing you in book one."

Book of Ivon and Ivoire

THE AUDIT	1
IVON	13
ROLAND AND THE TANK	19
IVOIRE	28
THE SOUND OF TRUTH	35
A CHILD'S GAME	49
STRENGTH OF FAITH	61
FRIENDS, FAMILY, AND FAITH	71
BEAUTY AND THE BOAT	87
RED IN THE SNOW	97
BULLETS AND BOOKS	107
THE GUILD	117
BEHIND ENEMY LINES	129
THE WATCH AND THE WIRE	141
PIT OF VIPERS	149
CLASS REUNION	163
COCKTAILS AND EXORCISMS	173
DEATH AS LIFE	189
BIRTH OF A DEMON	197
ROMANCE AND REVELATIONS	211
DROWNING IN THE DESERT	221
SHADOWS NO MORE	231
THE REAL MISSION	239
KNIGHTS AND DRAGONS	251
DEATH, LIFE, AND FACT	263
THREE ENTER, FOUR LEAVE	277
THE PLANS I HAVE FOR THEE	285
MOTHERS	297
NOW WE ARE 5	305
EPILOGUE	309
ABOUT THE AUTHOR	311

AUTHOR'S NOTE TO THE READER

  This is the second novel in The Record of The Paladins story. Some very important details are only revealed in book one, The Book of Oliver. If you have not read it, put this down and go read that. Concepts, ideas, and backstories are explained there that are needed to fully understand this novel.

  With that being said I need to address a few things revealed in this book. The title characters, Ivon and Ivoire, which are introduced in this book are from the countries Ukraine and Russia. I know that as of the release of this book, these two countries are at war, and some may find the references painful. The meat of this story takes place in 2014, long before the conflict in 2024.

  As I did with the prior novel I am not saying the following story is true. Even if I professed, as before, with all that I had, that it is true, you wouldn't believe me anyway. Even if, by some chance, you believed my profession that it was a true story, you would ask again, "Why has no one else met a Paladin or heard of them?" I could reiterate that they excel at staying hidden, or that you have met one and been so focused on your own life you missed it, or I could say the media is even more so controlled by demons. But, as before, that too would be a leap of faith, for if demons were real, then so is God.

  What I will say is I hope this novel expands your perception of events. That you look at what you see with your own eyes and think of them from the perspective of good versus evil, of God versus not God

RECORD OF THE PALADINS
BOOK OF IVON AND IVOIRE

THE AUDIT

Blue.

Waves of the deepest blue crashed on a black sand beach. The waves crashed on the rocks in their minuscule mightiness. The water retreated as tiny birds chased it away. The sun set behind the volcanic mountains cloaked in pink and orange clouds. Oliver walked along barefoot, carrying his boots and duster in his hand. His sleeves were rolled up, and a light rain cooled his skin. Somewhere on this beach, a demon waited.

Oliver paused for a moment and his gaze followed the waves rolling in. His eyes tracked back out to the endless horizon. His fascination with the sea still gripped him as his gaze followed to the end of the Earth. In another life, he could see himself content working as a hand on a boat coasting from port to port, the salt wind tangling his sandy hair. God had other plans.

"Where are all the tourists?" asked Oliver to his earpiece.

"You are walking along a southern beach in Kau," replied Persephone. "Most of the tourists are on the Oahu Island or the North part of this island. Many houses in this area don't even have power."

"They are missing out," said Oliver. "This beach is gorgeous."

"Focus, Paladin," said Persephone. "This is not a vacation."

"Yes, ma'am," replied Oliver. "Any updates from Melissa and Roland?"

"Melissa is visiting Hannah and has been out of touch. Roland is on his way back from Barcelona and sends his regards," answered Persephone.

"Thanks," said Oliver, "On to my mission. I am at the beach and looking for the altar. Any updates to share?"

"The parents of the missing girl are still at the police department hoping for answers," answered Persephone. "During your flight I read some more on the altar on this beach. It's for the deity Ku. In the Hawaiian religion, he is the god of many things, including war. Coolest of all, he usually takes the form of a man-shark. Are you going to fight a shark man?"

"Maybe," replied Oliver, "We fought that snake lady; why not a man-shark? Anything else that could help?"

"No identified weaknesses," answered Persephone, "but nothing about being impenetrable or being especially strong. King Kamehameha I built statues to honor Ku. The religion views him as a benevolent deity."

"We know that demons take many forms," replied Oliver. "This may not actually be Ku, but an opportunistic demon trying to gain some worshipers."

"Yeah," replied Persephone, snapping her gum. "Or a demon named Ku has been here for hundreds of years, growing stronger."

"Let's hope that is not the case," said Oliver.

"From the tracker, you are close to the altar," Persephone said. "Head away from the water. It should be about one hundred yards in front of you."

Oliver faced inland and walked towards the tree line. His feet sink into the loose lava-formed sand, slowing his pace. He saw the pre-shadow of something flying out of the brush and trees. He dodged as an arrow flew by. He drew his right-hand revolver and aimed at where the arrow came.

"Hello," called Oliver, "Please don't shoot any more arrows. I will shoot back."

Three more arrows fly out. Oliver ducked under and shoots at coconuts above where the arrows are coming from. Four coconuts fall, three hit the ground, and one hits something else with a soft thud. A moaning came from the trees, two figures step forward bearing bows. The figures are dressed in traditional Hawaiian clothing, loincloths, and leaves wrapped around their head and calves. The bodies are desiccated, and their skin was gray.

"Ghouls," said Oliver over his earpiece. He sent a bullet into each ghoul's head. They fall into the palmettos, splashing black blood on the leaves. The moaning continues from beyond the tree line.

"This confirms demons are here," said Oliver.

"Any sign of the missing girl?" asked Persephone.

"Not yet," replied Oliver. "I haven't found the altar either. I am going to head into the trees."

Oliver knelt to slide on his boots and don his duster, then walked to the palmetto brush. He pushed the leaves aside and found the source of the moaning. A ghoul lay with a broken neck from the falling coconut.

"Any interest in bringing a live ghoul home?" asked Oliver to his earpiece.

"What did you do?" asked Persephone back.

"I broke one's neck, but the head is still working," replied Oliver. "Should I see if I can bring it back?"

"Yeah!" exclaimed Persephone. "I have never seen a live one; maybe I can dissect it."

"Let me find the demon first," said Oliver. "This guy is not going anywhere."

Oliver binds the paralyzed ghoul's hands to its feet, *Just in case*.

He continued deeper into the brush; the rain had picked up, and it fell as a curtain of water on him and danced on the leaves. He came upon a volcanic rock that was eight feet tall, with an altar carved out of the side. The altar was decorated in pink and white pukka shell necklaces and long dead palm leaves.

"I found the altar," said Oliver.

"Any sign of Ku?" asked Persephone.

"No. I am going to document the altar, then keep looking," replied Oliver.

"Copy, Cowboy," said Persephone.

Oliver pulled a device from his pocket and took pictures of the altar. On the altar is a wooden figure about a foot tall. The figure has a humanoid body. The head is just eyes, nose, and mouth; all three are curved, exaggerated, and angry. Oliver takes a few pictures and then picks up the wooden figure.

"No!" yells a deep voice from deeper in the brush.

Oliver hears the sound of heavy feet running through the leaves. The palmettos split violently, and a live version of the Ku statue bursts out. The tiny figure first befuddles Oliver. Is this the demon Ku?

Ku leaped at Oliver, who pre-saw the movement and dived out of the way.

"Ku is only a foot tall," said Oliver over his coms.

"Really?" replied Persephone. "Can you capture it, too?"

"I already have one prisoner," replied Oliver. "I am going to kill this one."

Ku is running through the brush obscuring Oliver's view of him. Oliver calmed his mind and said Gerin's prayer.

Lord, make me swift and true.
Guide my hands with yours.
Let your will be my aim.

The noise of the rain and the rustling leaves faded, Oliver's vision focused, and the moment stretched out. He followed the wave of leaves as Ku ran circles around him. He saw his moment. A pre-shadow exited from the trees, and Oliver took aim.

"Stop!" yelled a girl's voice.

Oliver pulled his gun back and saw a girl exit from the brush.

"Don't shoot him," the girl continued. "He is my friend."

Ku ran out of the brush and hopped into her arms.

"Persephone," said Oliver, "read me that description of Kelani again."

"Sure," Persephone replied, "eight years old, long dark hair, dark complexion, brown eyes, she was last seen wearing a green and yellow flower dress."

"I found her," informed Oliver.

"Great! Is she ok?" asked Persephone.

"Physically, yes," answered Oliver. "Her mental state is still in question."

"Huh?" replied Persephone.

Oliver addressed the girl, "Your Mom and Dad are looking for you. They are very worried. Can I take you to them?"

"Ku says I should stay here," said the girl. "He is my friend and is nice to me."

"Isn't your Mom and Dad nice?" asked Oliver.

"Sometimes," said the girl. "Sometimes they are mean and make me do things like pick up dog poop."

"Kelani," said Oliver as he dropped to one knee while putting his gun in the holster. "They love you and are really worried. Can I take you home to them?"

"No, Kelani," said Ku, its voice now cute and soft. "Stay and play with me. We can make necklaces and stay up late and sing songs."

"Kelani," said Oliver, "that is not Ku. That is a mean and evil spirit. It means you no good will."

"No," said Kelani. "Ku is my friend. He made the bad kids scared and go away. He is nice to me."

"Any ideas?" asked Oliver to Persephone on the earpiece.

"Got any candy you can offer?" replied Persephone.

Oliver thought for a moment as he measured the situation. "Kelani," Oliver's voice softened. "My Dad died when I was young, and I miss him every day. I never had a Mom. But I know your parents are worried about you. Can you ask Ku if you can go visit your parents and come back later?"

"No," yelled Ku, its soft voice deepening. "Stay with me and play. We can play forever."

"Would your friend not let you see your Mom and Dad?" asked Oliver.

"No," replied Kelani. "Ku, I want to see my Mom. I can come back tomorrow."

"No," yelled Ku. "You will stay with me and play!"

"No, Ku!" yelled Kelani. "I want to see my Mom. I miss her."

Ku began to grow while in Kelani's grip. "No Kelani. We play forever." Ku continued to grow until it is too heavy for Kelani to hold. It fell to the ground and grabbed Kelani, lifting her as it burgeoned. Oliver's neck craned, watching it loom past ten feet.

"Here we go," said Oliver. He drew his weapons and fired rounds into Ku's growing head.

The creature screamed and rocked back. It loosened its grip on Kelani, who fell to the ground. Oliver continued firing. Ku began to shrink; it raised its hands in defense; bullets continued to tear through the wood demon, and splinters pelted the leaves. Ku took off in a run through the bushes, screaming. Oliver pursued, firing round after round into the demon as it shrank. The demon tripped on a rock and fell to the ground, back to its original size. Holes pepper the creature who lay dead.

"Ku, no!" yelled Kelani.

Oliver ran to Kelani and hugged her.

"You killed my friend," Kelani screamed and pounded on Oliver with her fists.

"He was not your friend," comforted Oliver. "That was a bad spirit."

"No," screamed Kelani. "He was nice to me, and we played games."

Oliver knew he could not reason with a tired and angry child. He put her head on his shoulder and carried her back to the SUV. She had broken down into uncontrollable tears and curled into a ball in the back seat. Oliver returned and grabbed the ghoul with the broken neck. He tied it as he learned in his SWAT training and gagged its mouth to stop the moans. He checks on Ku's corpse, and it has begun to dissolve into ash. Oliver dumped the ghoul in the trunk of the SUV. He enters the driver seat and punches in directions to the Police station where Kelani's parents wait.

"Oliver," it was Persephone on the earpiece.

"Go for Oliver," Oliver replied.

"We need you to head directly back here when you are done," Persephone's voice revealed some nervousness.

"I was hoping to see the sites," said Oliver. "Can it wait?"

"Sorry, cowboy," replied Persephone. "The Vatican is performing an audit."

After reuniting Kelani with her parents, Oliver was back in the private Vatican jet and not happy to be flying back so soon. He had wanted to spend some time exploring the Hawaiian Islands. The blue waters of the Pacific called to him. He knew duty and the souls of men took priority, so he left. He called Melissa while en route.

"So, what does an audit mean for us Paladins?" asked Oliver.

"The Vatican leadership will, at times, check in on us and see how we are doing," she answered.

"They want to see how their money is being spent?" asked Oliver.

"Yes," replied Melissa, "and to evaluate how we are doing."

"As in, 'are we killing demons effectively?'" joked Oliver.

"That," Melissa quieted her tone, "and to make sure we are not drawing too much attention."

"Oh," replied Oliver, recalling the Shanette concert. "How often do we get audited?"

"This is the first one since I joined," replied Melissa. "It has been a while."

Oliver was worried his actions at the concert may be why they were getting audited. During the flight, he cleaned his guns and prayed for guidance and courage for what lay ahead.

Father
Give me peace and guidance for what lays ahead
Guide my actions to be your will
Amen

The plane landed at the private airport, and Oliver loaded into the waiting SUV. The SUV dropped Oliver back at Paladin Headquarters. He exited the vehicle and dragged his ghoul prize to the main door. A new vehicle was parked by the door with a Swiss Army guard driver. *This must be about the audit.*

Oliver entered the main door to the sound of voices coming from the library.

"...is our primary concern. We can't have Paladins going *cowboy* on us." The voice was stern and direct, the Italian accent thick.

"We acted to save thousands of lives," replied Melissa.

"And millions saw the footage on the news," rebutted the voice.

Oliver entered and dropped the ghoul, "What news?"

Melissa was seated at a chair facing a man who paced the room. She was dressed in her klobuck, and her hair was up in a bun. Roland, on the other hand, simply wore a tank top and shorts; he leaned against the wall near the hallway leading to the gym.

"Ah, the American," the new man said; he stopped pacing and faced Oliver. He was short, fat, and balding. The circle of hair made him look like Friar Tuck from an old Robin Hood Movie. He was dressed in his priest habit.

"Oliver," introduced Melissa, "this is Father Angelo Conte. He is the auditor sent by the Vatican."

"A pleasure, Father Conte," Oliver stepped forward and extended his hand.

"As I was saying," continued Angelo, waving off Oliver's hand, "we can't just open fire into a crowd."

"Hey," Oliver raised his voice, "that crowd was mostly demons. They were trying to sacrifice the humans."

"They didn't look like demons," Angelo pointed a stubby finger at Oliver and jabbed into his chest, "It looked like you opened fire on a crowd of innocents."

"Father," pleaded Melissa, "we acted as we best saw fit- "

"Not good enough," interrupted Angelo. He turned and faced Melissa, "When a Cardinal wakes up, and the news network all show footage of a shooting, and that footage has Roland in it, I get a call. When I get a call, you get a visit."

"Roland wasn't the one shooting," rebutted Oliver.

"No," said Angelo, turning his attention back to Oliver and poking his chest, "you were. But he has a famous face that a Cardinal who has direct ties to the Pope himself would surely recognize…." Angelo's gaze moved past Oliver to the package he dropped. Something was moving inside. "What is that?"

"That is a ghoul," replied Oliver bluntly.

"You bring demon essence to the Holy City!" yelled Angelo as he moved closer to Roland.

"No worries," said Oliver, bending over the package, "he is helpless." Oliver removed the coverings, showing the ghoul beneath. It was still dressed in the traditional Hawaiian warrior leaves. Its arms and legs tied together like a calf. "I paralyzed him and brought him home for research." Oliver looked up at Melissa, her face not hiding her disappointment. "Not a good idea?"

Book of Ivon and Ivoire

Roland walked over and stomped on the ghoul's head. The head squished in a splash of black blood.

"Oliver," Melissa's voice stern, "put the ghoul's body into the incinerator. I am sorry, Father Conte."

"Ok," was all Oliver could say. He thought he had brought home a prize. He picked up the ghoul's body and headed to the maintenance room.

"You are all out of control!" yelled Angelo. "I have the authority to end your funding."

"Father, please," pleaded Melissa.

"But I won't," softened Angelo. "You do God's work. I have a solution that will please…."

Oliver turned the corner as the conversation faded. He was more embarrassed than angry. He reached the door to the mechanical area where Isaac and Persephone were waiting for him. Persephone had a sad look on her face that contrasted with her highlighted hair.

"I saw what happened on the cameras," said Persephone. "I am to blame as I gave you the idea."

"It's ok," replied Oliver. "I should have thought it through more."

"May I take that creature in for you, sir?" asked Isaac, his tone and demeanor stiff. To Oliver, he still came across as serious and direct.

"I appreciate the help," replied Oliver. "Can you open the door for me?"

Isaac and Persephone helped Oliver dump the ghoul into the incinerator. When they exited the mechanical area, Melissa was waiting.

"I am not angry, Oliver," started Melissa. "I know your heart was in the right place. I also know that you did not know Father Angelo would be here. With that said, we have a change in our next mission."

"Oh?" said Oliver.

"Yes," continued Melissa, "you, Roland, and I are going to follow a new lead we have on Ivoire."

"That's great news," smiled Oliver.

"Well," paused Melissa. "Father Angelo is going with us."

"Oh," sighed Oliver.

"He is waiting for us in the library," said Melissa. "Let's go back and go over the briefing."

"I'll prepare some tea," said Isaac.

Oliver, Melissa, and Persephone returned to the briefing room, where Angelo and Roland waited. Melissa took the chair at the main computer as the rest sat on the leather chairs.

Melissa pulled up a map of Ukraine and started, "We have found several instances of a woman named Ivoire operating for the Ukrainian government. We believe she is operating as a spy or informant in their continued tensions with Russia."

The image changes to a black-and-white photo showing a blonde woman wearing sunglasses. The photo is blurry, and the woman is far from the photographer.

"This is the only possible image we have of her," said Melissa, "and we are not one hundred percent it is even of her. We cannot trust descriptions of her as she often changes her appearance as part of her work."

"What makes you think she might be a Paladin?" asked Oliver.

"One report from an American agent states that she appeared to possess a nearly supernatural ability to know when someone is telling the truth," answered Melissa.

"And this is a Paladin ability?" asked Oliver.

"It could be," said Melissa. "Each Paladin is unique."

"What is our plan?" asked Oliver.

"Ivoire has frequently visited a small town near the Russian border called Dekhtyar. It was a hot spot during the Ukraine War of Independence, and we believe it may be her base of operations. Roland, Oliver, and I are going to the town and will stake it out, looking for clues on who she is. We might even luck out, and she shows up."

"Excuse me," interrupted Angelo, "we must not forget, I am coming too."

"Yes," replied Melissa, "Father Angelo is going as an observer."

"Thank you," said Angelo, "Just pretend I am not there and continue as you normally do."

"No worries, Father," said Oliver, "this will be a nice, quiet mission."

Book of Ivon and Ivoire

IVON

     Ivon's earliest memory is fighting for food in a Russian Army child education camp. As The Soviet Union fell, the Russian Army found its hands full with thousands of orphans. These children were sent to camps to be educated and indoctrinated into the greatness of Russia and the ideals of Communism. Life at the camp was brutal. These were the war orphans from a failing empire. Hundreds of children died from malnutrition, dehydration, neglect, or outright abuse. Those who survived grew to be hardened and vicious adults. Ivon was a survivor.

     The camp itself was an old Army base that had minimal adjustments to accommodate children. The children slept in one of two rooms, one for boys and one for girls. The former barracks were not temperature controlled; they did not even have proper windows. Glass was too expensive. Instead, bars were installed to keep the children from escaping. Beds were not assigned, there were no pillows or sheets, and there were not enough beds for every child to lie on. For a bathroom, they used a tool shed with a hole dug in the ground on the far side of a rocky field. The only source of water for hygiene was the rainwater that gathered in a drum next to the shed. The rocky field that housed the shed resided in was the only outdoor area the children had access too. The field itself was rocks and more rocks enclosed on three sides by barbed wire topped chain link fences. All other areas were barricaded off. The camp was perpetually cold. The children only knew of snow or no snow; there was no warmth. The only colors the children experienced were gray, brown, and red. Gray for the walls, rocks, and dirty snow. Brown for the rusted metal of the fences and barbed wire. Finally, red for the blood that was spilled daily among the children.

Adult supervision at the camp was sparse. The few Russian soldiers assigned to the camp never hid their distaste for their assignments. They would stay in their quarters and spend their time drinking and playing cards. They did not care if a few orphans suffered or even died.

Daily, the soldiers would kick open the door at sunrise. They would drop three things: a box of maggot-infested bread, a bucket of greenish-brown water, and a pan of mushy mess they called 'kasha.' Once the doors slammed closed the children would scramble for the food. Every day was a fight just to eat. The strongest ate and thrived, and the weak starved and died.

After dropping off the daily rations, the soldiers would normally not be seen until the next day. This gave the orphans free reign of the areas that were not cut off with metal fences and barbed wire.

Ivon was fortunate to survive the first few years; most children did not make it as the bigger and more vicious children ate, and eating meant survival. He survived off crumbs, bugs, and food he could steal from other children.

The concept of friends and family was foreign to Ivon. There was only self and others. Life was haves and have-nots. If others ate or drank more, he had less. There was no tomorrow. All that mattered was living through the day.

When a child would die, the soldiers did not notice until the next morning when they found their naked body by the door. It was an inconvenience, as now they had to drag the body out and dig an unmarked grave. No tears were shed as this meant one less in the competition for food.

Children of all ages would be dropped off at all hours. The very young would cry until a larger child beat them to silence. Older ones fared better, but not by much.

Beyond the hell of the camp, Ivon suffered from horrible voices that tormented him. He would spend sleepless nights in terror at the foul things the voices said.

Ivon did not count the years as there was only now, only life and death. One especially cold month, Ivon experienced a growth spurt. The sleepless nights of pain as his legs expanded signaled the change. Nearly overnight, he was now large for his age; he became the largest child in the camp. This extra size made the daily fights for food easier for him. He now regularly had enough extra rations to trade for favors and baubles. His large stature and extra food gained him a following in the camp. Ivon learned fear was a powerful tool. He and his gang of "golovorez" ruled the orphanage with cruelty and violence.

There was one thing that was peculiar about Ivon that benefited him in addition to his size. Sometimes, when someone spoke to him, their voice would sound as if they were underwater. At first, he did not think it was strange. He thought perhaps people mumbled sometimes or he had a hearing problem. He was also afraid it was a weakness and did not share it with the other children. It took a long while before he realized that when their voice would change, it was when they lied.

This realization became a new tool in his reign over the other children. If Ivon needed information from another child, he quickly learned that violence would produce answers. Someone stole the bread from Ivon? Just beat the other children until you find what you need. He would brutalize the orphans that had the 'lying voice' as he called it in his head. Once the answer came out sounding normal, he knew it was not a lie, and he had the information he needed.

Life went on like this for Ivon for untracked years. He was more animal than human. He had not heard music, read great works, seen art, or experienced love or friendship. His life was survival.

Visitors to the camp were rare. Russia was too busy falling apart after losing the Cold War for anyone to care about orphans. Sometimes, Russian Army officers would show up and leave new children or take a few children away. Those that were taken were never seen again.

One miserably cold day, the camp hosted a special guest, a Colonel.

Colonel Petrov was tasked with closing the war orphan camps; the Soviet Union had finished collapsing from the Cold War with the States, and the Russian Federation was working to hide the atrocities its former form had committed. These camps could be a public relations disaster.

The morning of the visit, the camp staff had lined the children up outside along the camp wall in preparation for Colonel Petrov's arrival. It was a gloomy, icy day. The children stood shivering against the frigid breeze that pounded them.

The Colonel's entourage arrived in a long black Mercedes-Benz W100 600 with colorful flags, followed by a giant green truck.

A stern and muscular woman with short dark hair exited first from the driver's side of the black car and ran around to open the rear passenger door. The Colonel stepped out. Petrov was tall and slender. He had dark, thinning hair, gray eyes, and an unnaturally small mouth. His dominant feature was his prodigious nose with a scar where a mole was removed. His clean, pressed uniform clinked with medals and brass buttons.

Petrov's walk was all legs, his arms held limp at his sides. He strode across the field and approached the children. He ignored the salutes of the camp soldiers and paced the line of children, looking over each one. As he reached the end, he turned to the camp staff, "Separate the boys and girls, then arrange them by height." His high pitched voice, not hiding the inconvenience of this errand.

"You heard him," yelled one of the staff, "Boys stay against the wall and line up by height. Girls move across by the outhouse and line up the same."

The children ran to follow the orders. They did not want a rifle butt to the back of their heads. Within a few seconds, the lines were established.

Petrov walked the girl's line first. There were only six. "The two older ones, put them in the truck."

One of the staff ran over and grabbed the two girls, each by the arm, and led them to the Ural-4320 parked behind Petrov's car.

Petrov turned his attention to the boys, smiled, and softened his voice, "Russia is going to care for you properly now. We have homes and families ready to take you in."

Ivon heard Petrov's voice as a lie. He fought his urge to react.

Petrov continued, "Today, we will take you away from this life of pain." It did not sound like a lie. Ivon relaxed.

Petrov turned and faced the children, "There is warm food, soft beds, and safety. There is nothing to fear."

The words had the lying sound. The lie of 'nothing to fear' had the opposite effect and drove fear into his heart like a dagger. Ivon was cold and tired and could not control himself. "He's lying!" he yelled.

The stern woman strode over and slapped Ivon across the face, "Do not speak to the Colonel as such."

Ivon recovered and gave the woman a hard look.

"This boy, he is the biggest of the group," Petrov noted. "He has some energy. Have him fight the next two biggest. The winner gets candy."

The two boys were Ivon's gang members, but survival and the promise of filling an empty belly were stronger than loyalty. The one next to Ivon grabbed him in a bear hug, and the other punched Ivon in the face.

Ivon screamed, the agony of surprise and betrayal coursing through his blood. He flailed wildly with his legs at the boy holding him; a foot caught, and they fell backward. The boy loosened as the wind was knocked from his lungs. Ivon was up facing the boy who had punched him. Ivon dove and clawed at his face, biting and tearing at his former comrade. The boy yelled in terror and tried to crawl away.

Petrov drew his pistol and shot the fleeing boy.

The other boy was still on the ground and still struggling to catch his breath. Ivon ran over, jumped, and landed hard on the boy's rib cage, bones cracking. The boy gurgled and sputtered.

Petrov walked over to the boy on the ground, gun aimed. After a minute of struggle against the inevitable end, the boy died.

The other boys and girls had all dropped and cowered against the walls. Ivon stood and faced Petrov, expecting a bullet. He would face his death.

"This one comes with me," said Petrov, pointing to Ivon. "Kill the rest, burn and bury the bodies. This building is now closed."

As the soldiers went about their work, Ivon was led away by Petrov to the black car with the Russian Federation flags. The sounds of gunshots and the screams of the children echoed off the building that was his home as he entered the car. Petrov entered the other side. Soft black leather welcomed him as he sank into the seat. The sudden luxury of the vehicle captured Ivon's wonder. He had never seen anything so clean.

An orange flash flickered against the window. Ivon turned to see the camp ablaze and the soldiers tossing the bodies of the children into the inferno. The inferno rose and engulfed the main barracks. Ivon's home for his entire life was now a hellfire fed by the children who had been his enemies since birth. No tears were shed, and no sadness touched Ivon's heart.

"Would you like some chocolate?" offered Petrov as he lit a long cigarette.

ROLAND AND THE TANK

Father Conte paced the aisle of the Vatican jet. "I question justifying the expense of this jet just to follow a hunch."

"This is more than a hunch," responded Melissa who was seated in an aisle seat. "This is actionable intelligence of a possible Paladin. A Paladin that a demon confessed to know of."

"And you trust the word of a demon?" quipped Conte.

"No," replied Melissa, "but they knew all of our names, and that makes anything they say worth investigating."

Conte stopped in front of Melissa, "Damn sloppy execution is how they know your names."

"Father," calmed Melissa, "please sit. We are landing soon, and we can discuss the value of this mission in the debrief."

Father Conte 'harrumphed' as he plopped into a seat.

The plane landed, and the Paladins gathered and prayed together. The team stood in a circle, and Melissa prayed for their safety and for God's help in their search.

Dear Father,
Protect us and guide us as we search for your chosen servant
Shield us from those who would bring harm
Lay peace on our hearts give us strength
Amen

They unloaded their gear. Oliver stepped out to the stairs and looked around at a familiar sight.

"This is the same airport from the time at the catacombs. We were this close to Ivoire?" asked Oliver.

"We are not sure if Ivoire is a Paladin. It could be a coincidence," said Melissa.

"Or the demon from the catacombs is how they found her first," said Oliver.

"We won't know until we find her," said Melissa.

"Yeah-" Oliver's eyes caught another familiar site. "The Land Rover is still here!"

"Would you like to drive?" Melissa teased.

Oliver looked at her and chuckled as he shook his head.

The team loaded into the vehicle. Melissa drove with Father Conte up front. Oliver and Roland sat in the rear.

They cruised along the desolate countryside. Winter had not produced the first snow yet, but the trees and grass had already shed their green. A recent rain had drenched the land in moisture. Small, quiet homes and farms speckled along the low mountains. They approached their destination when Melissa turned off the main road. They drove through a bumpy and rocky section that was more beaten path than road. They approached a lonely hill overlooking a shallow valley formed by a small river.

They parked the vehicle at the base of the hill that offered a view of the town and walked to the peak. At the peak, a lonely oak tree, barren of leaves and nuts, stood a solitary watch over the valley. From the base of the tree, they had an ideal view of the quiet town.

The town was a handful of houses hugging the river that flowed down from the mountains. A single dirt road that intersected the river split the town in two. At the far edge of the town were the remains of a church.

Melissa had a pair of binoculars out and was scanning the town. "I do not see any Paladin essence. The town's people I can see are all human, so nothing strange yet."

Oliver sat next to Melissa, who offered him the Binoculars.

"Do we know if there is a house she frequents?" asked Oliver.

"No," replied Melissa. "All we know is she comes here regularly."

"I see the remnants of what looks like a church," said Oliver. "Many of the buildings still show damage from a war."

"The far side of the river is Russia. It is likely this town was a hot spot during the Ukrainian war for independence. Let's get comfortable; we will observe the town from a distance for a day or two and then move in for a closer look," said Melissa. "Isaac packed some food. Are you hungry?"

They watched the lonely village until night fell. Isaac had prepared cucumber sandwiches and a fruity trail mix. Oliver and Melissa ate as they quietly watched the sunset. The moon chased away the day, and stars unfolded across the sky. At the base of the hill, Oliver could hear Roland singing quietly as Father Conte snored in the front seat of the vehicle. It was a peaceful moment that reminded Oliver of his Middle East trip with Gerin.

Near midnight, a car approached from the west. Melissa grabbed the binoculars and followed the car. It was an older model LuAZ that bounced along the dirt road.

"Anything?" asked Oliver.

"Maybe," said Melissa. "There might be something."

"Look... to the east across the river," said Oliver.

Multiple headlights shone in the darkness. They moved slowly, single file, across the plain towards the river. Melissa aimed her binoculars at the lights.

"Military vehicles," said Melissa. "Looks like some trucks... and a tank."

"Which military?" asked Oliver.

Melissa leaned in and scanned the vehicles. She put down the binoculars and looked at Oliver, "Russian."

They jumped up and ran down the hill to the vehicle with Father Conte and Roland seated inside.

"What is it?" asked Conte who was startled awake at the commotion. "Did you see her?"

"We are not sure," answered Melissa. "But Russian military vehicles are approaching the town."

"So, we are leaving," Conte more ordered than asked.

"No," said Oliver. "We need to help evacuate the citizens."

"We certainly are not," said Conte. He crossed his arms. "This sounds like a war, not a demon infestation. Besides, it may be nothing. They may just be passing by."

"If Ivoire is down there, and she is a Paladin, then we–" Melissa's words were interrupted by the sound of the tank firing.

"They are attacking!" yelled Oliver.

Roland reached forward and lifted Conte by his shirt out of the driver seat and into the rear next to him. "Rescue those who are being taken away to death; hold back those who are stumbling to the slaughter."

Conte sputtered in confusion and shock as Roland moved him.

Oliver jumped into the front seat while Melissa took the driver seat, started the vehicle, dropped it into gear, and tore off across the field.

"Stop this vehicle at once," demanded Conte. "I will not be taken into a war zone."

"You are free to exit anytime," said Oliver as he gestured out the side of the moving vehicle.

"Roland is going with us," added Melissa.

Conte looked at the ground speeding by, then at Roland; he leaned back and crossed his arms. "Fine. I am documenting all of this."

As they neared the town, the sound of gunfire, the tank firing rounds, explosions, and screams echoed between the homes and out across the plain. Melissa skidded the vehicle to a stop behind the first building. Oliver hopped out and ran to the corner of the building, his right revolver drawn. Roland was at the rear of the vehicle, donning his armor.

"Father," said Melissa. "Stay here in the vehicle. Honk the horn if you are threatened."

"You are going to leave me here?" protested Conte, "defenseless?"

"But the Lord is faithful. He will establish you and guard you against the evil one," replied Roland.

"The tank is at the end of the street on the far side of the town by the church," said Oliver. "The other vehicles have split and are circling. Looks like thirty soldiers."

Melissa ran over next to Oliver and peeked around, "I see demon essence mixed in with the soldiers and… Paladin's glow. A Paladin is here. Do you see any civilians?"

"There are a few still in the homes," said Oliver. "A few families drove off down the road."

"Our priority is to protect these people," said Melissa.

"Right," said Oliver, "Roland, is your armor tank proof?"

Roland stepped around the vehicle, his armor reflecting the light in the night. "No weapon that is fashioned against you shall succeed." He lowered his visor and stepped around the corner.

Oliver and Melissa stayed behind him as they walked down the street.

"Should we stay close to the buildings for cover?" asked Oliver.

"I beseech you therefore, brethren, by the mercies of God, that ye present your bodies a living sacrifice, holy, acceptable unto God, which is your reasonable service," replied Roland.

Oliver saw a pre-shadow of a soldier come around the corner to this left.

The soldier shouted in Russian and pointed his rifle. Two other soldiers joined him and pointed their rifles. Oliver fired three shots, and three hands were rendered useless with missing fingers. The soldiers dropped their weapons and grabbed their hands as they screamed in agony. From the right, five more soldiers ran out and opened fire on the Paladins. Roland raised his shield, and bullets twanged against it. Crushed rounds rained to the ground.

Oliver fired over the shield, blowing out kneecaps and elbows. "Melissa, do you see which house the Paladin is in?"

"Yes," she pointed. "The last one on the left. Her essence leads there."

The tank rumbled around the house she pointed at and aimed its cannon at the Paladins. Roland sprinted towards the tank.

Oliver fired at a door lock to his left and kicked open the door. "In here!" he yelled at Melissa. They dove in through the door and slammed it closed. Oliver spun to the window to cover Roland. A family was in the house hiding.

"Flip the table on its side and stay behind it," said Melissa to the family as she helped them create cover.

Other soldiers had arrived and were tending to the ones Oliver had shot. One raised his rifle at Roland, Oliver sent a round through both his biceps.

The tank fired a round. Roland, in full stride, angled the bottom of his shield forward, and the round ricocheted up off the shield and streaked up to the sky, where it exploded, casting a yellow-orange glow on the town. The force of the blast shattered windows.

Roland leaped and landed on the tank, the vehicle's suspension shifting from the impact. He swiped his sword down onto the primary weapon. The clang echoed deafeningly through the town. He lifted his sword; he had dented the barrel of the cannon, rendering it useless. The hatch popped open, and an arm aimed a pistol at Roland. Roland grabbed the arm, yanked the man out, and flung him to the side, smashing into the wall of a house and falling limp. Another man slammed the hatch shut. Soldiers outside of Oliver's view fired as bullets rang against Roland's armor.

"There is a demon in the tank!" yelled Melissa.

Roland thrust his sword into the tank, penetrating the steel. A voice inside screamed in pain. Roland stabbed the point of his shield into the seam of the hatch and leveraged it up, bending the lip of the hatch. He pulled his shield out and thrust a gauntleted hand under the opening, then stood, grunting. The gunfire stopped as the sound of metal straining screeched out. The area was still and silent at the sight of the impossible being made possible.

Roland rose, lifting the hatch and bending the steel. He yelled in his mighty effort until the hatch broke free; he tossed it aside where it fell with an earth-shaking clang on a Russian jeep, crushing the engine.

Roland reached into the tank and pulled out a soldier with one hand. He presented the soldier to the building Oliver and Melissa were in. The man had a gash on his shoulder, and blood was flowing out. "Whose likeness and inscription is this?"

"That is a human!" yelled Melissa.

Roland tossed the soldier to join the one he had thrown earlier. The soldier screamed in flight until the impact of the wall silenced him.

An arm wielding a pistol reached out and fired at Roland. The bullet impacted his armor and fell dead on the tank. Roland stepped on the arm, and the owner howled.

"That's the demon!" yelled Melissa.

Roland lifted the demon by the arm he had been standing on and pulled him to be face to face. "Behold, I cast out demons and perform cures today and tomorrow…'"

The demon was dressed in an officer's uniform and insignia. It laughed and spat on Roland's visor, "You tell your God that he tells beautiful lies." It pulled a knife and stabbed against Roland's armor uselessly.

Roland punched the demon in the chest, and the bones cracked with a snap. The visage of the commanding officer faded until a white-skinned demon lay bare for all to see. Four soldiers from different alleys charged at Roland with a hiss, firing their weapons, their disguises fading as they took their demon forms.

Oliver threw the door open and fired four times. Four demon heads exploded, and bodies fell to the ground, black blood flowing from their wounds.

Most of the rest of the soldiers screamed and threw down their arms and ran. Some retreated with the wounded. Others prayed in their native tongue as they fled. Back in their vehicles, the convoy sped off over the hill they came from, short one tank and a jeep. Oliver and Melissa exited the house and walked to Roland.

Roland presented the demon to Melissa and Oliver. It was pale and sickly with green eyes and sharp teeth. It coughed up black blood that spilled down to the Russian uniform that hung on its frame as a child wearing his father's clothing.

Melissa asked, "What are you here for?"

A female voice, thick in a Ukrainian accent, came from the door of the nearby house, "I think he is here for me."

An athletic blonde woman with hair that ran past her shoulders stepped out of the doorway with her hands raised. She had hazel eyes, a straight nose, and a small chin. A classical European beauty. She wore a black topcoat with a blue scarf around her neck.

The demon kicked against Roland and hissed. Oliver stepped closer to the demon and asked, "How did you know she was here?"

The demon swiped at Oliver and laughed as he dodged the attack. Roland punched the creature again, and it fell unconscious.

"What is that?" asked the woman.

"That is a demon," answered Melissa. "Sent here to kill you, we think."

Roland hopped off the tank and brought the demon in closer view to the woman.

"I don't believe in demons," said the woman.

"They're real," said Oliver. "Let me prove it." Oliver raised a revolver and held it against the demon's head. He looked at Melissa, and she nodded. Oliver fired a round into the demon's head; it burst with black blood splattering against Roland's armor.

Roland dropped the lifeless body.

"What does that prove?" asked the woman.

"Wait," said Melissa.

After an uncomfortable passage of time, the demon began to dissolve into ash.

"Do normal things die like that?" asked Oliver.

"No," replied the woman. "But it does not mean it is a demon."

"Perhaps," said Melissa. "I can offer this. Your name is Ivoire, and there is something special about you. A skill you have that makes you different. A skill that is not learned, a skill that can only be explained as supernatural."

"How do you know my name? How did you and this demon find me? How did you know about my ability?" asked Ivoire.

"I knew how to find you because the Russian government knew how to find you. I know many things that would be of interest to you," said Melissa.

The memory of Oliver meeting Melissa in his church swirled in his head.

Melissa continued, "Most importantly, I know that you are a Paladin."

IVOIRE

    It was a happy day. The sun was peeking through the clouds as the remnants of an afternoon storm moved east past the mountains. The air was fresh and cool. The ground was soaking up the last of the rain that came and went with a tease. Ivoire was walking home from her grandmother's house and their daily lesson. Her father should be home from work soon. Her grandmother had given her a special treat, a shank of ham. She planned on preparing it with the potatoes and carrots they received from their neighbor's garden.

    Today's lesson was caring for potatoes, how to plant an old potato, and how it grew into many more with care. While she could say that the daily lessons with her grandmother were her favorite, she loved every aspect of her life. She loved her small town, her house, and her room, which was warm in the winter and cool in the summer. Most of all, she loved her father.

    As she walked home with her prize, she recalled life with her father. He raised her alone as her mother died giving birth to her. Her father would often say she looked so much like her mother, especially her hair. Every night, she would brush her hair and keep it long, just like the picture she had of her mother. They have lived in this simple town near her grandmother since her birth. Her grandmother cares for her and teaches her while her father works repairing cars.

Book of Ivon and Ivoire

Ivoire smiled and waved at familiar faces as she walked. People who are as much family as they are neighbors. At the Bondar house, Mrs. Bondar greeted her outside and gave her a loaf of bread as she asked about her grandmother. She smiled at Mr. Witki, who was on his porch, smoking. He waved with a smile as the smell of cheap cigarettes wafted across the way.

Along her walk home, she passed many buildings that were damaged. Her father would often tell her stories of how the town earned its scars. Bullet holes adorned the buildings, and craters speckled the fields from explosions. Small hand-built homes lined a single dirt road that led from the river up to the church on the smaller of two hills that frame the town. This simple town is now part of Ukraine. Before she was born, the town was part of the Soviet Union. Her father shared stories of the war to free their country. He sometimes gets sad when he tells these stories, and he says many people he loved died.

Ivoire loved her father's stories. He is an animated and enthusiastic teller. Her favorite stories are how he and her mother met in the medical tent. How they fell in love. How they got married by a lake in France. How they worshiped God in the church before it was destroyed in the war.

The townspeople also loved and helped to raise Ivoire. She enjoys nothing more than listening to people tell stories of their lives. She has learned that people love to talk about themselves. They tell stories of the history of their town and the families that lived there. When people tell their stories, the sound of their voices has a pleasant and calming effect on her.

On Ivoire's tenth birthday, her father planned a surprise party for her. He tried his best to hide the details of the event, but Ivoire was able to know when her father was not truthful. The pleasant ring his voice normally carried was gone when he hid the details of the party. There were other times when her father's voice changed, each time when he was hiding something or wanting to change the subject. The people of the town would also have their voices change at times. Mostly Mr. Witki, his voice changed when he told stories about his time as a famous movie star. She was eleven before she put the pieces together and realized that people's voices changed when they lied. At first, she thought it was a normal thing; lies are a sin, and God is simply uncovering the sin. When she asked her father about it, he said that it was something unique to her. After testing it for himself and seeing it to be true, he was amazed but also cautious. He warned her never to share that she has this gift with others.

  She was twelve this year. The curly hair of her youth had straightened and thickened. She now had silky blonde hair like her mother. Her father kept telling her that her hair would darken as she grew older, but it only seemed to get lighter each year. She had only two photographs of her mother that survived, and they were among her most precious possessions. One was of Ivoire's parents' wedding and another was from behind of Ivoire's mother sitting on a bench looking at a lake. Her mother's blonde hair draped behind the back of the bench and almost touched the ground.

  Ivoire's father loved her and raised her in a supportive and loving home. He did the best he could being a single father in a third world country. Ivoire never knew hunger, always had a roof over her head, and always felt loved in her home. Her father worked until his fingers bled to ensure she was comfortable and happy. He was a kind and God-loving man, quick to laugh and slow to speak. When not working, he would sit in his favorite overstuffed chair and read his Bible until he fell asleep. He shared in the faith of his mother and daily read the Bible and prayed with Ivoire. They regularly attended a church service that was held on the field next to the remains of the old church. Ivoire enjoyed her life.

  As Ivoire approached her house, her pace slowed. It was a simple house that her father had repaired away the damage from the war. The front door was red and flanked by a pair of flower gardens that Ivoire would lovingly replant every spring. Her father loved lilacs and lavender, and the house always smelled of them. The yellow paint of the house was not perfectly matched in every area, and the black shingle roof had a few brown and red shingles. Spare parts are hard to come by in this part of the world and they had to make do. Next to the house was a carport that her father used to repair cars for people in the town and the nearby areas. Ivoire loved this house.

Today, there was a car parked in front and not in the carport. Her father did not own a car. The black car was clean and new, a rarity in this forgotten corner of the world. It had light blue flags with a yellow starburst cross.

She slowly walked by the car and approached the house. The car was shiny, she could see herself in the black metal. As she passed the car, she heard strange voices coming from inside the house. She peeked through the window and saw her father. She ran to the front door and opened it; inside, her father and a man in a brown uniform were seated at the table. The man at the table was chubby with gray hair. He had a happy smile and warm brown eyes.

Another man, also in uniform, was slender and serious, stood behind the other. Ivoire's father rose and rushed to greet his daughter.

"Hello, my love," her father picked her up into a hug. "How were today's lessons with grandmother?"

"Hello, papa," said Ivoire. "I had fun, and I learned a new song on the piano and how one potato can become many. Grandmother gave me some meat, and Mrs. Bondar gave me some bread, and I brought them for dinner." Ivoire pointed to the bag she dropped when her father picked her up.

"Wonderful," said her father. "We will have guests for dinner. Get cleaned up; we have much to tell you."

Ivoire and her father prepared a meal of ham, potatoes, and vegetables for their guests. Ivoire shared her day with her father, and he shared his with hers. She did not bring up the strange men in their house, and neither did her father. She lost herself in the ritual of making dinner and prolonged the moment. They were seated at the table when her father finally introduced the men as they ate.

"This is Major Koval," began her father. "He is the commandant of a school that our government has founded to train gifted children."

"Hello, Ivoire," said Koval, his voice warm and disarming. "Your father has told me much about you. May I tell you a story about my daughter?"

"Yes," said Ivoire. "I love stories."

"So your father has told me," Koval cleared his throat. "My daughter loves to pick flowers down by the river near our house in Toluna."

Ivoire's smile faded, and she looked to her father.

"You may speak freely, love," said her father.

"Father," said Ivoire, "he said 'pick flowers' in that funny way."

"What do you mean by 'funny way?'" asked Koval.

Ivoire looks to her father, afraid to answer.

"It is what we talked about in the letters," replied her father. "Lies sound funny to her."

"Interesting," Koval leaned in, placing his elbows on the table and tented his hands. "I am going to say some statements. You tell me which ones sound funny and which ones do not. Do you understand?"

Ivoire looked to her father.

"It's ok, love," he smiled. "I know I said not to tell anyone, but it's okay with this man."

"Yes papa," said Ivoire and looked at Koval. "Please begin, sir."

"I have a black car."

"That sounded normal."

"In my pocket is a silver key."

"That was not normal."

"This table is made out of water."

"That was not normal."

"Hmm...," Koval leaned back and brought his tented hands to his lips. "I want to try something." He turned to his assistant. "Give me a piece of paper and a pen."

The attendant pulled the requested items from his briefcase and handed them to Koval.

Koval wrote on the paper, folded it in half, and slid it to Ivoire's father, "Sir, please read these three lines to your daughter." Koval turned to Ivoire, "After your father reads a line, please let me know how they sound."

Ivoire's father unfolded the paper and began to read, "The door of the Commandant's office is green."

"That sounded normal," said Ivoire.

"The Major's cat has red fur."

"That was also normal."

"The Major has six toes on his left foot."

Ivoire giggled, "That was normal."

"Very interesting," said Koval. "Tell me how this sounds. 'I have blue skin.'"

"That sounded funny."

"Hmm..." Koval looked up at the ceiling. "I think I understand. Everything I had your father read was false. He did not know they were false. It would seem that when people speak the truth, the sound of their voice has one sound. She perceives this as normal. Your father did not know the things I had written were lies or truths; he read them, accepting them as the truth. I believe when a person speaks a purposeful falsehood, their voice sounds different to you. You have only known love and family, so to you, the truth is normal. Intentional deception is rare to you, so that's not what you hear as normal."

"Did she pass?" asked her father.

"Yes," smiled Koval. "We will take her."

"What do you mean 'take me'?" asked Ivoire.

"You are going to his school," said her father.

Ivoire's eyes teared up, "I don't want to go. I want to stay with you and grandmother." She ran to her father and jumped onto his lap, hugging him.

Her father pulled her in tight, "Oh, my love. You are not going away forever. You will stay at his school during the week. You will be back here every weekend to see Grandmother and me. We can go to church and have dinner together."

"I don't want to go, papa!" cried Ivoire.

Ivoire's father kissed her on her head, "I know love. This is a good opportunity to go learn from some of the finest teachers in Ukraine. You will make friends and see new sights. It will be fun, I promise."

Koval pushed back from the table and stood up, "Ivoire. You will see your father and your grandmother every weekend." He knelt next to Ivoire and looked her in the eye, his eyes softer; his words did not sound strange but pleasant. "Ivoire, I have spent many years teaching many children who are extraordinary. Great athletes, scholars, mathematicians, and logical thinkers. Children who grow and go on to do great and wonderful things. With all that said, I can say this after only knowing you for this short time. You are by far the most extraordinary child I have ever met."

THE SOUND OF TRUTH

      Oliver waited at the shooting range as Melissa introduced Ivoire to the history of the Paladins much the same way she did with him. The memory of his introduction to the Paladins, their origin, and their numbers flowed through him. He chuckled to himself as he recalled Persephone's reaction to revealing how they are "created" via a newlywed's marriage night consummation.

      The "outdoor area" was set to a "Western" setting that Oliver had customized. It presented a hot, arid desert with distant mountains that reminded him of the town of Drywell. Parched wind breezed and whistled through, flapping his duster. He was lost in reflection brought to him by the illusion. He wondered how Kevin, Cary, and the rest of the town fared.

      On the trip back from the Ukraine, Ivoire explained to the Paladins that she visited her childhood home as an escape from her work. Her grandmother and father had died years past, and the old home was her refuge from the world. Before leaving, she showed them their graves in the field by the wrecked church. Ivoire was easy to convince to come and seemed to be eager to learn more about the Paladins.

      Melissa, along with Ivoire and Roland, exited out the door leading to the gym and walked across the open field towards Oliver and the shooting range. As they walked, Melissa explained the details of the open training area. Oliver observed Ivoire as she walked. She was graceful and confident. Her eyes were always scanning and observant. She did not hide her beauty; she was open and embraced it. She was a contrast to the reserved Melissa.

"Welcome to the shooting range, Ivoire," said Oliver as they approached. "Did you enjoy Melissa's presentation and Roland's demonstration?"

"Hello, and yes," Ivoire answered. "A very impressive introduction. Now, It seems we are here to meet you formally."

"In that case," Oliver tipped his hat, smiled, and nodded at Ivoire. "My name is Oliver. I'm from the United States, and my Archangel is Michael. It is a pleasure to meet you.

"Hello, Oliver, a pleasure to meet you formally," Ivoire returned the smile. "I saw some of your shooting abilities the other night, most impressive. What is your gift?"

"I have predictive sight," answered Oliver. "Since you have already seen me shoot, Instead of me shooting some targets and wasting the bullets that Persephone goes through great pains to provide, what say we play a game?"

"Sure," replied Ivoire. "What is the game?"

"This is a simple game," started Oliver. "Put both your arms behind your back. Pick a random number of fingers for each hand. When ready, show us one hand. I will predict the hand and the number of fingers. Do you understand?"

"Yes," replied Ivoire, who positioned herself. "Ready."

"Left three–"

Ivoire played Oliver's game, and after Oliver correctly predicted the hand and the number of fingers six times, she commented, "You really are supernaturally skilled. I also see now why you use guns while Roland uses a sword and armor."

"Yeah, we complement each other nicely." Oliver looked at Roland, who nodded in agreement. "Are you a combat– I mean, what Archangel do you fall under?"

"Melissa showed me the Archangels and the pictures. Mine was under Uriel," replied Ivoire.

"Uriel," recalled Oliver. "The eyes of God. Spies and informants. So what is your gift?"

"When someone tells a truth, their voice has a pleasant sound to it," answered Ivoire.

"Can you explain that more?" asked Oliver.

"Let's go meet Persephone first," interjected Melissa. "Let her tell her story one time this way."

Melissa led the group out away from the shooting range and through the library to the armory where Persephone waited. She was loading bullets at the loading station when they walked in.

Persephone jumped from the loading bench and said, "Ivoire! Welcome to my domain, The Armory. I am Persephone, I come from Scotland, and my Archangel is Raphael. "

"It is a pleasure to meet you," said Ivoire. "But Persephone is not one of the names Melissa read to me on the list of Paladins."

Oliver laughed.

"What?" asked Ivoire.

"Persephone is her nickname," said Oliver.

"I see," said Ivoire. "So what is your Paladin name?"

"Ogier," blurted out Persephone. "And that is all I have to say about that."

"I see and shall ask no more on it," said Ivoire. "Please, tell me about your domain."

Persephone took Ivoire by the hand and showed her around the room. She danced along the walls from station to station. She opened the vault to Roland's armor and explained it with reverence. Just as she had done with Oliver, she guided her hand to touch it, and Roland quoted the Greek inscriptions. Persephone pirouetted across the room to the gate guarding the relic area and pulled it open.

"And these are the relics," said Persephone. "These are objects of significance related to the Paladins that we have collected over the years."

"These relics," said Ivoire. "Are they weapons and armor?" She paused at a bronze helmet.

"Not all of them are," replied Persephone excitedly. "While some, like Oliver's revolvers or Roland's armor, are quite effective in slaying demons, some are simple items that have no specific purpose. For example–" She twirled over and picked up a wooden plate. "This plate is made of wood from the cross that Peter was crucified on. The magistrate who ordered the execution had it made as a trophy, as you can see, no help in combat, but still of significance. Oh!" Persephone set the plate down and swirled again across the room. She picked up a piece of cloth. "This may be of interest to you. Ten generations ago, the Paladin Ivoire, this was her swaddling cloth when she was a baby." She danced over and handed the cloth to Ivoire. "It may 'do' nothing. But as it was 'yours,' it is yours again."

Ivoire accepted the cloth and held it in her hands. "This belonged to my ancestor?"

"Well–" said Persephone.

"Not a blood relative," answered Melissa. "I think it is time we told you about the blank boxes on the computer screen."

Melissa and the other Paladins walked Ivoire through the history of the Paladins and how the names work. Then, once again, to Persephone's embarrassment, how they are created and identified. Ivoire took each piece of information with a nod or an affirmative statement. Nothing seemed to phase her.

"So this cloth belonged to a prior Ivoire?" asked Ivoire.

"Yes," answered Persephone. "If you want, I can make it into something other than a small blanket. How about a scarf?"

"That sounds lovely," said Ivoire as she handed it back to Persephone. "What is your power, Persephone?"

"I would not call it a 'power' as much as a gift," Persephone said. "But if I focus on something I am able to see the parts, how it works, even the measurements."

"So you are not a combat Paladin?" asked Ivoire.

"Oh no," said Persephone. "I am an inventor under the Archangel Raphael."

"Alright," said Ivoire. "What about you, Melissa? What is your gift?"

"I can sense Paladins and demons," answered Melissa.

Ivoire nodded and breathed through her nose.

"You seem to be taking this well," said Oliver.

"I have seen many things that can only be explained by supernatural concepts," said Ivoire. "This is putting those things into place. I witnessed that Russian officer transform into that white creature that you said was a demon. I have seen how powerful Roland is and the magic of Oliver's vision. Most of all, with my 'gift,'" she smiled at Persephone, "all you say rings of truth, so you at least think this all to be real. I have long trusted my ability and have no reason to doubt it now."

"You started to explain your gift outside," said Oliver. "Can you tell us more about it?"

"There is not much to it," replied Ivoire. "When someone says a truthful statement, the sound of the words is pleasant to me; the back of my head tingles and relaxes me. If they lie or the statement simply has no bearing on the truth or lie, it sounds bland."

"So if I say, 'my hat is made out of spaghetti,'" said Oliver. "You would know it is a lie?"

"I would know you did not believe it is the truth," offered Ivoire.

"I don't understand," replied Oliver.

"Let's say that somehow you truly believed your hat being made out of spaghetti was the truth, even though it is not a fact. You believe it to be the truth. In that case, even though it is not a factually correct statement, it would still ring as a truth."

"So your gift has a blind spot?" asked Melissa.

"In a way, yes," replied Ivoire. "What people hold in their hearts as true can be hard to hide. If they have been deceived or misinformed and they believe something to be a truth, it does not have to be a fact to ring as a truth. So truth believed by a person is not always fact, and fact is not always what a person believes to be true."

"I see now why you fall under Uriel," said Oliver. "Such a skill would be invaluable to a spy."

"I think it's awesome," said Persephone. "Melissa, Oliver, and I have vision gifts, and you have an audio gift."

"Thank you," said Ivoire, who smiled at Persephone. "My gift does make getting information from people easier."

"Does your gift work over recordings?" asked Melissa.

"No," replied Ivoire. "It has to be live and in person. It does not even work on the phone."

"Just like you, Melissa," said Persephone.

"So if Melissa is a demon and Paladin sensor, then we could call you a truth sensor," said Oliver.

"That is as good a description as any," replied Ivoire.

"Is that what you did for the Ukraine government?" asked Melissa.

"You seem to know much about me," said Ivoire.

"We have resources at our disposal," replied Melissa. She turned to the other Paladins. "Let's go to the cafeteria, Isaac has prepared a welcome dinner for Ivoire, and if willing, she can tell us her tale."

They gathered in the cafeteria where Father Conte, who stayed to learn more of the new Paladin, was waiting with Isaac who had prepared a traditional Ukraine meal of borscht and pampushky.

"Where to begin my tale?" pondered Ivoire and she thought for a moment before she continued. "One day, a Major came to my father's house to take me to a special school."

The Paladins were enjoying the meal prepared by Isaac as they listened to Ivoire's tale of her childhood and meeting the Major. Father Conte had stayed for the meal and was very interested in Ivoire's story.

"Incredible," said Conte. "So if I say, 'There is but one true God,' you can tell if it is the truth?"

"I can tell you believe it to be the truth," answered Ivoire. "It does not make it a fact."

"Do you believe?" asked Melissa.

"In God?" replied Ivoire. "I am not sure. My father and Grandmother did. You all do. God's existence would explain much, but I have not seen any proof one way or the other."

"Is it possible for a Paladin to not be a Christian?" asked Oliver.

"It is," answered Melissa. "Remember, the only part faith plays in their creation is the faith of the parents."

"Has it happened before?" asked Oliver.

Persephone answered, "Yes, a few times."

"What came of them?" asked Ivoire.

"They eventually all accepted Christ into their heart," answered Melissa.

"For wisdom will come into your heart, and knowledge will be pleasant to your soul," said Roland.

"So," said Ivoire. "You expect me to be a Christian?"

"No," answered Melissa softly. "God has a plan and a time for everything. I have learned not to make any assumptions."

"Did you ever believe?" asked Persephone.

"When I was a child, yes," said Ivoire. "God was part of my life, part of my family. After my father died, well, I will just say that I had some doubts."

"I wish Gerin was here," said Oliver. "He explained God to me when we first met and I wish I could find those same words now for you."

"I am sure you will find them," said Ivoire. "I can tell you are sincere and wish the best for me."

"I must say," said Conte. "I have enjoyed this conversation, but my time is short. I have to get my report back to my superiors."

"And what is the summary of the report?" asked Melissa.

Conte's face hardened as she looked at the group. As he reached Persephone, he smiled, "The Paladins are a dangerous but righteous group who are doing God's work in ways others cannot." His scowl softened, "Funding shall not be affected."

Persephone smiled and hugged Conte, "Oh, thank you–"

She was interrupted by a beeping sound coming from the panel by the door.

"We are being paged," said Melissa. "There is an emergency."

The Paladins and Father Conte all moved to the Research room and activated the screen on the wall. An elderly man wearing red cardinal's vestments and biretta greeted them.

"Cardinal Sandri," greeted Conte. "What is the emergency?"

"Father Conte. We have a situation in the Republic of Cameroon. Cardinal Sepe was doing the pre-work for a visit by the Holy Father when he and his entourage were taken hostage. I want Roland to intervene and rescue Cardinal Sepe."

"This is most unusual," said Conte. "This seems more a matter for the UN."

"I am making this request," said Sandri. "Cardinal Sepe is a personal friend and the top candidate to be the next Pope. I want the finest warrior in the world to respond."

"Let each of you look not only to his own interests but also to the interests of others," said Roland.

"We can leave at once," said Melissa.

"No," said Sandri, "I want Roland alone on this. I do not need the 'American cowboy' making a spectacle."

"Roland and I can manage," said Melissa.

Sandri breathed through his nose, "No. Only Roland. I have already sent over the location and contact details. Leave immediately-"

The call disconnected.

"How odd," said Melissa.

"Maybe not," said Conte. "Cardinal Sandri is still upset about the shooting at the concert."

"But why not have Melissa go?" asked Oliver.

"I do not know," Conte paused. "Well, you have your orders."

Oliver smiled and patted Roland on the shoulder, "Roland, this one is all you. Have fun."

Roland was on a flight to the Republic of Cameroon within the hour and reviewing the briefing. The cardinal was taken hostage near the city of Yaoundé and moved to a fortified building two hundred miles east into rebel-controlled territory. The Cameroon government had provided a vehicle and driver to take Roland to the compound. Roland prayed through the flight, and as the plane touched down, he readied his gear. He exited the plane carrying his armor in its case. A wet, hot wind greeted him as the plane's door opened. Warm rain pounded down and thudded on his shoulders as he walked down the steps.

A dark-skinned man in a Cameroon military uniform was leaning against a green four-wheel drive vehicle and greeted, "Are you Roland?"

The man was tiny next to Roland, barely five feet tall.

"It is I; be not afraid," answered Roland.

"A pleasure, sir; my name is Jean," introduced the man. "Can I help with your bag?"

"For each will have to bear his own load," replied Roland.

"Sure thing," Jean opened the rear gate. "Here you go."

Roland placed his case, and the vehicle shifted under the weight.

"That better be guns in there," said Jean. "The place we are going is not friendly."

"Wisdom is better than weapons of war," said Roland.

"I suppose so," said Jean as he got into the driver's seat.

Roland sat in the back, and off they went.

"You ever been to Cameroon before?" asked Jean.

"I have been a stranger in a strange land," answered Roland.

"You talk funny, my big friend," laughed Jean. "Is English not your first language? It's not mine."

"Let your speech always be gracious, seasoned with salt, so that you may know how you ought to answer each person," said Roland.

"Sure," replied Jean. "Well, let me fill you in on a few things about where we are going. These are bad men. They have been a real pain for the government. They kill, they steal, they blow up buildings. All sorts of bad news. This is their first high-profile kidnapping, though. The Vatican only sent you?"

"Not that we are sufficient to think anything of ourselves, as of ourselves, but our sufficiency is from God," replied Roland.

"If you say so," said Jean.

They drove for another three hours when Jean stopped. The rain had stopped, and the first tease of the rising sun warmed the distant mountains to the East.

"We are about three miles away," said Jean. "You sure I can't take you closer?"

Roland exited the vehicle and pulled his case out of the rear.

Roland set his case behind the four-wheel drive vehicle, pressed a button on the side, and stepped back. The case split down the middle and expanded out, presenting his armor.

Jean exited the vehicle and walked back to Roland, "Is that armor?"

Roland strapped on his boots in front of the portable armor rack. His eyes were closed as he grabbed each piece and attached it to his body with practiced and graceful movements. He had his gloves, girdle, and breastplate on in a matter of seconds. He reached for his helmet and spoke.

"The Lord shall cause thine enemies that rise up against thee"—He placed the helmet on his head and lifted his shield—"to be smitten before thy face: they shall come out against thee one way"—He reached for the sword, tested its weight in his hands, and rose to his feet—"and flee before thee seven ways."

"You look like a Templar," said Jean. "But I do not see any guns. You think your sword is enough?"

"It is enough," replied Roland. He attached his sword to its magnetic holder on his back and tapped a button on his inner left wrist, "Your word is a lamp to my feet and a light to my path."

"Hello, Roland," chimed Persephone. "Hope you had a good flight. I have Melissa, Oliver, and Ivoire here with me. Conte headed back to file his report."

"Hello, Roland," said Melissa. "I hope your trip was comfortable. We have your video feed open now."

"Ok," said Persephone, "make your heading two-one-eight. Your distance is three point two miles."

Roland turned his body and burst into a sprint. His boots squashed on the wet ground.

Through Persephone's display, Ivoire could see Roland's dot moving across the map, "How fast is he running?"

"Thirty miles per hour, he will hit the base in about six minutes," answered Persephone. "The rain may be slowing him down."

Oliver whistled, "I will never not be amazed by his speed."

Five minutes later, Roland spoke on the communication, "They are almost ready to stone me."

"From what we can gather from the intel, the Cardinal is being held in the basement with his entourage. The government believes there are thirty to forty armed rebels between you and the Cardinal," said Melissa.

"I would quickly subdue their enemies and turn my hand against their adversaries," replied Roland.

"Good luck," said Oliver.

Through Roland's camera, the other Paladins could see him approach the building. It was a brown clay masonry building two stories in height. Rusty trucks were parked with men dressed in utility pants and t-shirts, carrying rifles standing behind. The men behind the vehicles saw Roland and yelled and pointed their weapons. More men pointed AK-47s through the windows and started yelling. When Roland was one hundred yards away, the men opened fire. He raised his shield, and bullets twanged dead against it. Roland ran to the man by the car to the left of the door. With his free hand, he slapped the rifle out of his hands and grabbed the man by his collar. He tossed the man into the other, and they crashed into the car, indenting the door of the vehicle to the sound of breaking bones and bending metal. Roland spun and kicked open the wooden double doors. The barred doors exploded, and wood shrapnel pummeled the men inside. Men poured into the antechamber, readying weapons.

A wooden walkway circled above the courtyard with men aiming down at Roland, and they opened fire. One tossed a grenade that Roland swatted out the front door, where it exploded and shook the building. Bullets thudded against Roland's armor and piled on the floor.

Roland roared over the gunfire, his voice amplified by his helmet, "Submit yourselves, therefore, to God."

The men continued to fire.

Roland dashed to the support beam on the walkway and sliced his shield through; the wooden structure wobbled and collapsed in a cascade of wood and nails, bringing the men down with it. Roland sprinted to a nearby man, pulled his rifle out of his hands, and clanged it against the man's head, sending him to dreamland. Roland tossed the rifle at a man to his right; it impacted against his arms, breaking them. Five men fled out the front door in retreat. Roland punched, tossed, and kicked his way through the men until only four were left standing. Men with broken bones and moaning mouths were scattered amongst the rubble of the building. Roland approached a man firing a .45 caliber pistol at him. Its bullets *clanged* in futility against the metal of his armor. Roland slapped the pistol out of his hand and lifted the man up by jacket.

"The one who seeks finds," said Roland, pulling the man close.

The man pleaded in French.

Roland spoke again in French.

The man pointed to a privacy screen leaning against the wall.

Another man closed on Roland and fired at his helmet point-blank. Roland backhanded the man, who cart-wheeled end over end, landing hard on his side.

Roland tossed the man he was holding at the screen, who crashed through and tumbled beyond. The last two men dropped their guns and ran for the front door.

Roland ran down the steps after the man he tossed. At the bottom, he stepped over the thrown man and entered a sublevel of a dirt room supported by makeshift wooden pillars and beams. The room was filled with crates of weapons and explosives. In the far corner, he found Cardinal Sepe on his knees, a man standing above him with a gun to the priest's head.

Roland commanded in French, "Thus says the Lord, the God of Israel, 'Let my people go.'"

The man yelled back and threatened to kill the Cardinal.

Roland dropped his shield and raised his hands in a surrender gesture. The man pointed the gun at Roland. Roland dashed and grabbed the gun, crushing it and the man's hand in his grip. Pieces of pistol and drops of blood fell to the floor. He lifted the man and tossed him against the wall. Roland reached down and helped Sepe stand.

"Thank you, Roland," said Sepe. "You were the right one to call."

"Everyone who calls on the name of the Lord will be saved," replied Roland.

"I have contacted your driver," said Persephone over the comms. "He should be there with the truck in a few minutes."

Four hours later, Cardinal Sepe, his entourage, and Roland were airborne, heading back to the Vatican. Sepe and Roland were seated at a screen talking to the other Paladins.

"Very well done, Paladins," Sepe said. "No one killed, and everyone rescued."

"Thank you, Cardinal," said Melissa. "We look forward to your feedback on the debrief at headquarters."

"That won't be necessary," said Sepe. "I will be going directly to my office."

"As you wish, Cardinal,' replied Melissa.

The plane landed, and Roland took the SUV back to headquarters.

"Welcome back," said Persephone, who greeted him at the entrance. "The video stream was a great watch."

They entered and Melissa was sitting in the library with Ivoire, "welcome back–" she paused and rose. "Roland, there is a faint demon essence coming from your case."

Roland set the case down, and Melissa approached. He pressed the button, and the case expanded.

"Were there any demons you ran across?" asked Melissa.

"Truly, I say to you, I do not know," replied Roland.

Melissa lifted Roland's right gauntlet. "This still has essence on it. You left the combat over five hours ago," Melissa said. "Only an exceptionally powerful demon could leave an essence this strong."

A CHILD'S GAME

Petrov and Ivon rode in the luxurious car, and Ivon enjoyed his candy. The dreary Russian landscape streamed by through tinted glass windows. They passed a security gate and drove down a long gravel driveway flanked by ancient oak trees growing in well-manicured grass. The driveway ended at a loop that led to a building that was larger than the facility where Ivon was raised. The tan masonry building was four stories tall with a red tile roof. The windows sparkled and reflected the setting sun in a glare. Russian Federation flags flanked the main entrance. The building was clean and well cared for. Far from the mess and negligence Ivon had known his whole life.

A stern woman in a Russian uniform ran down the stairs, opened Petrov's door, and saluted, "Greetings, Colonel. How was your trip?"

Petrov exited the car and half returned the salute, "Ahh, fine. I may have found a treasure. Come on out, boy."

Ivon exited the car after Petrov.

"This is Ivon," introduced Petrov. "Ivon, this is Captain Sidorov."

Sidorov was only a few inches taller than Ivon but broader by almost two feet. She was muscular with a hard face and short-cropped black hair.

"Hello, Sidorov–"

Captain Sidorov slapped Ivon, "You will address me as Captain Sidorov or Ma'am. Do you understand?"

Ivon dove at Sidorov and screamed, his face on fire with pain. She reached out and caught him by his throat in her massive hands. She lifted him as he struggled against her grip.

Petrov laughed, "There is the fire I saw in you. Yes, boy, we want that aggression. But I would not aim it at the Captain. She can crush an apple in her hands. Your throat would fare no better."

Ivon fought against her grasp and pounded on her arm. His vision blurred as his brain fought for oxygen.

Sidorov balled her free hand and smashed it into the side of Ivon's head. He fell limp.

When Ivon awoke with a massive headache, he discovered he was back in a bunk. The familiar sounds of children sleeping welcomed him.

Was it a dream?

The fog of head trauma had not cleared, and he sat up. He tried to survey the dorm. It was dark, but something was wrong. Gone were the smells of excrement and dirty humans. The air was fresh. The bunk had sheets and a blanket; not just these comforts, but they were clean. He tried to stand but was still dizzy. He shook his head and tried to see the child in the bunk next to him, hoping to see a familiar face. His vision came to focus, and it was a boy he did not recognize, he had short brown hair and a fat nose. He reached down and slapped the boy on the face.

"Ouch!" yelled the child as he woke.

The lights flickered on, and two Russian soldiers entered and grabbed Ivon. They dragged him to the end of the rows of bunks and pushed him to his knees. Children popped out of beds and stood at attention at the foot of their bunks.

Colonel Petrov sauntered in, "Good morning."

"Good morning, Colonel Petrov!" the children yelled back.

"We have a new recruit," Petrov walked to Ivon. "His name is Ivon. He has not earned a last name yet." Petrov spun and faced the child Ivon slapped. "Dimitri Golubev, you will be his mentor. But first, a lesson must be had."

The men holding Ivon stood him up and held him up by his arms.

Petrov began to pace the bunks, "What are the three rules?"

The children shouted in unison. "Number one, always obey a superior officer. Number two, do not act until ordered to act. Number three, all is done for the glory of Russia."

Petrov stopped at Ivon, "See, child—three simple rules. You broke rule number two when you attacked Dimitri. No one told you to slap him." Petrov looked to one of the soldiers and nodded. The man punched Ivon in the side. Ivon called out in pain.

"This is your first lesson, Ivon," said Petrov. "Life here is easy. You follow the three rules, and good things happen. You get candy, you get to watch movies, and you can play with toys. But," Petrov paused and lowered his tone, "you break the rules, and all you get is pain." He tapped his cane on Ivon's head, accenting the word pain. Ivon did not sense a lie in the man's words. "Now, if I have these men let you go, will you stand next to your bunk nice and quiet?"

Ivon breathed a few breaths and then nodded.

The men released him, and he glared at each as he walked and stood next to Dimitri.

"Very good," said Petrov with a smile. "Since we are up early… I say we go for a little run."

Petrov and his men led the children into the concrete block hallways painted red with a white drop ceiling and fluorescent lights. Along the walls were pictures of historical Russian men and Russian flags. Ivon walked in formation with the children past five other indoor barracks before passing a mess hall. They turned at the mess hall and followed the hallway past classrooms and, lastly, a gym. The soldiers led the children outside to the predawn darkness. They walked down the facility steps and followed a sidewalk a short distance until they reached a field with a wooden obstacle course. The children stopped at a white line painted on the sidewalk.

One of the soldiers stepped forward and commanded, "Double time, march!"

The children took off at a brisk pace; Ivon struggled to keep up; there was not much space for jogging in the confines of the old military base. Three miles later, Ivon broke from the group and vomited from the effort.

A soldier ran over and dragged Ivon to the group. "Catch back up!"

Ivon tried, but his body had reached its limit, and he fell to his knees.

The soldier walked over and kicked Ivon in the head. Blackness followed.

The first few months at Petrov's facility continued like this. The children exercised multiple times a day, usually running, push-ups, sit-ups, and the obstacle course. Any child who fell behind was beaten by the soldiers. When not exercising, the children attended classes on combat, weapons, vehicles, Russian history, and basic schooling. They were well-fed, and medical attention was available—only the weak received beatings. The strong thrived.

Ivon quickly adapted and learned how to survive and earn the extras. If he were the best at any activity, he would get special treats. Usually candy or a few hours at night where he could watch Russian made films about the heroism of its soldiers. The time at the school was a relative luxury compared to the military base he had come from. The voices that tormented him had even faded, and he finally found restful nights.

There were five other squads of children, three boys, and two girls. Often, they were pitted against each other in competitions. Sometimes, it was straight-up fights; other times, it was academic competitions. The winning squad was rewarded, and the losers went without food or sleep. Often children would fall

Book of Ivon and Ivoire

out from an exercise or were pulled from a class by strange men and were never seen again. Sometimes, children would show up left on a bunk, much as Ivon did. Ivon understood this reality better than the rest. Petrov rarely made appearances, but Ivon knew someone was behind the cameras who always watched, even in the bathrooms.

Ivon made special care to hide his ability to sense lies. He worried that he would be drug away like the other kids that never returned. His skill did teach him that adults lie at every opportunity and the children around them would take up the habit. The staff would lie about the strangest things. On one occasion, they said lunch was going to be sandwiches, and it was soup. Ivon could not understand how eager they were to lie.

Life like this continued for three years until one morning when Petrov entered the barracks as the children stood at attention.

Petrov passed the bunks in his gangly walk and inspected the children. Ivon's squad had been reduced to twenty children.

"Today is a special day," said Petrov as he spun away from the door and smiled with his yellow teeth. "We are going to play a game with every squad. The winning squad will move to a new school."

Ivon could sense the lie in Petrov's voice when he said the prize. He kept his composure. He knew what would happen if he brought attention to himself.

"Each squad will be given a piece of cloth with your squad number on it. You will hide and protect your 'flag' anywhere on the grounds. At the same time, you must find and capture the flags of all the other squads. When your flag is captured, you lose. And you know what happens to losers," Petrov sneered.

Petrov pulled a yellow piece of cloth about six inches square from his pocket. There was a red six sewn into it, "Here you go, squad six." He dropped the flag on the ground and exited the room.

"Dimitri," yelled Ivon. "Take that and go hide it. Take Maxim, Lev, Mark, and Rurik with you" Ivon turned to three others in the room, "You three with me, quick." He turned to the rest of the squad, "We are going after number 5; four of you hold this room; the rest split up and attack the other squads now!"

Ivon and the three boys he picked burst out into the hallway and went straight across into barrack number five. Petrov had just exited, and the door was closing. "Oh, Squad Six is here," he called into the room.

Ivon ran in and punched the first boy he saw, knocking him down. The other three from Squad Six poured in and followed his lead. They attacked any child in their path.

Ivon saw the purple flag with a white five dropped by Petrov still on the floor. He dove, slid onto the tile floor, and grabbed the flag. He stood and held it. "I have it, Five loses."

A voice came in on the PA, "You have to get it back to your barracks."

The members of team five, not injured by Ivon and his crew, all dove at Ivon. He swung wildly, punching and kicking. The other three from squad six pulled the boys off of Ivon. Ivon broke free and ran to the hallway and across to his barracks. He saw children from Squad Four entering the door to Barracks Six. Ivon reached the door, grabbed a Squad Four boy by his collar, and pulled him back, banging his head against the door.

He rushed into the barracks and held his prize high, "Squad Five has lost!"

The voice on the PA cracked, "Squad Five's flag has been captured. All Squad Five boys return to your barracks. Squad Six now has two flags. Any flag that is captured results in a loss."

The three Squad Four boys turned and faced Ivon.

Ivon balled the flag into his fist and yelled, "Come on!"

The ones that went with Ivon ran in and with the help of the other Squad Five boys, subdued the Squad Four boys, pushed them into the hallway, and barred the door with a bunk.

"Where is Dimitri?" Ivon asked to the room.

"He went out the window with two others," the one who answered pointed to the window that a thrown foot locker had broken. "They are hiding our flag."

Ivon handed the Squad Five flag to the boy. "Good. Hide this." He turned to the rest, who stayed behind, and the three who helped him with Squad Five. "I have an idea. You three stay here with me and catch your breath. Everyone else out the door and bring me captives from each team."

Ivon and the first three slid the bunk out of the way and let the others out.

"Wait," said one as he was about to exit. "How will you know it is us to let us in."

"I'll know," replied Ivon.

They closed the door and returned to the bunk. Ivon looked around. The room was secure with their captured flag. From the hallway, the sounds of children fighting, yelling, and crying could be heard.

I hope Dimitri can hide the flag well.

A few minutes later, someone knocked on the door and yelled, "I have a captive from Squad One."

Ivon did not sense a lie, "Let him in."

The boys at the door slid the bunk away, and a Squad Six boy, Arkadi, led in a girl by her hair; she had a black eye.

"Ok, now what?" asked Arkadi as he pushed the girl to the ground.

Ivon squatted down and grabbed her hair. "Where is your flag?"

"I do not know," she said defiantly. Her voice rang a lie to Ivon.

"She knows," he punched her in the nose, breaking it.

The girl started to cry, "I swear I do not know."

Ivon punched her again, blacking the other eye. "I know you are lying."

"Please, please, I'll tell," she said weakly.

"Well," said Ivon as he pulled her hair, lifting her head.

"The third hand-dryer," she said. "In our bathroom. We jammed it up in there."

Ivon looked at Arkadi. "Take her outside and go get the flag."

Arkadi exited, dragging the girl as a Squad Three boy tried to push his way in.

"Grab him," yelled Ivon.

The boys at the door pulled in the boy and threw him face down on the floor.

Ivon mounted the boy and pulled his hair. "Where is your flag?"

"It is in Petrov's offi–"

Ivon punched him in the back of the head, bouncing his face off the floor. "That is a lie."

The boy began to cry, "I don't know. I promise."

"That is not a lie," said Ivon. "Who hid it?"

"I don't know."

Ivon punched the boy again, and blood leaked from his ear. "Don't lie to me."

"Igor," the boy whimpered. "He hid the flag."

Ivon turned to a boy sitting on a bunk. "Take him to the hallway and bring me Igor from Squad Three."

A knock sounded on the door, "Let me in. It's me, Adrik."

"Wait," said Ivon. "That boy is lying. It's not Adrik. Grab him and pull him in."

The Squad Six boys slid the bunk out of the way, grabbed "Adrik," and pulled him in. Two others tried to push their way in. Ivon slammed the door on an arm; the owner screamed and pulled it back. Two Squad Six boys slid the bunk back. Two others held "Adrik" to the floor.

Ivon stood over "Adrik" and looked down at him, "Anyone know who this is?"

"Yes," answered a boy at the door. "That is Vassi from Squad Four."

"Perfect," said Ivon. "Vassi, where is your flag?"

"I don't know." It sounded like a lie.

Ivon kicked Vassi in the side. He heard a rib crack.

"Oh please…" begged Vassi. "I'll tell."

They were interrupted by the PA. "Squad Two has lost. All Squad Two children, return to your barracks. Squad Three now has two flags."

"Well," said Ivon, turning his attention back to Vassi.

"We buried our flag in the obstacle course."

"Any more specific?" asked Ivon.

"The pole by the rope climb, under the loose gravel."

Ivon looked at the two boys holding Vassi. "Take him there and get it."

A knock at the door sounded, "We are back from Squad One with the flag. Let us in."

"Let them in," commanded Ivon.

As the boys entered, the PA announced that Squad One had lost, and Squad Six now had three flags.

"Good," said Ivon. "Hide that flag. Three and four are all that is left."

Another knock on the door. "We have Igor!"

"It's them," said Ivon. "Let them in."

They dragged Igor in, who was unconscious.

"He is no good like this." Ivon punched one of the boys.

"He put up a fight," said the other. "It was an accident."

"Whatever," said Ivon. "Take him to the bathroom and turn a shower on him."

They tossed him in a shower and turned on the water. Igor jumped to consciousness and swore.

Ivon turned off the water. "Where is your flag?"

"I am not telling—"

Ivon kicked him in the face, driving his head against the tile wall. "Tell me where it is."

Igor, bleeding from his mouth, spat blood on Ivon.

"Drag him out here," Ivon said to the two other boys.

They pulled him out and laid him on his chest on the floor. Ivon sat on him and pulled his arm up to him. He grabbed the pinky and twisted hard, dislocating it.

Igor screamed and cursed, "Fine. This game is not worth it. The flag is in the duct above our door."

Ivon stood and looked at the two boys. "With me."

They went out to the main room, dragging Igor. The boys who went to the obstacle course to fetch Squad Four's flag had returned. The PA announced Squad Four had lost, and Squad Six now had four flags.

"Everyone with me," commanded Ivon.

He led Squad Five down the hall to the Squad Three barracks. The door was barred from the inside. The noise of fighting pierced the metal door. After a moment, the noise stopped, and the door opened; Dimitri stood there bloodied. He smiled, revealing a newly missing tooth as he let Ivon in.

"How did you get in?" asked Ivon.

"Same way I got out of our barracks," Dimitri looked over his shoulder at the broken Squad Three window. Between them were several Squad Three and Squad Six boys who went with Dimitri on the floor in various levels of pain and consciousness.

"Lift me," said Ivon to his squad.

They lifted him up, and he opened the vent. The Squad Three flag and the Squad Two flag fell out. They took the flags and walked down the hall back to barracks six.

"Where did you hide the flag?" asked Ivon.

Dimitri pulled it from his pants. "I just kept running."

Ivon smiled and slapped him on the back. They entered the door to barracks six, and the PA clicked on. "Squad Six has won. All children return to your barracks. Medical teams will be there shortly. Ivon of Squad Six, report to Colonel Petrov's office."

Ivon ran down the hall and up the stairs to the administrative office. He has never been up these steps. As he climbed, his spine tingled and grew cold. He walked past the olive-green secretary's desk and approached the door to Petrov's office.

He paused as another wave of chills gripped his spine. He closed his eyes and breathed hard, forcing movement back into his body, and knocked on the Colonel's door.

"Come in, Ivon." Petrov's voice slithered out the door.

Ivon stepped into the dimly lit room. The curtains were drawn, and all light came from the wall monitors showing views of every section of the compound. Petrov, seated at his dark wooden desk facing the monitors, was a shadow in front of the screens.

Ivon stopped at the desk and saluted the Colonel, "Reporting as ordered, sir."

Petrov waved off the salute and motioned to the chair in front of his desk without turning to Ivon. "Please, sit."

Captain Sidorov came in with a tray that had a glass bottle of soda, a piece of cake, and a sandwich and laid in on Ivon's lap.

"Please eat, Ivon," said Petrov. "That was a very impressive display. Tell me. How did you know when the other children were lying?"

"I have always been good at it," answered Ivon through a mouthful of sandwich. "I can hear when people lie."

"What do you mean?" probed Petrov

"People's voices change when they lie," Ivon answered and slurped down a gulp of soda.

"So if I say," started Petrov. "Every child here is going to live a long and happy life."

Ivon froze. He had been lured into this false security by weariness and the tasty food. Petrov knew his weakness and had exploited it. Worst still, Petrov was lying about the children living.

"Ahh," said Petrov and smiled. His yellow teeth reflected the light of the monitors. "You can tell I am lying."

"Am I in danger?" asked Ivon.

"No," paused Petrov. "Not today."

The words did not sound like a lie. Ivon relaxed and took a bite of cake.

"You are not going to a new school," said Petrov. "But you are getting a promotion. I want you to pick one child to promote with you."

Ivon swallowed the bite and said, "Can it be Dimitri?"

"Oh," said Petrov, who chuckled. "A good choice." He leaned forward and pressed a button. The PA clicked on, and Petrov's voice changed to the one that had been announcing the game, "Dimitri of Squad Six, please report to Colonel Petrov's office." Petrov leaned back and watched Dimitri on the cameras as he ran from barracks six to the staircase. When Dimitri reached the staircase, Petrov pressed the PA button and spoke in his normal voice. "All staff, spring cleaning has begun."

On the cameras, Ivon watched as a dozen armed soldiers ran down the hallway and split off, two each, into the barracks. Petrov turned and faced Ivon, who watched numbly as the soldiers opened fire and killed all the children, even the ones in squad six. The gunfire flashed through the monitors like fireworks.

"Today is your graduation day, Ivon Pravdivyy."

STRENGTH OF FAITH

Roland, Persephone, Melissa, Oliver, and Ivoire were gathered in the research room, watching the recording from Roland's helmet of his rescue of the Cardinal on the central monitor.

"So, who was the demon?" asked Persephone.

"It could have been any of these guys," said Oliver. "He punched or grabbed over a dozen of them."

"From the video, none of the men looked especially strong," added Melissa.

"Maybe the leader?" asked Ivoire.

"If the essence really belonged to something that powerful," replied Melissa, "Roland would have not been able to subdue him so easily."

"Can the essence rub off?" asked Oliver. "I mean the demon was there, left the essence behind, then Roland rubbed against it and carried it back?"

"I do not know," replied Melissa. "I have never encountered that scenario with my ability."

"What about the Cardinal?" asked Ivoire.

Silence grasped the room. The Paladins all looked at each other.

"You mean, is the Cardinal the demon?" asked Oliver, breaking the silence.

"Yes," said Ivoire. "Roland touched him when he helped him up."

"This Cardinal is favored to be the successor to the Pope," said Melissa. "He has been a popular man for many years."

"Have you ever seen him in person?" asked Ivoire.

Melissa thought and shook her head, "I cannot remember if I have or not."

"Wait," said Oliver. "Could it be? Have the demons infiltrated the Vatican?"

"I'm not jumping to conclusions," said Ivoire. "I am trained to be suspicious and to ask questions. This is only a possibility I offer with no supporting evidence."

"It does merit investigation," said Melissa. "As do these other things." Melissa looked at Persephone and nodded.

Persephone tapped on the controls next to the screen and the image changed to a picture of a house. It was a simple ranch-style, American suburban home with light green walls and a gray roof. A white wood railing framed a front porch.

"This house is reportedly haunted," continued Melissa. "The house is located in a suburb of Boston and has a bit of a history of hauntings. The owner was desperate enough to ask her church for help. The minister from her church has already visited the house and captured this video."

The screen changes to the recording. The camera showed a garage workbench illuminated by a work light. Screwdrivers, wrenches, hammers, and more are lifting off the rack and slowly floating to random spots around the garage. A middle-aged woman with short brown hair, wearing an apron and a blue summer dress, enters the screen from the right, and she points to the screwdrivers and other tools.

"This has been happening for a few days now," said the woman. "I called the police, and they thought it was a prank."

A man follows behind her; he is dressed in a light blue long-sleeve shirt and khaki pants. He is portly and thinning on the back of his head. He carries a Bible in his left hand and opens it and flips to a page.

"Yup," says the man. "You have a demon."

"Oh dear," says the woman. "Now what?"

"I can exorcise this creature," the man says. "But it may be dangerous. You go back in the house, and I'll do the rest."

The woman left the screen, and the man moved closer to the workbench.

"God of power, who promised us the Holy Spirit through Jesus your Son, we pray to you for these catechumens, who present themselves before you."

The tools that have been slowly moving across the workbench drop and clang on the bench and floor.

The man laughed, "Did not even need the 2nd verse…" He turned towards off-camera, "I think it is safe–"

The tools started gyrating on the bench, dancing over each other.

"Hold that," said the man. "This may need some more." He turned to the tools and continued, "Protect this house from the spirit of evil and guard them against error and sin so that they may become the temple of your Holy Spirit."

The tool's gyration intensifies; they bang on the workbench, causing the wood to chip and splinters to fly off.

"Save these your servants: free them from evil and the tyranny of the enemy. Keep far from them the spirit of wickedness, falsehood, and greed."

The tool's banging accelerates until it is a hum of noise.

"We ask this through Christ our Lord. Amen"

The tools stop in place, they rise, hovering in the air pointed at the man.

"I speak with the power of Christ," the man yells. "Leave this house!"

A wrench flew from the rest and crashed into the man's arm.

"I invoke the name of Jesus," his yell stifled by pain. "Return to Hell."

All of the tools fly forward, striking the man and the camera. The video ends.

"The minister, Robert Johnson, survived the ordeal," said Melissa. "He is currently at the hospital, and other than the police, no one has returned to the house."

"What did the police find?" asked Oliver.

"Nothing, just the scattered tools," said Persephone. "They think it is a stunt by the minister; he has a reputation."

"I want to take Ivoire and go and question the minister and the homeowner," said Melissa. "If this is real, I can exorcise the demon and give Ivoire a taste of our work."

"Want Roland or I to come for protection?" asked Oliver.

"Not needed," said Melissa. "This is a simple one. Instead," she turned to Persephone. "You have your own mission."

"Oh yeah!" exclaimed Persephone. "You two are going after a yeti."

Melissa and Ivoire leave the other three to brief on their mission.

"You do not have to come," said Melissa. "There is much to take in, and you have not had time to reflect."

"I am ok; besides, my curiosity is piqued," replied Ivoire. "Let's go exorcise a demon."

They took a Vatican jet to the executive airport in Boston, Maryland. From there, a self-driving SUV carried them on the ninety-minute drive through the suburbs to the hospital the minister was taken to.

They entered the hospital and identified themselves as parishioners of Pastor Johnson's church and were here as well-wishers. The triage nurse directed them to his room. Melissa paused outside the door to the Minister's hospital room. She placed a hand on the door, "would you pray with me?"

"Yes," answered Ivoire. "But I have not prayed since I was a child."

Book of Ivon and Ivoire

Melissa took both of Ivoire's hands:

Lord Jesus
Guide our actions as we help this man who is suffering
Guide our hearts to glorify your name
Amen

"Amen," replied Ivoire.

"I am going to let you take the lead," said Melissa. "Just ask him about what happened and follow your instincts on what to ask next."

Ivoire nodded, and they entered the room. The quiet beeping of the medical equipment greeted them in the well-lit room. The window curtains were open, and a few rays of sun peeked through. Pastor Johnson was reading a newspaper and looked up as they entered.

"Hello," said Johnson. "I am sorry, I do not recognize you. Are you members of my church?"

Ivoire looked at Melissa who had taken a seat at the far side of the room. Melissa placed her tablet on the cabinet next to her and started recording. She smiled and gestured to Johnson.

"No," said Ivoire. Her Ukrainian accent gave way to a Midwest dialect. "My name is Cyndi Smith. I am a reporter, and this is my producer, Stacy. We heard about your haunting and wanted to cover your story."

"Excellent," said Johnson, who gestured at his bandages. "Someone from the church must have called; they care so much for me. I am so happy my story is getting out. As you can see, it was quite the ordeal."

"It appears so," said Ivoire. "So there was an actual ghost there?"

"No," said Johnson. "A demon. An emissary from Hell."

"Goodness," said Ivoire. "Were you able to send it back to hell?"

"Yes," said Johnson. "I triumphed."

The 'yes' did not sound as truth, but 'I triumphed' did.

"How did you triumph?" asked Ivoire.

"I sent the demon back to hell," insisted Johnson.

None of the words sounded true.

"How did you send it back?" asked Ivoire.

"You know," said Johnson. "Read the Bible and told it to leave."

More lies.

"Exactly how did you tell it to leave," Ivoire moved closer. "Our viewers want more details. Can you act it out for the camera?"

"I commanded it," replied Johnson.

Another falsity.

"What words did you use to send it back?" asked Ivoire.

"My memory is a little fuzzy. It was a traumatic experience, and as you can see, I injured my head," replied Johnson.

The sound of his unaffected voice echoed in Ivoire's ear. She looked at Melissa with a worried face.

Melissa rose and walked to the door with her chair; she jammed the chair on the handle, barring the way. She said, "Ask him to say, 'Jesus Christ is Lord'."

Johnson scoffed.

"Say it," said Ivoire, her voice hardening, "say 'Jesus Christ is Lord.'"

"This is silly," said Johnson.

"Why is it silly?" asked Ivoire. "You are a minister of a church. Saying Jesus Christ is Lord should be second nature."

"I am an injured man," said Johnson. "I will not be treated as such."

"You do not speak the truth," said Ivoire. "What is your name?"

"Robert Johnson," said Johnson.

Ivoire turned to Melissa, "That is not the truth."

Melissa moved next to Johnson, "Help me hold him down, and when I say, 'We ask this through Christ, our Lord,' you must say, 'Amen.' Do you understand?"

"Hold him down and reply 'amen,'" said Ivoire.

"What are you doing?" demanded Johnson.

Melissa placed a hand on Johnson's shoulder and held his mouth closed against muffled protests with the other. Ivoire stood opposite Melissa and held down Johnson's other shoulder. Johnson struggled against Ivoire and Melissa. Melissa closed her eyes and began to pray.

God of power, who promised us the Holy Spirit through Jesus your Son, we pray to you for these catechumens who present themselves before you. Protect them from the spirit of evil and guard them against error and sin so that they may become the temple of your Holy Spirit. Confirm what we profess in faith so that our words may not be empty but full of the grace and power by which your Son has freed the world. We ask this through Christ, our Lord.

Ivoire replied, "Amen."

The minister yelled into his closed mouth. His racing heart beeped through the monitors. He struggled against the women holding him down.

Lord our God, you make known the true life; you cut away corruption and strengthen faith; you build up hope and foster love. In the name of your beloved Son, our Lord Jesus Christ, and in the power of the Holy Spirit, we ask you to remove from these your servants all unbelief and hesitation in faith, [the worship of false gods and magic, witchcraft, and dealings with the dead], the love of money and lawless passions, enmity and quarreling, and every manner of evil. And because you have called them to be holy and sinless in your sight, create in them a spirit of faith and reverence, of patience and hope, of temperance and purity, and of charity and peace. We ask this through Christ, our Lord.

Ivoire replied, "Amen."

Johnson shook violently. Ivoire mounted him, knees on his shoulders, and held him on the bed. The medical equipment sounded an alarm. Johnson struggled, then thrust his body; he elevated off the bed, lifting Ivoire with him, floating.

God of power, you created us in your image and likeness and formed us in holiness and justice. Even when we sinned against you, you did not abandon us, but in your wisdom, chose to save us by the incarnation of your Son. Save these your servants: free them from evil and the tyranny of the enemy. Keep far from them the spirit of wickedness, falsehood, and greed. Receive them into your kingdom and open their hearts to understand your Gospel so that, as children of the light, they may become members of your Church, bear witness to your truth, and put into practice your commands of love. We ask this through Christ, our Lord.

Ivoire replied. "Amen."

Johnson went stiff and collapsed to the bed. His heart rate steady and calm.

Melissa removed the chair barring the way and returned it to its place.

Ivoire dismounted and stood next to Melissa.

A nurse entered and checked on Johnson, "what happened?"

"He fell asleep while we were talking. He may have had a bad dream," said Melissa. "We will go now."

"Was that an exorcism?" asked Ivoire in the hallway.

"Yes," replied Melissa.

"You knew he was possessed," said Ivoire.

"Only once we arrived at the hospital," replied Melissa.

"You wanted me to figure out he was possessed by a demon," said Ivoire.

"I saw an opportunity to see you use your skills, to see what our mission is, and to see what we face," replied Melissa.

"You are so calm," said Ivoire. "Do you do this often?"

Melissa walked to the hospital exit. Ivoire followed, "This was a simple one. The demon probably took over this fool at the garage. A minister who was true of faith would have no issue doing what we just did. I could sense how weak the demon was. Even from the video, what most people call hauntings are usually weak demons. We will go and check the house to ensure there are no more traces of the demon. I feel confident we will find none."

"Why is the minister a fool?" asked Ivoire.

"If this minister had actual faith in Christ, no demon that weak could possess him," said Melissa. "He is probably running his church for money or fame and not out of service to God."

"You said from the video you could tell it was weak. How can you tell when there is a strong demon?" asked Ivoire.

Melissa paused and turned to Ivoire, "People go missing or die."

FRIENDS, FAMILY, AND FAITH

Major Koval informed Ivoire and her father that the next training session would begin in three months, and she could remain with her father until they returned. These were a hard three months for Ivoire. She was excited about the adventure but also hesitant to leave her father. She and her father spent more time together these three months than they had in years. Often, she would wake in the middle of the night from terrible nightmares full of foul creatures. Her father would rush in and comfort her until she returned to sleep.

The day came to leave for the first day at the school. Major Koval and his aide returned to Ivoire's house as she waited out front with her father. It was a cold day; winter had begun to approach, and the first few flakes of snow teased the ground. The black car stopped at the house, and Koval exited.

"Hello, Ivoire," greeted Koval. "Are you ready to go on this exciting adventure?"

"Hello, sir," answered Ivoire, her posture stiff. "Yes, sir!"

Koval smiled, "I see your father has told you how we do things in the military. This is good. Load your bags in the trunk, and we will go."

Ivoire's father helped her with her bags and lifted her in a giant hug. "I will see you every weekend."

"Yes, Papa," Ivoire's eyes tearing. "I know this is best, and I will make you proud."

"Go, my love," we will talk again in a week.

Ivoire ran to the car door and waved to her father, "Goodbye, Papa."

"We will care for your girl," said Koval as the aide started the car and drove off.

"This is a one-time thing," explained Koval as they drove. "On Fridays, you will take the train from the station near the school to the station near your home. From there, you can hire a ride or walk the rest of the way. Sunday night, you must return to school the same way. Please do not miss the train."

"Yes sir," answered Ivoire.

"I think you will like the school," said Koval. "There are many brilliant and special girls much like you."

A three-hour car ride later, and they were at the school. The car crested a hill, and Ivoire took her first look. The school was nestled on a hill in the open Ukrainian countryside. It was a long, three-story, tall, red brick building with a black roof. The building was clean and well cared for. Further down the hill was a metal building sitting next to a flat paved area. Past the metal building rested small wooden homes. The trees and grass were red and brown in preparation for the upcoming winter. They parked the car at the main entrance and walked Ivoire in.

She was shown past empty classrooms and presentation rooms. The sounds of someone exercising from the gym echoed through the halls. They passed a great cafeteria where a few girls sat at tables and talked as they ate. There were few children in her small town, and Ivoire's heart swelled with anticipation of making new friends.

They took her to the third floor, where the dorms lay. She was shown to dorm room number twenty-seven. The room had four wooden bunks on the walls, flanking a window that overlooked the countryside. Two gray closet lockers were on each of the near walls at the foot of the bunks.

"You are assigned bunk 'D,'" said Koval. "You also have locker 'D.' Please put your stuff in there. You can rest here for now. You will have three roommates who will be arriving over the next few hours. One of your roommates is Daryna, a fourth-year student and your room leader. Room twenty-seven is also your team for the upcoming year. She will explain the rest. Unpack and rest for now."

Ivoire unpacked her belongings and sat on her bed. The bed was small and firm, and sadness crept into her heart as she longed to return home. She had never been alone before. She hoped the other girls in her room would arrive soon and be her friends.

Her wait was not long. A short, stocky girl with short dark hair walked into the room. She wore a tan hooded sweater and baggy jeans. Her face was in a book as she entered and plopped her bags on her bed. It was an uncomfortable moment before she noticed Ivoire.

"Oh, hello," she walked uncomfortably close to Ivoire. "What is your name? Are you the first year for room twenty-seven?"

"Hello," said Ivoire. "My name is Ivoire, and this is my first year here."

"Welcome," said the girl. "My name is Sofiy. What is your specialty?"

"Specialty?" asked Ivoire. "What do you mean?"

"Oh, each of–" Sofiy was interrupted by a tall, athletic blonde girl walking into the room. Her golden hair was curly and ran in a single binding down to her waist. She wore red tight-fitting leggings and a matching long-sleeve top.

"Hello, Sofiy," said the girl. "Welcome back. Is this our first year?"

"Yes," said Sofiy. "This is Ivoire and... She was about to tell me her specialty."

"Oh yeah," said the tall girl. "Hello, Ivoire. I am Darnya, room twenty-seven's fourth year."

Ivoire rose out of her bed, "Hello, Darnya and Sofiy. I am very happy to meet you both."

Darnya turned to Sofiy, "Kalnya is our third year. Have you seen her?"

"No," said Sofiy. "Oh, she is an interesting one. Makes me wonder–" she looked at Ivoire. "What did you say your specialty was?"

"I do not understand," said Ivoire.

"Why are you here?" asked Darnya.

"My father wanted me to come and receive an advanced education," said Ivoire.

Darnya laughed, "Oh, it's advanced, all right."

Sofiy joined in on the laugh.

A tiny girl walked in the door. She was barely four feet tall and thin, with olive skin and black hair. She wore a black turtleneck under overalls.

"Oh hello Kalnya," said Darnya. "It seems room twenty-seven is complete." She turned to Ivoire. "Ivoire, this is Kalnya."

"Hello," said Ivoire with a wave.

"Hi," said Kalnya directly. "What do you do?"

"What do you mean?" asked Ivoire.

"Your skill," said Kalnya. "What makes you special?"

Ivoire thought about her father telling her not to share her abilities.

"She is a first-year," said Darnya. "She may not know what she can do yet."

"How do I know what makes me special?" asked Ivoire, trying her best to sound innocent.

Kalnya cleared her throat, "It's simple. You excel at some skill. Is there anything you're especially good at?"

"Nothing comes to mind," replied Ivoire.

"Well, we might be able to deduce it. You see, every room gets balanced. We get one girl from each year, each with complementary skills. We as a room are a team that must compete against the other rooms." She gestured to Darnya, "She is a world-class gymnast with total control of her body." She gestured next to Sofiy, "She is a computer and technology prodigy." She placed her hand on her chest. "And I am a logistician and math expert." She pointed to Ivoire, "Your specialty would complement us three. My guess is you are a historian or are very good at gathering data. Are you a voracious reader and researcher?"

"Not especially," replied Ivoire.

"What sort of hobbies do you have?" asked Sofiy.

"My favorite thing to do is talk with my grandmother," answered Ivoire. The grilling of her roommates was making her uncomfortable.

"She may not be special," said Darnya. "Remember that girl? What was her name? Mikhaila, I think. She was here at her parents' request and was just a normal girl. She ended up washing out."

"That may be me," said Ivoire. "My dad did ask for me to come here. I hope I can prove my worth."

"Me too," replied Kalnya.

Ivoire's roommates stopped their lines of questioning and showed her the facilities. They showed her where the bathrooms, classrooms, and cafeteria were. They helped her understand her class schedule and gave their tips on being on time.

The first six months at the school dropped into a steady rhythm. She studied the basics: math, literature, and history. The school hosted intense physical education and elaborate science labs that Ivoire found especially challenging. She returned home every Friday, and every Friday, her father met her at the train station. She spent the weekend sharing her stories from her time at the school with her family. Every Sunday, she would return and prepare for a new week of class. She enjoyed the time. She became friends with her roommates, Sofiy especially.

At her six-month anniversary, the school had its first team competition.

The girls were all gathered in the auditorium when the school Sergeant called them to attention, and Major Koval entered.

"Please be seated," started Koval. "I know you are each excited to begin the first school-wide competition of the year."

Excited murmuring flowed through the crowd and quickly faded.

"As you may recall, last year, the prize was an extra day at home. This year we think we have a better prize. The winning team will have a high-class dinner with their families at a very expensive restaurant."

Another wave of excitement rolled through the crowd.

Koval gestured for silence, "This year, the competition is pretty simple. There is a golden key hidden on the grounds. You will need to find this key. You can use any means to find this key. The team that finds the key then brings it to my office and opens the box on my desk with the key wins. I will give a few clues. The key is not in any toilets, it is not in any of the staff's pockets, and it is not in any administrative offices like mine. And with that," he paused. "Go!"

Most of the girls leaped from their seats and ran off in search of the key.

Darnya tapped Ivoire on the shoulder and motioned for her to follow. Sofiy and Kalnya were in the hallway looking at Sofiy's laptop.

"We are seeing if we can get into the security camera system and see if we can track the key being hidden," said Kalnya.

"Nice," said Darnya. She turned to Ivoire, "Where do you want to start?"

"The key is in his office," said Ivoire.

"Would he really be that dumb," said Kalnya. "He is a Major in the military and Commandant of this school. Plus, he said it was not there; what makes you think he lied?"

"Well," Ivoire stumbled over the words. "Can we just go and see?"

"It is a waste of time," said Kalnya. "Our best option is to follow sound evidence and leads. Not some *normal* girl's guess."

Ivoire looked down to her feet. She knew Koval was not truthful but feared sharing how she knew.

"I say we split up, and a few go to the office," said Sofiy, who smiled at Ivoire. "Maybe it is a double bluff. Maybe it is that easy."

Darnya crossed her arms, "Ok. Ivoire you and I will go. You two keep checking the videos."

Ivoire and Darnya made their way to Koval's second-floor office. Girls were running up and down the hallways, opening doors and removing ceiling tiles, searching for the key. At Koval's office, his secretary greeted them, "Can I help you?"

"Can we check Koval's office for the key?" asked Darnya.

"At the gathering he said the key is not in there," replied the secretary.

"Can we look anyway?" insisted Ivoire.

"Fine," the secretary rose. "I need to supervise you."

The three entered the office. The room was brightly lit, with sunlight pouring in from the window. The light-colored wood furniture was neatly arranged, and the office felt warm and welcoming. The prize box sat in the center of Koval's desk.

Ivoire turned to the secretary, "Do you know where the key is?"

"I do not," she replied. Her words did not ring of truth.

"I see," said Ivoire. "Are you permitted to give us a hint?"

"No," the secretary replied. It sounded as truth.

Ivoire pulled Darnya in close and whispered, "I think she knows. Any ideas?"

"I have one," Darnya whispered back. She began to walk around the room. "Am I permitted to open the drawers and cabinets?"

"Yes," replied the secretary. "I am just here to make sure everything is put back where you find it."

Darnya pointed to a cabinet, "is the key here?"

"No," replied the secretary.

Darnya looked at Ivoire, who shook her head. Darnya continued around the room. As she approached an object, she looked back at the secretary, who kept an emotionless face.

"Is the key in his desk?" asked Ivoire.

"No," answered the secretary. It did not ring true.

Ivoire smiled, "check the desk."

Darnya checked every drawer and found nothing.

"She thinks it is here," said Ivoire. "Where—" an Idea struck her. "May we inspect the locked box?"

"Yes," answered the secretary.

"May we lift it?" asked Darnya.

The secretary paused, "You may."

Darnya lifted the box and there under it was a golden key. She grabbed the key and placed the box back down. She slid the key into the lock and slowly turned it. It clicked and sprung open. Darnya and Ivoire leaned in, and it was empty.

From behind the secretary, Koval spoke, "That was too fast. I had hoped to play the game out longer."

Darnya and Ivoire turned to see Koval smiling.

"Could you tell I was lying?" asked Koval.

"I could tell you were not honest," replied Ivoire.

Koval breathed and sighed in disappointment, then turned to his secretary, "Announce that the game is over and room twenty-seven has won the dinner. Ask the other two girls from team twenty-seven to join us here. Remind the rest of the girls to return the school to its pristine condition."

"Yes, sir," the secretary said as she spun and exited the room.

Koval walked behind his desk and sat. He looked directly at Ivoire and taped his fingers on his desk, disappointment dripping from his face. Koval breathed deeply, "I spent the last six months training with the best vocal coaches, body language experts, actors, and liars in the world. I controlled my heart, the position of my eyes, the pacing and tone of my voice. I was convinced I was ready to get a lie past you. I had hopes of watching you use your skill on the staff. Only my secretary and I knew where the key was. I had this elaborate scheme set up where I told the staff all sorts of wild stories of where I hid the key, hoping to put you off the trail. Still, despite all my efforts, you saw through my lie all the way across the auditorium." Koval sighed and looked at his desk, "Anyway, please sit, both of you."

They sat as Koval continued, "Darnya, you are very fortunate to have Ivoire on your team. She is the most unique girl in the history of the school and your roommates were wise to accept her and help her even without any obvious special qualities."

Sofiy and Kalnya entered, and Koval waved them to join their team. "None of you three figured out Ivoire's skill?"

The three girls all shook their heads and looked at Ivoire.

"Well, I am impressed, Ivoire." He slapped the desk and leaned forward, "Enough of that—the matter of your prize. Beyond just the wonderful dinner we have planned, I am promoting your room to number one."

The girls all smiled and sat up.

"We are honored, sir," said Darnya.

Ivoire spent three more years at Koval's school. Each year followed the same pattern; three other girls would arrive to share her room, one from each year. Training would continue, and the rooms would compete against each other. Each contest centered around information gathering.

Major Koval tried more elaborate ways to test Ivoire's gift. He would bring in professional liars, actors, and linguistic experts. His schemes grew with expense and complication. None worked in the end. "The truth will come out," he would say and move on to the next plan.

As the years passed, friends she had made would graduate and leave. New girls would arrive, and the cycle continued. At times, girls would drop out or never return from break. Ivoire found it difficult to make close friends. She could always tell when the other girls were not truthful. While most people can have casual conversations and be told "little white lies" to maintain friendships, Ivoire never had this luxury. Word spread through the school that Ivoire was strange and could sense lies. Many avoided her for fear of their innermost secrets being laid bare. When she started her fourth year, she had no friends as her roommates from her first year had all moved on one by one. Her new roommates all felt distant and strange, and she never made the connections she had with her first three.

During the fall of her third year, her grandmother died. It was expected. She was far older than anyone else in their town, and during the last two years, she was plagued with painful aches and dizzy spells. Her death almost came as a relief. Her suffering had ended. The town honored her with a memorial and buried her under the tree behind the ruins of the church she loved so much.

Midway through her fourth year at the school Ivoire returned home the same as any weekend. She walked with a group of other students to the train station. She rode the train to the stop near her home and exited to a familiar cold. It was the dead of winter. Six inches of snow covered the ground, and freezing air wafted through the station. After retrieving her bags, Ivoire searched for her father. He was nowhere to be found. Each time she had arrived before, he was there, sitting on the third bench from the end by the ticket booth.

Maybe the snow is delaying him? I'll wait a while.

Hours passed, and there was no sign of her father. As darkness approached, the opportunity to hire a ride dwindled. She made her choice and hired a ride to her house. Each minute of the ride felt like an hour. She grew more anxious as to why her father had not picked her up. He had never missed before. *I hope he is not sick with this cold weather.* The driver dropped her at her house. Snow blanketed the town. A soft wind carried small flurries of the fallen snow. The car her father had purchased for the sole purpose of picking her up at the train station sat covered in a half-foot snow, long unused. The house was dark, still, and lifeless. It felt alien and strange, a dark reflection of her childhood home. The near silence added to her chill from the snow. Her breathing and footsteps in the snow sounded amplified against the stillness. She tried the front door, locked. It may have been the cold or the darkness of her house, but a chill ran down her spine and almost paralyzed her.

"Papa!" called Ivoire as she pounded on the door. "Are you home?"

Only the wind responded.

She walked around the back of the house, the kitchen door window was broken, the door slightly ajar. She stepped in; snow had worked in through the broken window and open door, and the house was cold, a far cry from the warmth the house normally radiated.

"Papa," called Ivoire again, "where are you?"

She pulled a candle out of a drawer and lit it. The orange light danced and flickered. She slowly walked to the main room. Someone was in her father's favorite chair, facing away from her.

"Papa?" she whispered.

She rounded the chair and found her father. He looked peaceful and asleep, his Bible in his lap.

She shook him gently, "Papa. I am home."

His arm fell off the armrest, and his body slumped. She moved the candle closer. Ivoire knew he was gone. He had been dead for a few days. She could smell the rot and feces. Tears welled behind her eyes.

"Oh, Papa…" She leaned him back in his chair and put his arm back on the rest. She kissed him on his head. She fell to her knees and cried into the lap she had sat upon countless times.

The town was remote and medical help would be hours away. There were no phones, not even power in this small town. She cleaned the snow off of her father's car and drove to the train station to use the phone. It was near noon the next day when what passed for an ambulance in this area arrived. The technicians said it looked as if her father had died in his sleep. They asked what she wanted to do with the body. She chose to have her father buried next to his mother and wife behind the church. The people of the town held a memorial and buried him on Sunday.

After the memorial, she sat alone in her house, empty and quiet. Her family was gone. She rose and wandered through each room. First, her own, filled with childhood memories. Next was her Father's room. The bed was still unmade from the last night he had slept there. She could smell him here. She closed her eyes and could almost feel his presence. She left the house, walked through the snow around the town, and wandered aimlessly until her feet carried her back to her family's graves. She stood before the headstones and cried until there were no more tears. Every friend she made at school had graduated and left. Her family was all dead and gone. She, herself, was about to graduate and did not know what was next for her.

"God," she said. "Why did you take my father? What do you want from me?"

She waited for an answer that would not come; all she received was cold wind and snow falling in her tear-stained eyes.

When her toes were on the verge of frostbite, she placed a hand on her father's headstone. "I miss you so much already, papa. We had more songs to sing. More meals to cook. More stories to tell." She sobbed.

Ivoire stiffened, and a revelation came across her. She grabbed the crucifix her grandmother had given her and pulled, breaking the chain. "You worshiped a God, the God of your mother. He only gave you pain and poverty, and now he has taken you before you could see a grandchild of your own. A loving God would not do these things." She placed the crucifix on her grandmother's headstone. "I return this to you, not out of hate but out of love. Your God has forsaken me. He has taken my family, whom he never blessed. He has cursed me with knowledge of truth that alienates me from others. If this is the will of your *loving* God. Then he is no God of mine."

She kissed her hand and touched her father's and grandmother's tombstones, saying, "Goodbye." She walked away from the headstones and back through the snow to her empty house.

On the following Monday, she returned to school. She walked the familiar halls and greeted the familiar faces. They all felt distant, almost unreal. She was in a haze as she attended classes.

The words of her instructors were the moaning of an out-of-tune trumpet. Her physical exercise did not offer relief as a distraction from her loss. She did not share her pain; there was no one left to share it with.

After three days of her "going through the motions," she was summoned to report to Major Koval. She sat stiffly in the comfortable leather chair in his warm office.

He smiled at her and asked, "I can tell you are bothered. Would you like to talk about it?"

The weight she had carried these days pushed and pressed the tears out.

"It's ok," said Koval as he offered a handkerchief, "cry as much as you need."

"I'm sorry, sir," sniffled Ivoire.

"No apology needed," replied Koval. "You can talk, or you can cry. Let it out."

"My father," Ivoire breathed in hard three times, almost gasping. "My father…"

"What about your father?" asked Koval.

"I found him," said Ivoire. "I found him at home. He was…"

"He was dead?" asked Koval.

Ivoire cried harder, and she balled up in her chair.

Koval let her cry. She cried and cried until she was sniffling and whimpering.

"I have something that may cheer you up," offered Koval. He pulled an envelope out of his desk.

Ivoire continued to cry but looked over her arm at Koval.

"The assignment for after you graduate has finally come in," said Koval. "I know you were worried when none had come in."

Ivoire sat up, tears still streaming down her face. She took a few deep breaths and attempted to compose herself. "Where am I going?"

Koval opened the envelope and pulled out the paper. He handed the paper to Ivoire, who accepted it. She read the paper.

> Attn: Major Koval
> Re: Ivoire Kravets
>
> Ivoire Kravets is to report to the
> Hil′diya Anthemoessa for
> induction and intake.
>
> From: Security Service of Ukraine

She flipped the paper over, hoping for more. "I have never heard of 'The Anthemoessa Guild,'" said Ivoire, curiosity and excitement swelling her sadness. "What is it?"

"In the book The Odyssey, the island of Anthemoessa was home of the sirens who would lure sailors to their death with their beautiful songs," explained Koval.

"Am I going to learn to sing?" asked Ivoire.

"No, my dear," said Koval. "Hil′diya Anthemoessa is under the umbrella of the SSU."

"So, what will I be learning there?" asked Ivoire.

"Isn't it obvious?" replied Koval. "As part of the SSU, It is the school that trains females how to identify, capture, and, if needed, kill enemy spies."

Book of Ivon and Ivoire

BEAUTY AND THE BOAT

Oliver was telling of his and Roland's adventure with the "yeti" in the research room when Ivoire and Melissa returned from the States.

"-so this guy was just pretending to be the yeti?" asked Persephone.

"Yes," said Oliver. "His costume did not even look convincing. He had stitched together goat hides to make the costume."

"Thank you both for going," said Melissa. "The local pastor was convinced he had a demon infestation."

"It was a fun trip," said Oliver. "We saved some lives, and the sight of Roland carrying the man in the yeti costume down the snowy mountain is not one I'll ever forget. How was your trip?"

"We exorcized a demon," said Melissa. "I also discovered that Ivoire's gift works on people who are possessed."

"I would love to test it on a full demon," said Persephone.

"I am still not convinced these creatures are demons," said Ivoire.

"What else could they be?" asked Oliver.

"I don't know," said Ivoire. "But I have decided to work with you for a while longer. Each of you has only spoken with honesty. I have not been around a group that talked to each other with such love and candor in a long time."

"Yay," exclaimed Persephone.

"Thank you for giving us more time," said Melissa. "We have an opportunity to test your skill set on a familiar foe." Melissa looked at Persephone.

"Yeah," said Persephone with a smile. She tapped on her tablet, and the screen changed to a picture of Senator Wiles.

"I wondered what happened to her," said Oliver as he took a seat at the table.

"For background," said Persephone to Ivoire, "she arranged a concert for a major demon and tried to sacrifice thousands of people. We stopped her."

"She is hosting a fundraiser on a yacht off the coast of San Diego," continued Melissa. "I think we can get Ivoire access, and she can help us find out what other plans the Senator may be involved in. Any interest in helping us?"

Ivoire studied the photo. "How do we get on the boat?"

Two days later, the Paladins, minus Persephone, who stayed at headquarters, were on a dock north of San Diego. It was a cloudy night, perfect for their mission. Roland and Oliver pulled a black canvas case out of the SUV and placed it on the end of the dock.

"This is going to rock," said Persephone over the coms. "On the count of three, push it in the water, ready?"

"Ready," said Oliver as Roland positioned himself.

"One, two, push," commanded Persephone.

As the case fell, it unfolded, and a six-passenger landing craft inflated, expanded, and splashed into the water.

"Load up," said Persephone.

The Paladins loaded their gear and pushed the boat away from the dock.

"How do we start it?" asked Oliver, who took position by the motor.

"Push the green button on the control handle," said Persephone. "It's electric and silent. You can pull right up, and they will never know you were there. It's only a two-hour battery, so don't take too long."

Oliver started the motor and accelerated off into the open water. Persephone guided them to Wiles' yacht. To their left, the lights of San Diego reflected off the waters. To their right, the waning moon peeked through the dense clouds. As they glided along the black waters, Ivoire changed into a black dinner dress. Persephone had packed a pair of fashionable glasses with an embedded camera, an earpiece, and an invitation. Her cover would be Leslie Carter, heir to the Carter Oil family.

Melissa handed her a small purse. "Tools from Persephone."

As they neared the one-hundred-meter-long yacht, *The Imperative,* lights and noise from the party drifted over the waters.

"Pull up along the boat near the rear and out of the wind and hold," said Melissa. "I need the wind to stop so I can finish Ivoire's hair."

Oliver pulled the craft to the leeward side of the yacht. Roland grabbed the frame of a porthole and held them steady.

Melissa gave Ivoire's hair a final swish of her hand, "that will have to do."

Ivoire looked up and saw the access to the boat was ten meters high. "How do I get up there?"

Roland presented his free hand, open with palm up, "He lifts the needy from the ash heap."

Ivoire stepped onto Roland's massive hand. Both feet could rest on it with ease. She placed a hand against the boat to balance herself. "Lift me slowly so I can listen."

Roland lifted her fully. She was not even half the distance up.

"I think it is clear," said Ivoire.

Roland lowered her a bit and drove his arm up. Ivoire flew up and grabbed the railing, rolling over onto the deck.

"Can you hear me?" said Persephone over the earpiece.

"Yes," whispered back Ivoire.

"Good," said Persephone. "I read you, too. I was able to obtain the manufacturing specs for the boat. There may have been customizations since, but we have a basic idea."

"I can hear the party noise coming from the fore section," said Ivoire. "I'll head there and try to blend in."

Ivoire walked along the boat; a waiter returning to the kitchen passed by with a tray of half-empty glasses of champagne. Ivoire swiped one. She dipped her finger in and patted a bit on her neck. She turned the corner and entered the crowd. Ivoire wasn't sure what to expect. *What sort of dinner party does a demon host?* What she found was a simple cocktail party. People in fancy outfits loitered around, drinking, eating, and talking—nothing evil of note. Ivoire weaved through the crowd and listened, her training in information gathering guiding her as conversations flowed by.

"-I think the production of plastic in Korea will-"

"-did you hear of the affair between-"

"-my summer home is getting the pool resurfaced-"

She worked through the crowd and tried to find Wiles.

"-Wiles barely survived the concert-"

Ivoire slowly paused at the food table and subtly inspected the speaker as she picked up a strawberry. He was a slight man with thinning brown hair and a widow's peak. He wore a three-button suit and fiddled with something in his coat pocket as he spoke. He was speaking to an elderly lady in a blue puffy dress with a miniature poodle in her arms.

"They are brazen enough to attack in a public venue," said the man.

"Who knows where they strike next," said the lady petting her dog. "I don't even think Foo Foo is safe anymore."

"These extremists are a threat to decent people," replied the man. "I hope the government does something soon."

"They are referring to the news story of our fight in the concert," said Persephone. "They blamed the shooting on right-wing Christian extremists. I would move along."

Ivoire continued through the crowd.

"I picked up Wiles' voice," said Persephone. "You are close to her. Be careful. She was possessed by a demon when we last saw her."

Ivoire found Wiles at the bar speaking to a group.

"-water shortage is the perfect opportunity." Senator Wiles said, "People want water. People need water. They will sign off on any law we pass if it brings back the water."

Ivoire moved to the bar and ordered a martini.

"What do we do when it rains so hard that the towns flood?" asked an eager young man.

"Too much water, we pass laws that promise to make it go away. People don't want their belongings washed away. We say it is all for 'climate change' or some nonsense that can't be disproven."

The people around Wiles laughed. The conversation continued around politics. Nothing of use for Ivoire. She drank her martini and listened until the boat sounded a signal horn of two short blasts.

"Oh, is it midnight already?" said Wiles. "Will you excuse me?" She left the bar and worked through the crowd.

Ivoire casually finished her drink and followed. Wiles headed through a set of automatic sliding doors. Ivoire watched her round a corner and then entered the doors after her.

"If they haven't remodeled too much," said Persephone. "This is the living area. Ten bedrooms, twelve bathrooms, a dining area, an office, an entertainment room, stuff like that."

Ivoire peeked around the corner and watched as Wiles entered the doorway at the end of the hall. "Where is the office?"

"First right, then last door on the right," said Persephone.

Ivoire moved to the door without making a noise. She stopped at the door and listened for a moment; then, she tried the handle. It was locked.

"In the purse is lipstick," said Persephone. "Open it and pull hard on the gloss. Stick the metal probe into the lock."

Ivoire followed Persephone's instructions and inserted the probe. After a few seconds, the lock clicked. She tried the handle again, and the door opened.

She peeked in and found the dark office empty. The sparse moonlight cast in from the windows.

"Glance around the room," said Persephone. "I am recording this and having the computer process what is in the room."

Ivoire scanned the walls from left to right. She moved behind the desk and found a laptop. She opened it and found it powered on and locked.

"In your purse is a small bubble gum case. In the case are three USB sticks," said Persephone. "Pull out the white one and plug it into the port on the left side farthest from you."

Ivoire found and inserted the USB drive.

"It will need a few minutes," said Persephone. "I am not the best at computer hacking."

"I am going to see if I can listen at the door Wiles went through," said Ivoire.

"In your bag, find the makeup mirror," said Persephone. "Under the makeup is a clear circle. Place it on the door."

Once Ivoire had found the circle, she checked the hall and stepped out, placing it on the door.

"I can forward the sound," said Persephone. "One second."

The conversation in the room fed through her earpiece.

"-the research." It was Wiles speaking. "What do we need next?"

"We need three voluntary sacrifices that have accepted you-know-who as their you-know-what," said a male voice with a Japanese accent.

The sound of something breaking, "Well, that explains why this part has only worked once before." Wiles was screaming. "I must be the one-"

Book of Ivon and Ivoire

"I hear the door opening in the hallway," said Persephone. "Pull the USB."

Ivoire returned to the desk, removed the USB, and tucked it in her purse. She stumbled out into the hall. The man approaching was dressed in a black suit with an earpiece, Secret Service.

"Oh, hello," Ivoire donned an American accent and acted inebriated. "Did you see a sexy man in a purple shirt walk by," behind her back, she pulled the listening device off the door. "He promised to show me his pet snake. I love snakes, don't you?"

The man spoke to his wrist, "We have a woman on deck one coming out of the office."

"Oh, you don't like snakes," said Ivoire. She wobbled away from the man, feigning inebriation, then shot forward, striking him square in the nose. His head reeled back, paused, and then came forward. He grabbed her by her neck and lifted her with inhuman strength.

"Move in now," yelled Persephone over the coms.

The ship thudded with a rhythmic sound. *BANG, BANG, BANG, BANG.* Then stopped.

The Secret Service agent spoke to his free wrist, "What is that noise–"

Ivoire wrapped her legs around the arm of the agent and pulled, trying to dislocate the elbow. The arm did not budge.

The door Wiles had gone through opened, and a man stepped out. "What is this commotion?"

"I have an intruder," said the agent.

"And the banging?" asked the man. "Did we hit something?"

"I don't know y–" The sound of screaming and gunfire cut off the agent.

"Lock Wiles down," said the agent to his wrist. "We are under attack."

The sound of shattering glass echoed down the hall. Ivoire looked over the agent's shoulder and saw her rescue. Roland, fully

93

armored, strode over the man he had just thrown through the glass door towards her.

The man from the room slammed the door shut. The agent pulled a 9mm pistol from his jacket and fired at Roland, but the bullets clanged uselessly against the armor. Roland closed and grabbed the pistol and the hand holding it. He squeezed, metal and bone broke. The agent dropped Ivoire. She landed in a crouch and punched the agent in the groin. His body contorted, not knowing which pain was worse. With his other hand, Roland grabbed the man's neck and lifted him, just as the man had lifted Ivoire. Melissa rounded the corner with Oliver in tow as he aimed back to where they came.

"Demon. Kill it," said Melissa.

Roland released the gun hand and clapped his gauntlet against the head of the agent; its skull cracked, and black blood splattered the wall.

Ivoire, gasping for air against her wounded neck, "Wiles is behind this door."

Roland dropped the agent, stepped past, and kicked the door in; the wood splintered and exploded into the room, pummeling those inside.

Gunfire erupted out of the room. Roland raised his shield and entered.

Melissa helped Ivoire up while Oliver covered.

"Let's get her to the boat," said Melissa.

"I am getting radio traffic from the Coast Guard," said Persephone over the communications. "A gunship is inbound."

Oliver fired over Ivoire and Melissa into the room, "Roland, we are leaving."

Roland punched, and a body thudded against the wall. The gunfire stopped. Roland exited the room and jogged to join the rest.

"Did you get Wiles?" asked Oliver as they followed Melissa and Ivoire back to the boat.

"They went out from us," replied Roland.

They exited onto the deck; it was clear save for unconscious bodies and broken glass. A body was dissolving as the Russian tank commander and his men had. They headed back and found the boat waiting ten meters below.

"How do we get down?" asked Ivoire.

Roland turned and offered his back to the other three. "I will carry you."

The three all clung to Roland's armor as he eased down the side of the boat. Ivoire could see the source of the earlier noise. Roland had punched handholds in the metal side of the boat and was using them to climb down now. They loaded into the boat and climbed off Roland's back. Roland turned and punched both hands into the boat below the water line. He pulled and opened the hole wider. The ocean streamed into the boat.

Roland surveyed his work, "Hast thou entered into the springs of the sea? Or hast thou walked in the search of the depth?"

Oliver smiled, "Nice. Keep the Coast Guard busy with rescue efforts." He accelerated the boat away into the night.

RED IN THE SNOW

After Ivon's "graduation," he and Dimitri were moved to a room on the second floor of the academy, among the faculty quarters. The change in accommodations was nothing short of transformative, introducing Ivon to a level of luxury he had never experienced before. Each boy was provided with a real bed, complete with soft sheets and pillows that offered a new world of comfort compared to the rough, utilitarian bedding they had grown accustomed to. Their room featured a large window that overlooked the expansive training fields. Beyond the fields, the horizon stretched out to the distant mountains, often shrouded in a veil of mist. The shared bathroom was his favorite upgrade. Unlike the communal facilities they had previously used, this bathroom boasted a bathtub and hot water. Both boys had been fitted with new uniforms, marking their promotion to the rank of Junior Sergeant. The uniforms were sharply tailored, the crisp fabric and polished insignia reflecting their newfound status.

Their first assignment was the removal of the bodies of the slain students. Dead bodies and blood were nothing new to Ivon; he had seen more than his share in his life. They dumped the bodies into a pit they helped dig. The pile of bodies was burned, and the ground returned, completing the unmarked grave. Even after the earth was returned, Ivon could still smell the smoldering flesh. Ivon looked across the field, and he could see dozens of small mounds from what he assumed were prior classes.

Once the school had been returned to pristine condition, Colonel Petrov and his staff were gathered in the auditorium. Ivon and Dimitri sat in the rear with the other enlisted.

"We have much work to do before our new cadre arrives," started Petrov. "This is going to be a different experiment this semester. Two of our former students have joined our ranks as Junior Sergeants. They are new to military protocol, so do not give them any allowance for this. If they perform any action incorrectly, you are to punish them," Petrov glared at Ivon. "Now, I want to find an interesting cadre of students this semester. I want to see what potentials we can bring in. That is all, get to work."

Ivon rose to leave with the staff when Capitan Sidorov stopped him, "The Colonel would like to talk to you in his office."

"Yes, ma'am," saluted Ivon. He turned to Dimitri, "I'll see you tonight in our quarters."

Dimitri nodded and headed to his duties.

Ivon climbed the now familiar stairs to the second floor, turned down the hall, and found Petrov's office door open. As he approached, a tingling cold chill ran down his spine. Ivon stopped at the door and peered in, only darkness.

"Protocol is to knock before entering," Petrov's voice pierced through as the monitors behind his desk clicked to life. Petrov was sitting at his desk with his head resting on his folded hands.

Ivon knocked, "Junior Sergeant Ivon Pravdivyy reporting as ordered, sir."

"Enter, Junior Sergeant," replied Petrov.

Ivon entered. He has only been in this office twice; both times, he could not fight off this sense of impending doom when he entered. This time felt worse as Petrov glared at him like a lion would a gazelle.

"Sit down, Junior Sergeant," Petrov gestured to the chair in front of his desk. "Let's have a talk, you and I."

Ivon sat yet remained stiff and at attention.

"Relax," said Petrov. "No danger will come to you from me today."

Ivon could not sense a lie. He breathed in and out slowly and tried to relax. It did not help. Even knowing that Petrov was not lying, he could not fight off this sense of unease around him.

Petrov turned and leaned back in his chair. He placed a hand on the desk and tapped his hand three times in a slow rhythm. "Do you remember the day we met?"

"Yes, sir," replied Ivon.

"I make trips like that often," said Petrov. "I am searching for special children much like you."

"Like me, sir?" asked Ivon.

"Yes," said Petrov. "You know when someone lies simply by hearing them. This is not common. I look for others with special abilities like yours."

"Other children who can hear lies like me?" asked Ivon.

"Maybe," replied Petrov. "I cannot be sure what skill they may have. Some can have special hearing or special sight. Some can be strong or fast, stronger and faster than any other human."

"Is Dimitri special?" asked Ivon.

"Not in the way you are," answered Petrov. "What we are looking for is rarer. You do not need to worry about that now. I am going to need your special skill to help in our search."

"How can I help, sir?" asked Ivon.

"It should be obvious," Petrov smiled. "You will stay by my side and tell me every lie you hear."

"It will be an honor, sir," replied Ivon.

"Now," said Petrov, waving away Ivon. "Return to your room and pack. We are going recruiting."

That evening, Ivon was on his first flight with Colonel Petrov and Captain Sidorov. It was a large military craft that could hold fifty men; today, it only carried three. Petrov and Sidorov sat near the front of the massive bay and conversed privately. Their voices echoed down the vast cavern of the plane and were swallowed by the noise of the engines. Ivon sat in the last seat, close to the rear door, and tried his best to go unnoticed. Petrov still made him feel uneasy, cold chills running down his spine when in his presence.

They landed in a whiteout of weather conditions. Freezing wind and snow blew in when the rear doors of the airplane opened. A rusty hulk of a snowcat waited for them at the base of the ramp. At the end of the half-foot deep tracks where the snowcat's tracks that towered over Ivon as he approached the ladder. They loaded into the snowcat, and Sidorov drove as they rumbled across the blank terrain—nothing but white in all directions. Ivon could not see more than a few dozen meters away.

Petrov and Sidorov did not talk to Ivon during the flight or the snowcat ride. They talked to each other only minimally when in his presence. The silence bothered Ivon. He was used to noise and talking. At the orphanage, noise was a constant. Children cried or fought at all hours. He also preferred constant talk as he could use his skill to evaluate situations and measure lies versus not lies. The growling of the snowcat, the grating of its tracks, and the howling of the wind only served to accent the silence from Petrov and Sidorov. This silence was further highlighted by the absence of the voices that normally tormented him.

After two hours of snow and more snow, lights crested the horizon. Ivon couldn't see at first, but as the snowcat drew closer, he noticed the light shining through barred windows. It painted the snow in Khaki-colored squares. A pair of doors sat to the left of the center of this three-story structure. What wasn't covered in snow showed gray concrete beneath, easily blending in.

"Junior Sergeant," said Capitan Sidorov, "you are not to talk during the inspection. If you hear a lie, clap your hands one time. Do you understand?"

"Yes, ma'am," replied Ivon.

As they approached the building, two men in Russian uniforms walked down the steps to greet them. They hunched over, shielding themselves from the onslaught of the blowing snow. Sidorov stopped the snowcat, hopped out, and ran over to open Petrov's door. Ivon opened his door and walked around behind her.

Petrov and Sidorov did not seem bothered by the cold. They walked casually and did not protect themselves from the wind. They held their faces high in defiance of the biting chill.

One of the men waiting saluted, "Colonel Petrov, it is a pleasure to host you."

Ivon could sense the lie and clapped once.

Petrov looked back at Ivon and grinned. He turned his attention back to the still saluting man, his grin dropped, "Take me to see the children."

The man lowered the salute unreturned and gestured to the opening, "This way, sir."

They were led into the building and down the unkempt corridors. Ivon knew the smell that greeted him. The smell of human waste, blood, and death. They rounded a corner and entered a large room. What was once a gymnasium with a basketball court now had rows of gray cots lined up. The children were all huddled in the center of the room. They were emaciated and pale with rags for clothing. *Had I looked as such?* Thought Ivon.

"Separate the boys and the girls and arrange by height," said Petrov, not hiding his boredom.

The two men followed the orders and had the children organized opposite each other.

"Is this all of them?" asked Petrov.

"Yes sir," replied the man who had not spoken yet.

Ivon clapped.

Captain Sidorov was on the man before the sound of the clap had faded; she carried him to the wall and flung him against it, "Do not lie to the Colonel."

The man pleaded, "I swear, all the children are here."

Ivon clapped.

Sidorov slammed her first into his face, breaking his nose and cheek. "Where are the other children?"

The man gurgled, the blood pouring from his nose.

The other man intervened, "Please. There is one more. I will grab her now."

Sidorov looked at Ivon, and he did not clap. She dropped the man. "Now!"

The other man ran off and returned with a twelve-year-old blonde girl.

"Ahh," said Petrov, "a plaything. Put her with the other girls."

Petrov paced the line of girls, "Anything odd about any of these?"

"No," said the man who could still talk.

Petrov looked to Ivon. He did not clap.

"Hmmm," said Petrov. He stopped before the three tallest girls. "Ok, I will take these three. You can keep your pet. Load them into our vehicle."

The man herded the three girls out of the room.

Petrov turned to the boys, "Which of you is the strongest?"

The boys all looked at each other until the tallest one stepped forward and said, "I am."

"Junior Sergeant," said Petrov. "Fight him."

Ivon ran at the boy. He barreled his shoulder into the boy's chest, and they tumbled down, knocking another boy aside. Ivon was on top and pounded the boy in the face. The boy got his hands up, blocked his punch, and countered. They rolled and exchanged blows, each taking dominance for only a moment. They rolled until they hit the wall. Ivon was on top. He landed a clean hit on the side of the boy's jaw, sending him limp. Ivon rose, his uniform ripped and bloody.

"Kill him," Petrov was behind him, presenting a pistol, grip first.

Ivon took the weapon; it was heavy and strange for such a small thing. He was not new to killing. He had never intended it, but when you fight for food or let others starve, it happens. He aimed the weapon at the unconscious boy. He pulled the trigger,

BANG. It was loud, louder than he had expected. A spot of blood began to pool on the boy's chest.

"See," said Petrov. "There is nothing to it. You pull a trigger, and a problem goes away." Petrov leaned in close and looked at the other boys. "Now, pick three more," he whispered.

Ivon turned to the boys. He knew if he disobeyed, Sidorov would harm him. He walked over and shot three times in quick succession. *BANG BANG BANG*

The surviving boys screamed as three fell dead. The man had returned from stowing the girls and ran in.

Petrov took the weapon from Ivon and gave it to Sidorov. "Take the three biggest still alive and load them into my vehicle. Kill the rest."

Ivon and Petrov exited the building as the sounds of gunfire and children's screams echoed across the snow.

"You did your job well," said Petrov to Ivon. "You followed my orders without hesitation." Petrov stopped and turned to the door.

Sidorov and the uninjured man had exited. Sidorov walked down the steps to join the Colonel. The man stayed in the shelter of the awning.

"Capitan Sidorov, give your rifle to the Junior Sergeant," ordered Petrov.

Sidorov did as ordered. Ivon tested the weight of the weapon in his hands. It felt huge, and it was almost as long as he was tall.

"Junior Sergeant," said Petrov. "Kill the man who was not happy to see me."

Ivon looked at the man. He was pulling his rifle off his back. Ivon readied his and pulled the trigger, but it did not move.

The man had his rifle up and aimed it at Ivon, *CLICK.* No bullets.

Capitan Sidorov offered to Ivon, "The safety lever is above your index finger."

The man ran down the steps, yelling.

Ivon turned the rifle over and found the lever. He pressed it up and aimed at the man. He pulled the trigger, and the rifle fired three times. One bullet hit the man in the leg, tripping him. The man rolled and began to crawl back to the steps. A trail of blood was melting the snow following him. Ivon stepped forward and took his time. He paced with the man below him, aiming for his head. He pulled the trigger, but nothing happened.

"No more bullets," said Sidorov.

"My order stands, Junior Sergeant," said Petrov.

Ivon stepped on the man's neck, pressing him into the snow. The man grabbed at Ivon's leg as Ivon wielded the rifle like a club and smashed it on the man's head. He continued to strike long after the man had gone limp, and the rifle started to hit soft innards.

"Lovely," smiled Petrov. "You have done very well today." He turned to Sidorov, "Capitan, let us return with Sergeant Pravdivyy. I believe he has earned a treat."

Ivon made several more trips with Petrov and Sidorov as they searched for children. Sometimes, it was to orphanages; other times, it was to the homes of families. Each visit, he had the same command, 'Clap if you hear a lie.' Petrov would order him to fight or to kill each trip. After the trip, they would bring the selected children back to the school and put them through the trials. If there were children Petrov found promising, they would be spared the end-of-semester slaughter. Some years, there was no "graduation." Others had several. These surviving children would either become part of Petrov's staff or be shipped off with other officers. Ivon stayed with Petrov, and he, along with Dimitri, was eventually promoted to First Sergeant as Petrov's and Sidorov's personal aide.

Life during these years was easy for Ivon. He lived in comfort, and his meals were plentiful. Petrov, ever the manipulative benefactor, rewarded compliance with treats like candy, movies, and small luxuries that had a disproportionately powerful effect on the young mind.

Ivon's new role granted him a certain power, one that came with a gradual but inevitable erosion of empathy. He learned to assess the students coldly, focusing on their utility and potential without regard for their individuality or suffering. Over time, he became numb to the idea that they were even human, viewing them instead as mere assets to be evaluated and optimized. The dehumanizing perspective was encouraged by Petrov, who praised his efficiency and rewarded his detachment.

When they celebrated Ivon's sixteenth birthday, Petrov hired a prostitute to "introduce him to manhood," it was an awkward experience that he found no real pleasure in.

They never found any other children with abilities like his. Over time, the search missions blurred into each other. Ivon lost count of the people he killed during these operations, each death becoming just another statistic in a long, bloody ledger. The end of each semester marked an especially dark period, with the systematic slaughter of children deemed failures by Petrov's ruthless standards. The bodies piled up, and Ivon obeyed, else he joined in the fates of those Petrov deemed "unworthy."

When Ivon turned eighteen, Petrov closed the school.

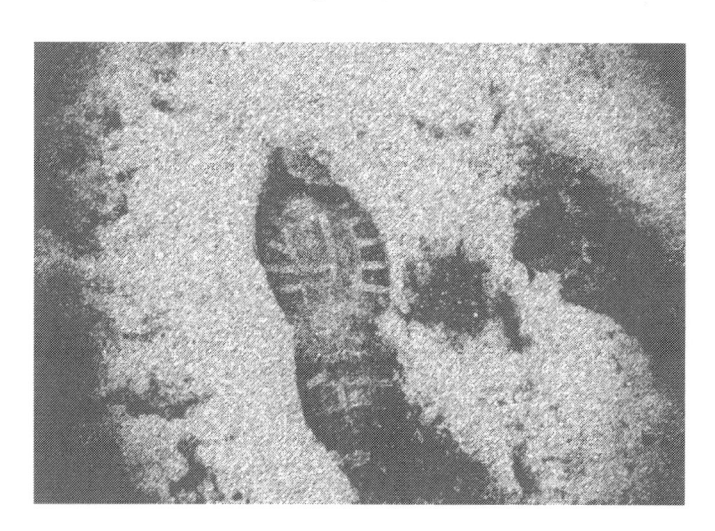

BULLETS AND BOOKS

While her throat healed from the fight on the yacht, Ivoire stayed with the Paladins and observed their workings. She attended the briefings and watched hours of videos of the Paladins' missions with Melissa and Persephone.

One morning, she accepted Persephone's invitation to watch some weapons testing. Ivoire met Oliver and Persephone at the shooting range at Paladin headquarters. The programmable room was set to a dense Canadian forest at night. A peaceful breeze and the occasional owl hoot drifted through the range. Ivoire marveled at the technology available to the Paladins. She approached the shooting range. Oliver was standing at the first stall with Persephone. Before them, on the shelf, were Oliver's revolvers and a collection of bullets.

"After the fight with the bullet-proof Valec, I wanted to see if I could give you some options," said Persephone. "It wasn't easy; the 380 ACP is a smaller bullet. What I have here is a selection of rounds I want you to try and get your feedback on."

Ivoire examined the six bullets on the shelf, placed on end before Oliver. The first had a green tip, the second had a red stripe on the casing, the third had small grooves on the bullet, the fourth had the number 00001 in blue on the casing, and the sixth had a silver-colored tip.

"What do these do?" asked Oliver.

"Load them up in one of your guns and find out," said Persephone.

Oliver loaded the bullets in the order they were set on the shelf as Persephone walked to the control room. Ivoire joined Persephone behind the protective plastic.

"As I bring targets out, fire a round with a standard bullet first, then fire with a new round," said Persephone.

"Got it," said Oliver. He pulled his left revolver, already loaded with a standard issue .380 ACP. Ivoire heard him recite a prayer.

Lord, make me swift and true
Guide my hands with yours
Let your will be my aim

"First target," said Persephone. "Standard steel plate."

Green tip recalled Ivoire. *That normally means armor piercing.*

The steel target glided out of the side opening. Oliver waited until it reached the center of the range before firing from his left pistol. The bullet impacted the center of the target and fell to the ground.

"Now fire the first test round," said Persephone.

Oliver fired, and it kicked harder, jarring his arm. Dirt flew up from the mound at the end of the range. Above the dent made by the first round on the target was a hole torn clean through.

"Most armor piercing uses steel rods in the bullet," said Persephone. "I made this rod out of tungsten. It had to be super thin to still be light enough not to damage your revolvers."

"It kicked hard," said Oliver. "But nothing I can't adjust to."

"Yeah," said Persephone. "Even being thin, it is still heavier than a standard round, so I had to amp up the accelerant. I would not use that too often as it could strain your gun a little."

The sound of the bullet and Persephone's lessons pulled Ivoire's mind back to her time at the Guild and the weapons training.

"Noted, what's next?" asked Oliver, pushing Ivoire's thoughts back to the present.

Red stripe, Ivoire recalled.

Persephone worked the controls, and a wooden board presented itself. "Plain ole' wood," she said.

Oliver fired a round from his left gun, hitting near the top. The wood splintered and cracked as the bullet passed through. Oliver aimed his right revolver and shot low on the board. The bullet left a bright trail as it streaked to its target. The board erupted into balls of fire that pelted the range. Fire retardant foam sprayed from the sides, extinguishing the flames. The flash blinded Ivoire for a second.

"Incendiary?" asked Ivoire as she blinked vision back into her eyes.

"Incendiary-tracer-high-explosive hybrid," said Persephone. "It pre-ignites on discharge, making the tracer effect; then a secondary ignition occurs upon impact. It's a special zirconium, magnesium, and uranium mix that burns at four thousand degrees for five seconds. Hot enough to melt steel."

"Uranium?" asked Oliver. "Is it radioactive?"

"Less than a cell phone," said Persephone. "But when it ignites, it creates a teeny-tiny nuclear explosion to damage the target and help reach the four thousand degrees."

"Awesome," said Oliver. "Next?"

The next round, the one with small grooves on the bullet, remembered Ivoire.

Three paper silhouettes slid out, two behind the first, which was centered.

"Fire at the head of the middle target," said Persephone.

Oliver fired from his left revolver, and a hole appeared where the nose should be. He aimed his right revolver and fired.

The head of the target shredded; the flanking heads each had holes in them.

"What was that?" asked Oliver.

"Sort of like buckshot," said Persephone. "The bullet breaks into six pieces and spreads in a tight cone. I had to configure it to spread after exiting your revolver to avoid barrel damage."

"Great for when the ghouls group up," said Oliver.

"Exactly," replied Persephone, working the controls. "Now for the last two."

A ballistic gel cube slid out.

"Don't fire a normal round at this," said Persephone. "Just fire the next test bullet."

The blue numbered one, thought Ivoire.

Oliver fired, no kick. A small pellet embedded itself into the ballistic gel.

"GPS tracker," said Persephone. "Goes about an inch into flesh. So, if you aim at a calf or bicep, it won't be lethal and will be tough to dig out. It's also sticky for shooting at vehicles and stuff."

"I like it," said Oliver.

"Fire the last—"

"Hello, everyone," Melissa was behind Persephone and Ivoire, observing.

"Hi Melissa," said Persephone. "Just showing Ivoire and Oliver some of my bullet ideas."

"Just in time for the last one," said Oliver. "Shall I?" he gestured to the target.

"No need," said Persephone. "It's a simple hollow silver bullet filled with holy water."

"Look out werewolves and vampires," joked Oliver.

Ivoire wondered at this: *What sort of creatures require holy water?*

"If you are done, I wanted to tell you I have a lead on what Wiles may be up to," said Melissa.

They gathered in the library with Roland.

"Remember that book that we found with a broken shield like Roland's in the Vatican Luciferin collection?" asked Melissa.

"Yeah," said Persephone. "I scanned about half of it."

"I want to get the rest," said Melissa. "It begins to describe a ceremony that requires a person who has accepted Christ as their savior."

Ivoire, whose throat was still injured, added in a husky voice, "Wiles mentioned such a ceremony on the boat. She was angry about the lack of a viable volunteer."

"Yes, if they are looking for a volunteer, they may be close to completing it," said Melissa. "I want the rest of that book."

"Oh boy," said Oliver. "Another library trip."

"Not this time, Cowboy," said Melissa. "I want Ivoire to come. An extra female to distract Mallory."

"Oh, you're going to love him," said Oliver to Ivoire.

They left headquarters and headed off to the library. As the SUV navigated the narrow Vatican streets, Melissa and Persephone filled Ivoire in on what to expect at the Apostolic Library—the foulness of the books in the Luciferian collection and the flirtatious Karl Mallory.

As they exited the vehicle, a voice carried across the parking area, "Melissa."

It was Father Mallory. "Have you come to take me to lunch?" Mallory paced past the vehicles with arms open. He closed on Melissa and kissed both cheeks.

Melissa held Mallory at arm's length. "Sorry, Father-"

Mallory gave her a dour look.

"Sorry," said Melissa. "Karl. We are not here for lunch. I want to show our newest Paladin the library." Melissa gestured to Ivoire. "Can you give us a tour?"

"Hello, Father Mallory. I am Ivoire," said Ivoire, presenting her hand for a handshake. "A pleasure to meet you."

Mallory looked Ivoire up and down. He accepted her hand and kissed it, "the pleasure is double for me." He turned to Persephone, "And there is my favorite 'punk rock princess.'" He pulled her into a hug. "I would adore to give our lovely new Paladin a tour," he said to Melissa over Persephone's head.

Mallory guided them into the library and waved the Swiss Guard away. He led them through the aisles and recited impressive facts of the library to Ivoire. Ivoire was not impressed. She had seen libraries and braggarts plenty in her life. As they passed the masonry spiral staircase leading down to the restricted collections, Melissa paused.

"Can we show her what's down here?" asked Melissa.

Karl paused, then sighed, "What is to show but foul books? Come, let's go eat; there is a lovely cafe I want to show you."

Melissa ran her hands down her habit and breathed in, "I think it is important for her to see what is there. Persephone also wanted to read more of a book she started on her last visit."

"To visit again so soon," said Mallory. "It may raise some attention."

Melissa moved closer and took Mallory's hand, "Please, Karl. For me, and then we can go to lunch at that cafe."

"Only for you, my dear," said Karl. "You know I would march straight into hell if it would simply make you smile."

Persephone turned to Ivoire and giggled. Ivoire returned a smile.

Mallory led them down the spiral staircase. The warm light from above faded as the dimly lit staircase reached a long, arched hallway. Electrical wires ran along the roof, connecting construction lights every few paces. They approached the plain steel door without a lock or handle.

Out of his robe, Mallory pulled out a device that looked like a cell phone. He pressed the device on the door in the center; its panel lit up. "Father Karl Augustus Mallory: seven, nine, four, seven, eight, six, three, two," he said to the device and placed his thumb on the screen. After a moment, the door clicked open softly.

As they entered, the nearest guard rose and spoke to Mallory in German. Mallory replied. After a few back and forths, Mallory's voice took on a hint of anger. He continued to speak with the guard as he turned and gestured to his three guests. The guard spoke and shook his head.

Mallory turned to his guests, "Only two may enter. I had hoped to have all three of you see. I must admit I am curious too and wanted a look."

"It is fine," said Melissa. "Persephone has been in there before, and she can show Ivoire the books. Let's sit, and you can tell me about the cafe we are going to for lunch."

Mallory smiled, "Oh, it is lovely." He guided Melissa to the sitting room.

One of the guards approached with a basket, and Persephone spoke, "Yes, I know. No phones or cameras." She emptied her pockets, and Ivoire followed suit.

The guard stowed their belongings and handed a pair of rubber gloves to Ivoire and a pair to Persephone.

"Good, good," said the guard, "you may go."

"Thank you," said Persephone.

"What are the gloves for?" asked Ivoire.

"Don't touch the books with your skin," answered Persephone.

"To preserve their integrity?" asked Ivoire.

"No," said Persephone. "To preserve your fingers."

The far guard turned to a console on the wall and pressed a few buttons. Machinery whirred, and the massive door hinged back. Blinding white light poured out.

Ivoire and Persephone stepped into the all-white room. The massive golden wooden crosses on all four walls remained on their eternal watch. The room had not changed since Persephone's last visit. The same white bookshelf in the center and two tables, each white with a golden cross embedded into the top, rested in the same place. They approached the shelf.

The books defied her imagination; Ivoire could feel what could only be described as Evil radiating from them. They were a grotesque menagerie of foulness and wickedness that made it hard for her to breathe. Only a golden chain adorned with crosses kept them in check.

"What are we looking for?" asked Ivoire.

"The book was just over here last time," said Persephone. "On the cover of the book is a crest that looks like Roland's shield but is broken."

Persephone stopped, "this is where the book was." She pointed to a section with no book behind the golden cross chain.

"Has it moved?" asked Ivoire.

"Let's check," said Persephone. "Look behind the books, but do not touch them with your skin."

They circled the bookshelf three times and checked behind every book, but it was not there.

"Now what?" asked Ivoire.

"I am not sure," replied Persephone. "Let's ask Melissa."

They exited and found Melissa seated with Karl.

"Melissa," said Persephone. "The book is missing."

"What do you mean missing?" asked Mallory.

"The book I read last time is gone," said Persephone.

"Are you sure?" asked Mallory.

"Yes," said Persephone. "We checked the whole room, even behind the other books. There's a blank space where the book was."

"Show me," said Mallory as he approached the white room.

The Swiss Guard spoke, and Mallory waved him off. He stormed in with the three Paladins in his wake.

"It was here," said Persephone, pointing to the empty spot. "Now it is gone."

Mallory was flush with anger. He turned to the guards and shouted in German. The flustered guards yelled back. Mallory stomped out of the room and pounded a finger on the registry tome. The guard opened it and went back and forth with Mallory as they argued and turned pages. Mallory pointed to the phone on the wall and yelled more. The guard picked up the receiver and spoke in Swiss to someone.

"Jetzt," yelled Mallory, and he pounded on the desk. He composed himself and turned to Melissa. "I apologize for this display. There is no record of the book being removed. The registry shows it should still be here. I have ordered an immediate investigation."

"Thank you, Karl," said Melissa. "I know you will find what happened to it."

"That is not the worst of it," said Mallory.

"What else is there?" asked Persephone.

Mallory sighed, "I will have to cancel our lunch date."

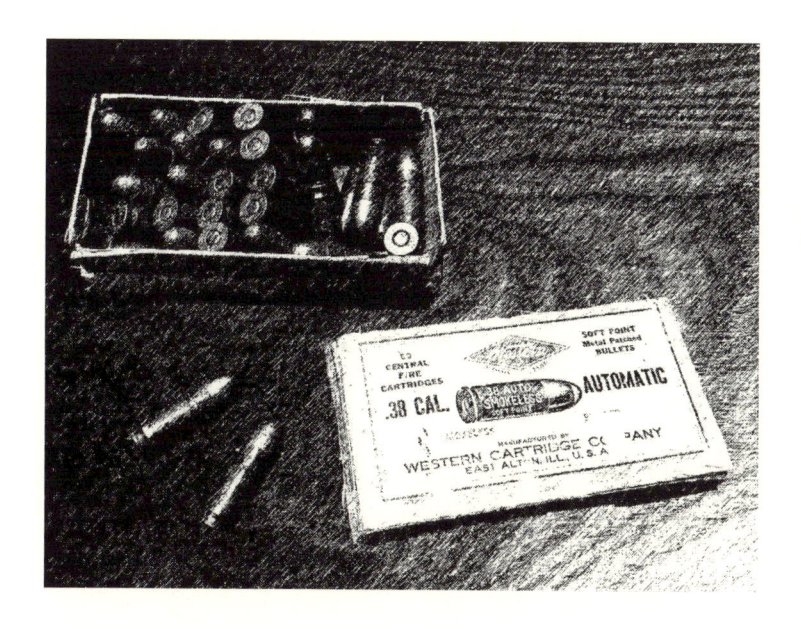

THE GUILD

After her graduation, Ivoire was transferred to the Hil′diya Anthemoessa, the Anthemoessa Guild. Ivoire was on her first airplane flight—the clouds cruised by as she looked out the window. The sun dripped light on the soft white fluffs. It was a peaceful moment. She was excited about having an assignment but nervous about the words of Major Koval, "kill spies." She had never committed a violent act in her life. Could she kill?

She pushed these concerns to the back of her mind and focused on the excitement of the adventure. When she landed, Ivoire worked through the busy airport and pushed against the flood of people. After she retrieved her bag, she made her way outside. A slight elderly woman in a military uniform with a captain's insignia waited with a sign that read Ivoire's last name.

"I am Ivoire Kravets," she said to the lady.

"Hello, daughter of a tailor," said the lady. Her voice was slow and cracked. "Load your bags into the rear."

"My father was a mechanic," said Ivoire.

"Your name, Kravets," said the lady. "It means tailor."

"Oh," said Ivoire. "What is your name?"

"I am Capitan Bula," replied the woman. "Bula means fat one."

"Hello, Captain Bula," said Ivoire. "Are you my new instructor?"

"No," replied Bula. "I am the chief of transportation for The Anthemoessa Guild. The usual driver was sick today, so I am helping out."

The statement of 'the usual driver' did not ring true. It seemed an odd thing to lie about.

"Oh," said Ivoire. "A pleasure to meet you."

Capitan Bula drove them out of the city through the countryside. It was fall, and the trees had just started to brown. The area reminded her of home, simple buildings hugging rivers and valleys.

As Ivoire approached the Anthemoessa Guild, the building looked like it hadn't been touched since it was built in the 1940s. Nestled in the rocks of the surrounding hill, the walls were a dull shade of gray, and the roof was missing a few shingles. The windows were cracked, and the panes were dirty and smudged. The front door was made of heavy-looking, weathered wood. A dirt and rock half-circle drive fronted the building.

Capitan Bula stopped at the peak of the circle drive and exited the vehicle. "Grab your bags, young lady."

Ivoire exited and retrieved her bags. She walked up the moaning wooden steps and stood before the weathered door adorned with a large brass knocker in the shape of a mermaid with the tail as the knocker.

Ivoire wondered if there had been a mistake. This ruined old building hardly seemed the place to train spies.

As she pushed open the creaky door, she was greeted by a manicured garden that was a riot of colors and smells, flowers of every shape and hue. The fragrance of the flowers was sweet and intoxicating and reminded her of her grandmother's garden. The exterior building ran up to the rocks and continued up. The garden was in a bowl of a valley, hiding the beauty that lay within.

Around the garden were open areas full of shade trees, tables, and benches. Flanking on all sides, the hills climbed up, blocking the view of the world beyond. Around the grounds, other students lounged and enjoyed the serene setting.

Beyond the garden lay the main building of the school, an enormous stone structure chiseled out of the rock, which dominated the gardens. The building was several stories high, with ornate carvings and intricate reliefs that decorated its facade. The windows were tall and wide, letting in the natural light and offering stunning views of the surrounding garden.

"This way dear," said Capitan Bula.

Ivoire was led past the gardens, into the main building, through the halls, and up the stairs to her quarters. This facility was vastly different from her prior school. The building was a repurposed castle, adjusted to accommodate its new mission of training female spies. The neat halls with white walls were adorned with photos and plaques. There were no open classrooms, only wooden doors and more halls.

They climbed a spiral stone staircase four flights up and veered down the hall. Captain Bula stopped at the sixth door, pulled a key from her pocket, and presented it to Ivoire.

"This is your room," said Bula, handing her the key.

"Thank you," said Ivoire, accepting the key.

Bula walked down the hall back to the stairs.

"What do I do now?" called Ivoire after.

"Instructions are in a folder on your desk," called back Bula.

Ivoire entered and surveyed her quarters. The private room had a spacious living area, a comfortable bed, and a large window that overlooked the surrounding gardens.

The room was decorated in a minimalist style, with light-colored walls and dark wood furniture. A small desk was positioned against one wall, with a comfortable chair and a lamp. A wardrobe was situated at the foot of the bed, providing ample space for her clothes.

Her private bathroom was attached to the room, with a sleek glass shower and a large bathtub. The marble countertops were spotless, and the large mirror provided ample space for her to get ready in the morning.

Ivoire unpacked her bags and put her clothes in the wardrobe. She sat at the desk with the waiting folder that Bula mentioned. She opened the folder that contained a stack of papers. It had a map of the grounds, a guide for when meals were served, and her lesson plan. At the top of the stack was a welcome letter from Commandant Witko:

Dear Ivoire,

    Welcome to the Anthemoessa Guild. I am Commandant Witko, and I would like to extend my congratulations on being accepted into our esteemed institution. You have shown exceptional dedication and commitment to your studies, and we are thrilled to have you as part of our community.

    As you embark on your journey here, I would like to emphasize the importance of time management, self-drive, and independence. Our curriculum is rigorous, and we expect our students to be self-motivated and to take initiative in their studies. We believe that you possess these qualities, and we are excited to see how you will apply them during your time here.

    Our faculty and staff are committed to helping you achieve your professional and personal goals, but ultimately, the responsibility for your success lies with you. We encourage you to take advantage of the resources available to you and to seek assistance when needed.

We believe that you will find our campus to be a welcoming and stimulating environment full of opportunities for growth and personal development. We look forward to seeing how you will make the most of your time here, and we are confident that you will excel in all that you do.

Once again, welcome to the Anthemoessa Guild, and we wish you all the best as you embark on this exciting new chapter in your life.

Sincerely,
Commandant Witko

Ivoire found her schedule of classes and read that she was to report to Logistics for uniforms and other sundries. She rushed off and began her training.

The first year at the Guild was mostly dedicated to building a foundation in the basics of identification, tracking, and capturing of enemy spies. The classes focused on infiltrations, unarmed and armed combat, information gathering, interviewing, and interrogations. Ivoire discovered that she had a natural talent for interrogations, thanks to her ability to sense truth. Her instructors were impressed with her ability to extract vital information during their exercises, and she gained high marks in this area.

Each day, she attended classes that delved deep into linguistics, history, and the rich tapestry of cultures from around the world. Her lessons were like opening portals to distant lands. She didn't just memorize vocabulary and grammar; she immersed herself in the rhythms and nuances of each language. Every phrase she mastered was a key, unlocking the stories of people she had never met yet felt she was beginning to know intimately. The histories she studied weren't mere dates and events; they were vibrant tales of triumph and tragedy that shaped civilizations. The cultures she learned about became vivid landscapes in her mind, places she longed to explore. She imagined walking through the bustling markets of Morocco, feeling the sun-warmed cobblestones beneath her feet, or tracing her fingers along the ancient stones of Greek ruins, each one whispering secrets of the past.

For Ivoire, these lessons were more than academic pursuits—they were dreams in the making. She reveled in the beauty of learning languages, seeing each one as a thread in the grand tapestry of human connection. She hoped to one day visit the places she read about, to use her linguistic skills not just as tools of communication, but as bridges to understanding and friendship. Her visions were filled with vivid scenes: chatting in flawless French at a Parisian café, haggling in fluent Mandarin in the vibrant streets of Beijing, and sharing heartfelt stories in Spanish with villagers in the Andean highlands. To Ivoire, learning a language was an act of respect, a way to honor and truly grasp the essence of another culture. Each new word she acquired was a step toward her goal of becoming a spy, someone who could navigate and appreciate the world's immense diversity with grace and insight.

She was permitted to travel home for the summers, but she chose not to. The notion of returning to the empty house, where every corner whispered memories of her lost family, was too painful to bear. Instead, she decided to stay at the academy during the "recovery months," as they were euphemistically called, a time meant for rest and rejuvenation between the rigorous academic terms.

The nearby city became her sanctuary, a place where she could lose herself in the anonymity of its bustling streets. She spent her days exploring its labyrinthine alleys and grand boulevards, immersing herself in the vibrant urban landscape. One of her favorite discoveries was a small, unassuming coffee shop tucked away on a quiet side street. The shop's exterior was modest, with a faded awning and windows fogged by the constant steam from the espresso machines inside.

The moment she stepped through the door, the rich aroma of freshly ground coffee beans enveloped her, mingling with the sweet scent of baked goods. The interior was cozy, with mismatched furniture and walls adorned with black-and-white photographs of the city in its earlier days. The barista, a middle-aged woman with kind eyes and a permanent smile, quickly came to recognize her as a regular.

Among the shop's offerings, it was the muffins that captured her heart. They were unlike any she had ever tasted—perfectly golden with a tender crumb, bursting with fresh blueberries that left a sweet-tart burst of flavor with each bite. She savored the way the top of the muffin crumbled delicately, revealing a moist, fluffy interior. Each morning, she would order one with her coffee, taking it to a small table by the window where she could watch the world go by.

The city outside the window was a study in contrasts. Businesspeople hurried past in tailored suits, their faces set in determined expressions, while street vendors called out to passersby, selling everything from handmade jewelry to aromatic spices. Occasionally, she would see a street performer—musicians playing soulful melodies on worn instruments or dancers moving gracefully to the rhythm of the urban heartbeat.

As she sat there, the coffee shop became her refuge, a place where she could momentarily escape the weight of her past. The regular patrons, with their own stories and routines, became a familiar backdrop to her solitary contemplations. It was in these moments, with a warm cup of coffee in hand and a bite of her favorite muffin, that she found a semblance of peace. The city, with its endless activity and hidden corners, offered her a sense of belonging, a new home where she could begin to heal.

The second year at the Guild shifted focus to advanced espionage techniques, including cryptography, counterintelligence, and sabotage. Ivoire found herself studying every waking moment.

She had little time for anything else, but she was determined to become the best spy she could be. With her family dead and her friends all moved on, her studies became her life.

Finally, in the third and final year, the school focused on using femininity as an asset. It was the most difficult year for Ivoire, who had never even kissed a boy. She grew up in a small town and was then moved to an all-girl school. The idea of sex was almost foreign to her. But her instructors made it clear that in the world of espionage, every tool was necessary. Sex, when properly applied, was the most powerful tool in her arsenal. They trained the students in seduction, social engineering, and other methods of manipulating targets. Ivoire struggled with this part of her training; every aspect felt as if it was a living lie- showing interest in a person you had no interest in.

It was near the mid-point of her third year, and she had been summoned for an examination she had feared for some time. She stood before the mirror in her room as she dressed. She had been given a red dress that hugged her athletic body. She had her hair up in a fashionable style she had learned from her instructors. She applied the makeup and perfumes and gave herself a final look over. She barely recognized herself. In the mirror was a beautiful woman. Long gone was the girl of her self-image.

She made her way to the assigned exam room and knocked on the door.

"Come in," said a male voice.

The door clicked open, and she stepped inside. She had been in this room before when she had taken a practical on cleaning a pistol. Gone were the tables and stools. The room had been transformed into a bedroom. Comfortable chairs and soft drapery adorned the walls. In the center of the room was a four-post bed with burgundy satin sheets.

"Come sit with me," said the man sitting on the bed.

He was handsome and wearing a black four-button dinner suit with a silk tie. He was tall and fit with short brown hair and gray eyes that reminded her of her father's.

As she approached, she could see the cameras in the corners. Her instructors were always watching.

Her first sexual experience with a man, an exercise in seduction that was recorded and evaluated, left her feeling empty and violated. It was a necessary part of her training, but the emotional toll was overwhelming. Her instructors had warned her that emotions were a liability in the world of espionage, and so she worked to bury her feelings deep inside.

The pain of the experience was worsened when the instructors had her watch the video with them and coached her on improving her skills. This was not the training she had visualized when she first arrived. She felt broken and empty, holding in tears until she reached her quarters.

She would repeat this experience many more times, with different men and in different settings. Eventually, she grew numb to the experience of sex, and it became just another tool.

Four months after the ordeal of her first sexual experience, an envelope waited for her on her desk as she returned from afternoon exercise.

Candidate Kravets:

Report to room four on sub-level two for your final evaluation.

There were no other instructions. Ivoire quickly cleaned and dressed in her utility uniform and ran down to sub-level two. She had never been down here before. This area of the castle had not been modernized. The bare stone walls dripped with moisture. It was dark, and the air stale. She found room four, the ancient wood door had a metal plate covering where a window once served.

She knocked then shouted, "Candidate Kravets reporting,"

The door clicked open and swung with a squeal on the rusty hinges.

In the room, a single light swayed slightly above a woman tied to a chair. The woman was blindfolded, blood stained her face, and a torn button-up shirt. Her ponytail was mottled and stiff. The floor and walls were covered in splashes of blood.

"Candidate Kravets," said a voice from a speaker in the corner next to a camera. "This woman has committed crimes against Ukraine and is a threat to the sovereignty of our nation. Take the gun from the shelf to your right and kill her."

Ivoire looked down and saw the gun on the shelf. She had been trained how to use it by the Guild but had never used one on a living thing. She lifted the weapon and tested its weight. It felt heavier than she remembered.

"Please don't kill me," pleaded the woman. "I am innocent."

The woman's words did not ring true.

"Her actions have led to the death of dozens of Ukrainian citizens," said the voice on the speaker.

"It's a lie," yelled the woman. "I am a simple waitress."

Ivoire could not read the truth or lies from the voice of the speaker, but she could tell the woman was not truthful about her innocence and profession.

"We will make this easy, Ivoire," said the voice. "Killing her protects more of your countrymen from dying. Kill her and graduate."

The woman began to sob, "I am sorry."

Her voice rang with truth.

Ivoire aimed the weapon at the woman's head, moved the safety selector, and chambered a round.

"Oh god," said the woman to the sound of the gun readying. Her sobs intensified.

Ivoire aimed the gun, and her arm began to shake, the weight of the weapon increasing.

"Do it. Do it now," commanded the voice.

Ivoire squeezed, and the woman fell limp. It surprised her how easy it was. A simple twitch of her finger and someone is dead. She dropped the gun and stepped back against the wall. The school had trained most of her emotions away, but this was still painful.

The door clicked open, and Commandant Witko entered, "Congratulations, Ivoire. Today marks the end of your training and the beginning of your real work as an agent,"

Ivoire breathed in deeply and kicked the gun across the room. "Thank you, sir," she replied, her voice shaking.

"With that mess out of the way, we have your first assignment from the SSU. They suspect a spy operation within our borders, and we need you to infiltrate it and gather as much intelligence as you can," Witko explained.

Ivoire stiffened and nodded, "Understood, sir. What are the details of the operation?"

Witko handed her a file. "Your cover has already been established. You will be embedded as a secretary for hire for the suspected front of the operation, an accounting office. Your mission is to discover the benefactors of the group and report back to us. If you fully validate the espionage operation, you are authorized to take whatever actions are required to end the operation."

Ivoire nods again, taking the file from Witko. "I understand, sir. I won't let the SSU down."

"I have every confidence in you, Ivoire. Remember your training here. Use the skills we have given you, and you will do great things for our country."

"I will, and thank you. I will leave at once," Ivoire replied

"Before you go, I have a parting gift for you," said Witko. "Major Koval informed us you wore one that looked similar to this." He pulled a golden crucifix on a chain from his pocket and tossed it to Ivoire, who caught it. "Press hard on one side of the base."

Ivoire examined the crucifix. It was near perfect recreation of the one her grandmother had given her, the one she left on the headstone. She pressed on the base of the crucifix, and a small knife folded out of the cross.

"That blade has a hollow tang," said Witko. "It can be filled with any matter of chemicals from poison to sleeping drugs, even truth serums. A simple poke or slice and the drug is administered. It will come in handy, I think."

"Thank you, sir," said Ivoire. "It is lovely."

"Good. Now, your handler is waiting. The details on their contact and your transportation are in the file. Good luck, Ivoire," Witko said.

"Thank you, sir," she said as she exited the room. She took a deep breath and placed her new necklace around her neck. She put the ordeal of the room behind her and hurried back up to the sunlight.

BEHIND ENEMY LINES

The Paladins were gathered in the library at their headquarters. Ivoire and Persephone shared the long couch. Oliver was relaxing on one of the overstuffed chairs. Roland, as was his preference, stood by the door and leaned against a bookshelf.

"Let's review what we know," said Melissa as she sat at the computer and worked the keyboard and mouse. "Senator Wiles and her followers are attempting some ceremony." A picture of Wiles fills the screen. "Twice now, we have been close to her, and she has eluded us. The Shanette concert and on her yacht." The computer screen changed to display Persephone's picture of the cover of the missing book. "It has to be more than a coincidence. There is a missing book from the Luciferan library that seems to describe the same ceremony she is referencing."

"What about the demon essence on Roland's armor?" asked Persephone.

"It may not be related to Wiles," said Melissa. "Most demons work independently of any grander schemes."

"Have you had any more consideration that Cardinal Sepe is a demon?" asked Ivoire.

The Paladins all looked at each other as the question hung in the air.

Oliver broke the silence. "I was thinking it, too. Sepe would have access to the library to get the book."

"Melissa," said Ivoire. "If you see the Cardinal in person you can tell if he is a demon?"

"Yes," said Melissa. "Or possessed even."

"Like the man in the hospital?" asked Ivoire.

"Exactly," Melissa replied.

"So," said Oliver. "How do we get you in eyeshot of Sepe?"

"I can work with my contacts at the Vatican and see if I can arrange an audience," said Melissa. "I still want to focus on Wiles. We know she is a demon."

"Any idea how to get close to her?" asked Oliver.

"We want to embed Ivoire as a volunteer for her political office," said Persephone.

"Are you up to it?" asked Melissa.

"What is the plan?" asked Ivoire.

Persephone answered, "Wiles is not up for reelection, but that does not stop her from fundraising and helping other candidates. All fifty-three representatives from California are up for election so this is an important year. Senator Wiles has turned her primary office into a Democrat campaign headquarters for California. They are on a hiring spree."

"You want me to get a job and see what I can find," said Ivoire.

"Yes," said Melissa. "There is a temp agency that Wiles' office frequently uses, and we are going to set you up as a translator. Do you know any languages besides English, Russian, and Ukrainian?"

"French, Italian, and Spanish, I can pass as a native," said Ivoire. "I have some trouble with Arabic and Hebrew."

Roland smiled. "There are doubtless many different languages in the world, and none is without meaning."

"Wonderful," said Persephone. "Being a translator will make it easier for you to get into some of the higher circles and conversations."

"When do I leave?" asked Ivoire.

Book of Ivon and Ivoire

"We have a flight booked three days from now," said Melissa.

Ivoire stood in front of the mirror in her room at Paladin Headquarters as she readied her new look. Her training at the Guild included deep cover and disguises. For this mission, she would become Martina Bucci, an Italian national who graduated from the University of Milan with a degree in Linguistics. Ivoire straightened the brown wig of wavy hair. She applied a tan foundation to darken her complexion. Under her clothing, she wore a padded girdle that made her breasts and hips larger.

As 'Martina' exited Ivoire's room, Melissa was waiting, "If I did not know it was you, I would not recognize you."

"Grazi," said Ivoire, donning her Italian accent. "I am Martina from now until the mission ends."

"The others are waiting in research," said Melissa. "Persephone has your kit."

They entered the research room. Persephone had laid out a collection of items on the central table.

"Wow," said Persephone. "You look so different."

"Yeah," added Oliver. "I am convinced you are not you."

"Grazi," said 'Martina'.

"The voice, too," said Persephone. "I do hope you decide to join us full-time."

"What do you have for her?" said Melissa, focusing on the briefing.

"Ah yes," said Persephone. "Here are some of my more genius designs. Each item before you is functional in its appearance but can be switched to be used for more covert uses."

Persephone picked up a hairdryer and clicked it on, blowing hot air onto her hand. "See, a normal hair dryer." She twisted the barrel back and forth and pulled it longer, and the dryer went silent. She plugged in a pair of headphones in a screw hole on the handle. "Now it is a long range directional microphone, able to pick up vibrations at three hundred meters."

Ivoire picked up a makeup mirror. "This the same as from the boat?"

"Yes," said Persephone. "Close-range listening pads."

"Tell her about the cigarettes," said Oliver.

"Oh yeah," said Persephone. "Oliver helped on these." She picked up a gold cigarette case and opened it. "See. Normal cigarettes." She closed the case and clicked the lock twice. She pointed the case at a metal target on the far wall, "Cover your ears." She squeezed the case, and a bullet fired, striking the metal with a clang.

"A gun?" asked Ivoire.

"Yes," said Oliver. "The case holds five .22 LR bullets. A little more range than your necklace."

"I am sorry it was so loud," said Persephone. "To keep it small, I could not add dampening to the case."

"It's wonderful," said Ivoire. "I wish I had this years ago."

"You can read about how the rest work on the flight." Persephone walked around the table and handed Ivoire a small box. "This is something special."

Ivoire opened the box to find a watch.

Persephone showed her wrist to Ivoire. "Now we match. The watch can take pictures, video, and record sound."

Ivoire strapped the watch on. "It is lovely."

"Lastly," said Melissa as she slid over a leather case.

"Oh yes," said Ivoire as she took the case and opened it. "My chemicals."

"I disguised them as simple hygiene bottles. Mouthwash, nail polish remover, stuff like that," said Persephone. "The Bible in your kit has an extra book called 'Preparations' that describes what else is in your gear and what chemical does what."

To help lower suspicion, Ivoire would be flown under her assumed identity on a standard airline. Her cover, Martina, wanted to come to America and gain experience as a translator. As she was an Italian Socialist, working for a Democratic campaign headquarters was a natural fit.

Book of Ivon and Ivoire

Ivoire landed at Sacramento International Airport in the dark of a Sunday morning. She collected her bags and presented her identification to the customs officers. She had rented a room at a hotel a short walk from the California Democratic Headquarters. She had slept on the plane and had the day to scout the location in advance.

She was dressed in comfortable walking shoes, jeans, and a loose shirt. She explored the pre-dawn Sacramento streets, memorizing her escape routes in and out of the California Democratic Headquarters. It was a modern two-story building built in the brutalist style. The surrounding parking lot had the parking spaces labeled with the "progressive" ideals, words like "diversity," "inclusion," and "equity." Even an agnostic could sense the evil radiating from the area.

After circling the building and making note of the entries and exits, she continued her walk away from the building and South down towards Saint Mary's Cemetery. She walked the aisles of beautiful headstones as the first rays of sun painted the cemetery in light. The morning dew was drying, and the smell of fresh-cut grass filled her senses. From the cemetery, she walked west along Fruitridge Road. Shops and stores had started to open as the city came to life. From the airport, she turned north until she reached the zoo. The sounds of the animals waking up and being fed their breakfast echoed out into the street. She had never been to a zoo, so she purchased a ticket, and spent the day among the animals.

In the evening, she walked north until she reached Midtown, where she found a cafe and enjoyed dinner. After dinner, she walked east and found her hotel. She settled in for the evening and prepared for her first day as a translator for the California Democratic Party. As she lay in bed on the edge of sleep, the hotel room reminded her of her accommodations at the Hil'diya Anthemoessa.

Ivoire woke from her memory-dream-filled sleep with a start. She collected herself by breathing in slowly three times and relaxing her body. She was in the hotel in Sacramento. She turned the bedside clock to face her. It was 5:49 am. As was her habit, she was awakened before her alarm. She dressed in jogging shorts and a tight-fitting shirt and went downstairs to use the hotel's fitness center. After a quick workout and light breakfast, she returned to her room to shower and to prepare. 'Martina' was out the door by 8:00 and walked south to the California Democratic Headquarters.

The city was alive on Monday morning. Cars filled the streets, pedestrians hurried to their destinations, and the sounds of a busy city swelled and swallowed Ivoire. She enjoyed large crowds; they are easy to get lost in. She was just another worker on her way to her office.

At 8:27, she arrived at the California Democratic Headquarters.

She entered the clean and modern reception area. People were coming and going, conversing as they went. She approached a chubby lady behind the counter.

"Welcome to the CDP Headquarters," said the lady. "Are you here to volunteer?"

"No," said Ivoire/Martina in a thin Italian accent. "I start today as a translator. My name is Martina Bucci."

"Oh yes," said the lady. "You are early, wonderful. Please, we need you right away." The lady turned to a younger woman behind her. "Paula. Can you take Miss Bucci back and get the HR paperwork done? We need her on the phones ASAP."

Ivoire was led back past reception. As she had been trained, she observed and memorized the building. She noted workers' body language and egress routes, and she sized up potential threats. Ivoire was processed, shown her desk, and asked to answer phones for donations in various languages she had been trained in.

It was a boring first week for Ivoire, but not without its benefits. She had learned the routine of the building. She had obtained a copy of a key she had seen work on the doors. She had made "friendships" with two other phone workers and was able to gain yet more information from their gossiping. Behind her glasses and in her ear was always one of the Paladins—usually Persephone. Oliver and Melissa had checked in on occasion and even Roland would drop in with a verse. She started to accept them more. She had not had a family since her father died, and in many ways, Roland reminded her of him.

In the evenings, she would pass the building at various hours to see if any late-night activity was worth attention. She also made use of the trip to enjoy the warm Sacramento weather. She strolled along the water and then relaxed with a simple dinner at a diner. Being a Paladin was different than being a spy; she had much more freedom. She did not need to check in or submit reports. They worked more on faith, trusting each other and their God instead of discipline and routine.

Towards the end of the second week, Ivoire was answering phones when a large group passed by the glass wall of the phone area.

"What is going on?" asked Ivoire to Isabelle, a fellow translator.

"It must be someone special," said Isabelle. "Maybe a senator."

"I see Secret Service," said someone closer to the wall. "Oh look, it's the President!"

"Oh, let me see," said another woman.

The volunteers rushed to the window to get a better look.

"Are you seeing this?" said Ivoire.

"Yes." It was Melissa. "It may be nothing. Presidents visit places like this all the time."

Paula came in from the side door. "Martina. We need you."

Murmurs of "lucky" and "why her?" rippled through the room as Ivoire followed Paula out. She was led to the main conference room. At the door, she was stopped by a Secret Service agent who patted her down and checked her identification. The agent waved her and Paula in. At the head of the round table was the President of the United States. He was flanked by important-looking people around the table. Ivoire was shown to a chair two seats away from the President.

The Secret Service locked the door and announced. "The room is secure."

"Thanks, Mike," said the President. He turned to Ivoire, "Is this our translator?" The president was charming and young; he had a non-threatening appearance with his dark skin and thin build. In her mind, Ivoire recalled all she had known about him and was ready to interact.

Paula, who was seated at the wall behind Ivoire, replied, "Yes, Mr. President. She speaks Italian and Russian."

"Perfect, and thank you for helping out. This was very last minute, and my normal translator is out on leave." The president smiled. "Let's get started. Is President Putin on the line?"

"Yes, Mr. President," answered the man next to the phone.

"And Prime Minister Renzi?" asked the President.

"Also on the phone."

"Stand by," said the President and signaled to the man on the phone.

"Muted, sir," said the man.

The President turned to Ivoire; his almost lyrical voice dropped into a serious, almost demeaning tone. "This should be simple. Each of them has their own translator, so you do not need to translate what I say. When they speak, I need you to translate. If Prime Minister speaks, say 'The Prime Minister says..' and if President Putin speaks, say 'The President says..' then relay the message to me. Do you understand?"

"Yes, Mr. President," replied Ivoire.

"Perfect," said the President, his lyrical tone returning. "Let's begin."

The man by the phone pressed the button to unmute.

"Greetings, President Putin and Prime Minister Renzi," the President stated. "Thank you both for being on the call last minute. We have had a development in project Garmr we need to discuss."

President Putin spoke first, and Ivoire translated to English for the President. "Has the States finally found its key?"

"Yes," replied the President. "We have just now secured the key and are transporting it to a secure location. Is the Russian key still good to go?"

"Of course," replied Putin with Ivoire translating, "We had ours first, and he is still good to go. Now ask Italy about theirs?"

Prime Minister Renzi replied angrily, "We are close to finding a replacement. We can't be held responsible for plane wrecks."

"You need to take better care to protect your key," replied Putin.

"Gentleman," interjected the US President, "we can't change the past, and accidents happen. We are back down to two keys, and that is our reality. Prime Minister Renzi, is there any aid that President Putin or I can provide?"

"No," said Renzi and disconnected the call.

"The Prime Minister dropped from the call," said the man operating the phone.

"That's fine," replied the President. "President Putin, take care of your key. We will take care of ours. Mind is one."

"Mind is one," replied Putin and disconnected.

The President turned to Ivoire, his tone once again harsh. "That was satisfactory. Leave your name with my staff. You are dismissed."

Ivoire went to rise and noted she was the only one leaving. As she pushed back from the table, she pressed the listening device Persephone had given her under the table.

"It's been an honor," she said and quickly left with Paula following her.

They exited, and Paula closed the door. "Great work, Martina," said Paula. "How exciting."

"Excuse me," said Ivoire as she pushed past Paula, and she went down the hall and entered the bathroom. She locked the door and faced the mirror.

"Persephone," said Ivoire. "Are you there?"

"Yup," replied her happy voice over the earpiece. "I already have the audio streaming."

Audio clicked into Ivoire's ear.

"...be like Italy…" It was the President's voice. "Keep our key locked down."

"Yes, Mr. President," replied another voice. "We have them- "

He was interrupted by a ringing. The room fell to a knowing silence.

"Sir," said a new voice. "It's-"

"I know," said the President. His voice did not hide his annoyance and nervousness. "Hand it here."

The phone rang twice more when the President answered.

"Senator Wiles," he answered. "What a pleasure."

The President was interrupted and could be heard pacing around the room.

"Can you get the caller's audio?" asked Ivoire.

"I can try," said Persephone.

The audio squeaked and the amplified voice of Senator Wiles came through in pieces.

"… help them. My master …. impatient. Get the third… and complete …."

"Yes, ma'am…" the President's voice blasted through the audio, deafening Ivoire.

"Sorry," said Persephone. "I'm not much of an audio technician."

"It's fine," said Ivoire. "Let's listen more."

"… could have gone better," said the President. "What assets do we have in Italy? Wiles wants us to help find the third key."

The sound of people getting up and packing muffled the conversation as it continued.

"They are exiting," Ivoire left the restroom and moved down the hall to be in the President's entourage's path. She stopped at the window to the phone room.

"If the President is talking to Wiles..." It was Melissa, now. "...he is working with the demons. We need to find out more."

Under her breath, Ivoire replied, "I have an idea."

As the entourage exited, the phone takers all rose to get another look at the President.

The crowd of the President's people flooded out of the conference room in a cascade of conversation. As they neared, Ivoire saw her chance. She acted as if she had tripped and fell towards the President. The Secret Service grabbed her mid-fall and restrained her.

"Hold," said the President. "This young lady was just helping us in the other room. Are you OK, miss?"

"I am fine, Mr. President," replied Ivoire. "You said to leave my name with your staff, and I wanted to do that."

"Do you have a business card?" asked a stern woman with short blonde hair, wearing glasses and carrying a binder.

"No," replied Ivoire. "I really want to work for the President." The guards released her, and she stood tall. "I think he is just about the most handsome President in history."

The President, who surprised Ivoire by being unphased by her charms, turned to the stern aide. "Take her name and number."

"Give them 831-555-5689," said Melissa over the earpiece.

"Martina Bucci," said Ivoire. "831-555-5689."

The aide jotted the number down. "Thank you. Let's go, Mr. President, we are late for the dinner."

The group continued down the hall in a hurry of noise.

"What was that?" asked Persephone.

Ivoire turned and headed to the breakroom. "I was seeing if I could charm the President."

"Well, from the look on his face," said Oliver, who had joined the call. "He was not into it."

"Guess I am not his type," replied Ivoire.

"Focus," said Melissa. "The President is working with Senator Wiles on some sort of project. If Wiles is involved, it must be something we stop."

"You think the President is a demon or possessed?" asked Oliver.

"It's possible," said Melissa. "It's worth looking into."

"I'm going to stay and see if I can learn more," said Ivoire. "They mentioned Italy needing help; we should follow up on that, too."

"Sounds like something a person who wants to be a Paladin would say," said Persephone. Ivoire could hear her smile.

"I thought I was one," said Ivoire.

"Even if you choose to go separate ways," said Melissa. "You will always have a home with us. Now, Persephone and I will start researching anything that has information about 'Project Garmr.' Ivoire, you see what you can find from the staff there."

"What about Roland and I?" asked Oliver.

"Business as usual," said Melissa. "We have a possible ghoul infestation in Chile."

THE WATCH AND THE WIRE

After Petrov closed his school, he and his select staff relocated to Santiago de Cuba.

Before they left for Cuba, Petrov and Sidorov took Ivon and Dimitri on a tour of Moscow. Petrov said he wanted Ivon to understand their mission better. They visited the State Historical Museum, the Kremlin Palace, Kolomenskoye, the Museum of Cosmonautics, Arbat Street, Armoury Chamber, Tverskaya Street, the Bolshoi Theatre, and The State Tretyakov Gallery.

At each stop, Petrov would stop at the statues and paintings and explain who they were and why they mattered.

When they were touring Red Square, Petrov took them to see Lenin's Mausoleum. Inside, Petrov led them to Lenin's preserved body. The glass case with Russian flags draped across it sat in the middle of a massive chamber with statues of the entombed leader surrounding it.

Petrov neared the display, smiled, and turned to Ivon. "Come closer."

Ivon obeyed and stood next to Petrov.

"Kneel," said Petrov.

Ivon, at first confused, hesitated then dropped to one knee.

"This man," said Petrov. "And one other, whose body used to rest here… had done more to advance the kingdom of our god than any other in all of human history."

Ivon stayed kneeling, his eyes on the floor. He knew better than to interrupt when Petrov was giving a speech.

"I plan to finish what they started," said Petrov. "The way of our god will be heralded as liberation in all corners of the world. But enough history and politics, warmer weather awaits us."

After the tour of the Russian capital, they got to the task of moving operations to Cuba. Their new headquarters would be housed in a massive white Spanish-style masonry building with a red clay tiled roof that overlooked the blue waters of the Caribbean around Cuba. Ivon and Dimitri were given a room on the top floor adjacent to Petrov and Captain Sidorov's rooms. Their room had a view of the city that the complex resided over. From here, Ivon could see the comings and goings of the people below. Dimitri even gave Ivon the bed with a better view of the ocean.

After the team had finished moving in, Sidorov had gathered his staff into the main dining hall, who were all seated at the table. Ivon counted only twelve, including Petrov, who sat at the head. The staff had closed the shutters, and the lights had all been replaced with dim yellow bulbs. The dining hall felt more like a dungeon in the belly of a castle than of a room only feet away from paradise. The column and arches of the great room had all decorations removed so only dull white blank stucco was all to be seen.

"We will be here for the next eighteen months. Our primary goal is training on interrogation and–" Petrov paused, "shall we say 'removal.'"

Three of the senior officers laughed.

"Lieutenant Volkov and Sergeant Belyaev will lead a resource-gathering mission," continued Petrov. "Lieutenant Zaitsev will run facility security. Everyone else, focus on physical fitness until you are called upon. Now, dismissed."

The officers and enlisted hurried off to their assignments.

"First Sergeant Pravdivyy," said Petrov. "Come with me. I have a gift for you."

Petrov and Sidorov led Ivon out of the dining hall through the kitchen to a staircase down below the complex.

Book of Ivon and Ivoire

"Cuba has such magnificent cliffs," said Petrov. "A great place to build wonderful rooms where we can work without drawing attention. The Cuban government has permitted us to work here. A family close to the Castros owns this house, and they are supporters of our work."

They continued down the staircase until they reached a stone-walled room that opened to cobweb-covered wooden racks with bottles of green, brown, and black glass.

Petrov pulled a bottle and examined it. "With the embargo, foreign wine is very expensive." Petrov dropped the bottle; it shattered, and wine ran across the floor. "I am not much of a drinker, but for the right occasion, I'll enjoy a cup."

Petrov pulled another bottle that stopped halfway. Machinery whirred, and the case hinged forward.

"This way," said Petrov.

They entered a cramped and damp stone-walled room with water dripping down the rock walls. Along the walls were worn wooden tables with tools placed neatly on top. On the far wall, four sets of chains were attached to the stone and rested in piles on the ground. In the middle of the room was a metal chair bolted to the ground. In the chair was a man with dark hair and an olive complexion. He wore a button-up cotton white shirt and brown khaki pants. His feet were bare, and a blindfold covered his eyes. His arms and legs were secured to the chair.

Sidorov walked across the room to a metal cauldron above an open fire. She pulled a metal ladle of the steaming liquid out and splashed the contents onto the man. He started to consciousness with a yell.

The man whimpered and spoke in Spanish.

"First Sergeant Pravdivyy, do you know Spanish?" asked Petrov.

"No, sir," replied Ivon.

"I figured as much," said Petrov. "Just let me know if anything he says triggers your ability to sense lies."

"Yes, sir," replied Ivon.

Petrov picked a clipboard off the table and looked it over. He spoke to the man in Spanish. The man replied. Some of the words may have sounded muffled to Ivon. He was not sure.

"Permission to speak, sir," said Ivon.

"Yes, First Sergeant," sighed Petrov in annoyance. "When we are in this room, you may speak freely until told differently."

"Thank you, sir," said Ivon. "I think some of the words sounded like lies. I cannot be sure as I am not familiar with his language, and it may be the way the words are pronounced."

"I see," said Petrov. "Capitan Sidorov, at my signal, punch him."

"Yes, sir," said Sidorov.

Petrov spoke to the man in Spanish, and the man replied. Petrov looked at Ivon. None of the words sounded muffled to Ivon.

"Nothing, sir," said Ivon.

Petrov spoke to the man again; this time, he only replied with one word, 'Que.'

Petrov pointed to Sidorov, who slammed her fist into the side of the man's head.

Petrov yelled at the man.

The man replied, whimpering, "soy mujer."

"That sounded like a lie, sir," said Ivon.

Petrov spoke to the man.

The man whimpered, "soy una gatta," and began to sob.

"Yes," said Ivon. "That is a lie."

"Very good," said Petrov. "I made him say, 'I am female.' Then he said, 'I am a girl cat.' Easy lies and your talent picked it up. It seems you do not need to understand the word, only to hear it. I will continue questioning him. Anytime he lies, signal to Sidorov. Understand?"

"Yes, sir," answered Ivon.

The interrogation of the man continued for hours. Petrov would read from his clipboard, and the man would answer. If Ivon heard a lie, Sidorov would injure the man in various ways. Even if he were not sure, Ivon would signal to Sidorov. If the man fell unconscious, Sidorov would pour more boiling liquid to wake him up. By the time every question on the clipboard was responded to, the man was whimpering, scalded, and bloody.

"That went well," said Petrov. "Our hosts have agreed to let us stay here if we assist in the interrogation of individuals. They give us use of this complex, and we give them information validated by your ability. Now, on to your gift."

Petrov pulled a watch from his pocket and presented it to Ivon. It was a simple metal banded watch with an analog face. There was nothing special about it; it was not even new. The only distinguishing feature was a large hoop attached to the winding.

"Put this on your left wrist with the hoop towards your hand," instructed Petrov.

Ivon did as ordered and admired his gift.

"Pull the hoop firmly, and some wire should come out," said Petrov.

Ivon pulled on the hoop. It did not move at first, but as he pulled harder, a thin metal wire followed it out. He pulled until it stopped at about one meter.

"This a garrote," said Petrov. "You use it to strangle someone. Wrap a bit around each hand and choke this man to death."

Ivon wrapped the wire once around each hand and stood behind the man. He reached over and pulled the wire back. The man struggled and turned his head, gasping.

"No, no," said Petrov. "You have to wrap it all the way around the neck. Otherwise, they turn and keep breathing. See if you can do it in one swift motion."

Ivon's first attempt resulted in the wire wrapping at eye level on the man.

"Again," said Petrov.

On the next attempt, Ivon was able to wrap it around the neck.

"Good," said Petrov. "Now he can't turn to breathe. Pull it tight and hold it until he stops moving, then hold it a little more to be sure."

Ivon tightened the wire. The man flailed against his restraints. Muffled grunts, blocked by the wire, jammed in his throat. Ivon held until the man went limp, then for another thirty seconds.

"And that is how that is done," said Petrov. "Practice with your watch at every opportunity. The garrote is a fantastic and silent weapon that is very effective in trained hands." He turned to Sidorov, "Capitan Sidorov, arrange a cleaning crew."

Life for Ivon continued like this for the next eighteen months. Petrov and his team would bring in people to interrogate. Ivon would assist in the interrogations and then 'remove' the victim. On the rare occasion that there was no one to interrogate, Petrov, Sidorov, Dimitri, and Ivon would cruise the Cuban cities in Petrov's car. They frequented late-night clubs and bars. Dimitri was never far from his side. They would find pleasure in picking fights with the locals and in the chaos it would bring. They shared drinks, cigars, and even women.

Dimitri was not much of a talker. Usually, he would drink quietly while Ivon engaged with the locals.

For a time, Ivon was able to start a romance with one local girl. She was a server at a cafe that he would frequent for breakfast. She spoke Russian as her parents had immigrated to Cuba from Russia. She had pale skin and light brown hair. Ivon would spend every free moment with her. He was bringing her gifts and taking her to fancy restaurants. Like everyone outside Petrov's circle, she, too, eventually died. One evening, he found her dead in her apartment, her throat opened from ear to ear. It was not a sadness for him, just a change that he accepted. Another thing that could be replaced. Death was a part of his life; he had been around it for as long as he could remember.

He enjoyed this time in Cuba. He had access to luxuries and vices. He felt powerful and useful. He had long forgotten the voices that tormented him in his youth. To Ivon, it was a good life.

When the year and one-half had ended, Ivon and Dimitri were in Petrov's office.

"You two have done everything I have asked since coming under my care," said Petrov. "Now look at you, men ready to conquer."

"Thank you, sir," said Ivon and Dimitri in unison.

"Now for your new assignment," Petrov pulled a manila envelope out of his desk. "You two are being promoted to 'no rank.' We are destroying all records of both of you, and you two will now work as a two-man team that doesn't exist."

Petrov threw the envelope into the waste bin and tossed a match after it. The flame popped to life and the smell of burning paper filled the room.

"You two do not exist," repeated Petrov. "You are ghosts. Phantoms who will travel to where I direct and who will do what I command without hesitation." He ended the statement with a pause of finality, glaring at each of the young men, then softened his tone. "All of your needs and any equipment you require will be provided. We shall spare no expense as there is no one accountable."

"Yes sir," said Ivon and Dimitri.

"Now, for your first mission," said Petrov and slid a blue folder across the table. "There is a Ukrainian spy who has been a pain in Russia's side this last year. Find her and bring her to me."

BP McCoppin

PIT OF VIPERS

The Paladins, save for Ivoire, who remained in California, were gathered in the library at Paladin headquarters.

"We have been forwarded a letter from a mission near San Pedro de Atacama," stated Melissa. "Near the mission, there is a nearly abandoned Copper mine that a small town has taken root near. Protestant missionaries were in the area building a school when the leader of the group went missing. Shortly after, there were more disappearances. The sponsoring church asked for help from the local government. The government was not inclined as they viewed the town and the mining operation there as illegal. After a few more rounds, the issue has come to us."

"What do you mean by 'nearly abandoned'?" asked Oliver.

"Chile has nationalized the mining industry and that mine was deemed not worth the time and efforts of the government with so many other mines producing well," answered Melissa.

"That explains why the government views it as illegal," said Oliver.

"Correct," said Melissa.

"So why us?" asked Oliver. "What makes you believe a demon is there?"

"The American missionaries have reported that their leader and the other missing people were now 'zombies,'" said Persephone. "They even sent some photos." Persephone loaded a picture on the library computer screen. It was dark, and three figures in tattered clothing could be seen. They had blank, sullen looks and cuts on their chests.

"When do we leave?" asked Oliver.

An hour later, Oliver and Roland were on the private jet cruising across the Atlantic. Roland prayed and read the Bible. Oliver noted it was a Spanish language one. Oliver also prayed and read the travel Bible that Gerin gave him. He cleaned his guns, had dinner, and slept.

They landed and exited the plane to a beautiful Chilean sunrise. The dense forests trailed off to the distant mountains to the east. To the west, the forest faded to long, flat planes. The air was thick and wet from a recent rain.

"Oliver and Roland?" called a thickly accented voice. The voice belonged to a woman in her thirties; she had brown, thick, shoulder-length hair and an olive complexion that framed her light brown eyes. She was dressed in tan utility pants and a white untucked button-up shirt with the sleeves rolled up.

"We are Oliver and Roland," called Oliver as he walked down the steps.

"Bienvenido and welcome to Chile," said the lady. "Thank you both for coming. My name is Emilia Alvarez."

"A pleasure, Emilia," said Oliver. "I am Oliver, and this," Oliver gestured as Roland exited the plane. "is Roland."

Roland strode down the steps, armor case in hand, his weight and power reverberating the metal structure.

Emilia stepped forward and presented her hand. "Hello Roland, it's a—"

Roland grabbed Emilia's hand, set his case down, pulled her close, lifted her up into a giant hug, and then kissed her cheeks.

"Salute one another with a holy kiss. The churches of Christ salute you," Roland said and then set her down.

Oliver could see Emilia blushing. "Thank you. It is a pleasure to meet you both," she said as she gathered herself. Her posture stiffened. "Please load your things into the back of the truck, and we can talk while I drive."

Emilia entered the driver seat of the white and green Toyota truck, and Oliver sat in the passenger seat. Roland loaded his case and himself into the bed.

Oliver slid open the rear window. "All set, Roland?"

"I'm ready, God, so ready, ready from head to toe," replied Roland.

Emilia turned to Oliver. "Your handsome friend talks funny."

Oliver replied, "Man shall not live by bread alone, but by every word that proceedeth out of the mouth of God."

Roland smiled, "This is my beloved Son, in whom I am well pleased."

Oliver interpreted, "he only speaks in Bible verses and is especially happy when someone else does."

Emilia put the truck into gear and, with a smile, said, "I can tell you two are going to be fun."

The vehicle trundled along the Chilean landscape. Oliver admired the vast green forest and distant mountains. A cool breeze blew in from the ocean far to the west.

"I hope you can help," said Emilia. "The Chilean government has no interest in helping, and the American government is afraid of an incident with the Chilean government. I was surprised when Melissa contacted me and said she would be sending help. She called you 'specialists'. Are you experts in missing persons?"

"We have experience with that," said Oliver.

"Do you have an opinion on the zombies?" asked Emilia.

"We will follow all leads and stories," said Oliver. "Our priority is the missing people."

"Ok," said Emilia. "Where do you want to start?"

"Take us to the mission," replied Oliver. "We should talk to them first."

"We are close," said Emilia and gestured forward. "Look, you can see the remains of the bell tower."

In the direction they were heading, a stone bell tower pierced out of the tree line. The dirt road wound through the trees until they reached the mission. The ancient gray stone building showed every year of its existence. Vines had taken root, and pieces of wall had fallen. The remaining walls and bell tower defied reason as they remained upright. Surrounding the mission was a collection of Quonset huts and a wooden building with a red cross marking it as a hospital.

A very American-looking man with light brown hair, a three-button green polo shirt, and jeans waved as the truck approached.

"Hola, Johnny," greeted Emilia.

"Hola, Emilia," replied Johnny. "Are these the specialists from the Vatican?"

"Si," answered Emilia. "This is Oliver, and the big hombre in the back is Roland."

"Hello and welcome," said Johnny. "We have prayed for assistance. Thank you for coming."

Oliver exited the truck. "Hello, Johnny. What can you tell us about the missing persons?"

"Right to it, then. Derrick went missing first," said Johnny. "He was heading back from getting supplies when we lost contact. We found his abandoned truck three days later."

"How were you in contact?" asked Oliver.

"We use radios," said Johnny. "Phones don't work here."

"And the other disappearances?" asked Oliver.

"Four went looking for Derrick and never returned," said Johnny.

"How long ago was that?" asked Oliver.

"Two weeks now," said Johnny, his face falling.

"Don't lose hope, friend." Oliver placed his hand on Johnny's shoulder and bowed his head. "Dear Father. We ask for your protection of your children. If it is your will, guide our paths to find them. In your eternal name, Amen."

"Amen," replied Johnny. "That was lovely. I am glad to have Christians sent to help us."

"Thank us after we find them," said Oliver. "Now, I saw some photos. Are they of your missing friends?"

"We are not sure," said Johnny. "We think so."

"Where were the pictures taken?" asked Oliver.

"My wife and I were out searching one night and took them," answered Johnny. "We were in the woods near where we found Derrick's truck."

"You have a map of the area?" asked Oliver.

"This way," said Johnny, and he led Oliver into one of the Quonset huts.

Inside, a blonde woman in a tan blouse and matching cargo pants waited, talking to four other people.

Johnny introduced Oliver to his wife, Jenn, and the remaining members of their group. He unrolled a map and placed it on a table.

Johnny pointed to a blue cross on the map, "This is the mission." His finger followed a curving black line. "This is the main road you came in on." His finger stopped near a curve." This is where we found Derrick's car. This is near where the others went missing, too."

"What is this?" Oliver pointed to a large orange blob.

"That is the copper mine," said Johnny. "It's mostly abandoned; the locals still dig up scraps to sell at the market."

"Brood of vipers," said Roland as he ducked into the Quonset hut

"I agree," said Oliver. "Are there caves in this mine?"

"Yes," answered Johnny. "It's an open strip mine, but sinkholes and caves have formed."

"Take us there," said Oliver to Emilia.

"I'm going too," said Johnny.

"It is safer if you don't," said Oliver.

"A shepherd will leave the ninety-nine and go after the lost sheep until he finds it," replied Johnny.

"I'm going to be straight with you," said Oliver. "We are here because we think a demon has taken your friends. An actual physical demon that is violent and sacrifices people in service of Satan."

"I am not afraid," said Johnny. "My faith in Christ shall protect me."

Oliver looked at Roland, and Roland smiled back. "Fine, but you do what we tell you to. Most importantly, if we say 'run,' do so and don't look back."

"Agreed," said Johnny, who offered Oliver a hand.

Oliver accepted the shake. "Let's go."

They loaded into Emilia's truck with Oliver up front. Johnny and Roland rode in the rear. As they drove, Roland offered a prayer.

Proclaim this among the nations:
Prepare a war; rouse the mighty men!
Let all the soldiers draw near, let them come up!
Beat your plowshares into swords
And your pruning hooks into spears;
Let the weak say, "I am a mighty man."

Half an hour later, Emilia turned off the road into the thick trees. The truck wound and bounced down the unused road until it cleared, revealing the copper mine. The gray scar on the Earth stretched across for a mile. The tired sections of dug-out land led down to a brown pool of water at the bottom. Pockmarked along the carved lines of earth black holes of cave mouths could be seen. Emilia skidded the truck to a stop overlooking the area. Oliver stepped out and approached the edge.

"We have to take ladders down," said Emilia as she walked over to Oliver. "I hope your big friend is not too heavy."

"Everything is possible for one who believes," replied Roland as he hopped off the back of the truck and opened his case.

He pressed a button, and the case split open and presented his armor, and he went through his donning ceremony.

"Gather round," commanded Oliver as Roland dressed. "Roland will lead. I will bring up the tail. I would prefer it if you stayed here and waited. If anyone insists on coming, I offer this warning again. These are vile creatures that will kill you if given the chance."

"We are not afraid," said Johnny. "I trust in the Lord."

"Ok," said Oliver. "Stay between us then and follow our directions."

Roland joined the circle, "For where two or three are gathered in my name, there am I among them."

"Yes," replied Oliver. "Let us pray."

Dear father
Guide our hands and hearts as we seek your wayward sheep
Protect us with your hands as we endeavor on this quest
May our actions glorify your name
Amen

"Amen," replied the group.

Oliver looked down and evaluated the ladder. The word "ladder" was loosely applied to a collection of wood and metal that was lashed together with a variety of materials that ran the thirty feet down to the next level.

Roland approached the ladder.

Emily said, "The ladders are not very–"

Roland stepped off the edge and slid down the wall of the mine down to the next level where he skidded to a stop.

"That's one way down," said Johnny.

"Oh," laughed Oliver. "Just wait until Roland gets going."

Emilia was next and climbed down the handmade ladder, Johnny followed, then Oliver. They doubted it could handle more than one climber at a time.

"Any idea where to start looking?" asked Oliver.

"There are dozens of caves," said Johnny.

"Any particularly large ones?" asked Oliver.

"There is one I can think of," said Emilia. "I used to explore these as a child, and one was more cavern than a cave."

"Show us where," said Oliver.

Emilia led them down three more sets of ladders and to a small cave entrance. Oliver and Roland had to duck into the entrance.

After a dozen feet, it sprawled open into a cavern. Its ceiling stretched up over fifty feet. Water runoff had cut a path through the floor that trailed off deeper into the darkness.

"This fits the bill," said Oliver. "Emilia and Johnny, stay between Roland and I."

Roland clicked on his chest light and Oliver clipped his hat light on. Johnny and Emilia turned on handheld flashlights.

Roland led, his cross of light guiding the way.

"How did you know about this place?" asked Johnny to Emilia.

"My father used to work these mines," answered Emilia. "I would explore the closed areas as he worked. This was the biggest and the coolest in the heat of the day."

"Any idea how deep it goes?" asked Oliver.

"No," replied Emilia. "I never went past where the light reached."

"The Lord my God lightens my darkness," replied Roland.

The group continued down, the path narrowing.

Roland raised his hand. "Wait for the Lord; be strong, and let your heart take courage; wait for the Lord!"

Roland stepped forward and examined a pile in the path with his light. It was a body.

"Julia," yelled Johnny as he knelt next to the body. "Oh God!"

Julia was long dead, her body torn and her clothing in shreds. Her left leg and arm were mostly torn off and missing.

Johnny looked to Emilia, "Could a puma do this?"

"Not likely," said Emilia. "It would not leave this much food behind."

From deeper in the caves, a moaning echoed out.

"Get behind us," said Oliver.

Roland planted his foot and took off down the cave path.

"Here we go," said Oliver. "Let's move."

Oliver jogged so Emilia and Johnny could keep pace. The cave opened up into a wide path. Roland stood above three bodies in a puddle of black blood.

"I smell sulfur," said Emilia.

"It's the demon blood," said Oliver.

"Are those demons?" asked Johnny as he pointed to the bodies at Roland's feet.

"Ghouls," answered Oliver. "Dead bodies that a demon has taken control of. Do you recognize the bodies?"

"No," said Johnny.

"I think so," said Emilia. "They look like locals who scavenge this mine."

"Quiet," said Oliver. "I hear something."

"The eyes of the Lord are toward the righteous. And His ears are open to their cry," said Roland in a whisper.

From deeper in the cavern, a rhythmic chant hummed through the rocks.

Roland charged forth, his armor clanking on the rocks.

Oliver ran after him with Johnny and Emilia in tow. "Stay close."

The path opened up into a vast section. Torches were placed along the walls and cast dancing lights across the area. Roland stopped at the threshold. Before him, a dozen ghouls in torn clothing revealing seeping wounds stood before an elevated section carved from the rock. They were swaying and chanting in a strange tongue.

On the 'stage,' a pair of figures wearing black robes stood before a crude wooden table. On the table, an unmoving body lay surrounded by candles.

The taller of the two figures raised his hands and then placed them on the body. The dozens in the audience raised their hands, and the room fell silent.

After a still moment, the body on the table let out a dry moan and sat upright.

"They have set their mouth against the heavens, and their tongue parades through the earth," yelled Roland and dashed forward.

The shorter figure pointed and shouted in a language Oliver did not understand.

Roland hammered into the crowd with his shield, and ghoul bodies exploded back. He swiped with his sword and cleaved into the group. Ghoul heads and blood splattered across the cave. He was again unleashed, God's wrath in physical form.

From the ceiling, demon-possessed bats swooped down and pelted against Roland's armor.

"Johnny," yelled Oliver. "Read from your Bible"

"What verse?" yelled back Johnny.

"Just pick a book," yelled Oliver as he fired into the crowd, picking off ghoul heads and bats.

Johnny pulled his Bible out and held it to his face.

"Read it aloud," yelled Oliver. "Emilia. Read with Johnny."

"Sorry," called back Johnny and started to read from Isaiah.

"I don't believe," yelled Emilia.

"Read or run," yelled Oliver over his gunfire.

Emilia took off back to the cave entrance.

Roland had reached the stage; a dozen ghoul bodies and countless bat corpses lay behind him.

From the darkness at the rear of the stage, a wet laughter echoed out. The two figures in robes had fled, and from the dark, a green-skinned demon stepped forward. Over twelve feet tall with a massive belly that sloshed with each step. Its head and face a warped pig's features, red bloated eyes, and thick teeth that flanked a pair of worn tusks. In its hands was a massive ax-cleaver weapon.

"What is that?" screamed Johnny in horror.

"What we came to kill," replied Oliver.

The demon laughed, and the deep rumble echoed through the cave. It readied its weapon and spoke, the voice oozing past obese lips, "Better Paladins than you have tried."

Roland leaped and sliced with his sword; the demon blocked it with its weapon. Roland spun off and rolled behind.

Oliver fired rounds that entered the fatty flesh, doing no harm to the creature.

The demon swiped its free arm with speed, un-matching its obesity, and struck Roland, who had raised his shield and was knocked off the stage.

Oliver emptied both guns into the demon, its bullets embedded harmlessly into the bulbous flesh.

The demon jumped off the stage with the ax raised and brought it down, aimed at Roland; Roland rolled out of the way. The cave shook with the impact of the gargantuan weapon.

Oliver pulled a red Prideaux loader and a black Prideaux loader from his pouch. His hands danced over each other as he reloaded and thought, *try these.*

As the demon struggled to pull its ax out of the ground, Roland stabbed his sword into its side; it was halfway in before it found something hard. The demon howled in pain and swiped at Roland, knocking him back and dislodging the sword still in Roland's titan grip. Out of the sword wound, black sulfuric blood flowed out.

Oliver fired, and two bullets found home, one in the demon's chest and one in its head. A millisecond later, the flesh at these spots exploded out.

"But as for you, be strong and do not give up, for your work will be rewarded," called Roland as he dashed forward and jumped. He swiped his sword horizontally and embedded it in the demon's neck above the back. He kicked both feet and planted them into the mushy flesh.

Oliver fired again, and both rounds entered the neck opposite Roland's sword. The bullets exploded, and molten flesh burst out.

Roland pulled his sword out and swung again. The sword drove deeper into the neck. With his free hand, he grabbed the demon's far ear and pulled back.

Two more of Oliver's bullets embedded into the neck, and more flesh exploded out.

The demon freed its ax and threw it at Oliver, who pre-saw the throw and easily dodged. The weapon continued its flight, and the handle struck Johnny, who was bashed back into the wall. With black blood pouring out of its neck wounds, the creature reached with its hands at its back but could not grasp Roland. It turned and ran backward into the cavern wall. The impact caused pieces of the cave to fall from the ceiling.

Roland cried out in pain but would not relent. He reached with his gauntleted hand around the demon's neck, grabbed the blade, and sawed at the neck.

A pair of bullets found each of the demon's eyes and erupted them out. The demon squealed in agony.

Roland had the sword up to his elbows, wrapped them around the blade, and pulled. The skin that remained stretched and tore. Oliver fired through the taut skin, and the standard rounds bounced off Roland's chest. Roland yelled and continued to pull the sword until the head was separated from the body.

The massive creature fell forward headless. Its head rolled down its form, a tortured look frozen into its unholy visage.

Roland tumbled after and steadied himself next to his slain foe.

Oliver, guns still aimed at the creature, moved next to Roland, "Is it dead?"

Roland thrust his sword into the detached head. "Victory rests with the Lord."

Oliver turned to the altar. "Let's go, Roland. We can still catch the other one."

"We who are strong have an obligation to bear with the failings of the weak and not to please ourselves," replied Roland.

"Yeah, you are right," said Oliver. He walked over to examine Johnny and crouched next to him, "I think he has a cracked skull. Can you carry him to the truck?"

"Come to me all who are weary and burdened," said Roland as he flicked the black blood off his sword and attached it to his back.

Oliver documented the scene with his camera and set a flame to the altar.

They found Emilia cowering near the entrance. She was mumbling, "I do not believe." Fear had taken her senses. Oliver helped her up and walked her, guiding them until she regained her composure.

When they reached the ladder, Roland scaled the mine wall carrying the unconscious Johnny. Oliver helped Emilia climb up the ladder.

They loaded into the truck and a still shaken Emilia slowly drove them back to camp.

CLASS REUNION

Ivoire spent the first years after her training at The Guild undercover at various Ukrainian businesses. She would be tasked to see if the business was working for a foreign government or if the profits were leaving the country. She would receive her orders, develop her disguise, and gain access as an employee or support member. Each mission fell into a rhythm, she would use her gift to find information, her training to infiltrate, then send her findings back to the handler. To her surprise, every business she investigated was legitimate. Just ordinary people trying to make their way in the world.

Her handler changed with every assignment. She rarely met them in person. Usually, the information was exchanged via dead drops, miscellaneous containers that would hold the message until picked up. Handlers were simply contacts who provided her with her orders and equipment. The only identifying marks were their unique handwriting in the margins of the typed messages.

It was a boring time for Ivoire. After what she experienced at The Guild, she expected to be using the languages and skills she had learned as she traveled the world. So far, she had not left Ukraine. She only had to use her martial skills once as she fended off a homeless man demanding money. Her one relief was she had not had to use the distasteful seduction training in the field. That training still disturbed her and haunted her nightmares.

The assignment she had just completed was a simple one. A company was suspected of selling foreign products as locally made ones. She validated their origin as local and delivered her findings to her handler. This mission felt like a waste of her skills. This was not spy work but work for the Department of Consumer Affairs. Any other agent could have completed this with a simple visit.

Why was the government not using her and her ability to sense truth in more impactful ways? As she dropped her findings into the dead drop, her next assignment was there waiting. She sighed in boredom as she cut open the tan envelope. As she read, her demeanor changed.

Agent,

Your assistance is requested in an investigation. Use the enclosed ticket. Your contact will greet you upon arrival.

Nothing else, which was pretty normal. The ticket is what grabbed her fancy. It was for a flight to Venice Airport.

She landed at night. The lights of "The City of Water" blended with the stars and moon in the clear sky and reflected off the encircling ocean. It was a beautiful sight that only added to Ivoire's excitement.

Stirring ideas ran through her head. *What was the investigation? Will I finally get to speak Italian?* She could barely sit in her seat.

After exiting the plane, a surprise she never imagined awaited her. There was no mistaking the diminutive figure waiting for her. It was Kalnya. She was dressed in a black suit. Her hair was short, parted, and slicked down.

"Greetings, Ivoire," said Kalnya curtly.

"Kalnya!" said Ivoire as she rushed over and hugged her. Ivoire now towered over Kalnya, who had not grown since their time at school.

Book of Ivon and Ivoire

"Please contain your emotions," said Kalnya. "We are here on an official assignment."

Ivoire straightened, "Apologies. It has been so long since I have seen a friendly face. What is the assignment?"

"We can talk in the car," said Kalnya. "Too many ears here. Also, Sofiy says hello."

"Sofiy!" said Ivoire. "You're still in touch with her?"

"She is my top asset," said Kalnya, who was briskly walking towards a black sedan. "I'll drive and explain more."

Kalnya drove them from the airport to a boat dock. During the drive, she revealed she was now an investigator for Ukraine's Foreign Intelligence Service. Her primary mission was investigating missing agents. Sofiy had been assigned to the newly formed Cyber Defense division and worked in all aspects of technology counterintelligence. Kalnya had not seen her in person, nor did she know how to contact her directly. Just that when she needs her, to simply say it out loud around any connected device and Sofiy reaches out.

They approached the dock and boarded a sturdy wooden power boat, the driver at the helm. The vessel surged forward across the expanse of the Venetian lagoon, the city shimmering in the darkness ahead. With deft precision, the driver navigated past boats and yachts, the wind carrying the tang of salt through the air, refreshing Ivoire's senses. As the boat crested each wave, her anticipation for what awaited her in the city only intensified.

They entered the narrow canals of the city and slowly wound through tight alleys and low bridges. The driver pulled into a dock under a four-story, tan and red masonry building. Three serious-looking men waited and helped moor the boat.

"Agent Truchan," greeted one of the men. "Is this the specialist you requested?"

"Yes," said Kalnya as she exited the boat. "This is Agent Kravets. Give her the same autonomy as you give me."

"Yes, ma'am," replied the man.

"This way, Ivoire," said Kalnya as she ascended the stairs.

Three flights of stairs later, they turned down a short hall leading to a double door that another man in a suit was standing outside of. Upon seeing Kalnya, he opened the door and let them pass.

Beyond the doors was an expansive suite. Soft linen and highly polished wood furniture were all askew. The signs of violence, blood, and broken objects stained the once comfortable room.

"What happened here?" asked Ivoire.

"One of our agents was murdered here," said Kalnya bluntly. She stopped before another double-door set. "We have the suspect in here. This is why you are here. To help us understand."

"He is not answering your questions?" asked Ivoire.

"He is," said Kalnya. "But we do not like his answers."

"And you think I can do better?" asked Ivoire.

"It's not in my nature to mince words," said Kalnya. "I only trust the logical, what can be proven, in all things except one." She paused and walked over to the window. "I spent two years at that school with you. I watched as Commandant Witko tried to lie to you, the dozens of experts he brought to our school to try to trick or deceive you. All failed. For two years, I watched as you could, without fail, discern truth vs falsehood. I have encountered no proof of anything supernatural, no event I have not been able to explain with science and logic. None except for one." Kalnya turned and faced Ivoire. "You."

"Me?" said Ivoire.

"Yes," said Kalnya. "Your ability to know the truth can't be explained by anything other than mystical."

"I can't explain it either," said Ivoire. "I have had this ability my entire life."

"I did not bring you here seeking an explanation," said Kalnya. "I have known of your skill and, in my pride, resisted believing. But Sofiy, she always believed."

"She knew, too?" asked Ivoire.

"She more than knew-" Kalnya was interrupted by a chime coming from her inner pocket. She pulled the phone out, flipped it open, and put it on the speaker. "Hello Sofiy." Her voice not hiding the annoyance of the interruption.

"Ivoire!" said Sofiy in glee. "You look stunning. You always had such great hair."

"You can see me?" asked Ivoire.

"Sure," said Sofiy. "Lots of phones and security cameras nearby."

"It's a pleasure to be seen," said Ivoire. "How have you been?"

"Oh, you know," said Sofiy. "Busy. Kalnya is always work, work, work."

"Ladies," said Kalnya. "We have a murder to solve."

"Does she know?" asked Sofiy.

"No," said Kalnya. "I was weighing if I should tell her now or after she questioned the suspect."

"Darnya is the victim," Sofiy blurted.

"Darnya?" asked Ivoire. "From school?"

"One and the same," said Sofiy.

"And you think the person in the next room killed her?" asked Ivoire.

"We know he did," said Kalnya. "You are here to help us understand why." She picked a folder off the table and handed it to Ivoire. "These are the pictures we took of this room while Darnya's body was still here."

Ivoire accepted the folder and opened it. She flipped through the photos that showed her old friend laying in front of the couch of the room she currently stood in. She was nude and covered in her own blood and bruises. Her face was swollen, and some teeth were missing.

"He beat her to death?" asked Ivoire.

"Yes," said Kalnya. "His story doesn't help explain it. Are you ready to try your ability on him?"

"Yes," said Ivoire as she handed the folder back to Kalnya.

Kalnya opened the double doors into the bedroom. The room matched the sitting area both in luxury and in signs of violence: more blood and broken furniture. In front of the bed, a nude man was tied to a chair. He was muscular with short brown hair and a full beard. He had tattoos on his chest and arms. He was beaten and bloody, both eyes blacked, and multiple contusions on his body. A muscular man in a white button-up shirt splashed with blood and the sleeves rolled up sat in a chair next to the door.

"Wake him up," said Kalnya.

The man in the white shirt rose and picked an ice bucket from the floor next to him. He walked over and splashed water on the bound man, who woke with a yell.

The white-shirt man slapped the nude man, "Time for more questions."

"I promise," said the man in English with an Irish accent. "I told you everything."

"His identification says his name is Quincy O'Donnell," said Kalnya in English. "From our research, he is a MMA fighter, the son of a wealthy whiskey maker in Ireland."

"It's true," said the man. "That's who I am."

"He is telling the truth," said Ivoire.

"Yeah," said Sofiy. "We were able to confirm it."

"Where we get fuzzy is how he ends up here with Darnya," said Kalnya.

"I told you," said Quincy. "My dad bought her for me as a birthday present."

"He at least believes it is the truth," said Ivoire. "Why did you kill her?"

"I didn't," said Quincy. "We went out, came back here, had sex, and I fell asleep. I woke up, and she was dead. I called my dad, but some lady was on the phone, and then you guys showed up."

"That was me on the phone," said Sofiy. "My scans heard Darnya call for help. I took over his phone."

"That's when we got involved," said Kalnya. "Sofiy messaged me, and I came straight here. That was yesterday."

"I changed your next orders and arranged travel for you, Ivoire," said Sofiy. "Kalnya did not want to involve you, but I did for the old 'Room Twenty-Seven' crew."

"What did you find when you arrived?" asked Ivoire.

"Just as you see it now," said Kalnya. "Except Quincy was dressed and packing."

"I was scared," said Quincy. "First, a dead hooker and then a strange woman on the phone."

"And the bruises on your hands and body when we arrived?" asked Kalnya.

"I don't know," said Quincy.

"Well?" said Kalnya to Ivoire. "Is he being honest?"

"He believes his story," said Ivoire. "Can I try something?"

"He's all yours," said Kalnya.

Ivoire pulled the travel kit from her bag, removed some bottles, and placed them on the table. She removed her crucifix and opened the blade. She opened two bottles and dipped the blade in both, one at a time.

Ivoire turned and approached Quincy.

"What are you doing?" asked Quincy.

"I know you are telling the truth," said Ivoire. "It's the blank space between we need to fill." She sliced the blade along the side of his neck. A small trickle of blood dripped down his chest. Ivoire looked at her watch. "Three minutes."

"Until what?" asked Sofiy.

"He'll be in a hypnotic trance to help his memory," said Ivoire. "Did Darnya have any possessions here?"

"They are all in a box out in the sitting area," said Kalnya. "This way."

They went back out to the room, and Kalnya showed Ivoire the box.

"Pretty normal stuff," said Kalnya. "We are going to send it out for analysis."

Ivoire dug through the box and pulled out a necklace and then a travel bag. She took the travel bag over to a table and dumped the contents. She examined the bottles of shampoo and tubes of toothpaste. She opened a bottle of acne cream and smelled it.

"I think I know what happened," said Ivoire. "It's been three minutes. Let's check on Quincy."

They returned to the room and Quincy was rigid with a blank stare.

"Quincy," said Ivoire as she approached. "Can you hear me?"

"Yes," said Quincy. His voice was drowsy.

"Do you recall falling asleep with the hooker?" asked Ivoire.

"I do," said Quincy.

"What happened next?" asked Ivoire.

"While I was asleep, she got up and went to the bathroom," said Quincy.

"Then what?" asked Ivoire.

"She came out with something in her hand," said Quincy.

"What was it?' asked Ivoire.

"I do not know," answered Quincy.

"What did she do with it?" asked Ivoire.

"She scratched my inner thigh," said Quincy.

"What happened next?" asked Ivoire.

"At first, it felt good," said Quincy. "Warmth ran up my leg." His eyes closed—a frightened look on his face.

"What is wrong?" asked Ivoire.

"The warmth," said Quincy as he squirmed. "It is turning to heat and then burning. I am awake and angry. Anger like I have never felt. Rage flows through me. I am in the octagon and fighting a title fight. I face my opponent; he is quick and flexible but not very strong. The fight is short. I have him on the ground, and I am pounding his face. The ref has not stopped the match, so I keep pounding. My opponent has stopped moving. I stand, exhausted, and go back to bed."

"He dreamt he was fighting?" asked Kalnya.

"Yes," said Ivoire. "He had a reaction to the LSD from the acne cream bottle that Darnya put into his blood. The LSD put him into a hallucinatory state. If you run blood work on him, you will find its traces."

"You can smell the LSD?" asked Sofiy.

"I can," said Ivoire. She held up the necklace from the box. On the end is an eight-pointed star; the point opposite the chain is longer than the other seven. Ivoire slid her finger along the back, and a needle popped out.

"Her necklace is like yours," said Kalnya.

"Sofiy," said Ivoire. "Where did Darnya go after leaving our school?"

"You don't know?" asked Sofiy. "She went to Hil'diya Anthemoessa just like you."

COCKTAILS AND EXORCISMS

"Can a ghoul be forcibly created?" asked Oliver.

"We are still learning the abilities of the demons," replied Melissa. "No vile act they can imagine seems past their means."

Oliver, Melissa, Roland, and Persephone were in the library. Ivoire, who was still in California, joined via the screen on the main monitor.

"If a demon can possess a body willingly, why the need to force it?" asked Oliver.

"It may be a way of helping demons too weak to do it on their own cross over," answered Melissa.

"Having access to such an ability would amplify their numbers greatly," said Oliver.

"Yes," replied Melissa. "We must investigate deeper and stop it."

"Melissa and I reviewed the video from Roland's helmet," said Persephone as she pulled up the video onto the display. "The language the one-robed figure spoke was Russian."

"What did he say?" asked Oliver.

"'Kill them,'" said Ivoire. "Did Roland's camera catch them leaving?"

"Not really," said Persephone. She advanced the video. "Here. The two figures step into the darkness, and a minute later, that pig demon steps out."

"Any information on him?" asked Oliver.

"The best we can surmise is that it is a 'Babi ngepet'," said Melissa. "An Indonesian boar-demon. In their legend, a man in a black robe transforms into the creature."

"That fits," said Oliver. "What of the ceremony?"

"We have long thought that it was possible to force a demon into a corpse and create a ghoul," said Melissa. "Normally, the demons are able to enter our realm of their own free will once strong enough but not do much more than what many would call a simple haunting."

"Like the garage of that lady the minister visited," added Ivoire.

"Correct," said Melissa with a smile. "If they are powerful enough, they can reanimate dead humans and animals. What we call 'ghouls'."

"In this case," continued Persephone. "This looks like someone is forcing the demons into the bodies against their will. The result is the weak ghouls that barely put up a fight."

"Why would someone do that?" asked Ivoire.

"They may be trying to forcibly create a ghoul army," answered Melissa. "They may be weak, but in sufficient numbers, it can be a serious threat."

"Is this the 'Project Garmr' that Ivoire discovered?" asked Oliver.

"Possibly," said Persephone. "Garmr in Norse Mythology is the guard dog of Hell. The story goes that as the events of Ragnarök (Norse end of the world) unfold, Garmr is said to break free from his chains in Helheim (Norse hell). This act signifies the collapse of the established order in the world, as the guardian of the realm of the dead is no longer confined to his post, and the dead can return to the land of the living."

"Unleashing a horde of ghouls on the Earth could bring about a societal collapse," said Melissa.

"Ok, so back to who are the robed figures. Anything else on them?" asked Oliver.

"The only lead we have is the language," said Melissa.

Book of Ivon and Ivoire

"The Russian that one spoke," added Oliver.

"On the call, I translated the mention of Garmr," said Ivoire. "The Russian Prime Minister was on the call, so there is a connection there."

"Unfortunately," said Persephone. "I was unable to pull anything from their faces. The robes kept them in the dark. I was able to pull one thing, though."

The video backed up and zoomed in on the hand that the robed figure raised and placed on the ghoul.

"M - N - P," read Oliver. "What is that?"

"It's Russian," said Melissa. "МИР, which means 'peace' or -"

"World," interrupted Ivoire.

"Yes, 'world,'" said Melissa. "Do you know this tattoo?"

"It is common enough in Russia," said Ivoire. "It is what you would call a 'prison tattoo.' It means 'menya ispravit rasstrel,' or in English, 'only execution will correct me.'"

"So this man was an inmate?" said Oliver.

"Only maybe," answered Ivoire. "It became fashionable among criminals and kids who played pretend gangster for a time."

"Not much there," said Oliver.

"Persephone and I will continue with this investigation on the ghouls," said Melissa. "Ivoire, what is the latest from your mission?"

"I have an upcoming event I want to bring to your attention. Senator Wiles is hosting a dinner party next month and I have been invited as an interpreter," said Ivoire.

"This is an opportunity to corner her again," said Melissa.

"Yes, and I have been given a 'plus one' invitation as well," said Ivoire. "What do you say, Oliver?"

"Me?" said Oliver.

"You are the only choice," said Melissa. "Roland is too obvious, and Wiles may recognize him from the Shanette concert or the boat. You are of a normal stature and easier to disguise."

"I may not be the best choice," said Oliver.

"Why?" asked Melissa.

"I've never learned to dance," answered Oliver.

Persephone giggled.

Roland responded, "I will instruct you and teach you in the way you should go; I will counsel you with my eye upon you."

"You, Roland?" asked Oliver. "You can dance?"

"Let them praise His name with dancing," said Roland with a broad smile.

"The party is in a month," said Melissa. "Roland and I will instruct Oliver in charm and civility."

Oliver's training began that night. He, Roland, Persephone, and Melissa were in the gymnasium.

Roland stood before Oliver and bowed, saying, "Praise Him with tumbrel and dancing." He stood and offered his left hand high and his right hand low. Oliver stepped forward, and Roland pulled him close.

Melissa played a waltz on her tablet, and Roland led Oliver. They stepped and swirled around the room. Roland's power forced Oliver to follow his lead.

As they moved around the room, Melissa kept time with a "one, two, three, four."

As they danced past, Oliver saw Persephone's smile and laughed to himself.

Once Oliver had the rhythm, he and Roland stopped, "Take your turn; no one person is taking over."

Melissa approached and bowed. "Bow and take my hands." She held her right hand high.

Oliver positioned himself, and Persephone started the music.

"Lead me," said Melissa. "Just as Roland led you."

Oliver let the music take him, and he guided Melissa around the room. As they danced around the room, Oliver saw Persephone's smile at the sight.

"Look at me," said Melissa, moving his head with her hand. "Your eyes should not leave mine."

"What if I need to scout?" asked Oliver.

"Keep your head on your partner," answered Melissa. "Look out the corner of your eyes."

Oliver's gaze settled on Melissa. As they swirled around the room, he stopped thinking and just danced in the moment. His whole world became him and Melissa dancing. It was a serene moment: no demons, no battles, just him and a friend swaying to music.

When the song ended, Melissa stopped and stepped back. "Very good. He has the rhythm now. We can dance more later. Now, let's have dinner and show Oliver how to act at a formal dinner."

When not training in dance, Roland and Melissa tutored Oliver on the protocol for fine dining and the social rules for the engagement. Training continued for a week until Oliver was a passable enough dancer and diner.

Persephone and Ivoire researched the location of the event and completed the planning. The following week, Oliver geared up and flew to meet Ivoire in California. Oliver stayed in a different hotel to minimize suspicions.

Roland and Melissa flew up separately and were going to be on stand-by if Oliver and Ivoire needed help.

The night of the event, Ivoire hailed a cab and took it to Oliver's hotel. He waited out front in his tuxedo; the outfit felt constraining. His discomfort was amplified as he only carried one revolver concealed in his suit in the small of his back. Persephone had made what she called "a Faraday cage for your guns." It was a mesh beyond Oliver's understanding, only that it would prevent the metal detectors from sensing the heavy metals of his weapon.

Ivoire's taxi pulled up, and Oliver opened the door. He was not prepared for what awaited him. Ivoire, as Martina, dressed in a form fitting black evening dress. Even seated, her athletic body radiated beauty.

"Hello, handsome," said Ivoire in Martina's accent. It was a sultry and seductive sound. "Are you just going to stand there all night?"

Oliver smiled. He realized he had been caught off guard and entered. "Hello, Martina. You look amazing." The words were truth and an act.

They rode the taxi through the street-light-lit roads out beyond the suburbs and up the hills to the cliffs overlooking the ocean. It was a clear and beautiful night. The distant moon hovered just above the water, and its twin reflections danced in the calm waves.

Roland and Melissa had taken an SUV and were parked in the driveway of an empty home that offered a view of the main gate.

Oliver and Ivoire reached the open main gate and were waved through when they got their first good look at Wiles' mansion. Seated at the end of a winding road up through a lonely hill, the building was an expansive structure challenging gravity as it hung out over the abyss down to the ocean. The white, column-fronted building was illuminated by red light, and decorations of gold glittered.

The taxi dropped them off at the top of the circle drive that was lined with expensive vehicles and flowed with people.

It was elegance beyond Oliver's experience. Fortunes untold passed him adorned with gems and finery. He felt naked and out of place—a simple man from a simple life.

Ivoire took his hand. "Let's go find some food." It was as if she could sense his discomfort. Her hand and words eased him as they approached the steps leading to the entrance.

At the base of the stairs, a Secret Service detail was inspecting bags and funneling guests through metal detectors.

Oliver's revolver felt warm under his shirt. As they walked he internally said a prayer asking for protection.

Ivoire handed her handbag to the detail and stepped through the metal detector.

Oliver stepped through next and fought a flinch as he passed the sensors.

When no beep sounded, he continued breathing.

Ivoire accepted her bag and took Oliver's hand again. "Let's go, babe."

They climbed the steps and passed by the great columns and through the massive doors. Inside, a small orchestra played as the guests mingled, drank, and danced. Red lights bathed the room in what Oliver could only call "evil light."

Oliver and Ivoire moved to the dance floor. Oliver pulled her close, and they danced around the room.

"We are free to talk," said Ivoire.

Persephone's voice rang through his earpiece, "I am scanning the audio for Wiles' voice."

"No need," said Oliver. "I have eyes on her."

Wiles was alone at the bar, drinking from a martini glass. She wore a red gown that hung on her emaciated frame.

"Move in, Oliver," said Melissa over the communicator.

"What?" he asked. "Take her now?"

"Don't 'take her,'" said Ivoire. "Talk to her. See if she shows any interest."

"Interest in what?" asked Oliver.

Ivoire stepped back and looked Oliver up and down, then looked at him with seductive eyes.

"Oh," he said, understanding what they wanted him to do. "I'm moving in."

"You got this," said Persephone.

"We will be in your ear," said Melissa.

How does one seduce a demon?

"Now, stand a few paces down from her at the bar and order a drink," said Melissa. "Don't greet her, don't even look at her."

Oliver weaved through the crowd across the room and sauntered up to the bar. "Beer, please."

"Now turn around and watch the dancers," said Melissa over his earpiece. "Pay no mind to Wiles. We can see you both through Ivoire's glasses."

Oliver did as instructed and sipped from his drink.

"Wiles is looking at you," said Melissa. "Do not look at her."

Oliver now understood what a gazelle felt like that was being stalked by a lion. He could feel Wiles slide closer to him. She smelled of vodka and expensive perfume.

"I do not know you," said Wiles. Her voice dripped with drunkenness.

"Don't reply yet," said Melissa. "Play hard to get. Look at Ivoire; focus on her."

Oliver let the noise of the room grow quiet in his mind as he focused on Ivoire. She was graceful, elegant, and confident as she walked closer. This vision of beauty was quickly blocked by the jarring ugliness of Senator Wiles.

"I said," said the inebriated Wiles. "I do not know you. Are you somebody? You look familiar."

Olivier worried she recognized him from the Shanette concert. "No, ma'am," replied Oliver. "I am here with my date, Martina." He pointed over her shoulder.

Wiles followed his point and found what it was aimed at. "Oh." She chuckled. "The translator."

Martina approached.

"Is this your toy?" asked Wiles.

"He is tonight's distraction," said Ivoire.

"Oh," Wiles looked back at Oliver. "And does this pet have a name?"

"My name-" Oliver started.

"She wasn't asking you," said Ivoire, interrupting Oliver. "Yes, he has a name," she said to Wiles. "But you can pick a new one if you like."

Wiles smiled, "Oh, you are a fun one. This is new. The times I have seen you at the office you have always been so shy, so reserved."

"You know what they say about the quiet ones," smiled Ivoire.

"No," smiled Wiles back. "What do they say?"

"They save all the noise for the bedroom," Ivoire quipped. She turned to Oliver. "Fetch the Senator and I two dry martinis."

Oliver turned to the bar as instructed. Ivoire and Wiles laughed as they flirted.

"Doing great," said Melissa over the earpiece.

"What's the plan now?" asked Oliver quietly.

"With any luck, Ivoire can convince the Senator to take her somewhere private," said Melissa. "Then you move in, and I will walk you through the exorcism."

Oliver waited for the drinks, then stepped back to Wiles and Ivoire, handing them their beverages.

"Thank you," said Ivoire who barely glanced his way. After a moment of him standing there, she waved her hand and said, "Go find something to do. I want to spend some time with the Senator."

"Yes, ma'am," replied Oliver and turned away.

"Nice," said Melissa. "Go find a place to keep an eye on them. If they move, follow at a distance."

"Why can't Ivoire just do the exorcism?" asked Oliver.

"She openly told us she is not a believer," answered Melissa. "You must have faith in Christ in order to do things in his name."

"Understood," said Oliver. "Hopefully, this goes smoother than the time in Estonia."

"I doubt she has an army of animals here," said Persephone.

"No," said Oliver. "Just an army of armed security guards and secret service."

"Yes," said Persephone. "And we have a Roland."

Oliver observed Ivoire in action. He could hear the conversation over his earpiece. They slowly moved across the room as they flirted back and forth.

"...this mansion is lovely," said Ivoire. "When is it open for tours?"

"I can make an exception for one as tasty as you," said Wiles. "Any area you are particularly interested in?"

Oliver watched in disgust as Wiles walked her fingers up Ivoire's arm.

"Why don't you pick?" said Ivoire. "I'm sure a place this big is easy to get lost in."

"Tell me," Wiles moves closer to Ivoire. "Are you a student of the arts?"

"I am a student of all things beautiful," replied Ivoire.

Wiles laughed and took Ivoire's hand. "This way, child."

Oliver watched as Wiles led Ivoire around the corner and out of view. He could still hear their conversation over the communicators.

"... down here is my favorite room in this house," said Wiles. "The Gallery."

"Now move," said Melissa. "Keep your distance, but try to keep them in sight."

Oliver left the drinks at the bar, moved across the room, and pretended to inspect a painting as Wiles led Ivoire down the hallway and turned at the junction to the left.

"I am moving down the hall," said Oliver as he followed.

"...this is my private art collection," said Wiles. "I think the centerpiece will be of special interest to you."

Oliver reached the closed door Wiles and Ivoire were behind. "Now what?" he whispered over the comm.

"Hold your spot," said Melissa. "This may work."

"What is happening?" asked Oliver.

"…this is a fascinating collection," said Ivoire. "I particularly am interested in the altar you have in the center."

Book of Ivon and Ivoire

"This," said Wiles. "... is my favorite piece of the collection. Archaeologists recovered this relic from a dig site from the peak of Mount Hermon. It is a Canaanite altar in nearly perfect condition."

Oliver could hear Wiles walking and then metal clanking.

"These straps were used to tie down the sacrifices," continued Wiles. "Human sacrifices to their Gods. This altar was specific for those who worshiped Ba'al. The story goes they would sacrifice twenty virgins on the altar, and then the king of the Canaanites would rape a twenty-first and impregnate her. These straps would be used to hold down both the sacrifices and the fertile rape recipient."

"Can you show me?" said Ivoire.

"Oh, you want me to tie you down?" teased Wiles.

"No," said Ivoire. Oliver could hear something soft hit something hard. "I want you helpless."

"Oh," said Wiles. "It always is the quiet ones."

"Oliver," it was Melissa over the coms. "Once she is tied down, we will start the exorcism. Wiles needs to hear you, so be ready to go."

"I'm ready," said Oliver.

"...this strap goes like this," said Wiles, and the sound of the clasp fastening could be heard. "And those are for my ankles."

The sound of the last clasp and Melissa said, "Go, Oliver!"

Oliver squared and kicked the door open. Ivoire was mounted on Wiles on the stone altar. The red-lit room was six-sided, with each wall adorned with a single painting. Each painting depicted horrific and demonic images—gory visions of pain and ungodliness. The altar was carved from a single piece of stone with dark stains and runic language carved into its sides.

"What's this," said a surprisingly calm Wiles. "Did your toy want to play, too?"

"Wait," said Ivoire, who pointed at Oliver and turned to Wiles. "What is Project Garmr?"

183

"Oh," smiled Wiles. "I see you have been eavesdropping in the office. You naughty girl."

Oliver approached and drew his weapon, aimed it at her head, and cocked it, "Answer her."

"Go ahead and shoot, toy," laughed Wiles.

"Let's just exorcise her," said Melissa on the com.

"Agreed," said Ivoire, her voice returning to normal.

"Agree?" asked Wiles. "Oh, you like some blood? That gets you hot?"

Melissa began to pray over the comm, and Oliver repeated.

God of power, who promised us the Holy Spirit through Jesus your Son, we pray to you for these catechumens who present themselves before you. Protect them from the spirit of evil and guard them against error and sin so that they may become the temple of your Holy Spirit. Confirm what we profess in faith so that our words may not be empty but full of the grace and power by which your Son has freed the world. We ask this through Christ our Lord.

Ivoire said, "Amen."

Wiles laughed. "What is this gibberish? You want to save my soul?"

Lord our God, you make known the true life; you cut away corruption and strengthen faith; you build up hope and foster love. In the name of your beloved Son, our Lord Jesus Christ, and in the power of the Holy Spirit, we ask you to remove from these your servants all unbelief and hesitation in faith, [the worship of false gods and magic, witchcraft, and dealings with the dead], the love of money and lawless passions, enmity and quarreling, and every manner of evil. And because you have called them to be holy and sinless in your sight, create in them a spirit of faith and reverence, of patience and hope, of temperance and purity, and of charity and peace. We ask this through Christ our Lord.

Ivoire said, "Amen."
Wiles continued to laugh. "Oh, I see. You are trying to exorcise me." Her voice jumped an octave and grew sinister. "You try your worst with your cute ceremony."

God of power, you created us in your image and likeness and formed us in holiness and justice. Even when we sinned against you, you did not abandon us, but in your wisdom, chose to save us by the incarnation of your Son. Save these your servants: free them from evil and the tyranny of the enemy. Keep far from them the spirit of wickedness, falsehood, and greed. Receive them into your kingdom and open their hearts to understand your Gospel so that, as children of the light, they may become members of your Church, bear witness to your truth, and put into practice your commands of love. We ask this through Christ our Lord.

Ivoire said, "Amen."
Wiles laid still, her eyes closed.
"Did it work?" asked Oliver.
"No," it was Wiles. The voice was a high-pitched squeal.
Wiles sat up, her hands slipped their bonds and knocking Ivoire off. She pushed Oliver with demonic strength, and he tumbled back and recovered.
"Why did it not work?" asked Oliver.
Wiles laughed and swung her legs off the table, slithering out of the bonds. "Exorcisms only work for the possessed."
Wiles' body began to swell. Her ancient skin first filled, then stretched, and finally tore as the creature underneath was revealed. Wiles' human skin and dress fell to the floor like dirty clothes. Oliver expected something taller. After the snake demon, the Ku demon, and the pig demon, each was massive. What was revealed was not even as tall as him. The creature reminded him of the children's stories of goblins. Grey-skinned with pointed ears and shark teeth. Wiles' eyes bulged out like a lizard's. Her torso was far too small for her arms and head.

"Roland." It was Melissa over the comms. "Move in now. Wiles is a full demon. Oliver, get Ivoire and get out. Don't fight it alone."

Oliver quickly said Gerin's prayer.

> *Lord, make me swift and true.*
> *Guide my hands with yours.*
> *Let your will be my aim.*

He fired at the bulging eye, but Wiles dodged. Her speed outpaced his predictive sight.

Wiles was on Oliver and punched him in the sternum. Pain exploded across his chest as he was blasted back against the wall. His breathing was shallow and fast. He felt suffocation taking over. His vision blurred, and he tried to aim. He could see Ivoire still lying on the floor across the room.

I must kill this beast and save Ivoire.

He fired again, and Wiles blinked away.

"I think I recognize you now," said Wiles. "You are the one who killed Valec. It's the guns, very unique. They are lovely. I think I will display them with your skull."

Oliver fired, his aim off, and the bullet flew wide.

Wiles laughed. "A fighter to the end. I am not going to kill you yet. First, I am going to bite off digits one by one and take away your favorite, your guns."

The house alarm sounded. Gunfire and screams echoed from down the hall.

Wiles approached, and Oliver's vision faded. He prayed, knowing that help would not arrive in time to save him.

I am yours, Father.

He fired again, but Wiles was too fast again. His vision faded, and darkness spread as Wiles approached. He was on the edge of a blackout; his mind flowed to Abby, Jimin, and Gerin. Peace washed across his body.

Bang!

Book of Ivon and Ivoire

He was jarred to consciousness as a gunshot pulled him back to focus, away from the peace.

Ivoire was up and aiming her cigarette case gun at Wiles. Black blood was streaming from Wiles' shoulder.

Oliver fired again; he aimed for the head but was weak, and his gun was heavy and hit Wiles's arm.

Wiles screamed and turned back to Oliver.

A roar! A silver flash and Wiles was on the floor.

Roland had arrived.

He had body slammed Wiles and had her pinned, gauntlet on her throat. "And he shall bring them down before thy face."

Her form shifted to a liquid and flowed out of Roland's grasp and under the altar. Roland punched into the puddle of Wiles as it streamed away.

Relief had come, and Oliver blacked out.

DEATH AS LIFE

"Wolf has eyes on the rabbit," said Ivon.

"Hawk confirms," replied Dimitri.

Ivon was weaving his way through the crowded sidewalks of Kyiv. A mild rain painted the city in water. It was the sort of rain that wasn't hard enough to deter people but just hard enough to annoy anyone walking through it.

Ten meters ahead of Ivon was the 'rabbit.' Even under her umbrella, the woman was hard to miss with her bright blonde hair. It ran down past her athletic frame to her legs. She dodged the oncoming pedestrians who hurried to their destinations. The rabbit took a casual pace, almost in defiance of the crowd rushing past her.

Staying slow to keep his distance was difficult for Ivon. The others out in the rain were in a rush and pushed against Ivon to swerve around.

Having no umbrella, the water had drenched his hair and was streaming down his spine. He tried to will the rabbit to walk faster so he could get out of the rain.

His prey had her umbrella and was spared the wet and chill.

He pushed the thoughts of discomfort aside and focused on his task.

"What's the play, Wolf?" asked Dimitri over Ivon's earpiece.

"Take the rabbit at mark four," said Ivon. "I'll tap and close. You pull and wrap."

"Confirmed," Dimitri replied.

Ivon moved faster with the crowd. He let the flow of the sea of people push him closer. The rabbit was twenty seconds from the alley that was 'mark four' when he closed in and paced with her, a stride behind. At the mark, he feigned a trip and knocked the rabbit into the alley.

Dimitri was waiting. As 'the rabbit' fell, he pushed a container into place, and she tumbled in. Ivon closed the lid, and Dimitri pulled their prey into an open door. Ivon checked to see if anyone followed. The crowd flowed by, too concerned with the rain and their lives to notice. He entered the building and closed the door.

They took the box deeper into the building. The soundproof container muffled the screams but not the pounding.

Ivon knew what came next and forced down a smile. He and Dimitri had done this dozens of times. They always say the same things. *Where am I? - Who are you? - Please, you have the wrong person.*

The rabbits will beg, barter, and lie, but Ivon and Dimitri always get the answers they seek. Always.

They had prepared the room for their arrival. Dimitri slid the metal door that scraped in protest against the concrete floor.

A muffled gunshot sounded from the box, and a bullet struck the wall, missing Dimitri by inches. The newly formed bullet hole let the sound of panting, then a yell escape.

"Let me out!"

Another gunshot and another hole. This bullet went left of Dimitri. The two dropped to the floor.

"The gas," said Ivon and pointed to the green cylinder against the wall.

Dimitri crawled over and dragged the gas cylinder and the two gas masks back. He handed one mask to Ivon.

Book of Ivon and Ivoire

A gunshot. A new hole appeared close to the hinge on the box.

Ivon took the hose from the tank and jammed it into the first bullet hole. Dimitri turned on the gas.

The gun fired again. The hole that appeared near Ivon's arm sent a metal splinter into his muscle and drew blood.

Ivon and Dimitri counted out five minutes as the gas flowed. No more gunshots. They opened the case and started the work of stripping the girl.

Dimitri loved this part. Ivon often caught him groping the pretty girls. He even caught him licking on occasion. Ivon never stopped him. It didn't affect their work.

Once they had the naked girl strapped to the table and gagged, Ivon turned on the ventilation. While he waited for the gas to clear, he observed the room. They had used countless rooms like this. They never stay in one area long. They would be given a target, and they would move in and set up a room like this one. Abandoned buildings were preferred. They would find some dank room and staple up a layer of soundproof insulation. The darker and messier the room, the better. They did not need power. They wore night vision sets and kept the prey in darkness. They used simple devices in the interrogations, Ivon's ability was better than any tool.

When the gas had cleared, they swapped gas masks for their night vision.

Dimitri grabbed her hand and broke her finger. She did not stir.

"We did use a ton of gas," said Dimitri and smiled. "Try again in thirty minutes?"

"Fine," said Ivon, knowing what Dimitri implied. "You have your fun."

Of all the things that Ivon did in service for Petrov, only rape felt distasteful. Dimitri enjoyed it enough for both of them.

Shortly after Dimitri finished, the woman moaned and slowly roused until she screamed against her gag.

Dimitri slammed his fist into her solar plexus, knocking the wind out of her lungs.

"I am going to remove the gag," said Ivon. "If you scream, I am putting it back on."

They always scream.

Ivon removed the gag, and she screamed as he expected. Dimitri pounded her ankle with a hammer, breaking a bone, and Ivon put the gag back into place. He let her scream and then whimper for a few minutes before he moved close, placing a hand on her head.

"Scream again, and we cut parts off." His voice was heavy and final. "We just want to talk. You answer some questions, and we will release you."

It was a tired old script he had said over and over again, but it worked.

He thought he heard a "uh-huh" through the whimpers and gag. He removed it, and she breathed hard and fast.

"Good," said Ivon. "The rest is easy. I will ask a question. If you answer with the truth, I move on to the next question. You answer everything, and you leave. If you lie… and I will know if you lie," he moved closer until his lips almost touched her ears. "Lie, and we cut stuff off. Stuff I know you will miss."

Everybody lies at first. Some learn after a few fingers or toes are removed. Others don't learn until they lose whole arms and legs. By the time they lose face parts, everyone talks. Everyone.

Two toes were enough to break this girl. She answered every question and, like the rest, begged to be freed.

Dimitri and Ivon incinerated her body with the rest of the room. The fire would burn and spread to the rest of the building. It may be hours before what passed for a fire brigade arrived. No investigations, no reports, just another abandoned building accidentally burnt down by the homeless squatting in it.

They returned to their hotel and readied their interrogation report for the drop. It was all mechanical at this point. Capture, interrogate, document, and deliver. Once the envelope was sealed, they returned to the streets. The rain had stopped, and the smell of the rain floated across the surface of the streets. The sun had burned through the clouds, and the evaporating puddles hugged the air with humidity. The drop location was a mailbox to a deserted cobbler's store four blocks from their hotel.

As they approached Ivon felt a chill down his spine and stopped and reached over to Dimitri, "that looks like Petrov's car."

The black Mercedes-Benz W100 600 gleamed in the wetness of the recent rain. Out of the driver's side, the familiar lump of a human that was Captain Sidorov exited. She opened and stood next to the rear passenger door and gestured for them to enter.

They hurried over and entered the car. Ivon had not been in it since Cuba. It still looked as new as the day Petrov picked him up from the military base.

"This is an honor, sir," said Dimitri.

"Yes sir," added Ivon and presented the envelope. "Here is the latest interrogation, sir."

Petrov grabbed it and tossed it out the door into the gutter. Sidorov closed the door and returned to the driver's seat.

"I have a new assignment for you two," said Petrov. He smiled and tented his fingers. "You have done exceptional work. We have something new that needs you," Petrov pointed at Ivon.

"Me, sir?" asked Ivon. "Some foreign agent needs to be handled?"

"No," said Petrov. "It would be easier to show you." Petrov turned over his shoulder, "Let's go."

Sidorov drove for six hours, only stopping once to replenish fuel and a second time at a checkpoint as they entered Russian-controlled land. Dimitri slept; he could sleep anywhere. The entire trip, Petrov stared at Ivon, wordless. Ivon grew more uncomfortable with each kilometer under Petrov's unblinking glare. As the night chased away the day, the dark grew in the car, and Petrov continued to stare in silence. Only the sound of the engine hummed through the car. A shadow grew with the night and enveloped Petrov's face. His yellow-eyed gaze pierced through the darkness. Ivon's skin felt hot, and the staring was pulling at him.

Ivon's relief came with the car coming to a stop and Sidorov exiting. His relief was short-lived when voices in the back of his head rang through his ears in isolated deafness. He was a child again as terror shot through his body. Ivon was out the door with Sidorov opening it. The voices did not relent.

They were at an old Jewish temple. The building was intact but dirty and uncared for. The paint had peeled away in spots from the masonry, and insects had started to ingest the wood of the windows. The familiar flicker of candlelight danced through the holes of the boarded-up windows.

"This way," said Sidorov and walked to the temple entrance.

A pair of Russian uniform guards flanked the ancient wooden doors. They saluted and held the doors open as Petrov's entourage entered. Petrov ignored the guards and led his group through.

The interior was in no better shape than the exterior. The smell of mold seeped through the air. The pews had been removed, only a pentagrammic altar with an onyx top and concrete sides adorned with candles at each corner in the center of the temple. Along the walls, more candles had been placed, and the light cast flickering shadows around the room. Four figures in black robes waited at the altar, two across from each other. They chanted in a strange foreign tongue.

Sidorov handed matching robes to Dimitri and Ivon. "Put these on. Say nothing." Sidorov handed a dagger to Ivon. "Take this."

Ivon took the dagger and inspected it. It was a single piece carved from bone. Strange writing was etched into the blade. He touched the ivory edge with his finger, and a tiny drop of blood formed, razor sharp. He tucked the blade into the belt of his robe.

Dimitri started to dress, and Ivon followed suit. Ivon looked at Dimitri, who smiled back. Once dressed, they joined the rest around the altar and stood in the last gaps. Each figure's face was in shadow, and he had lost track of which ones were Sidorov and Petrov. They were now all chanting in the strange language.

The two figures across from Ivon stepped aside, and two more in robes entered from the rear carrying something wrapped in black cloth.

Ivon knew a body when he saw one.

The body was placed on the altar and the two figures who had moved aside returned to the circle. The taller of the two raised his hands, and the chanting stopped.

Three figures grabbed Ivon from behind, one on each arm and a massive one holding his body. He had never felt such strength before. He was helpless, and his struggles did not flinch his captors. His right hand was pulled out and placed palm up on the altar.

Another stepped forward and took the dagger from his belt. "Relax, friend." It sounded like Dimitri.

With a flick, Dimitri cut a slash on Ivon's hand. It burned like a paper cut as the blood flowed out. Across the altar, the figures opened the bundle, pulled a lifeless arm out of the black cloth, and extended it towards Ivon.

Ivon's hand was forced closer to the dead body's hand. His blood dripped on the altar, leaving a trail of splotches. The two hands touched, and silence gripped the temple. Even the voices in his head ceased.

Ivon could feel his heart in his throat. His hand felt hot. Then the dead hand grabbed his.

The lead figure laughed. The ones holding Ivon released and backed away. Ivon jerked his hand out of the lifeless grip.

Dimitri offered a bandage to Ivon and removed his hood. "You did good."

"What did I do?" asked Ivon as he applied the bandage.

"Behold," the lead figure was Petrov. He removed his hood. "Life from death." He pulled the black cloth and unrolled the body.

The body was dressed in a Russian enlisted uniform, a bullet hole caked in dried blood in his chest. The body moaned and sat up slowly.

"How is this possible?" asked Ivon.

"Your blood," said Dimitri with a smile. "You are special and are going to help us build an endless army."

"All we need are bodies," said Petrov. "The fresher, the better. I am sending you and Dimitri out to find more. Places where no one cares if people go missing."

BIRTH OF A DEMON

Oliver woke to the soft beeping of his heart on the monitor. His vision was blurry, and his chest was heavy with pain. He moaned as his brain reconnected to his nervous system.

"He's awake." It was Melissa. She was at his side. "I am here, Oliver."

"Is Ivoire ok?" asked Oliver as he struggled to sit up.

"She's fine," said Ivoire, entering the room. "Just a mild concussion."

"Oh, thank God," replied Oliver. He let his head fall back on the pillow. "What about Wiles?"

"She oozed away again," said Melissa. "After she liquefied, Roland carried you and Ivoire back to the SUV."

"Where are we?" asked Oliver.

"A hospital," said Melissa. "We reported your injury as a car accident."

"So what's the prognosis?" asked Oliver.

"You have a cracked sternum," said Ivoire. "The doctor said nothing to do but rest. It's going to be painful for two or three months."

Oliver laughed and then winced in pain.

"You find this funny?" asked Ivoire.

"No, well, yes," said Oliver. He looked at Melissa. "It wasn't long ago our places were swapped. You in the bed and me sick with worry."

Melissa smiled and took Oliver's hand.

"So what now?" asked Oliver.

"Now that you are awake, we can see about discharge and moving you to headquarters," said Melissa. "For now, rest."

Oliver was returned to Paladin headquarters and stayed in the medical examination room under Isaac's care.

An injured Oliver and the Paladins were gathered in the library. Melissa sat at the computer. Persephone stood next to her, tablet in hand. Roland leaned against the doorway to the gymnasium. Ivoire sat on the leather couch with Oliver.

"I want to discuss a few things," stated Melissa. "I am still working to gain access to Cardinal Sepe to get a visual on if he is a demon. He seems to be purposefully avoiding me and it is only making me more suspicious. Persephone has also been following up on the book missing from the Luciferian collection."

"Yes," said Persephone. "I have been working with Father Mallory on the investigation. Still no leads. The camera feeds do have a gap that matches the time the book likely disappeared."

"Someone has deep access," said Oliver.

"Agreed," said Ivoire. "That points to someone like Sepe."

"I'll keep pursuing that avenue," said Melissa. "The third thing I want to investigate is Wiles' hometown of Lewiston."

"You think there may be some connection to the current events there?" asked Ivoire.

"Possibly," said Mellissa. "Persephone and I checked out the town, hoping to find more answers about Wiles, and we came across something strange. There have been no record of births for eight years."

"It might be nothing," added Persephone. "Many residents of small towns drive to larger towns with hospitals. It is just odd as there have not even been any record of home births."

"When do we go?" asked Oliver.

"You stay and heal, Cowboy," said Melissa. "Ivoire and Roland can handle this. This sort of investigation is perfect for her skill set."

"Why is Roland coming?" asked Ivoire.

"Just in case there really are demons in Lewiston."

Ivoire and Roland were in the private Vatican jet flying to Lonnie Pool airport in California, a short drive from Lewiston. Ivoire sat across from Roland in the comfortable seats. She felt oddly open around him. He was massive but had a quiet stillness about him. He seemed permanently calm.

"You and I have not really had a chance to talk. Can I tell you about myself?" she asked.

"For a man's ways are before the eyes of the Lord, and he ponders all his paths," replied Roland.

Ivoire told Roland her story, of her youth, of her time in the all-girls school. Roland did not interrupt but only listened intently, his eyes not leaving her. She shared the time when her grandmother and then her father died; sadness began to creep into her voice. When she revealed her time in the Guild, she fought back tears. When she recounted the seduction training, a trickle of tears started.

At her tears, Roland took her hand and said, "The scribes and the Pharisees brought a woman who had been caught in adultery, and placing her in the midst, they said to Jesus, 'Teacher, this woman has been caught in the act of adultery. Now, in the Law, Moses commanded us to stone such women. So what do you say?' This they said to test him that they might have some charge to bring against him. Jesus bent down and wrote with his finger on the ground. And as they continued to ask him, he stood up and said to them, 'Let him who is without sin among you be the first to throw a stone at her.' And once more, he bent down and wrote on the ground. But when they heard it, they went away one by one, beginning with the older ones, and Jesus was left alone with the woman standing before him."

Roland gently placed his massive hand on her chin, tilted her head up, and looked into her eyes, "Neither do I condemn you; go, and from now on, sin no more."

The emotions had won, and the tears went from trickle to flow. Ivoire hugged Roland, and he held her. Other men had viewed her only as a tool, a tool for a means, a tool for pleasure. Here, the strongest man she had ever met only viewed her as a sister or a daughter. He looked at her the same way her father did before he died.

Ivoire cried and slept the rest of the flight. Roland prayed and read from his Bible.

The jet landed at Lonnie Pool Airport, where the Stateside SUV waited for them. They loaded their gear and sat in the back as they rode to Lewiston.

This part of California was a contrast to the areas they had visited before. The port in San Diego and the Wiles Mansion felt like a different world compared to the hilly, sparsely populated Central-East California.

The town of Lewiston was a simple six streets separated by the main street, creatively named Lewiston Street. A simple and unkempt church greeted visitors at the edge of town. Next to the church was a faded wooden sign that welcomed visitors and proclaimed the town as the birthplace of "Senator Wiles." Six small brick shops adorned the main strip, only two were occupied, a pawn shop and a thrift store. The rest offered signs declaring their availability for purchase. At the far end was a not quite matching red brick building that served as the City Hall, Police Department, and Court House. At the other end was a diner in what used to be a gas station. The diner was the only building with lights on.

It was dark and nearing seven at night when they parked in front of the diner.

Ivoire turned to Roland, "Let me do the talking. I want to guide the conversation so they answer in ways that force them to lie or tell the truth."

Roland replied, "Commit your work to the Lord, and your plans will be established."

"Ok," she smiled. "My name will be Sarah, and yours can be Abraham."

Book of Ivon and Ivoire

Roland smiled at this.

"I am an investigative reporter doing a biography on Senator Wiles, and you are my husband tagging along," she looked around. "People love talking to reporters."

They exited the SUV and approached the diner.

The former gas station had been hollowed out and opened up to the connected garage. On the windows, a hand-drawn sign offering a "Blue Plate Special - $4.99" covered the faded "Oil Change - $14.99" sign.

Roland opened the door for Ivoire, and it hit a bell with a welcoming chime. Inside, mismatched tables and chairs of a variety of materials were placed in what could barely be called a pattern. The lone waitress was sitting at a table near the far door. At the sound of the bell, she tamped out a cigarette and called, "Sit anywhere."

Roland led Ivoire to a table and pulled out a chair for her. The act was almost foreign to her. Oliver and Roland treating her like an equal and not a means to an end was both offsetting and comforting.

She took the seat and spoke in a Boston accent, "Thanks, hun."

Roland took the seat opposite, facing the entrance.

The waitress approached. She was in her thirties and carried every year like a yoke. Her cigarette-stained fingernails and teeth almost matched her jaundiced skin. She wore jeans and a t-shirt that proclaimed her favorite motorcycle brand.

"What can I get you to drink?" asked the waitress.

"I'll have a diet soda," said Ivoire.

"And you, sir?" asked the waitress to Roland.

Roland replied, "Truly I tell you, anyone who gives you a cup of water in my name because you belong to the Messiah will certainly not lose their reward."

The waitress held her pose and blinked twice. "So water. The menu is on the board by the door." She spun back and headed into the kitchen.

"This place seems harmless enough," whispered Ivoire.

"It is not surprising, then, if his servants also masquerade as servants of righteousness. Their end will be what their actions deserve," replied Roland.

The waitress returned with the drinks. "What can I order you?"

"Well, I hear that Senator Wiles was born here in Lewiston," said Ivoire. "Did she ever eat here? What would she order?"

"This restaurant was opened after she left," replied the waitress.

"Does she ever visit?" asked Ivoire.

"Not that I know of," said the waitress.

The words did not ring of truth.

"That is too bad," said Ivoire. "I am a reporter and am looking to interview people about the Senator's youth." She pulled out a fold of twenty dollar bills. "I can offer compensation for information."

"I don't know who would know," said the waitress, her gaze locked on the money, her posture stiff, her words not sounding of truth. "I can ask the cook when I tell him your order."

"Thank you kindly," replied Ivoire. "We will have two of your blue plate specials."

The waitress moved much faster than before and returned to the kitchen.

"Now it begins," said Ivoire. "She is probably back there calling someone. Next, one of two things will happen: violence or talking."

Through the kitchen door, a bald man ducked. He was over six feet tall and close to three hundred pounds. His rotund belly pressed the limits of the black t-shirt he wore as it strained to remain tucked into his well-worn jeans. The man approached the table where Ivoire and Roland sat.

As he approached, Ivoire whispered to Roland, "They have chosen violence."

"I see you have left a nice tip for us," said the man, eyeing the money.

"Yes," said Ivoire. "It is yours if you have any information on Senator Wiles."

"Yeah, I do," smiled the man. "She's a bitch." He reached down for the fold of bills.

Roland caught the man's wrist before he could reach the money and held him still. The man looked at Roland and tried to free his hand. He could not budge from the grasp. With his free hand, the man pulled a 9mm semi-automatic pistol out from his belt. Roland intercepted the hand wielding the pistol, his massive fingers enveloping the gun and the hand.

"Let no corrupting talk come out of your mouths, but only such as is good for building up, as fits the occasion, that it may give grace to those who hear," said Roland as he rose from his chair.

Fear froze the man's face as Roland pressed him down, forcing him to his knees. He squeezed the hand holding the gun; the sounds of bones being crushed were followed by metal giving way to stress. Parts of the gun fell to the floor.

The man whimpered as a pain he had never even dreamed of washed down his arms.

The waitress ran out of the kitchen with a 12 gauge shotgun and leveled it at Roland, "Let Dwayne go."

Roland released Dwayne and was on the waitress, shotgun pulled from her grip. He pulled the slide up and off the gun, tossed the slide aside, and gripped what remained in both hands. He bent the weapon, and the barrel snapped in two; screws and metal shards pelted the ceiling.

The waitress cowered and then crawled next to Dwayne, who was on the floor, favoring his broken hand. "We are sorry, mister. We don't get many customers and money has been tight. Please don't kill us."

Kneeling next to the woman, Roland placed a gentle hand on her shoulder and softened his voice, "But my God shall supply all your needs according to his riches in glory by Christ Jesus."

Ivoire moved next to Roland. "We mean you no harm or ill will. We only wish to learn about Senator Wiles."

The waitress sniffed and wiped tears from her face, "The red building at the end of the street. The county sheriff has his office there. He can answer your questions."

"She tells the truth," said Ivoire to Roland. She turned back to the women and handed her the fold of twenties. "Take Dwayne to a hospital."

Ivoire and Roland exited the restaurant and stepped onto the street toward the Town Hall. They walked along the empty street past the abandoned buildings. This town, like many small American towns, once was a gathering place for farmers and ranchers to come, buy goods, and socialize. Now, where friendly faces once greeted them as they passed, only dead leaves skirted along with the wind, scraping the cracked pavement.

The City Hall was dark. Its clock tower, the tallest point for miles and long broken, displayed the wrong time. As they neared, a man exited the front door. He was slender and wore a tan long-sleeved button-up shirt with a gray trucker hat. There was a silver .45 revolver tucked into his faded jeans.

"Debbie called and said there were strangers in town," said the man.

Roland raised his hands and slowly walked up the steps, "Peace I leave with you, my peace I give unto you: not as the world giveth, give I unto you. Let not your heart be troubled, neither let it be afraid."

"What?" said the man.

Before the question was out, Roland closed the distance, pulled the revolver from the man's pants, and tossed it into the night. He lifted the man by the collar and pulled him close.

"Ask, and it will be given to you; seek, and you will find; knock, and the door will be opened to you."

"You want in?" said the man. "Yeah, fine. Go ahead."

Roland set him down.

"Where is the Sheriff?" asked Ivoire.

"He's inside," said the man. "Let me get the door." He pulled open the left of the double entrance doors and held it open.

Roland stepped through first, and Ivoire followed. The door slammed behind them, and the sounds of chains locking the entrance rattled the door.

It was dark inside. Ivoire could not see more than a few feet in front of her. Roland's hand took hers, and calmness washed over her.

Roland's voice boomed in the darkness, "For there is nothing covered that shall not be revealed; neither hid, that shall not be known."

Above them, a light flicked on and shone on a balcony above the entrance vestibule. In the light stood a man in his fifties. He wore a tan sheriff's uniform and a wide-brimmed hat. He was portly with a gray mustache on a chubby face.

"Debbie says you broke Dwayne's hand," said the Sheriff. "What brings you to our quiet town?"

"This has all been a big misunderstanding," said Ivoire. "I am a reporter and am here doing research on Senator Wiles for a biography piece."

"Uh-huh," said the Sheriff. "Where is the cowboy?"

"What cowboy?" replied Ivoire.

"Wiles said that three troublemakers might come asking about her," he explained. "A big, strong old man, a nosey lady, and a cowboy wannabe."

"I think you have the wrong idea," said Ivoire.

"Doesn't matter to me," said the sheriff. "Couple more bodies for the altar"

The lights flicked off. Out of the darkness, the sounds of guns cocking and readying echoed across the building.

Roland's hand released Ivoire's, and he placed it on her shoulder. "They Who Kneel Before God Can Stand Before Anyone."

Ivoire, having understood, crouched down and crawled over to the wall.

A gunshot rang and flashed light.

Ivoire heard Roland proclaim, "If you set a trap for others, you will get caught in it yourself. If you roll a boulder down on others, it will crush you instead."

She heard his heavy footsteps and flashes of gunfire, followed by a man screaming and then a body hitting the floor. More heavy steps, more guns firing, more screams, and more bodies falling. She tried in vain to follow his movements in the darkness.

With a final scream and slow footsteps, the lights flicked on. Roland stood across the vestibule over an unconscious man lying next to a rifle and night vision goggles. Ivoire looked around and saw eight other similarly equipped men unconscious scattered around.

Roland walked over to Ivoire. He had been injured. Blood ran from a wound in his left leg and one in his right arm.

"Oh God, Roland," said Ivoire as she rose and tore her sleeves off her shirt. "We need to get you to a hospital."

"For I will restore health to you, and your wounds I will heal, declares the Lord," replied Roland.

"Damn it," called the Sheriff's voice. "Who are you?" He was back on the balcony, surviving the aftermath.

"Thou comest to me with a sword, and with a spear, and with a shield: but I come to thee in the name of the LORD of hosts," replied Roland.

The sheriff pulled a .45 revolver and aimed it at Roland, and cocked it, "Well, I got better than a spear."

Roland dodged to the left as the sheriff's gun discharged, the bullet embedding itself into the floor. Still in stride, Roland seized a rifle and hurled it at the sheriff; it impacted the revolver, causing the sheriff's firearm to skitter away. With practiced ease, Roland leaped and pulled himself onto the balcony; he slapped the sheriff, who flipped sideways from the impact. With the sheriff in tow, Roland leaped back down to Ivoire, the blood from his leg wound staining the floor. He set the sheriff at Ivoire's feet.

"But now the Lord my God has given me rest on every side; there is neither adversary nor misfortune," said Roland as he applied Ivoire's torn sleeves to his wounds.

The Sheriff groaned in pain.

"Rest, Roland," said Ivoire and turned to the sheriff. "I can handle this part."

She sat the sheriff up and kneeled in front of him, "This could have been easy. We came just to ask questions. Now, tell me everything about Senator Wiles."

"Wiles is dead," said the Sheriff.

"This we know, replaced by a demon," said Ivoire. "What is your part in this? Why try to kill us?"

"Take me to the basement, and I can show you," said the sheriff.

"Fine. But if you try to trick us? My big friend won't be as polite as he has been," Ivoire looked at Roland. "Can you move?"

Roland rose with the makeshift bandages applied and said, "But they who wait for the Lord shall renew their strength." Roland lifted the sheriff by his collar and said, "Show me the way I should go."

The sheriff led them through the city hall to a stairway leading down. They continued down into the basement. The concrete foundation and walls of the substructure were moist and cold. The sheriff flipped a switch, and a scene unfolded.

Along the stone walls hand painted demonic runes were painted in a scarlet hue. The floor was splattered with stains of blood and violence. At the rear center of the room was an altar of skulls. Hundreds of skulls are stacked in a half pyramid topped by a pale statue. The statue was of Wiles in her demon form—a goblin with oversized, pointy ears, bulging eyes, and sharp teeth. The likeness was uncanny. The statue had one hand raised holding a skull.

Ivoire could feel Roland's wrath grow at the sight of the satanic temple.

"Time for stories," said Ivoire, pushing the Sheriff to the floor. "Go as far back as you can. Do not try to deceive me; I will know, and my friend is injured, and injury makes him quite angry."

The sheriff looked at Roland then back to Ivoire, "Nancy, Senator Wiles, was born here in Lewiston. I knew her as a child. A sweet girl, we attended school together. One day, a man came to town, and he promised great things for our town if we did what he said. He was convincing, and each time he said he would make a thing happen, it would."

"What was his name?" asked Ivoire.

"He went by Joe," said the Sheriff. "That's all we knew him as. As more of his promises came true, he gained a following. Soon, most of the town followed him in the hope of having their 'wishes' granted. Joe proclaimed himself a god, and his followers believed."

"How does Wiles fit into this?" asked Ivoire.

"I am getting to it," continued the sheriff. "After claiming godhood, the sacrifices started." He pointed to the skulls. "They started building the altar with the skulls of those who refused to follow," the sheriff paused, the memory painful. "When Wiles returned from college, Lewiston was a very different town. She tried to talk sense into the people, to stand up to the madness of Joe. Joe and his followers took her down here. They performed some ceremony. I do not understand it. All I know is one minute, Joe was standing, and the next, he was gone. Nancy was dragged down to this room, but something else walked out."

"How did the town react?" asked Ivoire.

"They moved their worship from Joe to Nancy," said the Sheriff. "The town elected her mayor and well… I guess you know the rest."

"Then the fire of the Lord fell and burned up the sacrifice, the wood, the stones, and the soil, and also licked up the water in the trench," said Roland as he approached the altar. He grabbed the statue of the demon, lifted it, and tore it in half. He tossed the halves aside and kicked over the mound of skulls.

"Let's go, Sheriff," said Ivoire. "We are taking your men to the hospital, and you are going to turn yourself in."

Roland carried the men, two at a time, and placed them into the Sheriff's jail transport bus. Through barred bus windows, they watched the building burn until it was ashes and rubble. They took the men to the Trinity Hospital in Weaverville, prayed with them, and stayed as they each confessed to the US Marshal of what happened in Lewiston.

ROMANCE AND REVELATIONS

After wrapping up investigating the scene of Darnya's death, Ivoire was at a cafe with Kalnya and Sofiy, who attended via phone.

"Darnya must have graduated before I reported," said Ivoire. "It was a three-year program, and she was three years ahead of me.

"Why would a graduate of the most well-hidden school for spies in all of Ukraine have a second life as a prostitute?" asked Kalnya.

"She may not have been," said Sofiy.

"What did you find?" asked Kalnya.

"The information was surprisingly well hidden," said Sofiy. "This made it even more compelling to get access to."

"Please skip the 'how hard it was' and get to the information," said Kalnya.

"Yes, sorry," said Sofiy. "She was assigned to investigate Quincy O'Donnell by her handler. The concerning part is I cannot find the order of origin."

"So we do not know why she was investigating Quincy?" asked Ivoire.

"Nothing beyond the orders," said Sofiy. "Just that he was a suspected spy, and she was to verify if he was or not using any methods."

"Including seduction," said Ivoire.

"It seems a big miss in intelligence gathering if they were investigating someone who was a borderline celebrity," said Sofiy.

"Anything else?" asked Kalnya.

"Only her next assignment," said Sofiy "She was to go to the city of Chernivtsi on the western end of Ukraine. There, she was to find a foreign national by the name of Matteo Bianchi. He was also a suspected spy. Her mission is to discover if he truly was a spy and, if so, what his mission in Ukraine entailed. Oddly enough, this one is also missing the order of origin."

"Send me," said Ivoire. "I am just as trained as Darnya. Maybe I can find more about this from Bianchi."

"Seems a stretch," said Kalnya. "O'Donnell was Irish and visiting Vienna. Bianchi is Italian and in Ukraine."

"But the mission is identical," said Ivoire. "A rich man suspected of espionage with no order of origin."

"I'll give you that," said Kalnya. "Fine. You investigate Bianchi. Sofiy, you keep cracking away at the order of origin on these two missions."

"What are you going to do," asked Sofiy.

"I have an old contact I want to talk to," said Kalnya.

Over the next few days, Ivoire was a mix of sadness and excitement. She was sad at the passing of an old friend but excited at the mystery of it. This was what she wanted. What, in her mind, was a real spy mission. This was her chance to travel to a beautiful city and test her skills while using her unique ability on a possible foreign spy and maybe unravel a larger conspiracy.

She flew back to Ukraine and took a train to Chernivtsi. Her trip on the train across the Ukrainian countryside enthralled her. The tracks wound through ancient towns and across green mountains. Ukraine was the 'breadbasket' of Europe. The vast fields of grain and quaint villages caressed the train as it coasted from stop to stop. She sipped her coffee and studied her dossier on Bianchi as she let the beauty of her country take her in.

She arrived at Chernivtsi in the afternoon. The city was alive with people coming and going and the station hummed with activity. It was a beautiful city at the foot of the Carpathian Mountains. A far cry from the simple and war-torn town of her birth. The locals lovingly called their home "Little Vienna."

The target, Matteo Bianchi, had an apartment that overlooked a public beach along the Prut River. He was known to walk the beach in the mornings after picking up a coffee at a cafe near the boardwalk.

Ivoire spent the first evening scouting the location, walking along the water's edge. The beach faced east and stretched fourteen blocks from the main road on the south end up to an industrial area marked by a tan concrete wall that extended into the water. Opposite the beach, across the river, beautiful waterfront homes of brown and red masonry lined the shoreline. The brown sand beach lay one hundred meters from the water to the boardwalk. Along the boardwalk, small shops and cafes offered knickknacks and snacks. She identified three stores that could be where Matteo purchased his morning coffee.

As darkness approached, Ivoire enjoyed a salad from a cafe and then found a hotel room with a view of the beach near the middle of the boardwalk. It provided a perfect vantage point for observing her assignment and to plan what openings she could use.

The sun rose the next morning and painted the beach in an orange glow. Ancient wooden fishing boats puttered along the river. Ivoire was already up and sitting on the balcony with a cup of coffee. She watched as the city slowly woke up. The crowds and cars slowly increased in density as the sun climbed the eastern sky.

Shortly after nine AM, she spotted Matteo approaching from the south, walking along the boardwalk. He was wearing leather sandals, a pair of blue knee-length board shorts, and a white button-up cotton shirt with wooden buttons. His shoulder-length, curly black hair shone as if it was in a consistent state of wetness. He was fit and handsome, more movie star in appearance than an Italian spy.

Approaching Ivoire's hotel, she retreated into the safety of her room to observe through the open sliding door. Pausing at a nearby cafe, Matteo requested an espresso with a friendly smile, striking up a conversation with the barista as he awaited his order. After settling the bill and leaving a generous tip, he found a table with a view of the water, where he sat, observing the sleepy boats for thirty-two minutes. Rising from his seat, he made his way down to the edge of the water, standing with his feet immersed in the river's minuscule waves for nineteen minutes before retracing his steps to the boardwalk.

  Ivoire was out of her room, down the steps of the hotel, and waited in the stairwell until Matteo was back on the boardwalk. He turned south and headed back to where he came. She followed as he walked with the flow of the late-morning crowd. He turned it into a small grocery store. Ivoire crossed the street and feigned shopping for some bathing suits while she waited for Matteo to exit. She watched him shop through the windows. He smiled and conversed with the shop owner as he paid his bill.

  While he checked out, she bought a simple and silky black bikini with narrow cups and thin straps that accented her slender figure.

  Thirty-three minutes after he entered, Matteo exited with a paper bag full of food. He walked back towards the boardwalk. He turned north on the street that ran parallel to the beach and then entered an apartment complex that faced the beach.

  Something bothered Ivoire. Matteo did not act like a spy. He was easy to spot and did not clear corners or check for being followed. Almost the opposite, he seemed desperate for attention. Even the way he walked seemed off; he meandered more like a person on vacation than a person on a mission. Then again, maybe it was an act. He may be trying to hide out in the open.

  Ivoire found a restaurant with street-side seating where she could watch the apartment entrance. She ordered coffee and a bagel and pretended to read a book. After three hours, six refills, and a dozen dirty looks from the waiter, Matteo finally returned to the street.

He headed south, then west, as he headed towards the heart of the city. He had lunch at a Greek restaurant. He spent the afternoon back on the beach in a lounger, people-watching and swimming. He chatted with people walking by and flirted with pretty ladies. At sunset, he returned to his apartment and had dinner on his balcony. Near 11 PM, his lights turned off.

His routine remained the same for the next three days. If he was a spy, the only thing he seemed to be spying on was attractive ladies on the beach.

On the fourth day, Ivoire was up early and out on the beach. She wore the new suit she had purchased along with a gray, nearly transparent, half-sarong draped on her waist and a pair of designer sunglasses. She let her blonde hair fall freely down her back.

She had to time this next part carefully. The seduction training in the guild talked about *implanting*, making your target think they saw you first. She made sure she was at the cafe Matteo frequented only a few minutes before he was to arrive. She took her order and slowly stirred in the creamer she added while she waited. Once he was in sight of the cafe, she found a table facing the water and enjoyed her drink. She made sure Matteo had a clear view of her body as she slid into the chair. She put on an air of boredom and aloofness. She was no longer Ivoire but a tourist here for some rest and relaxation.

Matteo ordered his drink and moved to a table next to Ivoire. They sat and drank in silence and watched the water.

After a long stretch of uncomfortable silence, Matteo spoke in Italian, "Excuse me. But do you speak Italian?"

"I do," said Ivoire back in Italian. "How could you tell?"

"I couldn't," replied Matteo. "I had just hoped. May I join you? You are the first Italian speaker I have met in weeks."

"Please do," replied Ivoire.

Matteo took the seat next to Ivoire. "What brings you to this lovely city?"

"I am just traveling," replied Ivoire. "Taking in the sites. What about you?"

"I am searching," replied Matteo, it rang of truth.

"What are you searching for?" Ivoire leaned in.

Matteo leaned in to match. "Oh, a sense of the miraculous in everyday life."

His answer did not ring of truth, but it was also nonsensical as he dodged her question.

"Oh, you seek miracles?" asked Ivoire.

"You could say that," he said with a truthful ring.

"What sort of miracles?" asked Ivoire.

"Maybe a miracle, like a beautiful blonde speaking Italian in a Ukrainian city," replied Matteo.

"Or meeting a handsome stranger?" asked Ivoire.

"What is your name?" asked Matteo.

"My name is Isabella," said Ivoire.

"Your name is beauty," smiled Matteo.

"Now, it is your turn," said Ivoire.

"My name is Andre," said Matteo.

"Oh, I don't like that name," said Ivoire.

"It's the only one I have," said Matteo.

Even without her ability, she knew he was lying. It made sense. A spy would not reveal their real identity.

They spent the day together, flirting and sightseeing. Despite it being a mission, Ivoire enjoyed herself. She had never been on a date and finally understood the appeal. It was made easier by the pleasantness of Matteo; he was handsome and charming.

After sunset, they had dinner at a restaurant with a view of the river. Ivoire had gotten no closer to finding Mateo's true purpose. She decided to take it to the next level.

They walked along the beach, and Ivoire took Matteo's hand. She stopped him and looked into his brown eyes. She leaned her head up. Having taken the clue, Matteo leaned down and kissed her. The kiss held for a moment then they pulled each other close. They kissed and ran their hands along each other's bodies.

Ivoire pulled away. "Do you live close?"

"Yes," said a nearly breathless Matteo. "This way."

He led her by her hand to the entrance to his condo building. At the door, Ivoire stopped to kiss him again. Inside, they continued kissing in the elevator and at the door to his condo.

Inside, they started to undress each other between kisses and flirtatious touches. In the bedroom, Ivoire pushed Matteo onto the bed.

"Get comfortable," she said.

Ivoire backed away from the bed and slinked into the bathroom and closed the door. She set her purse on the sink and undressed. She removed the cross from her purse and flicked the blade out. She pulled a mouthwash bottle out, opened it, and dipped the blade inside. She closed the knife and put the necklace on. She paused for a moment and inspected herself in the mirror.

She had grown much these last few years. The self-image of a little girl who adored her father did not match the reflection of an adult woman. With a final turn, she pushed open the door and stepped back into the bedroom.

Matteo was in the bed, topless. The bed sheet covered him from his waist down. The bulge between his legs revealed his nakedness beneath.

"Wow," was all he said.

"Thank you," replied Ivoire. "Now turn over."

"Turn over?" asked Matteo.

"Turn over," Ivoire repeated. "I want to give you a back rub."

Matteo smiled and obeyed.

Ivoire mounted his back and massaged his shoulders.

Matteo sighed happily and closed his eyes.

She teased him with the nails of her left hand while her right hand freed and opened her crucifix knife. She leaned forward and whispered into his ear, "Relaxed?"

"Very much so," he said.

"Good." She pushed her left arm around his neck in a chokehold and stabbed the knife into his right shoulder.

"What are you doing?" he demanded and struggled against Ivoire. She had him pinned against the bed.

In her mind, she started the three minute countdown. She tightened her hold. Blood from his shoulder wound had reached her hand and made her grip slippery.

Matteo fought for freedom.

Ivoire could feel him weaken, the chemical taking its effect. When the three minutes had expired, Matteo was too weak and drowsy to fight.

Ivoire climbed off. "Who are you?"

"Matteo Bianchi," replied Matteo in a drowsy and somber voice.

"What are you doing in Chernivtsi?" she asked.

"I paid for an experience excursion," he replied.

"Are you a spy?" she asked.

"No," he said. "I am from a wealthy family."

"What is an experience excursion?" she asked.

"I paid to meet a beautiful stranger and live out a fantasy," he said.

"Who did you pay?" she asked.

"A Ukrainian man named Andriy Bondarenko," he replied.

"How do I find this man?" she asked.

"He is the excursion coordinator for Hil′diya Anthemoessa," he said.

The words rang of truth, but she refused to believe them. *This can't be.*

"Where did you say?" she asked.

"The Hil′diya Anthemoessa in Ukraine," said Matteo.

"How do you know of this place?" she demanded.

"Many do," he said. "My friend recommended it as a once-in-a-lifetime experience."

"What do they promise?" she asked.

"To be seduced by a beautiful woman who had been trained in the arts of lovemaking," he trailed off.

Ivoire was off him and back in the bathroom. Anger flowed through her veins with intense heat. She pulled a bottle of ketamine disguised as cough syrup out of her purse, opened it, and stabbed her knife into it.

She returned to Matteo and stabbed the back of his left leg. He was unconscious in seconds.

I need to return to Hil'diya Anthemoessa and find out who sold my friend like a cheap whore.

DROWNING IN THE DESERT

Roland and Ivoire returned to Paladin Headquarters from Lewiston. Roland healed quickly from his wounds and was back to smashing base elements and lifting weights in the gym in days. Melissa had gathered all the Paladins in the research room.

"After the encounter in Chile," said Melissa. "Persephone and I have been looking into any small villages that either have had sudden reductions in population or numerous recent deaths. We have one we think is worthy of investigation."

"You think the demons are farming corpses by killing people?" asked Ivoire.

"It would make sense," said Melissa. "Think back to the ghoul from your church, dried and brittle. It had been dead for decades and could barely move. Compare that to the ghouls from the carnival; they were fresh, and that freshness gave them added movement and agility."

"Like you have said before," replied Oliver. "No foul deed seems beyond their imagination."

"Back to the village," said Persephone. "The village is called Rasbani in India, and it is near the Pakistan border in the heart of the Thar Desert. The town was an oil rig hub for the last two decades before the well ran dry. Those who could afford to leave did."

"Sounds like Drywell," said Oliver. "No ghouls there, I mean, until that one. Why is this one a candidate?"

"A former resident, Vihaan Nair, had returned to the village when he lost contact with his aunt," answered Melissa. "He found the town deserted and reported to the nearest authority at the city of Bharmer, two hundred miles east. They said it was out of their jurisdiction and to go to the regional government. The regional government blew it off as just another 'oil boom' town getting abandoned just like the dozens of others along the Pakistan border."

"Maybe they are correct," said Ivoire. "Maybe the man is just overreacting."

"After being rejected," said Persephone. "He went back, this time to record his findings." Persephone brings up a video on the main display. "He posted this on the internet."

The video showed the desolate sand-beaten town from inside a car as it was driven down the streets. It is night, and the car's headlight shine through the blowing sand. A man was driving, and another was holding the camera. The men were speaking in Hindi as the camera pans around.

"...that was my school," displayed the subtitles. "That was the diner where my cousin worked. There should be people here. My aunt and her family and dozens more I know live here."

"What is that?" said the camera operator, who focused on a building as the car came to a stop. The camera held on a building with flickering flights in the windows.

"That is the old recreation center," said the driver. "Maybe someone-"

He is interrupted by the sound of glass breaking, and the camera panned to the driver's side to show two figures who have broken the window and grabbed the driver. One is a middle-aged man with a dull expression and pale eyes; the other is a young girl with pale skin and purple lips.

"Get off me," yelled the driver as he hit the accelerator, and the car took off, freeing him of the figures.

"Go, go, go," yelled the camera operator. "What was that?"

"I think that was the old gas station owner," said the driver.

The video cut out.

"Nothing worth watching after that," said Persephone.

"If those are ghouls," said Oliver. "Those are a new type to me. They almost looked alive."

Persephone rewound the video and paused on the two figures who attacked

"Their features are consistent with someone who died of drowning," said Melissa.

"How does someone drown in a desert?" asked Ivoire.

"Let's go find out," said Oliver.

"I want Ivoire to come with us," said Melissa.

"How can my skills be of help?" asked Ivoire.

"I am more interested in growing your experience. You have witnessed an exorcism and a demon manifesting," said Melissa. "Now, you should witness a possible ghoul infestation. To see what can happen to innocents caught in the crossfire of this holy war."

"We'll keep you safe," said Oliver as he twirled his revolver into its holster.

The Paladins were on the Vatican jet and airborne within two hours. They landed in a stretch of hardpan twenty miles outside of Rasbani. From the cargo hold, Roland and Oliver unloaded two plastic cases that Persephone had prepared. They placed the cases and pressed a green button on the side. The cases unfolded, and a matching pair of all-terrain vehicles expanded out.

"Battery-powered and silent running with a hundred-mile range," said Persephone over the coms. "I had to tweak them some to handle Roland's weight and equipment; it has a 75-mile range."

"These are great," said Oliver. "Electric horses."

They rode two per with Ivoire and Melissa driving, Oliver and Roland sitting behind them in the passenger seats. They raced across the desert in the heat of the orange day. Sand and dry wind scraped across the helmets Persephone had stashed with the vehicles. Roland, whose proportions made outfitting difficult, wore his armor helmet. They rode away from the rising sun until they found a road, then turned and followed this desolate road until the village came into view.

The village was larger than Oliver had expected. Hundreds of abandoned homes encircled the downtown area. They passed sand-coated streets lined with empty homes.

"This town could house thousands," said Melissa. "Now, maybe two hundred still live here."

"Or lived here," said Ivoire.

The houses gave way to the city center. The wind subsided as they journeyed deeper, and the buildings blocked the wind. The sand piled into the yards and on the road, hiding the asphalt below. They reached the area from the video and parked their vehicles. Abandoned vehicles were scattered around, and the buildings all sat dark, even in the midday sun. A stillness gripped the area; the only sounds were the wind and scratching sand.

The main street was a two-lane road that separated matching sets of connected buildings. Former cafes, restaurants, and shops all sat empty. The years of harsh desert weather wear on the masonry, wood, and metal left every building a dull khaki color.

"I am sensing demons," said Melissa. "Ivoire, stay with me. Roland will lead, and Oliver will cover from the rear."

"He found him in a desert land and in the howling waste of a wilderness." Roland had donned his armor and approached Melissa. "For I have put my trust in you. Show me the way I should go."

"Let's head this way," said Melissa as she started to walk. "In the video, Vihaan identified a building as a 'recreation center.' There were lights there, and it was where he was attacked."

The group followed Melissa's lead and found the building from the video. It was the longest building in the area. It stretched for three blocks across and two blocks deep. The main entrance, a pair of glass doors, was boarded off. Along the twenty-foot-tall concrete walls were windows placed high, ten feet at the base, and each six foot tall. No lights showed through. The building was silent and dark.

"The demon essence is strong here," said Melissa. "As strong as the time in Estonia."

Over their communicators, Persephone's voice came through in broken and chopped, "..no plans... there is... find... nothing... signal..."

"The sand and remoteness must be interfering with the communicators," said Melissa.

"What do you suggest?" asked Oliver. "The direct approach or circle around back and check out the building first?"

Roland strode past them and kicked open the wood-barred glass doors. Wood, metal, and glass exploded back into the building, and Roland followed after.

"Direct, it is," smiled Oliver.

Inside was a reception area and a front counter scattered with pamphlets and signup sheets for the rec center activities. Sand dust had worked its way into the building, and a fine layer covered everything. There were doors to locker rooms to the left, a door leading to an exercise room to the right, and a wide open hallway behind the counter.

"What is that smell?" asked Oliver.

"I can't place it," said Melissa.

"It's algae," said Ivoire.

"Algae growing in this desert?" asked Oliver.

"Let's go deeper," said Melissa. "There are two trails of demon essence, a weak one to the left and a strong one leading back down the hallway."

"After you, sir," said Oliver to Roland.

Roland lowered his visor and moved past the counter into the open hallway.

"-Madad!" came a yell.

The group stopped and looked around, trying to locate the sound.

"Kya vah koee hain?" called the voice again. It was female and weak.

"The locker rooms," said Oliver.

Roland leaped over the counter and landed at the locker room doors; he pulled the women's room door open and dislodged the door off the hinges, tossing it aside. He was inside before the door fell to the floor. The rest followed after him.

The locker room reeked of death and feces. Green metal lockers circled the wall around an open-cornered square of four wooden benches. The only break in the lockers was a door on the far wall. Clothing, blood, and garbage were scattered on the dusty checkered tile floor.

"Madad!" yelled a voice from a locker.

"Over here," said Ivoire.

Roland stepped over, grabbed the padlock, and crushed it in his hands. Metal bits fell to the floor as the door swung open. An emaciated woman fell out, and Oliver caught her.

"Are you ok?" said Oliver.

The woman replied in Hindi.

"Go, therefore, to the main highways and as many as you find there," said Roland.

"Yes," said Melissa. "We must find anymore survivors and take them out before we engage."

Roland walked along the lockers and pulled every lock off. Doors swung open, and three more people fell out. He then turned to the first woman and spoke in Hindi. She replied.

"Those who diligently seek," said Roland as he exited back to the reception area.

Ivoire, Melissa, and Oliver helped the survivors to the exit. Roland entered the men's locker room by yanking the door off the hinges, matching the women's room.

"I came that they may have life and have it abundantly!" shouted Roland.

Oliver ran back inside and found Roland standing over a decapitated demon, white-skinned and androgynous, like the one from the carnival. It was wearing a black robe like the robes from the ceremony in Chile. Roland held a person in his shield hand, his sword dripping with black blood. The person he held groaned, and his head bobbed.

Melissa entered. "That is still human, as are the rest in here. Roland, can you ask if there are others?"

"I speak English," said a woman's voice from the lockers.

Roland placed the man on a bench, walked over, and removed the lock from the locker. An olive-skinned woman with black hair weakly stepped out dressed in a pink sari, "There are more in the woman's room, I think." She looked down at the demon Roland had decapitated. "These creatures have been taking us one at a time for days."

Roland got to work removing all the locks. Only two more survivors stumbled out.

"Where are they taking you?" asked Melissa.

"I do not know," said the woman. "Have you found others?"

"Yes," said Ivoire as she entered. "I took them across the street to the cafe. You should join them."

"Thank you," said the woman who turned to the survivors and spoke in Hindi. She led the survivors out and across the street.

"Surely the other demons have heard us," said Oliver.

"They may be too distracted with their unholy task," said Melissa.

"Or they expect commotion from the prisoners and mistook it for that," said Ivoire.

Oliver was at the rear door of the locker room. "The floor here is moist, and algae is growing. It is damp behind this door." He pushed the door open with a metal protesting screech and stepped through.

The next room was an indoor Olympic pool, light from the thinned sun pressed through gaps in the boarded high windows. Near the door was the shallow end. The pool ran away towards the deep end with a pair of diving platforms. Along the walls were pale, moaning bodies, like the two from the video. The water was green and swampy; slow ripples swirled around, and something was swimming in it. Between the diving boards was an altar. Three robed figures presided around it. On top of the highest diving board was a monstrous figure. A warped mermaid covered in dark blue scales. Its forearms had triangular flippers attached to its firearms, and a pair of legs flanked the tail. Its head donned four horns, two massive ones out the sides and a pair of small ones pointing upwards. Its yellow cymophanous eyes blinked with transparent eyelids.

A robed figure on the smaller diving board was holding a bound child and readying to drop them in the water.

Oliver fired, and the head of the figure exploded back; it dropped the bound girl.

Roland stepped through the door and announced, "I will cleanse you from all your filthiness and from all your idols." He took off along the left side, knocking the moaning figures down, trampling them, bashing them aside with his shield, and closing on the diving boards on the far side.

"Melissa," yelled Oliver. "Are any of the people still human?" He fired at the figures around the altar; two fell limp, one spun from the impact and dove behind for cover.

"Only the child on the diving board," said Melissa as she peered over Oliver's shoulder.

Oliver reloaded his right revolver, drew his left revolver, and shot the ghouls along the right wall in succession; sixteen splatters of black blood and sixteen heads gained a new orifice before Oliver reloaded again.

As Roland neared, he leaped over the end of the pool and landed on the alter; it was only a sheet over a table; the table crumbled from the impact, exposing the wounded figure who had taken cover.

The mer-demon jumped from its platform down onto Roland. Roland had his shield up and absorbed the impact. He impaled the beast with his sword.

The beast, which towered over Roland at twice his height, grabbed Roland and pulled him in close, pressing the sword in deeper. The creature began to bash Roland with its horns. They clanged against the metal of his armor.

Having finished off the last of the ghouls along the pool, Oliver reloaded and fired at the robed figures as they fled. Two fell as rounds found home. The last had escaped through the rear.

Roland and the demon pressed against each other. They slid and hit the diving board. The bound girl was knocked off and fell into the water.

Oliver ran along the pool and tore off his duster, hat, gun belt, and boots. He dove into the green darkness after the child. Thoughts of the girl he failed to save in Odessa darted through his brain. The water was thick with algae and other materials that Oliver tried not to think of. Only saving the girl mattered. He reached, guiding with his hands until he felt fingers, then a small hand. He grabbed and pulled it up and worked towards the surface. Melissa and Ivoire waited for him there; Ivoire grabbed the girl, Melissa grabbed Oliver's hand, and something else grabbed Oliver's foot.

He was pulled back into the darkness. More tiny hands grabbed him; he was swarmed by creatures he could only see water-blurred images of. He kicked and struck out; he thought of his revolvers, safely lying on the side of the pool. His lungs screamed for air; he started to fade as his oxygen-deprived brain reeled.

A new shape moved through the water with an unnatural swiftness. Unlike the hairy dark creatures, it was shiny and smooth. The creatures were in a frenzy as the new shape grabbed and crushed or tore them each in two. Black blood darkened the green water. A pair of metal hands grabbed Oliver as the last of his consciousness slipped away.

"--wake up, Oliver!"

Oliver was jolted to awareness and coughed acid-tasting water. Around him, the remains of otters, possessed by demons, rended and crushed by Roland, littered the side of the pool.

Roland was over him, his hand on his torso.

Melissa, Ivoire, and a young girl with black hair were kneeling next to him.

Oliver sat up and coughed more. "What happened?"

"You saved the girl," said Melissa.

"Then Roland saved you," said Ivoire.

Oliver laid back and breathed; it felt like learning to breathe for the first time.

"Did we kill the demon?"

"It is done," said Roland.

"How many people did we save?" asked Oliver.

"Eight in all," said Melissa.

"Are my revolvers ok?" he asked.

"Yes," said Ivoire. "Just a little wet."

"Good," said Oliver as he slowly stood with Roland's help. "Can we go? I want a shower."

SHADOWS NO MORE

  Another altar, another body. Ivon had lost count of the times he had completed the ceremony. The ritual, etched into the fabric of his existence, unfolded with a macabre familiarity. The lifeless form lay before him, an eerie silence hanging in the air. Chants in an ancient, guttural tongue reverberated through the chamber, creating an otherworldly ambiance. As the chants reached their crescendo, Ivon's blood began to flow, a dark river of sacrifice. The corpse stirred, animated by forces beyond mortal comprehension. This grim ceremony, death removed and life restored, had become the essence of Ivon's existence.

  Since the inaugural ceremony where Ivon's blood had breathed life into a deceased soldier, he and Dimitri embarked on their new mission. Their journey took them to remote corners of the world, performing the ritual over countless corpses. They became scavengers of death, seeking out fresh cadavers in obscure towns that would disappear overnight. These were places forgotten by the world, their inhabitants erased from existence as Ivon, Dimitri, and their crew moved in.

  The risen, revived by Ivon's sacrificial blood, were packed into shipping containers and shipped to unknown destinations. Dimitri, with an eerie power of command over the newly risen, orchestrated these creatures like a grotesque maestro. He would utter orders, and the risen would obediently file into the containers, standing shoulder to shoulder, a silent army awaiting their master's call. These risen bodies were indifferent to Ivon's commands, whose blood has given them new purpose. When Ivon questioned Dimitri about this ability control he had over the newly risen, Dimitri replied, "Petrov said your purpose is to create; mine is to command."

Petrov, the elusive puppet master commanding via letter, demanded more. The bloodletting shifted from ceremonial chalices to Ivon's own veins. Petrov's orders were clear – the life force coursing through Ivon's veins was the elixir that fueled their unholy enterprise. Ivon, almost perpetually prone, felt the sting of needles extracting the essence of his existence. Ivon watched as he grew pale and sickly from the blood loss, but he knew that it was for the greatness of his country that he sacrificed his health. The blood bags would be collected and sent off to Petrov, presumably for the same ceremony in other remote areas.

In return, Colonel Petrov continued to shower them with praise and gifts. Each time a new wave of risen soldiers was collected and shipped, a new reward would be delivered. For Ivon, the prize was mostly food, his favorite, and now a necessity as his body was drained and squeezed for every last drop of blood, just shy of killing him. For Dimitri, the prizes usually matched his carnal desires. No debauchery was too grotesque for his satisfaction. It was the one area where Ivon felt distaste.

Another town emptied, another chain of ceremonies going through the motions as another dozen bodies are resurrected. This time, once again, in a cave. Dimitri liked caves. He said he felt at home in them. Dimitri preferred dark, dirty, moist places, far from observance.

Like the forgotten number of times the ceremonies occurred and the risen gathered, today's ceremony blurred through like before.

That was until…

"They have set their mouth against the heavens, and their tongue parades through the earth," boomed a voice. The voice belonged to a massive man in shining armor. He wielded a sword taller than him and a shield with a red cross. Behind him were three more people: a man in a cowboy hat and two others.

Dimitri pointed and commanded the risen, "Kill them!"

The knight slammed into the gathering of risen with his shield, and those Ivon had sacrificed his blood to resurrect were beaten and sliced. The massive man swiped with his sword and cleaved into the group. Heads and blood splattered across the cave. Terror inexperienced before crashed over Ivon's body. He was frozen at the sight of this metal-clad monster unleashed on his creations.

Dimitri grabbed Ivon and pulled him to the rear of the cave. "You must run. Your blood is our treasure. I can delay. You must go."

"Come with me. How can you fight that?" asked Ivon.

"You are not the only one who is special," Dimitri said as his neck and arms bent in a strange way. "Go, this is not for your eyes." Dimitri's voice grew deep.

Dimitri's body bloated and grew; he expanded into a massive figure and started to laugh an unnatural, deep laugh. His friend's familiar features twisted into a new visage.

Ivon ran down through the darkness back to the staging area. He ran, compelled by fear. Fear of the metal man who attacked, fear of his friend's transformation. As he ran, he heard gunfire. He hoped his friend would follow shortly. *He transformed into that creature? Was that Dimitri?* He ran towards the daylight of the staging area, and he stopped when he smelled smoke. Worry for his friend had won, so he ran back.

He returned to catastrophe. The altar was ablaze. The people his blood had given new life to were shredded and burning. He found the transformed body of his closest friend engulfed in flame. He found what he knew to be Dimitri's head separated from his torso, the eyes gouged out, and a gaping wound in his skull.

Who were these monsters who attacked us?

Ivon returned to the shipping area. The crate was empty, its intended cargo smoldering in the cave below. Ivon entered the passenger seat of the truck.

"Where are the rest?" asked the driver.

"Dead," said Ivon. "We were attacked. Take me to Petrov."

"I don't know where–" the driver's lie was interrupted by Ivon's fist.

"You know," said Ivon. "Take me."

The driver dove for the glove box. Ivon pushed him against the dash and opened the box to find an MP-443. Ivon readied the weapon and aimed it at the driver.

"Take me to Petrov or die," Ivon's blood ran cold. His lifelong friend had been slaughtered. He wanted answers.

The driver drove through the night. Down from the mountain, they approached the capital city of Santiago.

The sun rose behind the city in an orange glow. It was a serene beauty that moved Ivon's anger to sadness. His only friend was dead.

The driver stopped at the President's mansion. "Petrov is here."

Ivon stepped out of the truck, and the driver sped away, not wanting to be a part of this. Ivon stood before The Palacio de La Moneda; its neoclassical facade rose with stoic elegance, columns standing as silent witnesses to centuries of tales etched into the very stones from which it was hewn.

Ivon approached the gate guard, "Tell Petrov I am here."

"There is no one–" his lying words were interrupted by a bullet from Ivon's pistol.

At the sound of the gunshot, an alarm sounded, and men poured out of the main building and quickly surrounded the guardhouse.

"Petrov!" screamed Ivon. "Where is Petrov?"

A voice slithered out of the public announcement system. Ivon knew it was Petrov's. It spoke in the native Chilean tongue.

Book of Ivon and Ivoire

The men surrounding Ivon lowered their weapons and parted a path leading to the main building.

Ivon tucked his pistol into his pants and walked through the opening. He entered the central courtyard, bathed in dappled sunlight filtering through ancient trees. The silent gaze of statues commemorating heroes and leaders seemed to follow Ivon as he passed. The main doors were opened by flanking guards, and Ivon entered. The guards inside motioned for Ivon to continue down the hall. The external silence of the soldiers and building pulled at Ivon, the internal voices of his childhood had returned, stronger than ever.

He continued to follow the guidance of the guards. Ascending a grand staircase, he found himself in the Hall of Mirrors, an expanse that reflected Ivon an infinite number of times as he passed. From the corners of his eyes, he thought he saw strange and grotesque figures. The ornate mirrors framed in gold leaf lined the walls, creating an illusion of endless space.

A final pair of guards opened a door, and Ivon entered the library. The room was only lit by a fire on the far side. Two figures sat on a leather couch. Countless books of red, brown, tan, and green adorned the walls. The only breaks in the books were massive paintings of former Chilean leaders. One of the figures on the couch rose, bowed to the other, and left through the far door.

"Do you remember when we met, Ivon?" the still-seated figure asked. It was Petrov.

"Yes," said Ivon. "You came to the Army base."

"I told you once I was there looking for special children," said Ivon. "Do you recall?"

"Yes," replied Ivon.

"Do you remember why I chose you?" asked Petrov.

"I could sense lies, and that had value," answered Ivon.

"No," said Petrov. "Try again."

"Because I fought the other boys?" asked Ivon.

Petrov rose and turned to face Ivon, "Close, your 'fire.'"

"My fire?" asked Ivon.

"Yes," said Petrov. "Your viciousness."

"Because I killed?" asked Ivon

"Exactly," said Petrov, his figure framed by the fire. "Your skill to sense lies is rare. But to have that skill and the rage in your heart? A further chance still that I could find you perhaps only one in a trillion."

"What are you going on about? I am here because Dimitri is dead," said Ivon. "We were attacked."

"I know, it was an inevitable event," said Petrov. "You met a Paladin."

"The monster in the armor?" asked Ivon. "That is called a Paladin."

"Oh, they take all shapes," said Petrov. "They serve their God and work against our God."

"Our God?" said Ivon. "I do not believe in such nonsense as gods."

"I know," said Petrov. "But they are real. Just as real as you and I. Dimitri served our God. Just as I do." Petrov stepped around the couch and let the fire illuminate his face. Petrov was the same, but not. His pointy nose had grown to an impossible length. His eyes were slanted and all black. His mouth extended almost to his earlobes, and his teeth were pointed and interlocked in his grin.

"This is the real me," said Petrov. "Just as I assume you met the real Dimitri before he died."

"Are you human?" asked Ivon.

"No," smiled Petrov. "I am something more."

"Am I human?" asked Ivon.

"Yes," said Petrov.

"What of Dimitri?" asked Ivon.

"He is like me," said Petrov.

"What God do you serve?" asked Ivon.

"Ahh, the question," said Petrov. "We serve a God of pleasure."

"Does your God make you powerful?" asked Ivon.

"Would you like to see?" said Petrov. "Take out your gun and shoot me."

Ivon pulled the gun and aimed. "Just shoot you?"

"In the leg or arm, please," said Petrov.

Ivon aimed for Petrov's right leg and fired. Petrov jolted and then stood firm. "Now watch."

Black blood flowed from a wound, and the air was tinted with sulfur; after a moment, the bullet was pushed out, the wound closed.

"If Dimitri was like you," said Ivon. "How were they able to kill him?"

"The God of the Paladins makes them strong," said Petrov. "They are the only ones who can kill us. They have killed many of our kind."

"What of the Paladins' God?" asked Ivon.

"They serve a God who challenges ours," said Petrov. "But enough about gods and powers. You think you came for answers but did not expect what was revealed. What you actually came for was vengeance."

"Vengeance?" asked Ivon.

"Yes," said Petrov. He moved closer to Ivon. "That fire inside you burns. It burns for vengeance against the ones who killed your creations. Creations born of your very blood. Vengeance against the ones who killed your beloved Dimitri, your only true friend. You are not here for answers. What you really seek is vengeance against the Paladins."

"Can I be made powerful like you or Dimitri to fight them?" asked Ivon.

"No," said Petrov as he walked behind Ivon. "But I can put you in command of more like he and I. Ones even stronger than him. Beyond that, I know where the Paladins are weak. I know where they are exposed. I can place you in their path when they are the least prepared. Would you like this chance?"

"Yes," said Ivon. "Help me to avenge Dimitri."

"Good," said Petrov. "Ready yourself, Ivon. I am unleashing you on the Paladins."

THE REAL MISSION

Melissa was in the cafeteria enjoying a meal of spaghetti and meatballs prepared by Isaac when Ivoire approached.

"May I join you?" asked Ivoire.

"Of course," replied Melissa. "Would you like Isaac to prepare another dish?"

"No," said Ivoire. "I am not hungry." She looked around the room at the empty tables.

"Was there something you wanted to talk about?" asked Melissa.

"I am not sure where to begin," said Ivoire.

"Just speak freely from your heart," said Melissa.

Ivoire let out a long breath, "When I was a child and would read the Bible with my grandmother, it brought me such warmth. She would read the stories of the great peoples with such passion and such love. I knew she believed with her whole heart in what the pages said. I adopted her faith, and with great joy, I would tell the stories and sing the songs with her and Papa, my father. After they died, I gave up on that faith, and my life has had little to offer to convince me of God's love since then."

Melissa did not interrupt; she let Ivoire continue with apt attention.

"Now meeting you, and Oliver, and Persephone, and Roland—" Ivoire searched for the words. "My whole life I have been used, my gift, my body, a tool for others." Painful memories flowed through Ivoire. "You four do not use your gifts for selfish gain but to help others. Roland could easily be the greatest athlete the world has ever known. Oliver could be a world-famous marksman or movie stuntman. Even Persephone could be a wealthy inventor. Instead, Roland and Oliver sacrifice their very bodies to protect those who cannot protect themselves. You and Persephone work tirelessly, searching and researching. None of you ask for anything but only to seek glory for God." Ivoire breathed in deeply. "I am here before you now to ask, help me to know why. Why did my grandmother and my father love God so? Why do you four risk and sacrifice so much for his glory?"

"That is not an easy question to answer," said Melissa. "To each, the journey is unique. God's ways are also mysterious. But I am glad you are here. In a few days, we are going to a pair of missions that we help support. I think meeting Kevin and then Hannah and her fellow sisters will give you some perspective. Would you like to go?"

"Yes," replied Ivoire. "I would love to meet Kevin and Hannah and see these missions."

Three days later, all of the Paladins flew to Utah and drove to Drywell. Ivoire had never seen such a dessert. Endless sands framed by blue skies and purple mountains were a contrast to the dark and dusty desert in India. The town had not changed much since Melissa first found Oliver. It was still fighting daily against the onslaught of the encroaching desert. The newest addition, a water tower, was possible from the financing provided by the support from the Paladins. Small green gardens now backed many of the houses.

At Oliver's church, shrubbery now flanked the entrance steps. Kevin waited for them at the church entrance as the SUV pulled up. Kevin had put on a few pounds of muscle and now filled out the robes of ministry much better than when Oliver had left.

"Oliver," yelled Kevin, who ran down the steps.

Oliver exited the SUV, met Kevin in stride, and embraced him in a hug. "How are you, my apprentice?"

"I am well," said Kevin. "I still practice daily. I have built new targets. I must show you."

"Later, friend," said Oliver. "I have people you must meet." He turned to the SUV and guided Kevin over.

Melissa, Persephone, Ivoire, and Roland all stood before the SUV.

Persephone waved, "You must be Kevin! I am Persephone."

"Hello, Persephone," said Kevin. "Oliver has told me about you in his letters, about each of you." He motioned to Ivoire.

"Hello again, Kevin," said Melissa.

"Hello," said Kevin. "I see you bring my master back in one piece."

Roland stepped forward and lifted Kevin up into a giant hug and then kissed his cheek.

"Salute one another with a holy kiss. The churches of Christ salute you," Roland said.

Roland set him down and looked into his face. "Abhor that which is evil; cleave to that which is good."

"There is no mistaking Roland," said Kevin, who turned to Ivoire. "Who is this? Oliver has not written to me about you."

"Hello, Kevin," said Ivoire. "I am Ivoire. I am a new addition."

"A pleasure," said Kevin.

When Oliver had left, Kevin was reserved and shy. His new role as the spiritual leader of the town had opened him up and developed his confidence. Oliver laughed with pleasure at this new behavior.

After the formal introduction, Kevin gave a tour to his guests and talked about developments in the town. He had upgraded the old shooting range with steel targets. The water tower had permitted them to grow plants and ensure enough water pressure for reliable plumbing. The town had also gained a family looking to live 'off-grid,' and the father was an engineer who was constructing a solar grid to power the town. Over dinner, Kevin shared an animated retelling of Oliver's rescue of the town from the Desert Demons.

Each Paladin helped in their own way while visiting. Roland helped pull a stuck truck out of loose sand. Persephone drew up plans to enhance the town's water supply with rain collectors and dew producers. Melissa worked with Kevin and added suggestions for his sermons. Kevin could do little to hide his attraction to Ivoire.

At the last sunset of their visit, Oliver and Kevin enjoyed a cigar on the back steps of their church. The reddish-orange sun crawled slowly to the distant mountains. The hot wind tousled Oliver's hair, and grains of sand tickled his cheeks. It was a peaceful reprieve from his work as a Paladin. He understood now why Melissa returned to Hannah's mission as often as she did. Watching Kevin flirt with Ivoire reminded him of his first love, Jimin. Now, he was the old man on the porch smoking and watching a sunset.

That evening the entire town had gathered to see Oliver. Each family had brought an item and what passed for a great feast was held. Oliver led them in a prayer.

Dear Heavenly Father

In Your infinite grace and boundless love, we come before You to lift up those who find themselves traversing the arid and challenging deserts of life. Lord, we know that the journey through the desert can be relentless, testing the endurance of the soul and the strength of the spirit. We humbly ask for Your mercy and guidance for those who face these struggles.

You, O Lord, are the oasis in the midst of the desolation. You are the source of living water that quenches the thirst of weary hearts. We pray for those who feel parched and depleted that Your life-giving spirit may fill them with renewed hope, strength, and resilience.

In the name of Your son, Jesus Christ, who Himself faced the challenges of the desert, we offer this prayer.

Amen.

When the visit ended, they said their farewells, and Oliver handed Kevin a small fold of money. They embraced again, and Oliver reminded Kevin to practice his shooting and martial arts each day. Kevin reminded Oliver to keep writing letters.

The Paladins took the SUV back to the airport, their next destination, Hannah's mission. On the flight, Ivoire found Oliver cleaning sand out of his guns.

"Oliver," said Ivoire. "Can I ask you about Drywell?"

"Sure," said Oliver. He motioned to the seat across from him and put away his weapons. "Please join me."

Ivoire sat and gathered her thoughts. "How did you end up there?"

"God sent me," said Oliver.

"How?" she asked.

Oliver retold his life with Gerin. How, after Gerin died, a final note told him to find Roland. He shared his quest to find Roland and how it took him to the orphanage of his youth. How he found it abandoned but still learned his birthdate and parent's name. He shared about the farmhouse he daydreamed about and how, inside, he found an old map with an even older town named Roland. He added to Kevin's telling of the Drywell rescue and of the time he stayed there until Melissa found him.

"You spent all those years in Drywell because you found an old map?" asked Ivoire.

"Sums it up," said Oliver.

"Did those years feel wasted?" she asked. "With your skills, you could have done much good during those years."

"Not at all," said Oliver. "I helped many during those years, most of all Kevin. God needed me to wait, to learn patience. I was where he needed me, waiting for when he led Melissa to me."

"But years of waiting?" asked Ivoire.

"In the Bible, God promised Abraham children," said Oliver. "It took twenty-five years before the promise was fulfilled. God has a plan, and it is not our place to understand sometimes."

"You follow a God and do not know his plan for you?" asked Ivoire.

"Exactly," said Oliver. "That is called faith. He has blessed me, and I have faith that when I meet him face-to-face, his plan will be revealed, and it will be a beautiful sight."

"I still do not feel it," said Ivoire. "Why do you and Kevin and the others work so hard to save a town when it seems like God is attempting to reclaim the desert?"

"Love and hope," said Oliver. "We love the residents. We have hope for a better tomorrow. God may be sending the sand, but He, at least we believe, wants us to work and labor for our fellow man. The labor creates fellowship and spiritual strength. We feel joy when our efforts bear fruit, and our land grows more beautiful."

"Is that what it means to be a Christian?" asked Ivoire. "To have faith in a God who keeps his plan a mystery, to love our fellow man when they give us every reason not to, and to have hope that tomorrow will be better when every sign points to it not being so."

"Yup," replied Oliver with a smile. "Let me offer this. Save judgment for now until we meet Hannah. She will give you a new perspective on the Christian mission."

They landed and drove to Hannah's mission. The SUV entered the small valley that was home to an even smaller village. Litter and sewage still lined the dirt street. At the end of the road stood Hannah's mission. There was a line of people at the door leading down the street. They parked the SUV behind the church, and Melissa led them through the back door to the filled kitchen.

"Sister! Welcome! How have you been?" cheered Hannah in her thick Italian accent as she approached Melissa and hugged her. Her hair was set in a pair of buns and she wore an apron over her habit that was filled with her corpulent frame.

Book of Ivon and Ivoire

"Hello, Hannah," replied Melissa. "I have been well and am very happy to be here. I want you to meet someone." She turned to Ivoire. "This is my new friend, Ivoire."

"Hello, Hannah. It is a pleasure—" Ivoire was interrupted by a hug from Hannah.

"Such a beauty," said Hannah after releasing Ivoire. "Welcome to my mission. Did you bring the rest?"

Oliver, Persephone, and Roland entered as if on command. Oliver and Persephone placed the boxes of food they carried on the ground; Roland dropped two skinned and wrapped goats onto the table.

"There is my man," squealed Hannah as she brushed past the others and scurried over to Roland. "Give me a kiss."

Roland picked up Hannah and kissed her on both cheeks.

Hannah turned her attention to Persephone. "And there is my sweet angel. Grown so much, I bet the boys just chase you all over."

Persephone rolled her eyes. "Sister...."

"And there is the handsome American," said Hannah, turning to Oliver. "Give me a kiss."

Oliver took off his hat. "Pleasure, ma'am," he said, and he kissed Hannah on the cheeks.

"Oh, my heart swims with joy," said Hannah. "We have quite the line of hungry people today. Let's get to work."

"Oliver," said Melissa. "You will work the floor with Ivoire. I need you two to bring food to the people and help them find seats."

"Yes, ma'am," replied Oliver and Ivoire in unison.

"Roland," continued Melissa, "you are in charge of cutting, prepping, and cleaning."

Roland replied, "If you ask me anything in my name, I will do it."

"Persephone." Melissa turned to her. "You help Sister Hannah and the others with the cooking. Follow her lead."

"Yes, ma'am," replied Persephone, who clanged a ladle on the stew pot.

The Paladins helped Hannah and the other sisters prepare and serve goat stew with vegetables and bread for every person who came seeking food. Hundreds of residents of the village and dozens more from the neighboring lands passed through the mission's threshold and were fed.

Ivoire followed Oliver's lead and helped the families find vacant tables and brought them food. It was a new experience for her, helping her fellow man and seeking nothing in return. These people were on the verge of starvation, and yet they smiled, they prayed, and gave thanks. She was helping a family, a father, his mother, and his daughter, find a table. They reminded her so much of her family, from when she was young and before her time training in the Guild. Once they were seated, she turned to fetch some food–

BOOM

An explosion blasted the main entrance open. Splintered wood sprayed inside, and people were thrown towards the rear. Ivoire regained herself; she could hear screaming and crying through her ringing ears.

Oliver was out first, revolvers drawn. "What hit us?"

"We did," creeped out a raspy voice. Through the hole created by the blast, a demon stepped through. An eight-foot-tall monster covered in black hair, a disfigured bear on its' hind legs. Its head, too small for its body, was bald with feline features. It carried an RPK-74 and aimed it at Oliver. "And the boss says no survivors." The creature swung its weapon and aimed at a family.

Oliver fired, bullets tearing into the fur. The creature fired, its rounds finding a toddler boy. Oliver yelled and closed, his rounds finding home more as he unloaded on the bear demon. It dropped its weapon and raised its massive arms to protect its face. Oliver reloaded red Prideaux; he fired, the explosions effectively tearing the arms off the creature as it fell back. Oliver fired more, emptying into the creature's tiny skull. The skull exploded in a burst of black goo. Oliver was on top of the bear, facing out in the open.

"Roland!" shouted an accented voice.

The smoke and dust from the explosion cleared, and the sight before Oliver grasped him. Five figures, four demons and a human, stood in a semi-circle, each with weapons drawn. The demons, each a distorted animal shaped of disjointed parts, an obscene menagerie from a hellish circus.

On the farthest left, the first demon was a massive elephant's body on its hind legs with the arms of a man and the head of a fox but retained its elephant nose. It was reloading an RPG-7.

Next to the elephant was a voluptuous tiger-woman in white and gray fur. A pervert's blend of feline and exaggerated feminine features with twitching ears and black fangs. It wielded a Vityaz-SN.

On the far right was the tallest, a giraffe standing on its four legs. Extra appendages, a set of three-fingered arms, attached to the neck baseline. Its deformed and bloated head, far too large for the tiny neck, swayed as if in a drunken stupor. The creature aimed a Saiga-12 automatic shotgun at Oliver.

Next to the giraffe was an emaciated Gorilla. Pale and sickly. Its head was missing, but a face was embedded in its chest. In each arm was an AO-44 with steel wire stocks.

In the center was just a man. He was tall and broad-shouldered. His head was shaven clean. His face was sharp and chiseled, with a scar on his jawline. He had an AK-47 in one arm resting on his shoulder.

The bald man spoke to the tiger lady. Oliver did not recognize the language; he thought it might be Russian

"The boss says," started the tiger lady, her voice a purr. "Where is the knight? We are here to kill the Paladins, but mostly him."

From the hole in the Mission created by the explosion, Roland's voice announced, "Here am I." He stepped out, his armor fully donned, sword and shield in hand. "When you come looking for me, you'll find me."

Oliver's heart was boldened in his presence.

'The Boss' spoke; before the tiger-lady could translate, Roland answered in the same tongue. Oliver did not know what was said, but the animal demons all aimed at Roland. Roland readied his sword.

"Roland," called Melissa from the mission. "The man in the middle. He is a Paladin."

Something happened Oliver had never witnessed before. Roland hesitated.

"What of the others?" asked Oliver.

"Obviously demons," replied Melissa.

"You get the families to safety," said Oliver.

The elephant trumpeted and leveled its RPG at the mission and fired. Roland dove and intercepted the rocket-propelled grenade with his shield. The explosion rocked him back, but he stood his ground. Oliver opened fire on the gorilla and the giraffe as he dove behind the wreckage of the mission's wall for cover. One of the Gorilla's chest eyes burst out, and one of the giraffe's arms dropped limp; it aimed the automatic shotgun with its good arm at Roland. The demons all opened fire. The bullets twanged in futility against the impenetrable armor. Roland closed on the elephant as it reloaded its RPG-7. The elephant swiped its trunk, and Roland caught it and pulled. Roland impaled the beast in its midsection with his sword and jumped, slicing up with the blade, exiting through the head. A river of black sulphuric blood poured out as the elephant fell back, defeated and nearly bisected.

The creatures continued to fire in futility at Roland. The leader commanded the remaining demons in Russian. In response, they all turned and aimed at the mission.

Oliver fired at the gorilla's other eye, matching the first and blinding it. It reeled and spun, firing in all directions. Bullets impacted the wall by Oliver, and he was pinned down. The firestorm of bullets was too much to track with his predictive sight.

Pellets from the 12-gauge penetrated his calf. Oliver cried out, steadied himself, and then took a deep breath. He focused on the moment to let the Holy Spirit guide him. He recited Gerin's prayer as he reloaded with the last pair of red prideaux.

Lord, make me swift and true
Guide my hands with yours
Let your will be my aim

The world around him calmed and slowed. Through the pre-shadows of the bullets streaking all around, he found a gap, peeked around the open wall, and fired four times into the giraffe's swaying head. A moment passed, and the head exploded like a jack-o-lantern filled with firecrackers. The beast fell dead.

Roland landed from his elephant-cleaving leap and was in full stride, closing on the tiger lady. The creature turned and fired on Roland, bullets sparking off the metal. Roland had nearly reached the tiger lady; she dropped her empty guns and pounced on him with claws bared. He caught her and skewered her with his sword. Not yet dead, it swiped at him. He swung his shield and decapitated her. He flicked his sword down, and the headless tiger-lady plopped into a mound at his feet.

The gorilla continued to fire blindly in all directions. The leader dove and covered himself as the gorilla turned towards him. Oliver fired his last twelve explosive rounds into the chest of the beast. The explosion erupted where the head should have been, a geyser of black goo spraying Roland and the leader.

Standing over the leader, Roland stabbed his sword into the ground, millimeters from the leader's nose. Roland picked him up and pulled him face-to-face. Roland spoke in Russian. The leader kicked, punched, and yelled in anger against Roland's impenetrable armor. His hands were bleeding from their impact.

"Roland." It was Melissa who spoke. She exited with Persephone, who was in tears. "We evacuated and protected the families that survived the blast." She paused. "More were killed by gunfire." Her voice trailed off.

"Where is Ivoire?" asked Oliver.

"I am fine," Ivoire called. She exited, covered in blood. Hannah's apron in her hand. "I tried to help her."

Roland roared and threw the leader to the ground, his ribs audibly cracking at Melissa's feet. He dropped his shield and tore off his helmet as he stomped over to a stump of a long, dead oak tree and punched it. The ancient trunk exploded, and he roared again. He turned to the man and pointed at the prone man. "Jesus, I know, and Paul, I know about, but who are you?"

Always the personification of calmness, Melissa answered, "He is a Paladin like us, but he has been corrupted by Satan's minions." Melissa turned to Ivoire. "We need you now to help us untangle this mystery. Will you help us?"

"Yes," answered Ivoire. "I also need you to do something for me."

KNIGHTS AND DRAGONS

Can't this train go any faster?

Ivoire paced the aisle of the train. Anger, rage, and hatred still poured through her veins. The discovery of The Guild selling her friend burned like an itch, an inch under skin she could not reach. She hadn't eaten or rested, only boarded this train bound for the Guild.

A flood of angry questions flowed through her brain. *How long before they sold me out for a sick man's pleasure? How many other girls were forced into seduction training?*

The train twisted through the Ukrainian landscape. A storm had formed and seemed to follow the train, cloaking it in darkness. The rain tapped the windows in an endless rhythm broken only by the distant thunder.

Knowing hundreds of kilometers of rail waited ahead, Ivoire slammed herself into her seat. She focused on the moment, reached deep, and sought calmness, just as she had been trained at The Guild–

The Guild!

Her mind flamed with fury, reminded of a life that had been a lie. It all fits together. It explained the years of boring assignments. *Researching Industrial Espionage, ha!*. There was no way the SSU believed in her supernatural ability to sense truth. She was just another 'pretty girl,' valued more for her body than her mind.

They knew not what they missed out on. Ivoire smiled a hateful smile. *I am their puppet no more!*

She fumed as the train coasted along the winding rails. She tried to sleep, to rest, to put these destructive thoughts behind her. She focused on the now, the rain tapping the window, thousands of unique water molecules dashing against the glass. She felt the rhythm of the train's motion through her chair, and she let her body flow with the sway of the curves. She sought calmness, peace, and respite. All she could find in her mind was the Guild and its missions; there was nothing else. She pressed deeper past the pain, past the anger, she leaned in and found her father, his eternal smile, the warmth his body radiated, the comfort in his hugs. She could smell him (motor oil and coffee), hear his voice, and feel the cracked leather of his favorite jacket. She pushed deeper into her memories and found her grandmother in her garden singing her favorite hymn. She let go of the world around her and focused on the memory.

In her memory, her grandmother spoke, "Hello, my little flower."

Ivoire let the memory envelop her, to hold her like a blanket swaddling an infant, "Hello Grandmother."

The memory felt real; she could feel the warm afternoon sun and smell the lilacs, lavender, and rosemary of the garden. Her knees rubbed in the moist dirt. She breathed it in, and relaxation washed across her body.

"I miss you, grandmother," said Ivoire.

"I know, my little kohana," her grandmother replied. "I miss you too."

Ivoire had not been called 'Kohana' since her grandmother died. The word was forgotten to her, but the sound of her grandmother's name pulled her deeper into the memory.

"I'm so alone," Ivoire looked down. She was twelve again, wearing the dress her grandmother had made the week before the Major came to her house.

"I know it feels that way," Grandmother smiled. "But love follows you. God only wants you to look."

"I have forgotten how to love," said Ivoire. Her voice changed. She looked down, she was nine and wearing the blue dress she wore so often it fell apart one day. The dress was new again.

"Your mother made that dress the week she learned she was pregnant," said grandmother, her voice softened to sadness. "I failed her, Kohana."

"What happened to my mother?" Ivoire's voice changed again; she was seven, wearing overalls that matched her father's.

"Your father loved her so," said Grandmother. "When he thought half his family died, his love expanded and focused on you. He put behind his old life, and you became his life."

Tears welled in Ivoire's eyes, "Papa…" Her voice lightened again. She was five and dressed in a yellow dress. "What do you mean; he thought half his family died? What happened?" Ivoire asked.

"This next part is going to be difficult," said Grandmother. "Healing is always hard. Hold fast. God is with you, my Kohana."

"What is going to be difficult? What healing?" asked Ivoire. She was three in a tiny white dress. "Harder than it has been? Harder than losing you and Papa?"

"Do you remember the story of the dragon and the princess your father used to read to you?" asked Grandmother.

"Yes," said Ivoire. "I asked Papa to read it every night when I was young. He would dim the lights and use a wrench as a sword as he performed the story all over my room."

"What happened in the story?" asked the grandmother.

"The dragon took the princess to the mountain to force the princess to marry it," said Ivoire. She was now two, wearing a raincoat and boots. "The princess was afraid, and the dragon was mighty. The picture of the dragon always scared me."

"The dragon is frightful," said Grandmother. "But what happened to it in the end?"

The memory of her father's voice swirled in Ivoire's mind, "Then a knight in bright and shining armor climbed the mountain. He stopped the dragon's fire with his shield and slayed the dragon with his magic sword. Then, with a kiss, he rescued the princess and carried her off happily ever after."

"There are still knights and heroes in the world, Ivoire," said Grandmother. "They come for you. They seek you. But so does the dragon."

"What are you saying?" Ivoire asked.

"Always remember, God, Papa, your mother, and I love you so much. We are with you." Behind her grandmother, apparitions of her father and a lady, her mother, appeared. Her parents embraced, and her father placed a hand on her grandmother's shoulder. Their visages slowly faded away.

Ivoire was one year old, wearing a pink onesie. "Don't leave me…" Her tiny arms reached for her family.

"We wait for you," said her mother.

"We love you so much," said her father.

"We are always with you," said her grandmother.

"Come back," whimpered the infant Ivoire.

DING DONG

"We apologize passengers," said a voice over the train public announcement system. Ivoire had drifted to sleep. "We have been ordered to hold here."

The dream lingered in her mind as she regained her consciousness. The train had stopped. The passengers were looking out the window and pointing. The storm had ended, and it was a bright and beautiful day. A pillar of smoke rose from the West. Ivoire looked out the window. The source of the smoke was from where The Guild would be. She ran to the door and out into the sunlight. Through the muddy woods, her feet carried her past exhaustion. She found the road and ran along, her legs burning. The Guild neared, its walls damaged, a hole where its main doors once hung. She sprinted past the entrance into the garden, the flowers torched and trampled.

A man with an AK-47 was at the far end, looking away. Ivoire picked up a piece of wood debris, closed on the man, and whacked him on the back of his head. He crumpled. She turned him over and worked to get his weapon strap off his shoulders.

Pain at the base of her skull, then blackness.

She awoke tied to a chair and blindfolded. She did not know how much time had passed. Her head throbbed.

"—I said, are you awake?" said an unfamiliar voice. "I hope you speak English. I don't know Ukrainian."

"What?" said Ivoire in English. "Where am I?"

"Oh, good, you do. You are in no danger," said the voice. "You are aboard my ship." His voice sounded of truth.

"A ship?" Ivoire's head reeled. "What happened to The Guild?"

"We destroyed it," said the voice. Ivoire thought she had the accent now, Israeli.

"Destroyed it? Why? Ukraine is not at war with Israel," said Ivoire.

The man laughed and removed her blindfold. "My war is not with your country but against any who would defile the innocent."

She was in a ship's brig, tied to a metal chair that was bolted to the deck. A metal bed and a metal urinal were to her right. To her left, the man stood in the open hatch, blindfold in hand. He had dark, curly hair and a squat face with light brown eyes and a pronounced nose. He was short but muscular, wearing a tan button-up shirt, black cargo pants, and boots.

"What do you want with me?" asked Ivoire.

"Depends. Are you a victim or a participant?" asked the man.

"If you're asking if I worked for The Guild," said Ivoire. "The answer is no. I was trained there. I am a graduate. I had not been there in years."

"Why did you return?" asked the man.

"I learned that I was sold out for sex," said Ivoire. "I came seeking answers."

"Untie her," said the man.

Another man entered and removed the bindings.

"I believe a formal introduction is in order." The first man bowed curtly. "I am Benjamin Blau, captain of this ship, *The Merciful*. Welcome aboard."

Ivoire rose. "my name is Ivoire Kravets. Why did you attack The Guild?"

"Please," said Benjamin. "Join me for dinner. I believe we can share stories."

Blau gave Ivoire a tour of *The Merciful*, the luxury yacht transformed into a war vessel. He introduced her to his pirate crew of marines and sailors.

Dinner was an Indian feast of chicken masala, basmati rice, and garlic nan bread. Over dinner, he shared his story and explained his mission of seeking out and destroying all the sex traffickers of the world.

"For years," explained Blau. "I had heard of the mysterious Hil'diya Anthemoessa and how it offered fantastical escapades with beautiful young women trained in the art of seduction. Then one day–" he was interrupted by a chime on his phone on the table. "No one has this number but my wife." He clicked ignore.

The phone rang again; he turned it over and saw the caller ID say, "Blau-Answer-Me."

"Who is this?" said Blau as he answered on speaker.

"I am a friend of Ivoire's," said Sofiy over the phone.

"Sofiy," said Ivoire. "How did you find me?"

"I have your voice pattern in my scanners now," said Sofiy.

"I am here, too," said Kalnya.

"I know that voice," said Blau. "You are my mysterious little friend."

"Hello, Blau," said Kalnya. "I hope you did not harm my old classmate."

"I am fine," said Ivoire.

"Well," said Blau. "I seem to be at a disadvantage here. I am the only one who does not know everyone's name."

"Our names are not important," said Kalnya. "We thank you, Blau. You have helped us avenge our friend's death."

"It was all in a day's work," said Blau. "Your final pieces of information led us right to the Guild's location."

"Ivoire," said Kalnya. "Did you learn anything?"

"Yes," said Ivoire. "Bianchi purchased a girl through a man named Andriy Bondarenko."

"That is what we found, too," said Sofiy. "He and Captain Bula were the ones who picked the girls from the guild to be sold and brokered the deals. Commandant Witko had found out, but instead of stopping it, enhanced it and profited from it."

"We must find these people," said Ivoire.

"Witko and Bula are dead," said Blau.

"How?" said Sofiy.

"Shall we say," smiled Blau. "Enhanced interrogations."

"I hope they suffered," said Kalnya.

"Your hopes are fulfilled," replied Blau.

"And Bondarenko?" asked Ivoire.

"We have him in custody," said Kalnya.

Realization suddenly hit Ivoire "So the training, The Guild, it was all a lie?"

"I do not believe so," said Blau. "We interrogated many staff members, including Bula and Witko already and learned much of The Guild. It was still a legitimate training facility for young spies. Even to this day, they kept the base curriculum. The Ukrainian government, like so many others in this damned world, soon became overrun with *Shedim*. These foul perverts want nothing more than pleasures of the flesh. A whole school full of beautiful girls, how could they not pervert it? They added seduction training and shared videos of the training to advertise."

"Oh god," said Ivoire. "They recorded me during the training. I was forced to watch it. They shared the videos with others?"

"I am afraid so," said Sofiy. "I have done what I can to scrub the databases. But videos may still exist."

"I want to thank you again, ladies," said Blau. "It took us years to get this far; you point us to a nest of traffickers. You all would make a fine addition to this crew."

"How much does it pay?" asked Kalnya

"More than a government agent earns," said Blau.

"I'll follow Kalnya," said Sofiy.

"What of you?" said Blau to Ivoire.

"Thank you, no," said Ivoire. "I think the best thing now is for me to return home. I need some time."

"Where is home?" asked Blau.

"A small town on the Ukrainian-Russian border," said Ivoire.

"It will be a while before we can take you," said Blau. "We have escaped to the safety of the Aegean Sea. We will be returning to the Black Sea and the Sea of Azov in a few weeks. Azov is near your home. Would you sail with us and enjoy the few luxurious areas of the ship until then? Besides, we could use your help."

"How can I help?" asked Ivoire.

"Many of the young girls we rescued only speak Ukrainian," said Blau. "We could use a translator. But more than that, they need a friendly face, someone who knows what they have gone through. A shoulder to cry on."

"Agreed," said Ivoire. "For the girls."

As promised, Ivoire helped Blau's crew with the girls they had rescued from the guild. They were cared for and entertained as best a pirate crew on a war vessel could. Simple games and sing-alongs usually.

Ivoire witnessed Blau's crew interrogate the remaining staff from The Guild. Any they discovered to be complicit were executed and dumped overboard. The few they deemed innocent were promised a return to their homes and asked to help with the rescued girls.

The Merciful returned to the Black Sea, and children were dropped off at ports. Those that knew how to contact their parents did after being dropped off. Those who they did not know how were handed off to a former staff member who took them to local authorities.

When they entered the Sea of Azov, of those pulled from The Guild, only five children, one staff member, and Ivoire remained. During the time spent on *The Merciful,* Ivoire grew in understanding and appreciation of Blau's mission. He demonstrated a way to help those who were helpless, even if his means were a little violent.

Blau's dingy escorted Blau, Ivoire, the last staff member, and the final five children to the port of Mariupol. Ivoire had been here on assignment once and knew her way home from here. She said her goodbyes to Blau and the children. Kalnya and Sofiy were present on the phone and also said farewell. Sofiy reminded Ivoire she would be watching and, if she ever needed help, just to call her name near any connected device.

Ivoire purchased a ticket on a rail to the station near her house and boarded when it arrived three hours later.

The train stopped at the familiar station where she found her father's car. She had been using it when she returned home, her escape from her profession. It started and hummed as it always did. Her father's care was evident in every rev of the engine. As she drove under the star-filled sky, her mind wandered. First to the sad and unexpected reunion with her friends, next to the charming Capitan Blau, then to closure on the Guild and that part of her life. As her mind reached peace, she thought back to the dream on the train. *Did my grandmother really speak to me? What do I do now? My time as a spy is over.*

It was near midnight when she crested the hill that led to her small town. The town was dark. Everyone was asleep. In the distance, she saw lights across the river; it *may just be a passing patrol,* she thought. She parked the car in front of her house and entered to settle in. The smells of her family welcomed her, and she locked the door. She was too tired to shower and lay down in her childhood bed, still dressed.

BOOM

An explosion rocked her house and pulled her from her short sleep. She was up and scrambling. Gunfire and screams filled the night. *I have to help my town.* She found her shoes and was at the window putting them on. She could see Russian soldiers across the street. They were firing not at her house but down the street. Someone was shooting back, and the five soldiers all dropped as bullets tore through their limbs.

Voices were yelling in English; she could not make it out.

A medic, escorted by another soldier, had started to tend to the ones shot. The escort aimed his rifle and his biceps erupted as he dropped his rifle.

They purposely are not killing them?

The tank fired a round. In the flash, Ivoire saw its target, a giant knight in full stride. He angled the bottom of his shield forward, and the round ricocheted up off the shield and exploded in the sky, casting a yellow-orange glow on the town. The force of the blast shattered her windows, leaving her ears ringing.

When she looked again, the knight was on the tank. He swiped his sword down onto the cannon. The sound was deafening, louder than the explosion. The cannon had been dented by the blow. He raised the sword, undamaged.

His weapon can cleave a tank?

A soldier in the tank opened the hatch and aimed a pistol at the knight. The knight grabbed the arm, yanked the man out, and flung him to the side, smashing into the wall of a house and falling limp. The hatch slammed shut. Bullets twanged against the knight's armor from unseen weapons.

"There is a demon in the tank!" yelled a female voice. She could not place the accent.

The knight thrust his sword into the tank, penetrating the steel, and a man inside screamed. The knight struck the hatch with his shield and wedged an opening. He then grasped the bent opening and stood pulling the hatch.

His strength is impossible!

The gunfire stopped as the sound of metal straining screeched out. The area was still and silent as the knight ripped apart the tank with his bare hands.

Ivoire remembered her dream. Her grandmother said, 'There are still knights and heroes... They come for you. They seek you. But so does the dragon."

Is the tank the dragon?

Ivoire refocused, and the knight reached into the tank and pulled out a soldier. He held the soldier in his outstretched arm and spoke to someone down the street. "Whose likeness and inscription is this?"

"That is a human!" yelled the female voice.

They seek humans?

The knight tossed the soldier aside when an arm wielding a pistol reached out and fired. The knight stepped on the arm, and the owner howled.

"That's the demon!" yelled a female voice.

A demon? It looks just like the others?

The knight pulled the soldier to his face. "Behold, I cast out demons and perform cures today and tomorrow..."

The Russian officer laughed and spat on the knight, "You tell your God that he tells beautiful lies." The soldier struck the knight with something metal that clanged against the armor

The knight punched the soldier, its appearance blurred and re-focused. Where there was a human, now, there was something else white-skinned and emaciated.

With a hiss, four other white figures closed on the knight, firing their weapons.

Before they reached the tank, each of their heads exploded as gunshots rang, and their bodies fell to the ground, black blood flowing from their wounds.

More screaming and vehicles leaving, then silence.

A man in a cowboy hat and duster, accompanied by a woman in a dark gown, walked to the tank.

The knight held the pale Russian soldier to the woman. "What are you here for?" she asked.

Ivoire called out. "I think he is here for me."

DEATH, LIFE, AND FACT

The Paladins stayed and helped repair Hannah's mission. Few words were spoken as work commenced. Sadness at the loss of a friend weighed on each of their hearts. People from the town helped as well, the people whose lives have been touched by the mission paid back in thanks the only way they could, with their hands. The mission now had new scars, bullet holes, and burns to commemorate the passing of Hannah and others who died in the attack.

They kept the new Paladin restrained and confined to a room that overlooked the repair efforts during this time. He refused to talk unless Roland was present, at which he would scream nasty and hate-filled words.

Once the mission was restored, the Paladins began the task of laying Hannah to rest. The viewing was held at dusk. They had placed her casket in an open field on the crest of a hill outside of town that overlooked the valley. A collection of mismatched chairs were placed in rows, viewing the open casket, which was next to the hole in the ground it would soon be placed in. The line of people waiting to pay their last respects wound down the hill back to the town and passed by Hannah's mission. The Paladins sat together in the front. Persephone next to Oliver. He comforted her as she cried through the celebration of Hannah's life.

When the hundreds of people had passed and said their goodbyes, Melissa stood next to Hannah.

"My grandmother died when I was eleven," stated Melissa. "She left a hole in my heart that was filled with regret and pain and anger at God." She paused and looked down at Hannah. "When I was thirteen, my parents and I came to Hannah's mission. That's when I first met Hannah. She was so full of love for all people. She reminded me so much of my grandmother. She hugged everyone, and she loved to cook and feed others. She was never shy to call you beautiful or handsome." She turned to the audience. "She filled that hole in my heart with love and purpose. She was more Christ-like than any person I have ever met. We must not linger on how she died. Our memory of her should be how, with every word, with every action, she lifted up her fellow man. She lived and loved unconditionally." She turned back to Hannah, kissed her hand, and placed it on Hannah's forehead. "Thank you, Hannah."

Rebekah, the sister who had taken over the mission in Hannah's place, rose from her seat and approached the casket. Rebekah was similar in age to Melissa. She was tall with long, full brown hair she had tied in four places as it ran down her back. She spoke in Italian to the audience as she fought back tears.

Lastly, it was Roland's turn. He rose from his chair and then kneeled at Hannah's coffin in silence for a moment. He then rose and turned to the audience; the trail of a single tear shimmered on his left cheek. "To everything, there is a season, and a time to every purpose under the heaven: A time to be born, and a time to die; a time to plant, and a time to pluck up that which is planted…" He paused and looked down the hill toward the mission. "A time to kill, and a time to heal; a time to break down, and a time to build up; A time to weep, and a time to laugh; a time to mourn, and a time to dance; A time to cast away stones, and a time to gather stones together; a time to embrace, and a time to refrain from embracing; A time to get, and a time to lose; a time to keep, and a time to cast away; A time to rend, and a time to sew; a time to keep silence, and a time to speak; A time to love, and a time to hate; a time of war, and a time of peace." He looked at his Fellow Paladins, and a smile crossed his face. "What profit hath he that worketh in that wherein he laboureth? I have seen the travail, which God hath given to the sons of men to be exercised in it. He hath made everything beautiful in his time: also he hath set the world in their heart so that no man can find out the work that God maketh from the beginning to the end. I know that there is no good in them, but for a man to rejoice, and to do good in his life. And also that every man should eat and drink and enjoy the good of all his labor; it is the gift of God. I know that whatsoever God doeth, it shall be forever: nothing can be put to it, nor anything taken from it: and God doeth it, that men should fear before him. That which hath been is now, and that which is to be hath already been; and God requireth that which is past." His gaze floated past the audience onto the horizon. "And moreover I saw under the sun the place of judgment, that wickedness was there; and the place of righteousness, that iniquity was there. I said in mine heart, God shall judge the righteous and the wicked: for there is a time there for every purpose and for every work. I said in mine heart concerning the estate of the sons of men, that God might manifest them, and that they might see that they themselves are beasts. For that which befalleth the sons of men befalleth beasts; even one thing befalleth them: as the one dieth, so dieth the other; yea, they have all one breath; so that a man hath no preeminence above a beast: for all is vanity." He looked down at the audience and gestured with open arms. "All go unto one place; all are of the dust, and all turn to dust again."

"Amen," answered the audience.

After the celebration of Hannah's life, the Paladins were gathered at the stream that cut the valley of Hannah's mission. A small crowd had gathered, and a familiar ritual unfolded.

Melissa and Roland, dressed in white robes, had waded out to waist-deep water. On the shore, Oliver, Persephone, and Rebekah, each holding a lit candle, stood with Ivoire, who also wore a white robe.

"Ivoire," said Melissa. "Please come forward and join Roland and I."

Ivoire stepped into the water and waded out to meet Melissa and Roland.

Melissa addressed the crowd, "Recently, Ivoire approached me and shared with me the foundation of her faith. Her grandmother and father loved her and raised her in God's word. It was a loving time, and she knew no hunger, pain, or sadness. Then, her father and grandmother left her at an early age, and she had doubts about God's love. She said that since then, her life has been full of hundreds of reasons why she should not believe in God. What she had seen, and worse, what she had been forced to do, only added to the doubt of a benevolent deity forming her by hand. But something pulled at her. At first, she thought it was simple morality, knowing right from wrong. Over time, she came to realize that the world is not separated by right from wrong, but by good and evil." Melissa focused her gaze on her fellow Paladins. "After talking to each of us and now in light of what has occurred, she came to me and asked, well," she greeted Ivoire as she finally made it out to her and Roland. "What did you ask?"

Ivoire said, "I want what you have. I want the same feelings I had when I was a girl with my father and grandmother."

"And what did I say?" asked Melissa.

"You said," Ivoire wiped a tear from her eye. "The love you all have for each other is not of this world, but from Jesus and his promise of eternal life." Her voice hesitated with sadness. "My father used to say that to me. I knew then that I was a sinner, but forgiveness was possible."

Melissa pulled Ivoire into a hug. "and now, we are here to celebrate her return to the family of Christ in the same way Christ has demonstrated for us."

Rebekah called out, "Ivoire Kravets, do you renounce Satan and all his ways?"

"I do," replied Ivoire.

Persephone called out, "Ivoire Kravets, do you reject the ways of the world?"

"I do," replied Ivoire.

Book of Ivon and Ivoire

Oliver called out, "Ivoire Kravets, do you accept the sacrifice of Jesus Christ openly?"

"I do," replied Ivoire.

Melissa called out, "Ivoire Kravets, who is your one true savior?"

"Jesus Christ," replied Ivoire.

Roland took Ivoire, placing a hand on the back of her head and one on her chest. He submerged her in the water and spoke, "I baptize you with water for repentance, but the one who comes after me is more powerful than I am, whose sandals I am not worthy to carry." He took her out of the water, let her catch her breath, and submerged her again, "He will baptize you with the Holy Spirit and fire. His winnowing shovel is in his hand, and he will clean out his threshing floor and will gather his wheat into the storehouse, but he will burn up the chaff with unquenchable fire." He took her out of the water again and, after a moment, placed her in again, "Therefore, go and make disciples of all the nations, baptizing them in the name of the Father and of the Son and of the Holy Spirit." He released her from his grip, and she sprang from the water.

Melissa hugged her as those gathered cheered.

That night, a great feast was held; they celebrated the life of Hannah and the new life of Ivoire. People from the mission and surrounding areas all joined in. It was a sight as Jesus once described heaven; friends and family sharing in God's love.

The next morning, the Paladins said their farewells and returned to headquarters with the new Paladin. He had not spoken, only glowered at Roland. He had watched the baptism from the room he was held in. He was even in attendance at the celebratory feast, and food was offered to him, but he refused it.

Back at headquarters, they had secured him in room seven of the sleeping quarters. He was not bound, and food was offered. He continued to refuse to eat any food.

Oliver, Melissa, Ivoire, Persephone, and Roland were gathered in the research room.

267

"Has a Paladin been hostile like this before?" asked Ivoire.

"Yes," said Melissa. "Not all are from loving backgrounds. I imagine the same can be said for him."

"So what do we do?" asked Oliver.

"I have an Idea," offered Ivoire. "Let him out of his room and let Roland and I show him around, freely without bonds. I want him to formally meet each of you as I have. I do not think he speaks any language but Russian, so I can translate. If he tries anything, Roland can contain him."

"Yes," said Persephone. "Let's show him love."

"I agree," said Melissa.

Roland and Ivoire went to the new Paladin's room while Melissa, Oliver, and Persephone took their places around the facilities.

Ivoire pushed the button, and the door to room seven opened.

"Hello," she said in Russian. "My name is Ivoire. What is yours?"

The man rose and ran at Ivoire, he was stopped by the massive grip of Roland. The man pounded on the arm and tried to free himself.

"Please," said Ivoire. "This is Roland. He is far too strong to be injured by mere fists."

The man pounded a few more times, then stopped. Roland set him down.

"We mean you no ill will," said Ivoire. "Please, what is your name?"

"That man is a Мудак," said the man. "He does not deserve my name."

"Who is?" said Ivoire. "Roland?"

"Yes," said the man. "He and any of his friends are Мудак."

"Why do you say this?" asked Ivoire.

The man looked away.

"It's ok," said Ivoire. "Would you like to walk around and get out of the cramped room?" She stepped aside and opened a way for him.

He stepped through cautiously and stopped when face to face with Roland. The man was nearly a foot shorter than Roland and easily less than half his weight. He did not look afraid, only angry.

"Before we begin," said Ivoire. "Would you care for a shower and some fresh clothes?"

The man looked at Roland and then down at himself and nodded. He was shown to the showers and given fresh, clean clothes - a simple work jumpsuit and boots. Isaac took his old clothes and mumbled something akin to "... the washer or the incinerator..." as he walked away.

Their first stop was the cafeteria, where a selection of fruits, meats, and cheese was made available. The man gathered a handful of sliced meat and a bottle of water. They then continued to the Library, where Melissa waited.

"Hello," said Melissa as Ivoire translated. "My name is Melissa and I welcome you to the headquarters of the Paladins."

Melissa guided the man through the known history of the Paladins, starting with the fall of Satan. The man mindfully ate his meat and drank his water. He did not interrupt and only occasionally glared at Roland.

From the library, the group went outdoors to meet Oliver at the shooting range in the outdoor area. He had set the simulation to a bright afternoon overlooking a loch in Ireland.

"Hello, sir," said Oliver as Ivoire translated. "My name is Oliver, my Archangel is Michael, and I am from America. What is your name?" Oliver offered a friendly handshake.

The man looked at it and then at Oliver's guns.

"Interested in these?" said Oliver as he motioned to his revolvers.

The man spoke in Russian.

"He says," said Ivoire. "The weapons that killed my friends. I want to use them to kill all of you."

"Not a great start," said Oliver. "Does he know his friends are demons?"

Ivoire spoke to him, and he replied.

"He says," said Ivoire. "They were humans who had been altered by science."

"Interesting," said Melissa. "Let's take him to Persephone. I want her perspective on this."

"So, no demonstration?" asked Oliver.

"He has seen enough of your shooting, I think," said Ivoire.

They escorted the man to Persephone's research room. She waited inside with Father Conte.

"So this is the new Paladin," said Conte. "I would love to hear all about him."

"He has not said much," said Melissa. "Only that the demons are his friends, and he wants to kill all of us."

"And he thinks Roland and all of his friends are Мудак," added Ivoire.

"What does that mean?" asked Conte.

"Basically 'shithead,'" said Ivoire.

"How crude," said Conte. "What is his name?"

"I think it is Ivon," said Melissa.

The man shot a stare at Melissa.

"I guessed correctly," said Melissa.

"How did you come to this?" asked Ivoire.

"For starters, the demon in the carnival said his name tied with yours, Ivoire," said Melissa. "Secondly, the demon said Ivon was out to get you, and this man attacked us at Hannah's mission. Thirdly, Ivon is the most common Russian name, so we had those odds. Lastly, Ivon is a Paladin name… so I took a chance."

Ivoire spoke to the man, and he replied.

"That is his name," said Ivoire.

"Hello, Ivon," said Persephone as she ran over and hugged him.

It was a tense moment; Roland and Oliver were both poised for violence. Ivoire held her breath. Melissa smiled. Ivon did not return the hug but did not push the tiny girl away.

After a moment, she released and said in Russian, "Добро пожаловать в семью."

"Close," said Ivoire, who repeated what Persephone said and accented the nouns a little softer. She turned to Melissa and Oliver. "Persephone learned to say, 'welcome to the family' in Russian."

The group then talked through each of their unique abilities and asked Ivon about his. He refused to answer. After learning of the unique powers of each Paladin they took Ivon back to the kitchen where Isaac had prepared an Indian meal of butter chicken, garlic naan bread, basmati rice, and tamarind drink.

Each Paladin, Isaac, and Father Conte took a hand of another around the table. Ivon sat between Ivoire and Roland, who each took a hand of his gently as Oliver offered a pre-meal prayer.

> *Bless us, O God, as we sit together,*
> *Bless the food we eat today,*
> *Bless the hands that made the food,*
> *Bless us, O God. Amen.*

"Amen," replied the group, except for Ivon and Ivoire. They sat, still hand in hand, with blank stares.

"Ivoire," said Persephone. "Are you alright?"

"Yes," said Ivoire and Ivon in unison, their voices steady and toneless.

"What is happening?" asked Oliver.

"This is our gift," they said. A pained look crossed their faces. "When we make contact, our gifts from God amplify, and we can move past truth and lies into fact."

"They look to be in pain," said Melissa. "Does it hurt?"

"Yes," they said. "The more impactful of the fact we reveal, the more it injures us."

"Separate them," said Melissa.

Roland reached over and pulled their hands apart. They both collapsed.

Ivoire woke first. The Paladins had moved her and Ivon to the medical bay. They were in beds on monitors. Oliver, Roland, Melissa, Persephone, and Conte were all present as Issac cared for Ivon and Ivoire.

"Take it easy," said Isaac as he was checking her blood pressure. "You were unconscious for three hours."

"I feel fine," she said. "I remember what happened, too. Ivon and I held hands, and the world around us softened and grew distant. It was peaceful."

"You appeared to be in a trance to us," said Melissa. "You did respond to questions, though; you two even spoke Spanish."

"I heard English," said Oliver.

"Me too," said Persephone.

"I heard them speak Italian," said Conte.

"When they heard this sound, a crowd came together in bewilderment because each one heard their own language being spoken," added Roland.

"The answers flowed from us," Ivoire said. "We had no control over it. I was aware of the questions and compelled to answer them. I knew it was hurting my body, but I did not feel any pain."

Ivon groaned.

"Hello, brother," said Ivoire.

"Brother?" asked Oliver.

"When we were holding hands," said Ivoire. "We could see each other's life laid before us, like a line of statues in a garden. We walked through the garden and shared each other's story."

Ivon spoke, and Ivoire translated, "twins, in fact."

"Incredible," said Conte.

"I am not sure of the extent of the damage," said Issac. "Your symptoms are comparable to a mild concussion."

"This is a powerful tool," said Ivoire. "Unlimited knowledge."

"You also said it injured you," said Melissa. "And the more impactful the fact, the more damage you receive. I advise against using it again."

"I feel fine now; besides, we could learn so much," said Ivoire. "About Garmr, about the plans the demons have."

Ivon spoke for some time before he stopped, and Ivoire translated, "He has been part of ceremonies where his blood is used to raise dead bodies. The ceremony that you," she gestured to Roland, "and you," she gestured to Oliver, "interrupted and killed the pig demon. That was his friend, Dimitri. That was one such ceremony."

"Does he know his friend was a demon?" asked Oliver.

"He does now," said Ivoire. "When we touched, we were able to move beyond communication and know each other deeply. For you, it may have been hours; for us, it felt like days." She turned to Ivon and spoke in Russian. They went back and forth when Ivoire stood up and moved to his bed.

"Don't touch him," said Persephone.

"It's ok," said Ivoire. "He had been sending liters of his blood to his master, Colonel Petrov, for months. The ceremony only needs a few drops. They may have thousands of reanimated soldiers."

"Does he know more?" asked Melissa.

"No," said Ivoire. "Petrov never let him in on anything. But he wants to try the trance again and see if we can find the answer."

"I am not sure," said Melissa.

"I am with Melissa," said Oliver. "We can find Petrov with other means, let's not risk any more brain damage."

"Just three or four questions should be fine," said Ivoire. "We may not have much time. Petrov must know by now that Ivon has failed."

"What do you think, Roland?" asked Oliver.

"Trust in the Lord with all your heart, and do not lean on your own understanding," replied Roland.

"I agree with Roland," said Persephone. "This is God's gift. We must use it to do his will."

"Just three questions," said Melissa. "Then we pull you apart."

"Agreed," said Ivoire.

Roland and Oliver moved her bed next to Ivon's, and Ivoire laid down.

Ivoire looked at Ivon and offered her hand and spoke in Russian. He replied with a soft smile and took her hand. They went stiff, and their eyes glazed.

"What is Colonel Petrov's plan?" asked Melissa, getting right to the point.

Ivon and Ivoire spoke in unison, "he has raised an army of nearly a hundred thousand strong. He plans on starting his own country."

"Where is he and this army now?" asked Melissa.

"He is in Brazil with his army," the twins spoke in unison, agony pulling at their faces.

"Last question," said Persephone.

"What is his next move?" asked Melissa.

"He is going to unleash his army on the World Cup match between Brazil and Croatia and raise the thousands killed there to double the size of his army."

"Enough," said Melissa. "Separate them."

Roland reached down, but before he could separate them, Conte yelled, "Is there a God?"

Ivoire and Ivon arched as their bodies twisted in painful angles, the lights of the building flickered, and their heart monitors raced. Roland tried to pull apart their hands, but even his titanic strength could not separate them. They moaned in ultimate agony, blood streaming from their noses, ears, mouths, and eyes, and yelled a final word before collapsing.

"Yes."

THREE ENTER, FOUR LEAVE

It was the dark hours before dawn as Captain Kravets walked the path between his men's tents. The surrounding jungle was quiet. They had seen heavy conflict the last three weeks, and today was the first day after a quiet night since he arrived.

He was the commander of a motor division of the Soviet army. His men were conscripts from his homeland, the Ukrainian Soviet Socialist Republic. They were a proud and rambunctious group he took great pride in leading. He had seen combat on three continents and was now back in Africa helping defend the Republic of Cameroon from a warlord who had built an army in the Central African Republic. He didn't even know the warlord's name and didn't care to learn it. It seemed every month, a new warlord would rise and get put down. This warlord was driven out of the Central African Republic and now retreated west through the small Cameroonian towns.

The Russian Army had scored a major victory, with help from an artillery division, and bought some rest as the warlord's army regrouped from the barrage in the dense forest miles to the East.

Capitan Kravets loved the hour before sunrise. The Earth felt still, quiet, and empty. The stars showed brighter, especially on a night like tonight when the moon was new. He walked with no purpose other than to be present for any of his men who woke early. None had. He smiled at their earned rest and turned down a lane to head to the medical tent. He had hoped that the French field nurse, Delphine, was up and attending to the wounded.

The French had sent a support medical detachment at the request of the Cameroon government. They brought with them field doctors, medical supplies, and Delphine.

As he walked, Captain Kravets recalled the first time he ever laid eyes on Delphine. He had brought in one of his corporals who broke his ankle when a vehicle he had been working on fell off the lift. The corporal was fine and in good spirits. Capitan Kravets had just finished scolding him on safety and precautions when down the row, between the beds, Delphine approached. He first noticed her hair, long golden blonde hair she had secured in a tight ponytail. He had never seen hair that color before. He thought it was like the brightest part of a candle's flame turned to oil and painted across strands of flax.

"What happened here?" she asked in her heavy French accent.

"Truck fell on my foot," said the corporal.

"Lucky for you, we no longer cut hurt feet off," laughed Delphine. She checked his blood pressure, pulse, and temperature and asked him his height and weight. She handed him two pills. "Take these."

She kneeled next to the bed and examined the swollen foot. "His tibia and fibula are both broken. We will need an x-ray to be sure. But he will be in a cast for six months or so." She looked down the row of beds. "Orderly, need x-rays on an ankle. Can you move him?"

"Sure thing," called back someone.

Delphine turned to Captain Kravets. "Are you his commanding officer?"

Kravets stared at her, transfixed.

"Captain?" she said, then waved. "Are you ok?"

Kravets shook his head, "Yes. Sorry. You were saying you need to cut off his foot?"

Delphine laughed, "No, we can save the foot. I just need you to sign off as his commanding officer." She handed him a clipboard.

Kravets looked at the papers. His body seemed unable to respond.

She leaned close and pointed. "Just sign here."

He could smell her: lilacs and lavender. He scribbled on the line, and she grabbed the clipboard.

"Thank you," she said. "You can leave him with us. We will have your corporal back under trucks in no time."

She whirled away and headed back down the aisle, her hair flowing in her wake.

He was in love from day one.

Beyond her beauty, he was impressed by how nothing phased her. Her face carried a permanent smile, and she beamed in caring for those she mended. She never grew angry, surprised, or shocked. Each time he brought in a gushing wound, it was just another day at work for her. Other doctors and nurses barked orders and panicked around the tent. She was an obelisk in the tempest—a granite fixture unmoved by the emotions around her.

For the last two months, he found reasons to visit her daily. He memorized her schedule's pattern and built his days around planning a visit to the medical tent.

Today, he had no crew in the tent that he had not already visited. Today, he had another purpose. He was going to ask Delphine on a date.

He pressed past the flap of the tent and immediately spotted Delphine. She was seated at the triage table, reading. As he approached, he noticed her book was a Bible.

"The fruit of the righteous is a tree of life, and he who wins souls is wise," he said.

She looked up. "Proverbs 11:30. Have you studied the Bible, Captain?"

"Yes." His heart raced. "Are you a Christian?" The question hung in the air. He had prayed to meet another believer. The moment stretched out.

"Yes," she smiled. "My family has attended the same church for generations."

"Me too," he said as he finally started to breathe again.

After an uncomfortable silence, Delphine spoke, "So, where are we going tonight?"

Their first date went as well as their first encounter. Captain Kravets was a quiet man under normal conditions. Delphine intimidated him. He found it hard to breathe around her. There were not many options for a date on the edge of a warzone. He had his Sergeant drive them an hour into town to the nearest restaurant, a simple local place offering Cameroonian cuisine. Delphine did most of the talking; Captain Kravets listened and smiled. He could listen to her talk for the rest of his life.

Three months later, his unit was disbanded as Ukraine ramped up their war for independence. Two months later, they married on the banks of Lake Doubs near her hometown of Le Vézenay near the French and Swiss border. They honeymooned there in a cabin overlooking the lake.

Two months later, they receive more news. Almost nine months later, to the day of the wedding, was Delphine's due date. As Delphine was an only child and her parents were long dead, they had decided to move to Ivon's hometown to be near his family. Namely his mother. She was a retired nursemaid, and they both wanted a home birth, so it all seemed planned by God.

They each had grown in their faith since meeting. They felt as if they completed each other and fulfilled God's plan for them.

Ivon had teased that he knew Delphine would bear him a boy, and his name would be Ivon like his and his father's before him. Delphine teased and said it was a girl, as her family always had girls, but he could name her Ivoire.

Book of Ivon and Ivoire

Two weeks prior to the due date, the war for Ukrainian independence was in full swing and approaching their town. They were loading the car to flee when Delphine's water broke.

8/23/1991 11:50 pm local time.

"Push!" screamed Ivon's mother.
"Gahh!" replied Delphine.
Ivon's mother popped her head from behind Delphine's open legs. "Here comes the child; the head has crowned. You are doing wonderful."
"Come on dear, push," coached Ivon as he held Delphine's hand.
An explosion sounded outside, and Ivon ran to the window. He could see the lights from gunfire cresting the hill and approaching their town.
Delphine screamed in agony as the child fell into the nursemaid's hands. The nursemaid quickly tied the umbilical cord, cleaned the crying child, and wrapped him in a towel. "It's a boy," she said with joy.
Delphine gasped for breath.
The nursemaid handed the boy to his father.
"I am a father," said Ivon. "His name shall be Ivon, and he shall carry on my name."
"How far away is the fighting?" asked Ivon's mother.
"Too close." He looked at his wife. "Once she is able, we must go."
"I am still having contractions," yelled Delphine in pain.
"It is not uncommon to have a few after the birth," explained Ivon's mother as she wiped her hands with a towel.
"No!" She lifted herself on her hands. "They are getting stronger!"
Ivon's mother moved back between Delphine's legs. "Oh my, it is going to be twins!"
Delphine screamed again. "Something feels wrong."

Ivon's mother felt Delphine's belly and listened for a moment. "The second child has not turned, and her body is pushing it out; we risk losing the child; I must cut her open."

"Here, in our bedroom?" Ivon Sr. yelled.

"Yes," answered his mother sternly. "if we do nothing, the child will likely die, and your wife too."

Ivon closed his eyes and shook his head. "Fine, please save them both."

Ivon's mother pulled her leather medicine bag over and laid out the tools.

"There is no time to sedate your wife; this is going to hurt a lot." She grabbed a scalpel and looked up at Delphine, "Are you ready?"

Delphine nodded her head, the sweat dripping down her face.

8/24/1991 12:07 am local time.

Ivon's mother handed the second twin, a girl, to the now-widowed father. They did not exchange words. She suffered in her shame of not foreseeing a twin birth and from losing her daughter-in-law. Ivon was awash in grief; his best friend, his lover, and his wife had died. He was not prepared for this. Ivon looked down at the two babies in his arms.

"Ivon and Ivoire," he said quietly to them and pulled them close.

BOOM

The wall of the house was blasted open. The fighting had reached the town.

"Mother," he yelled, "get to the car."

He carried his children out the door. He stopped and looked back at his wife's body. *I'll come back for you. I promise.*

He ran outside; his car was the source of the explosion that tore apart his house. He had to run.

"Mother," he yelled. "Can you run?"

Book of Ivon and Ivoire

"Yes," she called after. "Don't wait for me. Protect the children."

He was in a full sprint, away from the hill and towards the woods. An explosion detonated to his right, and he was thrown to his left. One of the children was knocked from his hands. He was down, and a piece of shrapnel is embedded into his arm. His ears ring, and he was up, searching for the missing child. He was frantic. The child is nowhere to be seen.

"Oh God!" he yelled. "Help me find my child."

He saw soldiers approaching, and they open fire. He covered the child still in his arms and is off running again into the safety of the woods. He ran until his legs are numb. His body was cold from loss of blood. He tripped on a trunk and tumbles, blackness.

He was awoken by his mother. He was unsure how long he had been out. He can hear a baby crying.

"I have the child," said his mother. "Can you move?"

He stood up, "yes."

They continued through the forest through the night. They reach the next town at daybreak and took shelter in the church.

Ivon collapsed again. He had lost his wife and a child this night.

Junior Sergeant Belikov got out of his vehicle and chased the man he saw leave a house. He yelled for him to stop as a tank round exploded next to the man, sending him flying. To his surprise, the man was up quickly. He was looking for something. Belikov fired his rifle at the ground, and the man turned and ran off to the forest. He headed back to his vehicle to check in when he heard a sound. He followed the sound to find an infant, freshly born, still red and wet, crying. His commanding officer approached.

"What do you have there, Junior Sergeant Belikov?" the Lieutenant asked.

"An infant, sir," answered Belikov. "Looks like he was born today."

"Well," said the Lieutenant. "Put it out of its misery, and let's get on."

"Sir?" replied Belikov.

"Do I need to write it down?" asked the Lieutenant. "Kill it."

"I can't do that," said Belikov.

"Fine," said the Lieutenant as he drew his gun.

"I won't let you kill a baby," said Belikov as he shielded the baby with his body.

"Out of the way," said the Lieutenant as he aimed his gun at Belikov. "Or I shoot through you."

"What is this?" screamed a new voice, Colonel Gromov. "Lieutenant Petrov. Put away your gun."

"Yes sir," said Petrov and holstered his weapon.

"Junior Sergeant Belikov," said Colonel Gromov. "What have you got there?"

"A baby, sir," said Belikov.

"Well," said Gromov. "Take it to the medical tent. They can put it with the others."

"Yes sir," saluted Belikov. He ran past Petrov. He never liked Petrov. He was *smarmy,* and his pointy nose made him look more goblin than human.

THE PLANS I HAVE FOR THEE

"What was that?" asked Oliver.

"I'm sorry," said Conte. "I could not resist."

Oliver, Roland, Persephone, and Conte were in the library at Paladin headquarters.

"They said 'the more impactful the fact, the more it injured them,'" said Persephone. "And you ask the mother of all questions."

"I am truly sorry," said Conte. "Please. I meant no harm."

Roland stood and faced Conte. "Let all bitterness and wrath and anger and clamor and slander be put away from you, with all malice, and be kind to one another, tenderhearted, forgiving one another, as God in Christ forgave you." He picked Conte up in a mighty hug.

Melissa walked in. "They are in a coma. Their vitals are normal except for their brain patterns."

"Are they brain dead?" asked Oliver, who looked at Conte.

"No," said Melissa. "There is activity. But it is not like any we can decipher. It does not match dreams, comas, or anything else. They are stable, but we need an actual doctor. This is beyond Isaac and I."

"If they are stable, we will have to search for a doctor later," said Conte.

"Why?" asked Oliver.

"The Brazil-Croatia World Cup match is in two days," Conte explained.

"Are you sure?" asked Persephone.

"Yes," said Conte. "I am a big fan of football; I follow Italy. The Brazil-Croatia match is the first of the cup."

"Too late to get tickets, I wager," said Oliver.

"Oh yes," said Conte.

"We have no choice," said Melissa. "Oliver, Roland, and I have to go. Persephone, you stay here and help Isaac with Ivon and Ivoire. We will need your support as well."

"Yes, ma'am," said Persephone. "I'll start pulling all I can on the arena."

Melissa, Oliver, and Roland were airborne that night. Oliver had packed every bullet he could carry, two hundred and fifty-six. Sixteen reloads. It made his belt and pack heavy. He wished he could carry more; the army being one hundred thousand strong drove a fear into him unlike any before.

Roland walked down the aisle of the jet and sat next to Oliver. "God is our refuge and strength, a very present help in trouble."

"You're right, Roland," smiled Oliver. "Besides. I'll kill three hundred or so, and you can take the nine-hundred-ninety-nine-thousand-seven-hundred that I can't."

Roland looked at Oliver with a serious face, "And Asa cried out to the LORD his God, and said, 'LORD, it is nothing for You to help, whether with many or with those who have no power; help us."

"Thanks, Roland," said Oliver. "Will you pray with me?"

"May I join?" asked Melissa, who had snuck in behind Oliver once again.

"Please," said Oliver.

They joined hands, and Oliver prayed.

Dear Father
Guide our hands, hearts, and eyes as we go forth in your name

Book of Ivon and Ivoire

Give us strength to push back those who would harm your people
Carry us through the battle and lead us into victory
Divine is your name
Amen

They landed at Sao Paulo Campo De Marte Airport and exited to the hot Brazil afternoon. It was the day of the match, and the charter airport was busy with jets flying in for the festivities. Their local contact was Father Fermino; he ran a church on the outskirts of town, had a vehicle, and knew the area around the arena. They walked down the steps of the plane and Father Fermino was nowhere to be found. A vehicle backfired, and a rusty white van screeched to a stop before them.

The driver, a young woman, yelled out the window, "Você é Melissa."

"Sim," replied Melissa. "Onde está o Padre Fermino."

"Ele está doente," she replied. "Eu sou a sobrinha dele, Elissa."

"This is Elissa," Melissa said to Oliver. "Father Fermino is sick." She called back to Elissa, "Você pode nos levar para a Arena de São Paulo?"

"Sim," Elissa replied.

"Let's load up," said Oliver.

"You understood that?" asked Melissa.

"Just the 'sim,'" Oliver smiled.

Elissa drove them through the busy traffic; she honked and shouted at the other cars. To Oliver, it seemed there were no traffic rules to follow, only pavement to claim. As the arena came into view, the traffic came to a standstill. Cars, motorcycles, bikes, and pedestrians, all in their team's colors, made their way to the festivities around the arena.

After an hour and only moving a block, Melissa said, "It may be faster to walk?"

"I say hoof it," said Oliver.

"But I say, walk," added Roland.

"Obrigado, Elissa," said Melissa. "Nós vamos sair daqui."

"Você vai sair daqui?" said Elissa. "Tudo bem, vinte dólares."

"'Dolares?'" said Oliver. "She wants money?"

"It's fine," said Melissa and handed Elissa a twenty. "Obrigada."

They exited the vehicle, gear in hand, and followed Roland as he swayed through the crowd. The crowds grew denser as they neared the arena. Vendors shouted and hocked their wares. People cheered and celebrated. The arena was massive, more coliseum then stadium. Persephone had told them that it could hold nearly seventy thousand spectators.

Melissa pulled Oliver close as they walked so he could hear. "There are a few demons in the crowd."

"Any sense on where Petrov or his army is?" asked Oliver.

"Nothing that strong," said Melissa. "I say we get to the arena. We only have two hours until the match starts."

"Lots of people in costume," observed Oliver. "You think anyone will pay Roland a second glance if he gets changed?"

They walked down an alley and found some space for Roland to don his armor.

Roland set his case behind some crates, pressed a button on the side, and stepped back. The case split down the middle and expanded out, presenting his armor.

Three men who were walking down the alley came over, "O que você está vendendo?"

"Não vendendo," said Melissa. "Vestindo uma fantasia."

"Ah, uma fantasia." said one of the men. "Mostre-nos."

Roland strapped on his boots in front of the portable armor rack. His eyes were closed as he grabbed each piece and attached it to his body with practiced and graceful movements. He had his gloves, girdle, and breastplate on in a matter of seconds. He reached for his helmet and spoke.

"The Lord shall cause thine enemies that rise up against thee"—He placed the helmet on his head and lifted his shield—"to be smitten before thy face: they shall come out against thee one way"—He reached for the sword, tested its weight in his hands, and rose to his feet—"and flee before thee seven ways."

When Roland rose, the three men applauded. "Lindo. Onde foi feito?

Roland answered, "Sabei que o Senhor é Deus! Foi ele quem nos fez, e somos dele; somos o seu povo e ovelhas do seu pasto."

The three men cheered and continued their drunken walk through the alley.

The Paladins made their way back into the crowd and pushed through towards the arena. From the arena, a great cheer erupted. Music flowed out.

"Has the game started?" asked Oliver

"The opening ceremonies," said Melissa. "Petrov can move anytime."

When they were a block away, Melissa stopped them. "I am getting a strong demon essence from this building." She pointed to a warehouse down an alley off the main road.

As they walked down the alley, the crowd grew thin. A semi-truck trailer was backed into a loading bay. As they approached, the world seemed to grow quiet. The noise of the crowds faded.

Oliver felt a chill run down his spine, "I feel it, too."

Roland was in full stride and hammered the door next to the bay with his shield. The wooden door tore open like paper, and Roland was through.

Oliver and Melissa followed. Inside was quiet.

A man came running out and yelled in Russian.

"Demon," said Melissa.

Roland stepped forward and lifted the man, "Where is he?"

The demon in a man's form smirked and said, "he who?"

Roland slammed him against the truck, "Satan might not outwit us. For we are not unaware of his schemes."

Upon impact, the demon's form shifted from a man to a pale, sickly creature. From inside the truck, a moaning seeped out. First, it was small, and then it grew as more joined the call.

Oliver walked to the rear, "Should we open it?"

Roland carried the demon around to the back, grasped the lock, and crushed it in his free hand. He dropped the pieces of metal and looked over his shoulder at Oliver.

Oliver drew his weapons and nodded.

Roland pulled the lever and swung the doors wide.

Bodies poured out. Moaning, clawing, climbing over each other. The trailer was full, top to bottom, front to back.

"Ghouls," gasped Melissa.

Roland threw the demon aside and drew his sword; he cleaved into the throng and tunneled into the trailer. Tearing, slicing, slamming, and crushing the ghoul bodies. The trailer rocked with the force of each blow.

Oliver held the demon at gunpoint with one revolver and picked off any stragglers that escaped Roland's fury with the other.

When the last ghoul was slain, Roland walked off the back of the truck, squishing into a pile of body parts; a river of black blood and viscera flowed from the trailer.

"Are there more of these trucks?" asked Oliver to the demon.

"Yes," smiled the demon. "Dozens. This is the last. You are too late."

"Where did they take them?" asked Oliver.

"I'll never tell," the demon laughed.

"Just kill it," said Melissa. "We know they are going to the arena. We waste time here."

Oliver pulled his knife from his boot and stabbed the demon in the side of the skull; he wiped the black blood off on the creature's overalls. "Any more demons here?"

"No," said Melissa. "Look at the bodies. They are in uniform."

Roland kicked one over, face up.

"Chinese Army," said Melissa.

"Petrov plans on framing the Chinese for this," said Oliver. "This is his plan: raise a mercenary army he controls and can grow with each battle, then kick off a war."

"Persephone," said Melissa over the comms.

"Go for Persephone," she replied.

"You have the stadium schematics?" asked Melissa.

"Yes," Persephone said. "What do you need?"

"Are there delivery areas that could handle semi-trucks?"

"Yup," she snapped. "Far east side, twenty bays for delivery trucks."

As they exited the warehouse, the cheers from the stadium slowly changed from cheers of excitement and joy to screams of horror and pain.

"Nevermind," said Melissa. "It has started."

Roland tore off through the crowds, barreling down all in his path. There was no time for tenderness; the few he trampled, and the small injuries he caused were a fair trade as the thousands in the area were now facing slaughter.

Oliver and Melissa followed in his wake. "Desculpe!" she yelled, and "Fugir!" she warned.

They had reached the arena, and Roland barreled through the gates and metal detectors. People dove away as he continued to push through. He had demons to slay and innocents to save. Oliver and Melissa steered through the path he hewed. From ahead, a wave of people flooded out to escape from the massacre within. Roland's pace was slowed as he pushed through the crowd. They worked up the ramp and found the clearing. Before them was pandemonium. Ghouls in Chinese uniform, thousands of them tore into the crowds. Blood and bodies littered the stands.

Roland bellowed, amplified by the electronics in his helmet, "Do not think that I have come to bring peace to the earth; I have not come to bring peace but a sword." He leaped into a nearby group of ghouls and tore into them.

Oliver calmed his heart and recited Gerin's Prayer.

Lord, make me swift and true
Guide my hands with yours
Let your will be my aim

    The world slowed around him, and he took aim. His priority was to save. He picked off the heads of ghouls, splattering black blood. He swirled and sought, looking for those in imminent danger. He loaded the scatter ammo Persephone had made and fired into crowds of ghouls—clouds of black blood puffed from eviscerated heads.

    Melissa stayed by Oliver and read from her Bible, praying for protection and help for those still in peril.

    Roland cleaved through the crowds, moving from group to group. The numbers of the ghouls seemed endless.

    Over the loudspeaker, a voice echoed across the stadium. "It seems Ivon has failed, and the Paladins are now here. Kill them! Kill the knight, the cowboy, and the nun."

    More ghouls flowed from the entrances—thousands upon thousands.

    "Roland," said Oliver over the comms. "Drive them down to the field away from the people."

    The whirlwind of violence that was Roland shifted direction and cut down to the field. The ghouls focused on him and moved down to meet him. A black trail of innards and outtards was left in his path.

    "That's it," said Oliver, who fired at ghouls in the upper rows. "Let's lead them down to the blender."

    "Sidorov," said the voice over the public announcement. "Move in, now!"

    From the home entrance, a short but broad woman with close-cropped hair stepped out. She lowered her head, and then she swelled, stretching her uniform; it filled and then burst as she expanded into a demonic shape. Twenty feet tall with a bull's legs and a lion's head. Its yellow skin covered in sparse fur of a darker yellow. It roared in challenge.

Oliver opened fire on it. The rounds found a home, and small streaks of blood formed on the yellow skin.

Roland had closed the distance and leaped, sword aimed forward. He handed on the creature's chest, his massive frame minuscule against the demon.

The demon batted Roland off, and he flew across the field, where he landed hard and splayed onto the grass.

From the visiting team entrance, dozens of figures ran out, weapons in hand. More demons like the ones from Hannah's mission, grotesque abominations of animals armed with guns. They fired at Oliver and Mellissa, who dove behind a short wall. More ghouls rushed down from all directions and swarmed Roland. He bashed at them with his shield, feet, and hands. The piles of bodies around him grew, slowing his steps as his footing became unstable.

Oliver fired back at the animal demons with his explosive rounds. Six fell dead. The rest focused on him and Melissa and laid down a blanket of bullets, suppressing them.

Roland was trudging through the piles of bodies, moving towards the demon unarmed as his sword remained wedged in the creature's chest.

"Can you take out the gunners?" asked Oliver.

"I waited patiently for the Lord to help me," said Roland, "and he turned to me and heard my cry. He lifted me out of the pit of despair, out of the mud and the mire." His breathing grew heavy. An explosion impacted on Roland's chest and sent him back to the ground.

"We are pinned down," said Oliver. "Any ideas?"

A surge of ghouls pressed down through the stands and entrances and piled upon Roland. In a moment, the mound of ghouls was over thirty feet. Roland, at the heart of the pulsating hill of flesh, roared in fury and struggled to gain a foothold; the sound of his fists slamming, his shield bashing, and his armor striking flesh echoed across the field.

Roland yelled again in frustration.

Oliver fired at the throng coming down the stands towards him and Melissa—an endless wave of ghouls.

"We have them!" screamed the voice on the public announcement.

The concrete wall protecting Melissa and Oliver was being chipped away by the gunfire. They did not have long before they were exposed.

Melissa prayed. Oliver could hear Roland join, and then he, too, joined.

> *Let us then, with confidence, draw near to the throne of grace, that we may receive mercy and find grace to help in time of need.*

"Amen," they said together.

A stillness washed across the arena. The hair on Oliver's arms stiffened, and his body tingled. A sound like distant thunder. No, a trumpet. A trumpet of more power than any man of this world had heard grew until it was deafening—a flash of blinding light, then an explosion of force. The ghouls in the stands were knocked back. Oliver was pressed flat, even behind the concrete wall.

After a moment, the pressure of the force subsided, and a voice called out, "For he will command his angels concerning you to guard you in all your ways." The voice boomed across the arena and echoed through the stands, shaking the very structure. It was almost like Roland's voice, but different. Oliver could not place it.

The gunfire stopped, and Oliver peeked over the concrete. Standing before Roland, who was kneeling, was an Angel. Wings of light radiated from his armor. A flaming sword in his hand was aimed at the demons, who were frozen in terror and awe. He wore a blue tunic over his armor, an armor that was a white metal that shone with its own light. He was shod in knee-high boots of the same metal, white with gold trim. His golden hair flowed over his pale face. Around them, the ghouls were crushed into a black paste.

The weapons in the hands of the demons glowed with a white light, and they dropped them. The angel flew at them and sliced them all. The motion was instant and complete. All collapsed, bisected to the ground. The angel threw his sword, spinning it; it glided across the field and decapitated the great lion demon. The angel flew up and through a glass window and returned with a man in his grasp. He dropped him to the ground, pointed his hand at the man, and pulled something invisible into his gauntlet. The man's visage changed, and a goblin-like creature, no bigger than a small child, cowered before the might of God's servant.

"This is the fiend you know as Petrov," spoke the angel. "He has another name that I shall not speak, for to God, he is now nothing."

He reached out with an open hand, then pulled it back, closing it. He opened his hand, and there was a small spark of light, like a candle whisking to life. The light grew in strength but not in size. It grew into an intense light, like a miniature sun that hovered over his palm. The sun pulsed, and a wave-like wind splashed as if a pebble had been dropped into a still lake, extending in all directions. As the wave returned, the bodies of the demons and ghouls were lifted and pulled into the tiny sun. Lastly, Petrov was pulled in; he screamed in agony as his body collapsed upon itself, swirling into the light. When all trace of their foulness was pulled in, the angel closed his hand and crushed the singularity in a spray of sparks. He pointed his palm out, and his sword returned to him.

"You may approach me," said the angel, "Remove your shoes, for this is now holy ground."

Oliver helped Melissa up, and they walked down the steps, removing their shoes before stepping on the grass.

Roland removed his sabatons and helmet but remained kneeling before the angel.

"Rise, Roland," said the angel. "Your deeds have reached the halls of Angels who sing your praise."

Roland stood, and a single tear flowed down his face.

"You as well, Oliver and Melissa," said the Angel. "You kneel only before God."

"Oh, give thanks to the Lord, for he is good, for his steadfast love endures forever!" said Roland.

"The deed was my pleasure," said the Angel. "I have not tested my sword in a time. But I am not here for aid but to deliver a message. Your time to find the rest is drawing short. The time of our Lord approaches. There are still six more to find and a seventh. Here is my Lord's word: Heal the one who heals by sacrifice, listen for the voice in the chaos, see the one who cannot be seen, feel for the one who feels everything, add to your number the one who lives among them, find the one who can't be broken."

With a flash of light and a trumpet's sound, the angel vanished.

MOTHERS

Ivon awoke, lying on a white sand beach. It was a warm morning, and a cool breeze caressed his skin. The sun was rising and casting an orange glow across the water. The sand was soft on his hands, and the waves teased his feet. It was a peacefulness he had never known. The last thing he remembered was holding Ivoire's hand and going into the trance again. He sat up and looked around and saw no signs of anyone else. He stood and could see nothing but beach and water as far as his vision could reach. *Am I dead?*

"Far from it," came a voice.

A man in gray work overalls walked from behind him on the beach. He smiled and stood before Ivon. The man was clean, except for his hands; grease covered his fingers as if he had been working on a car.

"It's hard to pick your first words to say to your son," said the man.

"Are you my father?" asked Ivon.

A tear formed in the man's eye, "Yes. I thought you were dead. If only I had been braver." The man smiled. "It's ok, though. God showed me why."

"Why what?" asked Ivon.

"Why your life was the way it was," said the man. "Why it is this way for all of us. Walk with me." The man offered his hand to help Ivon up. Ivon hesitated, then accepted, still unsure if the man was real or another deception.

They walked along with the water to their right; the rising sun seemed stuck halfway up. As they walked, something rose from the sand. The sand itself shaped into figures. A scene was laid out as the sand took shape and color. A man in a Russian army uniform was holding a baby, shielding it from another soldier pointing a gun.

"That baby is you," said the man. "Do you recognize the man with the gun?"

"Colonel Petrov," said Ivon.

"He was only a lieutenant then," said the man as he walked up to Petrov. "His lust for power had already cost him his soul."

"He later came and saved me from that hell of the children's camp," said Ivon.

"Not for your benefit," said the man. "When he found you in the camp, he did not know you were a babe he had almost killed years before. He had killed so many other children. It was just one more." He walked more and motioned for Ivon to follow.

As they left the scene, the sand behind them fell to the beach, leaving no trace, and a new scene assembled as they approached. It was of the soldier who protected the baby standing with a nurse, baby in her arms.

"You never knew her name," said the man. "But she saved you from death. She had saved many children during that awful war. She, like many others, was a believer who did God's work, even if in the employ of an evil army. Because that man showed you compassion, the nurse fell in love with him, and a new family was formed, all because of you."

"She was the one who sent me to that hell?" Ivon asked.

"Yes," the man replied. "But she did not know it was so. She believed it was a safe and loving place. She was deceived." The man continued down the beach.

Ivon followed as a new scene was built while the scene behind them collapsed. The sand took the shape of two small boys standing in front of a metal-framed bunk bed.

"You recognize this little fella?" asked the man.

"Is that Dimitri and I at Petrov's school?" asked Ivon.

"Yes," said the man. "Now, look closer."

As Ivon approached, the figure of Dimitri swelled and swallowed the sand around him until it was the pig demon.

"This is Dimitri's true form," said the man. "He was a demon, a servant of Satan."

A wave of sand came and crashed into Dimitri; when the crashing sand cleared, Roland was abreast of the creature, sword across its neck.

"And this is a Paladin," said the man. "They are humans with angelic powers who serve the one true God."

"Ivoire showed this to me, too," said Ivon. "She showed me the Paladins and Demons and the war they wage. Dimitri may have been a demonic creature, but he was still my friend."

The man turned and walked more as a new scene assembled. It was of a girl in a hotel room lying on a bed. Dimitri stood over her with a knife.

"Remember the girl in Cuba?" said the man. "The woman you cared for, perhaps the first person who showed you true affection and asked nothing in return. Petrov feared you had grown too attached and needed you as a weapon with no distractions."

The sand shifted as Dimitri sliced her throat and splattered blood. Dimitri approached the dead woman's body; Ivon already knew what his intentions were next. He turned away, and the sand fell.

"Your sister was also used by men who desired power," said the man as he walked.

The sand shifted and showed a man in a chair. A figure stands before him with a syringe.

"They killed me to manipulate her," he said, his voice verging on anger. "They forced her to…" His words trail off. He relaxed, composed himself, and looked at Ivon. "Some things a father should never know about his daughter."

"Ivoire and I discovered we were twins through our gift," Ivon stopped and looked at the man. "What happened?"

"I suppose I have delayed this long enough," said the man. "Follow me."

The sand collapsed as it did before, and as they walked, a new scene opened up. It was a woman on a table giving birth. Another woman has a scalpel out and had a hand on the mother's belly. Behind her, a worried-looking man held a child.

"This is the first and only time I held you," said the man, his voice soft with sadness. "We did not expect twins. Your mother died, and you and your sister lived. A few minutes later, I lose you."

"What do you mean lose me?" demanded Ivon.

"Watch," said the man.

The sand shifted, this time with movement but the replay is slow, highlighting the moment, stretching it out. The man is carrying two children, and an explosion sends him flying. One of the children flew from his grip and landed hard.

"I searched," said the man. "But you were not crying."

The sand shifted and showed soldiers firing at the man.

"I ran to save your sister," said the man. "I thought you dead. I know you can never forgive me."

"I am not angry," said Ivon. "I am just unsure. I have never had a family other than Petrov and Dimitri."

"They are not your family," said the man with a stern voice. "They used you for your gift and your blood."

They walked more, and the sand shaped into a new scene. It was the Paladins: the cowboy, the knight, the nun, and the punk.

"There are more like these," said the man. "More of God's divinely gifted warriors. Chosen to fight Satan and his hordes. More like you."

"Petrov said something like that," said Ivon. "Does your God want to use me too?"

"No," said the man. "My God just wants to love you and for you to love him in return. If you choose to use his gift to help others, it only serves to expand his love. It is your choice."

"What if I choose to reject your God?" asked Ivon.

"My God is so loving he will honor your choice," said the man. "From now until eternity. But we have more to see. Let us continue."

The sand unveiled a miniature scene of a stadium. Ivon stood over it and observed the action below.

"The Paladins fight innumerable odds," said the man. "Not for personal glory, but to save their fellow man in the service of God."

The sand expanded around them and the arena is full size. Ivon and his father stand next to Roland; he is swinging his sword at a group of ghouls.

"These creatures that Petrov used your blood to animate are not humans brought back to life," said the man. "These are dead bodies being controlled by demons. Your blood, which has an angelic essence, was used in a profane ceremony. Petrov raised an army and planned to unleash it onto the world."

"What do you mean planned?" asked Ivon.

"While we speak," said the man, "the Paladins have already moved in, and an angel of the Lord has even stepped in to help."

The sand whirled, flashing the scene forward to the angel's arrival. The angel stands before a cowering Petrov.

"Now, Petrov is dead, too," said the man.

The sand fell flat and they are alone on the beach.

"All I have known is gone," said Ivon. "I have nothing now."

"Only your false family is gone," said the man. "Are you ready to meet your heavenly family?"

"Your heavenly family has nothing I want," said Ivon.

"Perhaps I only offer love," said the man. "Same as him." He pointed over the ocean where a man approached—walking on the water. He was dressed in a simple tunic belted at the waist and plain sandals. His bearded face smiled and had a soft glow.

"Hello, Ivon the third," said the new man. "I am Jesus."

"The third?" asked the man.

"Yes," said Jesus, his smile broadening. "Your father is also Ivon, as is his father."

Ivon, the second, looked at his son, "Yes. My namesake and my lineage."

"You don't seem impressed by me," said Jesus.

"Should I be?" said Ivon. "If this is a dream, I am not sure what to believe."

"How does it feel?" asked Jesus.

"More real than any dream before," Ivon said.

"Good," said Jesus. "Now for the punctuation mark. Turn around." He pointed behind Ivon.

Ivon turned slowly. The beach behind him had formed into a pond. Facing the pond was a bench. On the bench was a woman with long blonde hair that almost touched the ground as she sat.

"Go say hello," said Ivon the second.

"Who is that?" asked Ivon.

"Go and ask her," said Jesus.

Ivon approached the woman. He rounded the bench and saw she was reading a Bible in French.

"Hello," he said. Something pulled at the pit of his stomach. He was nervous and could not tell why.

The woman looked up. She was piercingly beautiful. She smiled, tears welling in her eyes, "Hello son." She rose and pulled him into a hug. "Oh, how I have watched and waited for this moment."

Ivon let the hug envelop him. A foreign and new feeling washed over him. It was a warmth and love that only a mother could produce. He fought back tears, uncontrollable tears that soaked his face.

"Mom," he sobbed.

"Yes, my son," she replied.

"Oh, Mom." His voice shook as the tears flowed down his face. "I have not been a good son."

She held him at arm's length, "A mother can always forgive her son."

She pulled him in again, and they held each other and cried.

"Moms," said Jesus to Ivon the second. "Moms get them every time."

"It is you," said Ivon, his face buried in his mother's shoulder. "I know. I can feel it in my whole being. In my soul." He looked at his father and Jesus. "You are who you say you are. I wanted not to believe it, but I couldn't fight it. You are my family, and you are the one true God."

"Welcome home," said Jesus. "But I have work for you still. My angel has given a message to your fellow Paladins. You must bring one more message when you awake."

"What message is that?" asked Ivon.

"When you are ready, I will reveal it to you," smiled Jesus. "The Paladins will find a way to wake you, so time here is short." He pointed down the beach. "For now, spend some time with your family."

From down the beach, a figure approached. "Hello, brother."

Ivon ran and hugged his sister. "We are a family again."

Their parents came over and they embraced as a family for the first time.

BP McCoppin

NOW WE ARE 5

The flash of light had faded, and the Paladins were alone on the field. All traces of the ghouls and demons were gone.

Over the comms, Persephone reached out, "-issa, Oliver, Roland. Are you there?"

"We are here,"

"What happened?" asked Persephone. "I heard you three pray, and then the link went dead. Did we win?"

"Did you have any video feed from Roland's helmet the last several minutes?" asked Melissa.

"It went dead with the comms," said Persephone. "He was under the pile of ghouls, then nothing."

"Then a spirit passed before my face; the hair of my flesh stood up," said Roland. "It stood still, but I could not discern the form thereof: an image was before mine eyes, there was silence, and I heard a voice."

"Did you say something appeared?" asked Persephone, her voice not hiding the excitement.

"He did," said Oliver. "An angel. He came down with a trumpet blast and obliterated all the demons."

"We need to see if there are any injured we can help," said Melissa, looking around. "Then we head back to headquarters before the authorities show up."

The Paladins checked the entire stadium and found no trace of the demons. Only the violence they caused had remained.

Medical teams and police had moved in and were assisting the injured. With no more threat looming, the Paladins slipped out with the surviving fans and called for their ride.

Elissa picked them up three blocks away, "você estava no motim?"

"Que tumulto?" asked Melissa.

"Quando as gangues avançaram e atacaram as cerimônias de abertura," said Elissa as she careened through the busy streets. Emergency vehicles sped by, heading to the arena.

Melissa turned to Oliver, who had a puzzled look on his face. "She said people are calling it a gang-caused riot. It's already on the news."

"God's work?" asked Oliver.

"More likely the demons are covering their loss through the media," said Melissa.

The Paladins returned to the airport and flew back to headquarters. They were gathered in the library.

"An actual angel," said Persephone. "What a story!"

"He was unbelievable," said Oliver. "He massacred the demons, then said Roland was awesome and left." Oliver thought he saw a slight tint of blush on the giant man's cheeks.

"He gave us a message, too," said Melissa. "Our time to find the rest is drawing short. There are still seven more to find." Melissa paused in thought. "Heal the one who heals by sacrifice, listen for the voice in the chaos, see the one who cannot be seen, feel for the one who feels everything, add to your number the one who lives among them, find the one who can't be broken."

"That's what I recall, too," said Oliver. "The memory of the event is so clear. I can recall it with such detail."

"Whoever belongs to God hears what he says," said Roland.

"It's only six clues," said Persephone.

"You are correct," said Melissa. "He said there are 'six to find and a seventh.'"

Book of Ivon and Ivoire

"We have Oliver, Gerier, Ogier, Ivon and Ivoire," said Persephone. "Turpin, Otton, Berengier, Engelier, and Anseis are still missing."

"Also, the next Roland," added Melissa.

Persephone and Oliver looked at Roland.

Roland smiled, "For death is the destiny of everyone; the living should take this to heart."

"We have bigger problems than the missing Paladins," said Mellissa.

"Wiles is still out here," said Oliver.

"Yup," said Persephone. "Her 'Project Garmr' is still an unknown."

"You don't think Garmr was the ghoul army?" asked Oliver.

"No," said Melissa. "Nothing connects Petrov to Wiles. The Garmr legend is more about the gates of hell, not an army of undead."

"There is also the missing book from the Luciferian collection," said Persephone. "And the demon essence on Roland's glove from his rescue of Cardinal Sepe."

"Too many unknowns," said Melissa. "I have not made any progress on getting an in-person meeting with Cardinal Sepe. And we have no more leads in where the missing book may be."

"If only we could ask Ivon and Ivoire," said Oliver.

"If we find a way to wake them, I would advise caution," said Melissa. "We don't know yet what sort of damage the trance causes."

"Has there been a gift with negative effects before?" asked Oliver.

"I would offer every gift comes with some sort of sacrifice," said Melissa. "Us three," she motioned to Oliver Persephone and herself, "have vision-based gifts that caused us suffering in our youth."

"What of Roland?" asked Oliver. "Has he suffered?"

"Gentleness and self-control," said Roland. "Against such things, there is no law."

"Roland lives in a glass world," said Melissa. "He has had to learn to temper his power not to injure those he cares for."

"So what is our next move?" asked Oliver.

"The first clue the angel left us, 'heal the one who heals by sacrifice,'" said Melissa. "A Paladin healer might be able to wake Ivon and Ivoire."

EPILOGUE

Images of riots flash across the screen. A message runs across the bottom, "Riots break out at the World Cup." The screen flashes, and a stern-looking woman with short hair is the center of the screen.

"I am Rhonda Matthis," said the Stern Woman. "And this is Rhonda Matthis Speaks. From schools, to concerts, from churches to stadiums. No gathering place seems safe. Tonight's discussion is violence at public events."

The camera panned to an elderly man with white hair and floppy ears. Rhonda continues, "My guests tonight are Ryan David," the camera panned to a young man with dark skin and a bald head, "Mayor Leroy Williams," the camera panned to the final guest, a familiar face, "and Senator Nancy Wiles."

The camera zooms out, and all four are sitting at a table with microphones and cups of coffee.

"Ryan," said Rhonda. "You have the first say tonight. What are your thoughts on the riots at the World Cup?"

"Thank you, Rhonda," said Ryan. "Obviously, large groups are going to attract undesirables. The only way to curb violence is stricter gun laws. No guns, no violence. It is that easy."

"Mayor Williams," said Rhonda, "what say you?"

"Thanks for having me on Rhonda," said Williams. "I agree with Mr. David. A part of my re-election campaign is I am running on my record of getting guns off the street. An unarmed society is a safe society."

"Well said," replied Rhonda. "Senator Wiles. My audience may recall that you are a survivor of violence being perpetrated at two events—the shooting at the Shanette concert, and your private yacht. You have a unique perspective on the issue. What say you?"

"Thank you, Rhonda, always a pleasure," said Wiles. "Yes, we need more common sense gun control; yes, we need more legislation taking the dangerous weapons away from those who would do harm. But we also need to get to the heart of the matter. The attacks I survived was perpetrated by a Fundamentalist Christian Nationalist. Now, we have the attacks in Brazil, a very Christian nation. I say now that when the dust settled, we will see it was, once again, Christian Nationalists who were behind these attacks. Is there no surprise that this archaic religion is pushing ideas that threaten our very society? Yes, we must ban the guns, but we must also ban the ideas that aim to use them. We must ban Christians."

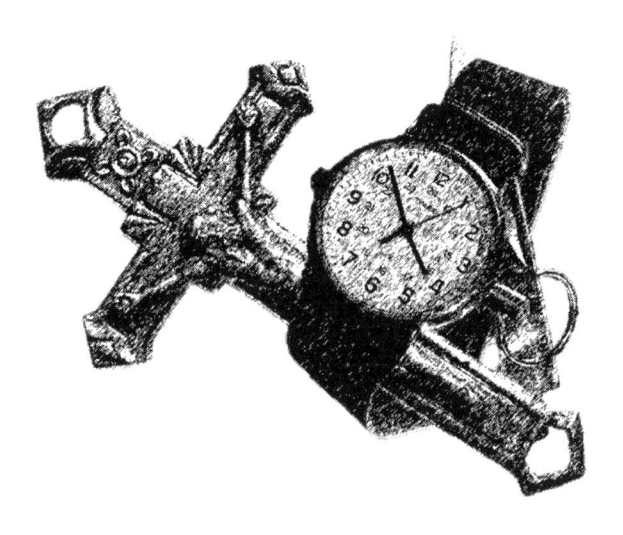

ABOUT THE AUTHOR

BP McCoppin is an international-selling author. He is a father of three and lover of his wife and Jesus. He is also the modern "Florida Man." He spends most of his time working on his boat or practicing karate.

The Paladin Books are his love letter to the Christian who wants solid action grounded in glorifying God with faith-based heroes.

Look for the comic adaptation with art by Kevin John Jacobs

RECORD OF THE PALADINS
BOOK OF ANSEIS

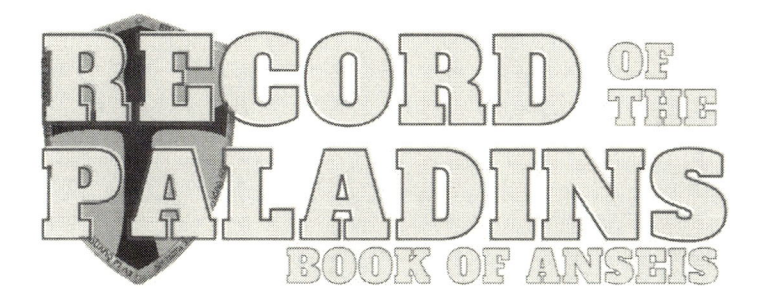

The next book in the epic series.

Thepaladinbooks.com